NMcliff

D0274084

:cwn.

Queen & Country

Other titles in the Hew Cullan Mystery series

Hue & Cry
Fate & Fortune
Time & Tide
Friend & Foe

Queen & Country

A Hew Cullan Mystery

~

Shirley McKay

Polygon

This edition published in Great Britain in 2015 by
Polygon, an imprint of Birlinn Ltd
West Newington House
10 Newington Road
Edinburgh
EH9 1QS

www.polygonbooks.co.uk

ISBN 978 1 84697 312 3

Copyright © Shirley McKay, 2015

The right of Shirley McKay to be identified as the author of this work has been
asserted by her in accordance with the Copyright, Designs and Patents Act, 1988.

All rights reserved. No part of this publication may be reproduced, stored, or
transmitted in any form, or by any means electronic, mechanical or photocopying,
recording or otherwise, without the express written permission of the publisher.

British Library Cataloguing-in-Publication Data
A catalogue record for this book is available on request from the British Library.

The publisher acknowledges investment from Creative Scotland towards
the publication of this volume.

Typeset by 3btype.com

Printed by Bell and Bain Ltd, Glasgow

Prologue

St Andrews, November 1586

The pedlar came to Scotland once or twice a year: in springtime when the leaves were opening in their buds, and sometimes when they fell, before the way was bared and bound in winter frost. In the year of the plague – a bad year that was – he did not come at all. In the course of a good year he crossed from his home in the midlands of England its length and its breadth, and then up north and down again. He brought his haberdashery to manor, fair and farm. He was welcomed in the houses landward of the towns, for his toys and baubles and his scraps of news, where news was slow to reach. In the burgh markets, he was made less welcome, and those he came to only for the annual fairs, when he would pitch his stall, and voice, among the rest.

This year, it was not until September that he crossed the Scottish border, to return to his old ground on the well-worn cadgers' paths. Here, he was assured to find a rousing cheer, comfort, meat and drink. He knew that his customers, after months of plague, would be glad to see him. The pack upon his back was as heavy as himself, lumbered with delights, when he first set off.

And yet, and yet, he did not find a welcome there, but a shifting silence that he could not comprehend. Wherever he went he was met with mistrust. Coming to each town, where he was turned out, he expected the good wives to follow him in droves and cry to see his wares; that did not happen now. And when he wandered landward to the little cots, expecting warmth and cheer, he found their doors were closed to him. In vain, he waved his paper proving he was hale, and free from pestilence. He could not understand it. Starved as they had been, had their hopes and wants withered in the plague?

For once, he was behindhand with the news. The news had swept before him, like a line of fire that shrivelled to a husk all in its path, so that his trudge was through desolate landscapes, all solace closed to him. The news had gone before, closing every port, and darkening every brow that once had offered friendship. And no one thought to tell the pedlar what it was.

He came at last, at the end of November, to the South Street of St Andrews, for the last of the fairs before winter came, St Andrew's Day itself. The people here he knew would be flocking to its stalls, *flocking* for the first time in a full year since the plague, looking to stock up not simply on commodities, but on a mirth and lightness now in short supply. And if the crowds were depleted, and a little more subdued, than the last time he was here, the pedlar's spirits still were high that he would find a market for his buttons and his beads, his crudely painted soldiers and babies wrought of lead, his rattles and his pins. There were people enough, craftsmen and labourers mellow in drink, students and schoolboys truant from schools, good wives and masters in holiday clothes. There were scholars also, from the university, who wanted books and paper, sealing wax and ink. The pedlar would have liked to purchase those things too, to carry back down south, but until he offloaded the goods he had brought, he had no hope of that. The merchants had forestalled, picking off the cream that came from overseas before it left the ships. He saw the town apothecary, filling up a sack with spice and painters' colours, long before the man who brought them from the Orient had opened up his stall.

Yet he was not deterred, for in a restless horde, that hankered after novelty, there was room for all; and if he could not hope to have a prime spot for his stand, he had the advantage that he could slip among the crowd, nimble as a pick-purse, to ply his stock-in-trade.

The town drummer and piper had set up their roll, and the

swelling of a crowd, with ale in their bellies and money in their pockets, encouraged the pedlar to stake out his claim in a little corner not far from the kirk. He opened up his pack and began to cry his wares, with a perennial favourite. 'Coventry. Coventry thread. Ye will not find a finer, nor a purer blue. For your caps and your cuff work. Your linens your embroideries. Will not run. Will not stain. No blue more true. No counterfeit stuff. Finer than gold. Mistresses, come buy. None is more true blue than Coventry blue.'

He was gratified to find that he had drawn an audience. Not, it was true, so many of the good wives who made up his target group, but several likely lads around the age of twenty, who had sweethearts, doubtless, targets of their own. 'True blue,' he appealed to them, 'to win a leman's love.'

One of the young men stepped forward. 'Well met, billie boy,' he said. 'Coventry, ye say? What kind a place is that?' The pedlar could smell the sour ale on his breath.

'A fine place, my master, where is spun the finest thread.'

'Aye? Is that a fact? In England, is that place?' the young man answered, pleasantly.

'Why, yes sir. At its heart. The very life and heartbeat of that brave green land.'

'An' wid ye be, yourself, fae *Cuventrie*, my friend?'

'From Warwickshire, sirs. From a place that is not far from it. And I can vouch, upon my life, that you will not find a blue thread of a finer quality.'

The young man grinned at that, turning to his friends. '*Ur-pon his loife*, he says.'

The pedlar, appealing, held out his thread. 'True blue,' he tried again. 'The ladies like it, sirs. An ever welcome gift, and the lady will be yours. I have ribands, too.'

'Did I hear that right?' the young man asked his friends. He was not smiling now, but a keen glint in his eye sent a signal to the pedlar something might be wrong. He took a small step back.

'Did that rusty bully call my lass a whore?'

'No, as I assure you, sir,' the pedlar stammered now. 'I did not say that.'

'I doubt he did he say that. I heard him quite distinctly, Tam,' came back the young man's friend.

'I heard the limmar too.'

'Good masters, what I meant . . .'

But what was meant, or not, was stopped by the flowering of a fist, that burst out into blossom in the pedlar's mouth.

Above the outer entrance to the St Andrews tolbuith a single glove was pinned. This signified the session of the Court of Dustifute – the pie-powder court, which ruled upon transgressions at the fair, the common law suspended for the day. Convened to that court were the stewards and the bailies appointed to the task, who took their role there seriously. They were chosen from the burgesses and merchants in the town, and chief among them, who spoke now, was a leading beacon in the baxters' gild.

'Ye are charged wi' disturbing the peace of the fair. What do you say?'

The pedlar peered through an eye that was bulbous and closed. His face had swollen up, to a shiny sullen purple, tight as a plum. His answer was muffled by the swelling of a lip, blubber to the touch of his shy protruding tongue. He swallowed on a tooth, a gobbet of slick blood, his answer indistinct.

'Whit dae ye *say*?'

'He says, it was not he that started the affray. That he was set upon.' The pedlar had a man to speak for him. It was only right and proper that a stranger at the fair should have a countryman of his own to take his part; that was the point of a dustifute court, that none should find himself thrown upon the mercy of a foreign law, without a friend to speak for him. The friend was hard to find. At last, they had pressed into the service a cadger from the south, who had been quick to point out he had not witnessed the assault. He had come reluctantly to support his countryman. Was that not like the English, after all, the baxter sniffed. Cowards, every one.

'He says that he was set upon. Well then, was he robbed?'

The pedlar had not been robbed. He had still, and plain for all to see, his same pack full of its cheap tricks and toys, his ribands and his laces and his true blue thread. His purse kept the pittance it held when he came with it.

'This court concludes,' the baxter said, 'that ye are guilty of affray, and of disturbing the peace of the fair, and of slander and provokement of a guid man of this place, in that that ye cried his lass a whore, and assaulted him, when he tuik offence at it.'

The pedlar replied to this, in some sort of speech, that the thickness of his accent and the thickness of his lip slobbered to a slur.

'He says,' his friend reported, 'that was not how it was, at all.'

'Aye, but ye see,' the baxter leaned across the desk, and looked earnestly into the pedlar's eye, the one good remaining one, yellow and red, 'there are fifteen witnesses that swear that it was so, besides those lusty fellows in the vault below; and ye, as I believe, have not one witness that will swear the contrary. Wherefore, you must see, the case is found and proved.'

The pedlar mumbled again, and the baxter found himself irritated by his smoothly stubborn face, bulging like a haemorrhoid. What business did he have in persisting in his obstinacy?

The countryman interpreted, sulking and reluctant, and the baxter found that he was prickled too by the southern cadger's whining English voice. Why did they think they were never in the wrong?

'He says that there was a boy, a student from the college, came to wipe his face when he was lying on the ground. A boy with black hair. And, he thinks if enquiries were made in the colleges, that boy might be found, to tell the truth of it.'

'Absolutely not,' the baxter said. 'That maun be a lie, else he was dreaming on the ground. There was no student there. For the very guid reason that, the masters at the colleges prohibit them the fair.'

The last thing he would sanction, in his court, was the risk of an appeal to the university. The collegers he knew would argue black was white. His gild had wrangled hard enough, in troubles in the past, with the man Hew Cullan. And while *that man* no longer troubled them at large, Giles Locke was as bad. The scholars had no business with the powder court, and the powder court would have none with them.

'This court finds the charge against you to be proved. And ye will spend the rest of the day, and the night, in the goif stok,' he said.

The cadger asked, wearily, what that might mean.

'The pillorie or jougs, whichever one is free,' a bailie spelled it out.

The southerner shrugged. 'Then, you will have his death on your hands.'

'Come, I will not hae that,' the baxter remonstrated. 'You will not tell me, cannot tell me, that a man who is fit to tramp the length an' breadth of Scotland is not fit enough to last a few hours in the goifs or jougs.' Lily-livered loun, he thought. 'What age is he, then?' he considered at last. With a man that was so weathered, it was difficult to tell. Fifty, perhaps? Three score and ten? The man had been a dustifute no doubt for thirty years. And that leathered a man, and made him impervious. Perhaps, after all, a night in the goif stok was not punishment enough, for such a kind of man.

'How should I know? I do not know him.' The cadger was surlier now. His part in the process was done. 'But you can surely see that if you put him in the stocks your bangster bullies' stones will kill him in an hour. You might as well tie the beggar to the butts, and have them shoot their bows at him.'

There was truth in that. The baxter looked for answer to the other bailies, scratching at his head. They had locked the hot youths in the strong room for a while, to let them cool off. But it was plain that no charge would be levelled against them.

'We could keep them there, until he serves his time,' one of them suggested. The baxter disagreed. 'We cannot do that. Sin they have done no wrong, there would be a riot, see?'

Injustice of that kind would wreak havoc in the town. The powder jurisdiction would vanish in a puff, and its failures would be tested in a higher court. The baxter chose instead a more expedient course.

'Then he shall pay a fine, and be whipped out from the fair. You shall gang an' a.''

'What have I done?' the cadger whinnied then. A snivelling sort of man. His kind were all alike.

'You provoke us, by coming at an unpropitious time, when any decent man would have had the judgement to have kept away. Go, sir. We have been guid to you. Ye shall have an hour, to set upon your path, before we loose the men whom you have so offended, they bay for your blood. Go, and thank us, now.'

The cadger saw his cause was lost, and he was himself complicit in offending them, by no more certain cause than his sorry Englishness.

'Show up your purse,' the pedlar was told. And he drew it out, wordless, from under his cloak.

A handful of coins, not amounting to much, that were Scots, and a single English one. The baxter scooped this up. The Scots pennies he tipped back in the purse, and handed it back to the pedlar. 'Now, on your way.'

He was not a cruel man. And he would not send a pedlar out into a world that was hard on him enough, without the means to prove that he was not a vagabond.

The bailie beside him suspected his softness. 'Why did ye dae that?'

'Because we do not want the death of a stranger, here, on our hands. If he will die, let him dae it in a parish far from here.' His kindness, his softness, must not be suspected. The man could not help it that he was an Englishman. Though he could, and should, have helped his coming here.

'That is not what I meant. Why did you take the coin that has the English whore on it? That bastard Jezebel?'

The baxter turned over the bright coin in his hand and scrutinised the portrait of the English queen Elizabeth. He was a pragmatist at heart, which made him the perfect judge for the powder court. He was surprised that his friend had to ask. 'D'ye not ken? Their money is worth more than ours.'

Part I

Chapter 1

The Queen's Highway

Tout commencement est difficile
[French proverb, written in the glass at Buxton Hall:
Every beginning is hard]

London, July 1586

The house had a stillness Hew mistook for quietude, its inner life in shadow at the close of day. The windows were shut fast against the hum of flies, the vapours of the river bed, swollen after months of rain, swilling to the surface of a heavy heat. He expected, at this hour, to find the family freshened from their evening walk, coming from the cooling air to settle down at cards, the green baize in the parlour cleared of supper things. But the boiled beef platter had been left untouched, the wheaten loaf uncut, the primrose pat of butter melting in its dish. The cards were closed up in their box, the lute lay in its corner, soundless. The Phillips family sat reflective, silent and apart.

'Mary has miscarried her child,' Frances said, her slight voice a brittle and strained note of brightness, resonant still in the gloom. Frances had wrapped in a white muslin square a translucent-skinned boy, whose whole she could hold in the palm of her hand, light as a leaf and as perfectly formed, while Mary had turned her small face to the wall, and drawn up her shoulders, narrow and hard.

'The midwife says she will not have a living child, that there is a fault, deep inside her womb. It cannot be helped,' Frances said.

Joan Phillips clicked her tongue, distant in the haze like the strumming of a grasshopper. She was vexed at the midwife, at Thomas, her son, who confounded her hopes, at Mary most of all, her fault gaping wide like a cleft in a rock. They had been married for less than a year.

Joan's husband William looked up from the chiselled oak settle, where he sat brooding and hunched. 'Thomas must be told. Indeed, he must be told.'

The loss of a grandchild was vexing to him, though Thomas was a boy he found difficult to fathom, secretive and staid. He set himself apart, spelling out his surname in the manner of the French. That *Phelippes* was a person William did not trust, whose purpose was obscure to him, a sad thing in a son. Children were a blessing, and indeed, a trial, for his daughters were more loving and expansive than his sons, yet their chitter-chat and prattle sometimes frayed his nerves. They had cost him dear enough, in frippery of gowns. If there was one among them, closest to his heart, then it must be Frances, his dead brother's girl. And that was like his perverseness, Joan would have said. He had brought Frances up to attend to his accounts, and in the careful rows of reckoning that lined his record books, in a neat, narrow hand, lay all that William Phillips wished for in a child. Yet he knew what was right, and proper to be done. The woman upstairs, with her face to the wall, had troubled his conscience. Her fault was a grief to him, in his old age.

Phelippes was at Chartley, on business of the state. And Hew had his suspicions what that business was. 'How does Mary now?' he asked.

Frances said, 'She takes the loss hard, but will not for the world have us send for Tom.'

'Thomas does important work, and must not be disturbed,' said Joan. 'The child will be dead, still, whenever he returns.'

William Phillips shrank from the starkness of this confidence.

'Though that may be true, he should be informed. We look to Tom Cassie, his servant, to take to him a letter, but that idle friar-fly is nowhere to be found.'

Tom Cassie could be traced within the hour, if he were still in London. Had word been sent to Walsingham?

'No, indeed,' sniffed Joan, who held the Master Secretary in a high esteem.

Hew sensed the warming up of an earlier argument, left to stew and simmer through the afternoon. William Phillips shifted, troubled, in his chair. 'We did not think it right, to cumber such a man with so small a thing.'

Frances asked, quietly, 'Should we have done?'

Hew was in no doubt. It was well-advised to put the case to Walsingham, who would take the trouble of it safely from their hands. Instead, he chose to offer, 'I can go myself, if Cassie is not found.' He told himself he saw, and understood the consequence. Frances smiled at him. And William Phillips leapt upon it, reckless in relief.

'You are an honest friend, Hew. Have I not said so before? It is proper that Thomas should hear this from someone he knows and loves well. Take the grey gelding. Set out at once. Or stay, twere better to hold fast until the break of day, for little shall be won by riding in the night, of safety or of speed. You shall have a purse, and a letter for my son, and whatever else you will that shall expedite your going, and relieve our burden here.'

Frances whispered, 'Thank you. For surely, she will want him. She cannot be unfeeling, as my aunt Joan thinks.'

Whatever Mary felt, her answer went unheard. The old man laboured at his letter, sorrowful and ponderous, and Hew made preparations to ride out to Staffordshire. He had time enough to call at Seething Lane, and lay the business bare, time enough to search out Francis Mylles, to call up Phelippes' servant from the pits and shadows where he knew he lurked. However, he did not.

Hew was thankful to escape the soup of that great city, before the dust and throng began to stir and stream into the morning sun. He liked the waking hour, when tousle-trousered prentice boys unlocked the shuttered workshops, when the clear-skinned milkmaids clattered through the streets, and the country market sellers filled the air with flowers. He bought bread from the baker, still warm, and set north to the Bishopsgate, and the Berwick road. He would follow the highway to Grantham, over the course of three or four days, resting for a while at Ware, and at the Crown in Caxton. At Grantham, he would find a guide to ride with him to Staffordshire. And if the grey horse flagged, he would hire another. Grey Gelding was accustomed to him, and the path ahead; he could fall back in the saddle and rely upon the horse to follow in the footsteps of the royal post boys, whose hollow hooves and horn blasts sounded out the way. In the warming sunlight, he allowed his thoughts to drift.

Three years had passed since he had travelled for the first time on that stretch of road; then, he had been bearing south, and borne against his will, kenned nothing of the highway that had swept him southwards but the stony brack of rubble rattling through the carriage to the marrow of his bones.

It had baffled him to see, when he was set on foot to walk upon the path, how broad and flat and fair it was, burnished by the dust of a thousand years of horses, kicking up their hooves. For all that, he had found that he could neither walk nor stand – like a shipwrecked seaman, falling on his feet, his limbs had lurched and floundered, thrown him to the ground.

He was kept there in that coach for breathless hours on end, hidden from the ranks of Walsingham's own party, let loose at night for sake of nature's easement, washing in the rain that had puddled in the stable yard and shaking loose his limbs. His body had been bowed and buckled, crueller than the rack.

'I assure you, not,' Walsingham had said, with a mirthless smile, when that case was put to him. Walsingham had suffered too. It had sorely pained the man to have to share his cart. From Berwick, he had ridden with his men on horseback, while his strength allowed. When his strength gave out – for he was far from well – he had come banked in a thick raft of furs, sniffed at a nosegay, closing his eyes, repelling all offer of comment or question. Once, he had vomited, discreet and disdainful, into a cloth-covered bowl.

It had taken Hew a while to come to understanding it, and to his proper self. He came upon it helpless as a newborn child. He had been stolen from the guards who had taken him from prison, on his way to trial, and forced to undertake a bruising, jagged journey, that had ended here in London, at the house in Seething Lane. There, he had been placed inside a panelled room, left with bread and blanket, lying in the dark, to make sense of the turmoil swilling in his mind, through what pleading or prayers could keep him from madness. He had fallen to a fever, caught upon the road, and had come to his beginning there exhausted and discomfited. The house in Seething Lane appeared a soothing sanctuary, following the deprivations of the coach.

Later, there were books, paper, pens and ink. In those first few days, he was not allowed to write, and struggled to make sense and shape of what he found. His impressions of London, first formed in that place, were muted and confused. Gradually, he saw the house at Seething Lane become the opening to a world, of which, in that beginning, he had known nothing at all.

In Walsingham's house, he had never heard the raising of a voice, nor seen a sharp blade glimmer, from the safety of its sheath. Yet within its vaults, and quiet trance of doors, where keys turned smooth and soundlessly, he felt a deep unease; the locking of those doors came after in his dreams, and woke him in a sweat. The house saw constant traffic, quiet and enduring as the sluggish Thames, the oil slick revolution of its smooth machinery, turning through the night. When he was shown its heart, and saw its inner works, he was astonished to find out how fallible it was, how much of it depended on a line of human frailty, a balancing of aspirations, promises and fears.

Walsingham himself he did not see for months. He had gone to court, reporting to his queen what little grace and kindness he had found in Scotland, and how the earl of Arran, insolent and proud, insinuated sly hooks round the Scottish king, whose tender youth bent easily to his insistent snares. He had gone to Barn Elms, his mansion at Richmond, to recover from the hurt to his pride and to his health that the Scottish trip had dealt him, and attend to some affairs, arising from his daughter's recent marriage, his private life as fraught, and pressing in its purpose, as affairs of state. Else he was at Whitehall to confer with Robert Beale, or with Burghley and his councillors, on what had taken place while he was abroad; and in this dizzy trail, he had no time for Hew, nor, it seemed, a purpose for him. Yet he was not forgotten. Walsingham had marked him as a note of interest, a postscript to a letter, to be answered still.

At Bishopsgate, the parched bones of the priests had fallen from their posts; their skulls, long since picked clean, made footballs in the dust. Here Grey Gelding slowed, pushed back by the traffic crowding at the wall. To the mouth of the city came a surge and swell of melancholy sheep. A foot post passed them by, blowing on his horn, and crying to the wind, 'Mind, make way, for life!' In moments, he had disappeared, deep into the current of the waking city, to the river, or the court, or the house at Seething Lane, where the flow of letters did not ever cease, but endlessly revolved.

Seething Lane was aptly named, for the still of human life that boiled and bubbled quietly, the fervent undercurrent, coursing through its vaults. So it seemed to Hew. Laurence had corrected him, in his patient way: it was former *Sieuthienstrate*, named for those who lived there. Laurence Tomson was a scholar, of the purest sort. He was Walsingham's own secretary, and the first true friend that Hew had found in London, loved and trusted still. It was Laurence who had taken him in charge, in those bewildered days, who had brought him from the darkness to a place of wonder, to begin again, who taught to him his alphabet, and showed him how to read.

To Laurence fell the task of filtering the flood of letters and despatches which were sent to Walsingham, or which were intercepted, copied and sent on. There were others in that office to assist him with the load, but Laurence was the only one who did not leave his desk to go into the field. His life was lapped in paper banked up by the ream, a far returning tide which threatened to engulf, but which he called to order there and quietly controlled. Daylight hours brought letters, in a thousand hands, from footmen, knights and courtiers, beggar boys and clerks, dressed in silk or rags, and every paper passed through Laurence, under his command. Those letters that were written in the hearts of men were ushered in by night, to be opened secretly in pockets of the house that Hew had never seen. Their bearers had been brought up, blinking, from their beds. Some left wearily by morning, of their own free will. Others were escorted out, to Newgate or the Tower.

Laurence had the patience of the mildest Puritan, gentle in his inquisitions, thoughtful and exact. He was interested to hear what Hew could report of Andrew Melville and his nephew James, whose teaching he admired. Laurence had made translations of Beza's New Testament and of Calvin's lectures, which he gave to Hew. And though Hew understood it was a kind of test, that Walsingham had primed him for the quiet purpose of finding out Hew's faith, he was touched at the gift, and had accepted gratefully. 'I had a friend, Nicholas Colp, who looked after my books. He would have liked to have had these.' But when Laurence had answered, 'Perhaps one day, he shall,' Hew had shaken his head, 'Not in this life. For, he is dead,' and had turned to escape from an unwanted kindness, that brought to him too poignantly the tenor of his loss, and what was left behind.

He had been set to work, at first upon the letters from the Netherlands and France, in English or in French, which he had supposed to be the simplest sort. Laurence had explained to him that this was not the case.

'You may think that a cipher is more difficult to read. And that may be so. But a message set in cipher is more often unequivocal, when you have the key to it. We shall come to those. Here we have despatches from ambassadors abroad. You will find them filled with matter, news of every kind. It takes a little practice to discern their worth. These others, from their wives to their friends and families back home, increase that worth tenfold, if you have the patience to look between the lines.

'A man will tell you what was done, by whom and when, and why. His wife will tell you *how*. She will notice more, and write it to her friends. Imagine that you see a flock of birds, rising from the ground and flying to the trees. A superstitious man would take it for a sign. But you and I will know they sense the coming of the hawk, long before our own ears have become attuned to it.'

The letters, with their flow of tattle, gossip and complaint, 'is pleased to welcome Master John' . . . 'has suffered from a distillation since he had your last' . . . 'is presently in Paris' . . . 'fallen from his horse' . . . 'did not eat the plums' . . . 'a skein of dark red silk', gave up little at the start. But gradually, Hew learned to sift, and find small specks of gold. Sometimes, it was buried in a mutual understanding, of the sort that goes unspoken, has no want of words. The signs the writers chose were close among themselves. But when Hew had their measure, through the slips and streams of a longer correspondence, he could work them out. It was more than language, he had come to see. It was holding up a mirror to the secrets of their hearts, which secrets might be hidden, even from themselves.

Others chose to write obliquely, concealing of their true intent, knowing they were overlooked: 'Our hope and trust', 'your honest friend'. The key was hard to find. By careful inquisition, sometimes it was wrung out from the man himself, who brought it to their door. There were lists of such words – *nomenclators* – for the use of Walsingham's men.

Once, he had found a letter for the queen of Scots. Laurence, in a heartbeat, had stolen it from sight. 'You are inquisitive, my friend, and that is what we want. But not quite yet. It is too soon.'

On the road to Staffordshire, Hew shook his head. Three long years, adrift. He had been an outlaw, exiled from his home. Now, he had licence and the freedom to return. What was it that kept him here? In part, it was the fear of what Phelippes did at Chartley, and the hope of finding out.

English Catholics, he had learned, were in a state of flux, of conflict, fraught and perilous. They fought among themselves. 'It is impossible for them to be true to their country and to their religion. Wherefore they are lost,' Laurence Tomson said. 'It is the fault of the Pope, who when he excommunicated our sovereign lady Queen Elizabeth, made it lawful in their eyes to seek for her destruction. Elizabeth is a queen beloved of her people, who will not rise against her, and she is the true defender of the faith. There are good Catholic families who honour and respect her, and young Catholic nobles welcome still at court, for their grace and wit. Yet though their only trespass were to pray for her conversion, that were treason in itself. Some are English to the bone, and would rather die than see these green lands fall to foreigners. Some see no other course but to sacrifice their country to protect their faith. The younger sons of gentle folk are easily allured and tempted into plots, by those who would latch upon small discontents, and stir them to rebellion, who are reckless, fierce and hot, who in their youth's confusion do not know themselves, or know where they belong.'

'For that, they might be pitied,' Hew had said.

'Not pitied. Stopped.'

He had been moved to confess, 'My father resisted reform to his faith. He was what you call now, here in this place, *recusant*.'

'We are aware of that.'

'Yet he had me brought up as a Protestant, grounded in a faith that he did not embrace. It was a bone of contention between us.'

Laurence had corrected him. 'It was an act of love.'

Threat came from all sides: uprising from within; invasion in collusion with the Spanish or the French; the captive insurrection of the queen of Scots, whom traitors hoped to set upon the English throne. 'Do not underestimate that woman's reach and influence. She is the devil's handmaid, hunkered in our midst.'

The Jesuits, and those who were in league with them, came cloaked in secret garb and wrote their dark intentions down in secret inks, of alum or onion juice, in ciphers and false script. The riddle they had made of it hid their living hearts, and made their deaths a game. The first cipher Hew had solved had come with its own alphabet. It took him several minutes to discover it was French, and less than half an hour to make a perfect copy of it, which he had presented to Laurence with a grin. 'Child's play.'

'And very fine it is. Now turn it into English.'

'What do you think it is?' Hew had objected.

'I should have said, Scots.'

It was a shrewd enough rebuke, from one who spoke twelve languages, and Hew took more care with the rest of his work.

The simplest of the ciphers were based on substitutions, and could be worked out on the basis of their frequencies. Hew had shown some skill in sounding out their secrets, and it brought him satisfaction. Confinement gave his mind the quietness to work, and the ciphers had distracted him from other, darker thoughts. He took a simple pleasure in the spaces filled, clear and unequivocal, and if the end and purpose of it was to hang a man, he did not think of that.

Sometimes, in those early days, Laurence took him out with him to explore the streets and stairways to the Thames. The walks took place at dusk, the flagstones in the market places bared to bone and blood, or at the breaking dawn, the milky vapours of the river rising in each whisper of their frozen breath, where Hew could see the waking city, stripped down to its flesh, before the pink-tipped sunlight warmed it back to life. They travelled from the Tower, by boat, to London Bridge, or wandered by St Pauls, to browse among the bookstalls at the close of day, where Laurence once bought a psalter and the Book of Common Prayer, which he gave to Hew. 'They are not the same, as those you may be used to. You should know the difference.' And Hew had thanked him, touched, and grateful for the gifts. They had walked among the houses of the potent and the great, by Fleet Street and the Strand, while Laurence gave accounts of those who worked and lived there. Once upon a dusk, they had turned into a quiet little street, and stopped before a door that was plain and unremarkable, like many others tucked behind the highway of fair mansions, as a good man walks in shadow of the grand. 'Whose house is this?' Hew had asked, and Laurence had answered, it was his own.

He had taken Hew inside, to a white-washed chamber stark in its simplicity, with nothing to adorn it but some cloths of black work and a shelf of books. Hew had shared a supper there with Laurence and his wife, and a little daughter, who had thrown herself at Laurence, squealing in delight, 'Daddie, Oh, my Daddie!'

'She is generally asleep, by the time he is home,' her mother Jane had said, while Laurence had lifted her to settle in his lap. 'This is my friend, Hew Cullan. He is far from home, and he has no little girl, so we must be kind to him.'

One trouble had disturbed him in those early days, and robbed him of the pleasure he had found in the deciphering. Among the siege of letters that he dealt with day by day, he had had no word of Giles and Meg. He had asked whether he might write to his family, to tell them he was safe. Laurence had refused.

'But they will think that I am dead.'

Laurence had answered, 'Better that way. Then their own lives are not drawn into danger. What they do not know, they cannot hide. They are in the care of Sir Andrew Wood, the coroner. He will have to work to extricate himself, and your family too, from any implication in your escape. It will take him some time to build up credit with the king.

'Better, for the while, if you are counted dead, until your family has been cleared of all possible suspicion, and the king no longer frets upon these strange events. Your escape must not be linked to Master Secretary Walsingham. Play dead for the while. When it is safe to write, be assured that we shall tell you.'

'But why should Andrew Wood have risked so much for me, in bringing me to Walsingham? To stop me speaking of his dealings to the king? It were simpler, surely, to have had me killed.'

'Now that I cannot say. I do not know the man. Perhaps he has a liking for you,' Laurence had replied.

The question of what force had moved the crownar's mind came back to Hew, and troubled still. Sometimes, in the night, it would not let him rest.

For all that, he took solace in the work to which he had been set, and the friendship he was shown, at the house in Seething Lane. A day had come at last when he was sent alone, with a letter to be taken to the French Ambassador, to his house at Salisbury Court. That packet, he was certain now, had been of little worth. But the value of it lay in the introduction; the understanding that he was deserving of that trust, in Laurence Tomson's eyes, was lifting to his heart. He was ready to go out, to be tested in the world.

The first command is patience, Laurence had instructed him. Patience was prerequisite in any kind of spy. But it was not the kind of patience that suffers and endures. It was an endless restlessness, tempered and alert, pricked to wait and watch, alert to any sign. The patience of the cat that fixed upon the mouse-hole watches it for hours, each twitching hair and sinew taut and tightly poised. That kind of patience Phelippes had, that left no pause for doubt.

Chapter 2

Leadenhall

Grey Gelding kept his course, coming into Ware a little after ten, where Hew had resolved to rest for a while, out of the heat of the sun. He entrusted the horse to the ostler at the White Hart Inn to be watered and fed. 'For he is cold and moist, and serves best in that element. I would keep him cool, and sheltered from the glare.'

At twelve, he took his dinner at the common board. Sixpence at the White Hart bought a satisfying ordinary, of bread and cheese with beef, or mutton in a broth, buttered eggs and beer. He played a game of dice with a group of merchants who were travelling home to Yorkshire, and at their invitation left among their company, safer in a crowd.

Though Grey Gelding was well rested, Hew let him straggle at the tail end of the group. He had no wish to be drawn into a closer confidence. 'Trust no one,' Laurence Tomson said. 'Not you? Nor Thomas Phelippes?' Hew had teased him once.

'*Anglicus Angelus est cui nunquam credere fas est. Dum tibi dicut ave, tanquam ab hoste cave.* The Englishman an angel is, which trusted will deceive thee. Beware of him as of a foe, when he doth say God save thee,' Laurence had retorted. 'Phelippes, most of all.'

He could not recall when first he heard the name. He had read it in the letters, carefully endorsed, over and again. Phelippes wrote a small, distinctive hand. Hew came to know the shape of it, familiar as his own, before he met the man. Some while into his stay at Seething Lane, Laurence had produced a page of script in cipher.

'Cut your teeth on this. The quick is dead and gone, the answer is no longer now of any consequence, but it is knotted tight enough to put you to some exercise. It took Phelippes months to read the Latin script. What your hot brain makes of it, I will wait to see.'

He had worried day and night for a week upon the text, but found that he could make no shape nor sense of it. It was, he saw at once, a simple substitution cipher, play for any child. A schoolboy could have solved it, he concluded furiously. Then he understood.

Phelippes was a Cambridge man, his Latin pure and faultless. While Phelippes was a scholar of the first degree, those Jesuits, who wrote the ciphered text, were not. Their secrets had been framed in a pattern of mistakes, in grammar so contorted, incomplete and villainous, it defied all sense, but the method in its working showed itself to Hew. Alerted to the errors there, he solved it easily.

His courage had been lifted to discover he could read a darkly ciphered script, to hear the very heartbeat of the man who wrote it, and to know his mind.

It was not long after that, in November of that year – 1583, and a vicious winter then – when Walsingham returned, to notice him at last. This notice stilled in him a shiver of excitement, stirred by his success, a surge of foolish pride. He smiled now to recall how supple he had been, how tender to the blade on which he would be whet, how willing to be shaped and put to sharp effect. Sir Francis had not mellowed to him, nor improved in health. His words were brief and brusque, and spoken under cover of a wafting handkerchief, as though he might breathe in some malheur of the Scots, though Laurence had equipped Hew with clean water, soap and shirts. 'You have been in this house now, how long? Two or three months? Then tis more than time for you to earn your keep. I have found a place for you. Master William Phillips, a merchant in cloth, seeks a privy clerk to assist him with his business at his place at Leadenhall. And also at the custom house.'

In his greenness, Hew had echoed, showing his dismay. 'I am to be a clerk?'

'What say you, sir? Too proud? Perhaps,' Walsingham had pricked him, cruel in his rebuke, 'you have some other friend, to keep you in that state in which you would be found?'

'By no means,' he had answered, 'should I be so proud. But I had thought . . . I had hoped, that the singular learning to which your honour has put me in the past two months, might have equipped me for a more singular service.'

At that, the man had smiled. 'And suppose that were the case, would you have expected I should advertise the fact? "This man is Hew Cullan. I have trained him for a spy." I should not loose you on the world, as an honest clerk, whom no one would suspect?'

Hew had begged his pardon then. 'I did not understand.'

'That may be excused. But what I cannot let pass, is that you let your feelings show so plainly in your face. You have much to learn. Consider this a trial. William Phillips is one of the customers for wool in the port of London. In name at least, for in the last years pleading frailty or else by idle negligence, he has farmed his post out to a series of deputies. His deputy reports a strange occurrence in the custom house; an unusual case of fraud.'

The custom house, by common knowledge, was rife with theft and fraud of every shape and kind from the petty to the grand, with the full collusion of the officers who worked there, most of whom were merchants too, and who had little recompense for service to the Crown. It was a tacit understanding of a man in public office, that the office he had paid for, or won by rank and privilege, was his to put to such advantage as could there be found.

'It is not common,' Walsingham had said, 'that the customer himself is heard to make complaint of it. In this most curious case, a theft is taking place under his very nose, and he is baffled by it. Monies are placed in a locked chest, in a strong vault in the custom house. The key to the chest is kept by the collector – or in this case, his deputy – locked in a box. The key to that box is kept by the controller. The box is opened only in presence of them both. Each time they open the chest, the monies inside are diminished. And each of them swears he does not know the cause. The chest has a leak, through which gold runs like sand. Or else there is witchcraft involved.'

'Or else, they are lying,' Hew had suggested.

'That, I confess, had occurred to me. Master William Phillips swears it is not so. He requires our help. This riddle of concealment, I shall leave you to detect. Since I have it on authority that you are an expert in resolving mysteries, you shall use your skills to find the matter out. Report to Laurence Tomson what you find.'

As always, Hew was spurred and quickened at the thought of mystery. Doubtless, there was nothing to it but a web of lies. He would soon find out. But his interest in the case was dampened at that time by his fear for the friends of whom he had no word. He had appealed to Walsingham, for any small intelligence.

Walsingham had made a great show of remembering, as though he had the information somewhere in his mind, but could not have expected to have ever had a call for it.

'Our foothold in Scotland is slidder as glass. The king persists in his affection for the earl of Arran, and despite better counsel, will not be put off from his course. There is stirring against the Protestant ministers. Your friends at the New College are fallen from grace, when it comes to their king, in spite of their faith,' he had acknowledged at last.

'But what of my sister, and Giles Locke, her husband?' Hew had demanded. 'What news of them?'

Walsingham had answered, wryly, that he did not think their names had occurred in the despatches. 'As I understand, they are in the compass of Sir Andrew Wood. He is at present building up his credit with the king, which is by no means assured. You should be aware, that the chain which links us to him, and him to your family, is a tangled and delicate one. Were it to be broken, I cannot assure the consequence. You may play your part, by doing as you're told.'

Hew had understood. The safety of his friends and family rested in a man he neither liked nor trusted. His hopes were held to ransom by the traitor, Andrew Wood. He could not help but say, 'Sir, I know not what you heard of me, from such as Andrew Wood who care little for their country, but I must tell you that my allegiance is first and foremost to the king of Scotland, and will remain so, though I die for it.'

Walsingham had frowned, but had not seemed displeased. 'I bear that in mind. But you do Sir Andrew a disservice, when you call him traitor. His allegiance, to speak truth, is not at odds with yours.'

'He sold you secrets,' Hew had objected.

'You may parry words. What you class as secrets, I should call intelligence.'

'I do not think the king would care to call it that.'

'Ah, perhaps not. But you will be the first to acknowledge, that particular young man is a poor judge of character. We shall agree on this; while you are here, and under my protection, I shall not ask of you anything that may call into doubt your loyalty to that king. We are careful, too, to see his trust restored in you. Meanwhile, it can do no hurt to place you in the custom house. I have told William Phillips you are an inquisitor, and of some renown. It is worth your while to know, that Thomas Phelippes is his son. For the sake of the engagement, I have told them you are known to him. That is not a lie, for so you shall be, presently.

'Laurence Tomson tells me that you have made remarkable progress in steganography. When you can compose a cipher of your own, that Phelippes cannot solve, then I will believe it.'

And with those words, that stage was passed; Hew found himself dismissed.

The further north they rode the thicker came the mud that clogged the horses' hooves and splattered over flanks to stop the roll of carts, the furrowed slough of months of rainfall burying their wheels. As the merchants slowed, Hew drove Grey Gelding on, and in space of half an hour, left them far behind. He was conscious of the loss of progress as the path went on, stony, sparse and narrow as the grey horse tired. He could not gather speed, in darkness or in rain, nor hope to find momentum in the coming days. Therefore he determined to drive on to Caxton, so to steal a march upon the road ahead. For did not forget the purpose of his ride, the leaden hopes and faces left at Leadenhall.

He felt a fond affection for the Phillips family, by force of their simplicity, their failure to collude in the conspiracies around them, to be caught up in intrigues. They had little understanding of the secrets of their son, or the work he did for Walsingham, though they were staunchly proud of it. Only William Phillips sometimes fostered doubts. Once, in failing health, he had confessed to Hew, 'It would not give me ease, to see Thomas in the custom house. I do not say, you see, that he would not be honest. There are in that place so many more temptations . . . a thousand ways a man can treat to serve himself and not the state. . . . I do not say he would, but he has wit and will, and only God can know what he may choose do with them. He keeps his secrets close. I cannot know his heart. And that, you see, is troubling in a son.'

The house at Leadenhall rang out clear and shrill when all his children came, though that was rare enough. They were brought up in the country, on the Lavenham estate where the second son kept watch upon his sheep, and on the Suffolk cloth men in whose cloths he dealt. A third son travelled for his father's business over sea, to markets which had shrunk and shrivelled hard in recent times. His letters were read out, a source of news and comfort, though little was divulged in them beyond the price of wool. However slim the thread, his mother spun it deftly, woven into gossip to share out among her friends. The letters were antithesis to those that came to Walsingham, so little were they filled of matter and of worth. And yet beneath the ink was carried on a life, the filtered, fractured figment of an absent son.

William, on the whole, preferred to be in London, wife Joan at his side, and without that brood, to which she seemed to him unreasonably attached. Wherever else he ventured, Frances was the one most often in his company, and the only one he could not do without. In London, she kept house, as well as his accounts, and when the younger children came, she kept them too, as quiet in their place as might be effected, and as well amused.

Together in one bed slept the five youngest sons, and Frances shared a second with the daughters of the house, in a narrow closet next to Joan and William's own. From the boys' bedchamber led a ladder to the storeroom in the loft, where a feather mattress had been laid for Hew.

'It is quiet, at night,' Frances had said, 'and at least, warm.'

Packed to the rafters with sheep's fleece and fells, the loft was close and suffocating in the summer months. In winter, Hew had shivered to the scrabble of the mice, who made their nests and burrows in the pelts, until Frances had extended there the service of the cat, a sleek and savage mouser by the name of Tybalt, beyond his natural manor by the kitchen fire. The plague of mice, receding, was replaced by fleas, for which she brought a candle, in a bowl of water, to be lit at night. 'They will leap to the light, and be drowned. By no means let it burn close to the wool, or where it may be knocked, or you will start a fire.'

The candle was illicit, and a mark of trust between them, at which he had been touched. By such small acts of kindness, Frances had consoled him through the winter's bane. And sometimes, lying wakeful in the flicker of that light, a weak and gentle flame, he felt content to lie lapped in the wool, when the wind blew its draught through the rest of the house, or rain drummed at the roof with its close, urgent beat.

It was early in the evening, on a foul November fish day, when he first quit Seething Lane, and was shown in to the parlour of the house at Leadenhall, over and above the busy marketplace. The children had been absent, yet their shadows felt, in every crack and corner of the timbered house, had left him an impression of a well-loved family home. The parlour was cluttered with boxes and baskets spilling out silks and half-finished works, with games of chess and cards, and old and new books that bulged from their spines kippered and split in the blaze from the fire. Countless cushions had been stitched, no folding chair or footstool came without its pillow worked with flower or bird, no shelf without a mantle cloth, no floor without its slippers, poppy red and gold. The walls had been hung with crude Flemish landscapes, painted onto cloths, bought by the dozen at the winter fairs. Though little of it grand, or of the finest sort, it gave the house a pleasing colour, and a homely warmth.

William, Joan and Frances had been settled down to supper of a spinach tart with currants, and a sugar glaze, a confection of a kind they particularly enjoyed, oversweet and perfumed to Hew's foreign taste. They had received him warmly, with a searching inquisition, and, on William's part, a faint note of defence. The old man had been cautious, wary still of Walsingham, and Joan unexpectedly keen, in her will to have news of her son.

'Master Secretary tells me,' William had informed him, swilling down the spinach with a draught of wine, 'that you are an expert, in detecting thieves.'

'I think it very like,' Joan had suggested, 'that Scotland is a place that is overrun with villains. For so much have I heard, that there is not a man among them to be trusted. All of them are thieves.'

'Not all, for certain, aunt,' Frances had protested.

'I do not say that Hew here is a villain. Only that, and he a Scotchman, he is well qualified to know one when he sees one.'

'Such are his credentials,' William had retorted, who would not have this credit challenged by his wife, 'and since he has the recommendation of the queen's own secretary, we take him at his word. He is besides, a friend of Tom's.' It was not clear whether he viewed this as an advantage.

'Now that, I count as strange,' Joan Phillips had persisted, 'For I never heard Thomas speak aught of a Scotchman, nor has he been in Scotland, to my best account.'

'You know that Thomas does not like to speak about his work,' Frances had defended him. Hew had thanked her for it, secret in his heart.

'Not to you, perhaps.'

'Nor, indeed, to *you*.' William had observed. 'He is, for a son, most intricate and secretive. It must be deplored.'

'The less, since we have Hew here, to tell us what he knows of him.' The mother would not be deterred. 'Was it in Cambridge you met? Or perhaps it was France?'

Hew had remembered what Laurence had taught him – speak as much of the truth as you can, say as little as possible, when you must lie – and answered, 'It was in France, where I lived for some years.'

As far then as he could, he had told them all: his father had been an advocate in the Scottish courts, and had sent him to study law in Paris – the Scots had no equivalent of English inns of court. In Paris he had met the Scots physician, Giles Locke, who had become his brother-in-law. They had returned to the university at St Andrews, where Giles had become principal of St Salvator's College. Hew's father had died, and he had tried to honour him by concluding his studies at the bar, in service of an Edinburgh advocate. He had not had the stomach for the work. He had worked at St Andrews as professor in the law. But he had found in himself a restless urge to find out a particular kind of justice, which the law did not satisfy. His brother-in-law Giles had been appointed Visitor, with the task of examining unnatural deaths, in which he had assisted him. Where Giles had found the final cause, Hew found himself adept at finding the efficient one; he had discovered murderers.

Mistress Phillips had gasped. How many murderers had he unmasked?

He had considered. 'In the space of four years, over four cases, I should say, six.'

'Lord save us! Six murderers! Then St Andrews must be a most bloody, lawless place. There are not so many murders in the whole of England, and in the whole of London, no unnatural deaths!' Joan Phillips had exclaimed. Hew smiled at that now, and wondered if the traitors spiked up on the Bishopsgate might have disagreed.

William, with a shrewdness copied in his son, had asked, 'And of those six murderers, how many of them did you bring to justice?'

Hew had hesitated then, as he hesitated now. 'Justice is served in many different ways. But I suppose you must mean, brought before the courts.'

'Do not prevaricate with me, sir. I have that from my son, and Tom will tell you plainly, as he is your friend, I will not stand for it. I mean, as you must know, how many were there hanged.'

He had answered *one*, quiet then, and fierce. That one death he kept still in conscience and in mind, and he was far from proud of it. 'That was the man I had served at the bar, who turned out to be false, and wicked in his heart.'

It had been direct, a challenge to his host, who took it in good part. 'Small return, no doubt, is preferable to none. A fraud has been detected in our custom house. Until the thief is found, we are all of us under suspicion, and most of all, myself, since I have the charge of it. And since I cannot work the matter out, I must answer for it, or give up the thief. Therefore am I resolute, and grateful for your help.' The worry and the strain of it showed clearly in his face. 'I suspect a clerk. But I cannot for the world fathom out which one.'

'Then,' Hew had promised, 'we shall set a trap.'

He had done his best to allay the clerks' suspicions, and to engage their trust. But the presence of a stranger was sufficient in itself to bring the thief in check. And though he had succeeded in uncovering the evidence, as carefully the culprit had obscured his trail; before he could be caught, for want of certain proof, the perpetrator fled.

William had been satisfied. It was enough for him that his office had been cleared of collusion in the fraud. The same could not be said of Phelippes and of Walsingham. The placement was a test that Hew both passed and failed.

On that first day, he had felt that he had answered them sufficiently, for what there was deficient there, they answered for themselves. They saw what they would see, believing what they wanted to believe. Helpful in the matter was the seal of Francis Walsingham.

32

Joan Phillips in particular, perked up at the name. Hew thought it quite unlikely they had ever met. William was less sure. He shuddered in the glare of the Secretary's suspicion, from which no one but the queen of England, and perhaps, her treasurer, was thoroughly immune. At times, he had to appeal to his son Thomas to intercede on his behalf in his business interests, in representations to that great man. And so, while he welcomed Hew's help in this matter, he viewed the intervention with a cautious circumspection. His instincts had been sound. He had believed, nonetheless, that Hew was placed in his household as a personal servant, as a cover for his investigations in the custom house. He had never quite grasped that it was the other way round.

'I do not understand,' Frances had remarked at last, on that first occasion when he told his tale. 'Why you are come to England, when it is so clear to see how much you miss your home. Surely, since it grieves you, you ought to return there.'

For he had been too free and open with the truth, of the parents he had lost, of his sister Meg, who lived upon the land, and of her husband Giles, whom he had assisted working for the Crown, and of his work and teaching at the university. And all of which convinced, as it was meant to do, and coloured in the telling with the rawness of his loss, his exile from the country he had called his own, so moved and impressed them that they took him to their hearts.

He had answered simply, there was nothing for him there, since he did not like the law. 'In my heart, I have learned that I am not a scholar.' He had dared to suppose, their son Thomas was the same. 'He stilled in me that spirit of adventure, that he has himself. When Master Secretary Walsingham came on embassy to Scotland, I applied to him, whether with my learning I might be of service, in some poor application of my studies in the law. It pleased him to accept me as a servant in his household. At Thomas' request, he has sent me on to you.'

'You see, there,' Joan had said, comforted at this. 'That is a thoughtful boy. Indeed, it is the essence of a loving son.'

Chapter 3

A Quiet Man

They came to Caxton village on the cusp of nightfall, as the clock struck nine. Both were hot and tired; the grey horse had begun to hang and falter, picking over stones, fretful and fastidious. They were thankful to find shelter at the Crown, William's favoured resting place on forays into Cambridgeshire. Grey Gelding was familiar with the stable here, and well assured of welcome. On credit to his master, Hew had the indulgence of a private room underneath the eaves, where he took his supper, with a stoup of ale to wash away the dust and rigor of the road. There he lay to rest, to quiet introspection in the rising darkness, muffled from the drinkers who made merry down below. The bed was sweet and clean, and presently he felt the willing bands of sleep, and closed his eyes to doze.

It had been at night that he had first encountered Phelippes, not long after Christmastide, lying in his bed in the loft at Leadenhall. He was woken at the crack of a brittle winter's dawn by the wrenching of the blankets that were wrapped around his feet.

'Jesu, thou art sluggish as a Scotsman's fart. Make shift will you, sirrah?'

He dared not strike a light to look upon the face, which, dredged up from his dreams, he knew belonged to Tom. But when the morning broke, and he saw him clearly, Phelippes was so like, and unlike, his imagining, he had to look again. He was small and slight, in his narrow-waisted doublet, slender as a woman, or a young boy half his age. He wore his fine hair long, a darkened shade of sand that tapered to the yellow of a sculpted beard, tenderly exact. His fair complexion scabbed and pitted with the pox had deepened to a rose of a more livid shade. His eyes, a clear blue-grey, looked blandly on the world, and kept their secrets close. In looks, he and Frances could well have been brother and sister. Yet they were nothing alike. Frances wore her flaxen tresses pinned back from her brow, the bloom upon her cheekbones delicate and clear, the gaze in her grey eyes intelligent and frank.

By morning they were close, though not exactly, friends. It had been a bold and thoughtful course of action, for if Phelippes had arrived home in the fullness of the day, they would not have had the chance of private talk alone. By breakfast, they had known each other more than well enough to convince the Phillips family that they had been friends for years.

'Tomorrow, you begin your schooling,' Phelippes had declared.

Hew had pointed out he had already started it.

'Ah, and you may think so. So much have I heard. Your Latin is beneath contempt, Laurence Tomson says.'

So Phelippes had begun a calculated rivalry, and by mercilessly pricking at Hew's strengths and skills, had shaped and sharpened them. As tutor, he would spare no stricture nor waste words on praise.

'I shall want some time to play with my old friend, and show to him the town, that he is ill acquainted with,' he had told his father. William Phillips, Hew remembered, had not been best pleased. In the space of a month, he had found Hew's service indispensable, in his trade at home as much as in his dealings in the custom house. Though he relied on Frances in the keeping of accounts, Hew could write a letter with more plenitude and force, the full weight of the law, resting in his hands, while William Phillips' own hand, riddled with the gout, struggled to adapt to the holding of a pen. Wherefore he resisted: 'He is acquainted with the markets and the custom house, and with Leadenhall. I cannot think where else he would wish to go. At sixpence a day, he is here to work.' Hew was retained as his clerk for eight pounds a year, with full bed and board, sheets and a blanket, shirts, coat and hose. If nothing else, the cloth merchant was generous with his clothes.

'At *five* pence a day,' his son had corrected, 'you may bear the loss. Besides, he belongs to Master Secretary Walsingham, and is here on loan.'

The old man had bridled at this, but despite his objections, Hew was released two days weekly to Tom, without loss of a place more open and respectable, or remit of pay.

In those days, he was worked as hard as ever in his life. Phelippes had a house in Holborn, where he taught Hew how to make up ciphers of his own, convolute and intricate, some of several layers. Of such ciphers, Walsingham required an endless new supply, for they were changed as quickly as his agents could get used to them. They must be opaque enough to baffle anyone who did not hold the key, yet clear enough to spill their secrets easily, to anyone who did. Hew had built his first attempt upon the Book of Common Prayer, and had been dismayed when Phelippes solved it easily. 'You could not choose a key more indiscreet and obvious. Why not write it plain, in English, and be done with it? Or if you would be cryptical, in your own vile Scots?' He meant no lasting malice in his piercing wit, which was his natural voice; Phelippes was a perfect mimic, and his cruelties were dispensed with careless generosity, often ending up in helpless fits of laughter. His mimicry had taught Hew to amend those imperfections which had marked him as a Scot, and return to the refinements he had learned among the French, which Phelippes, even-handed, ridiculed in turn. His scorn had the effect of spurring on Hew's efforts, which was his intent.

Hew's education, under Phelippes' hands, took him to the belly of that teeming city, to taverns, bull and bear pits, dank and fleshly stews. When he surfaced, he could taste it, sawdust, iron and blood, and a new kind of excitement quickened in his veins. With Phelippes, he had played at dice and dealt in corners, dimly lit, with a stream of dark-lipped strangers, who slipped by like ghosts. Phelippes had a liberal purse, which he dispensed in drink, though he was rarely drunk.

Nor was he ever drawn into a tavern brawl, for even when it seemed to Hew he started one himself, he somehow had the knack of sliding out from under it. In all things, he was quick. His shrill wit and incisiveness were often turned to charm; and no one could deny he made engaging company. Yet though Hew was aware he owed a debt to him, for all his time and care, he did not feel at ease with him, or count him as a friend. When he could escape, he went to Seething Lane, and sometimes in that winter left the filth and stew to walk with Laurence once again through quiet lanes and streets, or row upon the river that was white with frost. On those rare occasions, he felt clean, at peace. One day at a fair he had bought a little horse of sugar-gilded gingerbread for Laurence Tomson's child. Frances found a ribbon for a halter round its neck, a little scrap of red. Phelippes had remarked upon it, watchful and amused. 'You have won the friendship of the quiet man. That is rare indeed. No other man but Walsingham ever saw his house.' By habit, he referred to Laurence as 'the Quiet Man'; sometimes, too, the 'Muscovite', which Hew, when he first heard it, had not understood. He took the sugar horse to Seething Lane, for he would not for the world disturb him at his rest. But Laurence had insisted he must come himself, to give the child her gift. Hew had gone to dine with them one Sunday after church on cold cuts and a cheese, and a salad made of roots. The little girl had said the grace, and Jane had sung a psalm. The child had clasped the horse. 'He is too good to eat. I will keep him safe, in my treasure box. May I fetch it, now?'

Jane had smiled, why not? The child had disappeared into the sleeping space, returning with a box. And Hew, who had expected to be shown a pebble or a shell, was astonished at the toys the little girl brought out. A pocket wrought in silver with a clasp of pearl, a psalter set with emeralds, in a case of gold, a ruby like a gull's egg in a golden nest.

'My Daddie got these for me. The bird's nest was a gift, from the king of Russia. He is called the Czar.'

'Put those away, now,' Laurence had said. 'They are not for Sunday play. The little horse too. You can eat him at supper.'

His daughter had kissed the gingerbread horse, sucking the sugar that clung to her lips. 'I will keep him for ever. I never will eat him.'

Her mother had laughed. 'Do not make promises that you cannot keep.'

When Jane bent low to fill his cup, Hew had confessed to her, 'I feel foolish to have brought her such a trifling thing.'

'Indeed, you should not. You can see by her face how much she loves him, though I fear he will be gone by bedtime.'

'I had no idea she had such precious toys.' He could not reconcile it with that modest house.

'Precious?' Jane had echoed. 'I suppose they are.'

'But you must know their worth.'

'To Laurence, they are worth that they make our daughter smile, like your gift of gingerbread, and little more than that. They were given to him by some great men on his travels. He went, in his time, to many far places. Moscow is the place he remembers most of all. But he does not care to mention it. Katherine and I are glad he does not go there now. We do not see enough of him.'

'What do you speak of?' Laurence had smiled at them, helping his daughter to close up the box.

'I was telling Hew, of the travels you once made.'

'Once.' It was plain enough that he would not be drawn. *The Muscovite*, Hew thought. What Laurence had been once was buried in the past. Phelippes might allude it, but would never tell.

'See how modest he is,' Jane had laughed. 'He does not care at all for precious things.'

Laurence had glanced at his small daughter's face. 'Do I not, though?' he had asked.

Hew had worked hard, and learned quickly. He was rewarded at last. Walsingham sent word to him that he might send a letter with the despatches to Scotland to his brother-in-law, Giles Locke, at the university. The terms of the letter were carefully prescribed by Thomas Phelippes: the ambush at Dysart had surprised Hew, as much as his captors. The outlaws had left him for dead. By God's grace, he had survived, and crept into a wood, where he lived on roots and berries for the space of several weeks. Once the clamour had died down, he had made his way through shadows to the English border, which he had crossed buried deep inside a cart of dung.

'Why dung?' he had objected. Phelippes had grinned at him. 'Because the Scots will swallow any kind of shit. You want a story that is credible, that does not leave a trace, with just enough of the implausible to test their disbelief; that small, contentious detail will persuade them it is true.'

Hew had not been convinced. Phelippes was indulging his own foul sense of humour. Yet he had no option but to comply. To send a private letter of his own – even if it did not pose a danger to his family – would cost more than he earned in a year.

At Berwick, Phelippes' version of the tale went on, he had met with old friends of his father, who had helped him with money and clothes – you were a sore sight to them – Phelippes had sniggered – and set him on the way to London, where he found employment in the custom house, by virtue of his education and his skill in languages. A letter by return could safely find him there.

He sent his love to his sister, and assured them both that he was safe and well, and whatever else they heard, he denied all accusations that were made of him, maliciously, and falsely, and swore before God who had saved and sheltered him, that he was loyal still, as ever, to God and King James.

That, Phelippes said, was all. He was not permitted to include a private line for Meg, but the letter must be sent to Giles at the College of St Salvator, where there was no doubt it would be read and noted, by whatever spies were working for the king. There was, of course, no mention made of Phelippes or of Walsingham, the house in Seething Lane or of Leadenhall.

Even then, Phelippes would not be content, scouring through the letter he had made Hew write again, with no subtle piece of Scots, lest some secret might be hidden in a foreign word. The result was anodyne, squeezed dry of its sentiment, and all that had remained to assure Giles of its writer was the sureness of its script, in Hew's familiar hand, that was framed and tempered in the time they shared in France, no other mark remaining of the sender's heart.

Hew had questioned, at the time, the direction to the custom house. 'For surely, nothing sent there can be thought secure?'

'It will never reach there,' Phelippes had assured him, and the answer, sure enough, which Hew awaited eagerly, had never graced the place to which it was directed – 'Her Majesty's customs at the port of London' – but came to him direct, shorn of string and seal, from Seething Lane itself. Giles had written also under some constraint, in phrasing Hew felt certain had been overlooked in Scotland. Giles and Meg gave thanks to God that Hew was safe. They prayed that by God's grace he would be returned to them. Sir Andrew Wood, the crownar, had captured four men who took part in the raid on Hew's party at Dysart; the four men had been hanged at the side of the moor, where their corpses hung still, to creak in the wind, a warning to all who passed by. One had caught fire, by itself; a sure and certain proof that they were now in Hell. Before they were hanged, the four men had confessed; they had slaughtered the king's men for their bright swords and doublets, and had left Hew for dead. Therefore his escape must be thought fortuitous, and nought to do with them.

Andrew Wood, as it seemed, had hanged his own men. Why had they confessed? Because, as Hew supposed, the killing of the king's men was an act of treason, and there were other, less appealing, ways to die. Andrew Wood the sheriff hanged them quick and high. He caught them with the bridles of the horses in their hands, and that was his prerogative. Perhaps, the king would say, his actions were impetuous, his hastiness presumptuous. Sir Andrew would reply he acted out of loyalty to his Grace, a will to keep the peace, in that unruly place, a thirsting for revenge. He trod a dangerous path. In his waking consciousness, Hew remembered little of the dark and frantic night, when he was wrested from his captors' grip on Dysart Muir, the outer vale of Hell, where earth was turned to fire. Two of the king's men had perished in the fray. Of those others, who fled, God knew what hopes they had now.

Phelippes had asked him, what was the matter, conscious of the shadow that had crossed his face.

'Six men died to bring me here. Two that were guards of the king, and four that were charged with their deaths.' Hew had no control, no kenning of the ambush, and as little hand in what was his own fate, yet that did not absolve him of his sense of guilt.

'Then let us hope that you are worth the cost.'

The rest of Giles' letter dealt with slight domestic things: the land at Kenly Green, the keeping of the farm, 'We pray to God that all may be restored to you, as you must be to us. Sir Andrew Wood attends to us, and takes care of our claim. God willing, you may once again find favour with the king.'

'Amen to that,' Phelippes had said.

The channel had been opened then. And there were further letters, to and from both Giles and Meg. It was a relief to him to know when they were safe, which as the years had passed, he had not always known. Yet relief had been tempered with guilt. He had carried those deaths on his conscience for days. Phelippes, while he mocked, was sharp enough to see where a man might be most vulnerable, and careful enough to attend to his needs. He had taken Hew out to drink at the Bull, drowning his sorrows in sack. There he had asked him if he had a lass, someone back at home. Hew had not thought of, *would not think of* Clare, and had answered, no.

'In a service such as ours,' Phelippes had observed, 'a man should have a wife, or at least a wench. It does not serve him well, to be quite alone, as you seem to be.'

'You and I are the same,' Hew had pointed out. 'For I do not see you with a wife yourself.' In age and education, they were both alike, then twenty-eight years old.

'That is a fault that I intend to remedy, now that I am home. But for you, whose life is thrown in turmoil, I can recommend the widow of a friend, who will keep you company these chill winter nights, and offer consolation in your present grief.'

'I thank you,' he had answered, 'but I do not want a whore.'

'Audrey is not a whore. And, if she were, you could not afford her. She will like you, I think, and you will like her. She is a breath of fresh air.'

She was not that. But what she was, was billowing, open and voluptuous. He found between her sheets a dark, familiar scent, sweaty, stale and sweet, fleshly warm and comforting. Audrey's husband had been killed in the service of Lord Cobham's brother, while he was ambassador in Paris. It had not, Phelippes said, been a glorious death; he had lost his life in a drunken brawl, but Sir Henry had been moved to subscribe to a small pension, in view of Audrey's plight. She had given birth to her husband's child, eleven months after his death (her womb being stopped on account of her grief). The infant was lodged with foster parents landward from the city, and on Sunday afternoons, she would walk out to see it, sometimes taking Hew, to admire its fat fists and fair apple cheeks. She had taken Hew to bed with a willing heart; she had sorely missed a husband's conversation, by which she meant nothing he said.

Audrey's conversation, vigorous and frank, had restored Hew to himself, and brought relief from a burden that could not be shared. Phelippes had been right. There was comfort in the flesh. Thomas, for his part, had wanted something more. He had sought a wife in whom he could confide. His parents' choice had not been Mary, who was dark and saturnine. Frances had confessed, she found her cold and strange. She was, in every way, a perfect match for Phelippes. They shared an inner life, of perfect understanding. And Mary doubtless knew what Thomas did at Chartley, while she lay bereft, in his father's house.

Chapter 4

Chartley

Hew arrived at Stowe-by-Chartley five days after leaving London, in the afternoon of the eighteenth of July. On departure from Caxton, the grey horse had slowed, weathering listlessly in the fierce sun, which gathered in force as the steep road inclined. Somewhere north of Stamford, they had left the track, diverting to the west through a maze of paths, to follow on the trail of the post from Loughborough. They came into that place to find the post long gone. A farmer's boy, eventually, had walked with them for miles through thickets, weeds and mud, straddling streams and ponds, and left them in the village leading to the hall, in shadow of the castle higher up the hill. Grey Gelding, plodding softly through a haze of heat, came to rest at last. The manor here belonged to the earl of Essex and the family Devereux, whose crest was traced on every door and lintel post in gold and crimson lake. His mansion was built around a cobbled courtyard, settled in a moat that on this summer's day sank deep and still and soundless as the sky above. Like the scattered cottages the manor overlooked, its timbered slats were closed, and seemed to be asleep. No one took the air, or water from its fountain, no one kept the watch above the wooden parapets, cock-eyed and incongruous upon its gabled roofs. A path had been cut to the edge of the moat, felling and clearing the earl's copse of trees, and here Hew dismounted and let the horse loose. He walked on alone to that smooth flank of water, and stood there a moment, reflective, to look, when he sensed at his back the stirring of leaves, and catching the sunlight, the glint of a sword.

'If you care for your life, do not move.'

Grey Gelding, driven from the shelter of the wood, harried by his halter in a stranger's hand, passed by him so closely he caught his hot scent, the sliver of sweat, a diamond-drop glistening across his sleek back. 'Please treat him well. He has come a long way.'

There were four men at his back. Doubtless, they had watched him as he rode up through the wood, hidden by the trees. One among them asked. 'What business have you here?'

'I have a letter,' he said, 'for Thomas Phelippes.'

'Who told you he was here?'

'The man who sent it to him.' He had learned from Phelippes how to be impassive, to present a coolness, stubborn and reserved, in response to questioning. He applied that learning now, and was rewarded by confusion in his captor's face, the flickering of doubt. They stepped back to confer. They were, he thought, makeshift young soldiers, unsure of their command. One of them said, 'You must come to the keep, to speak with Sir Amias.'

Hew agreed. 'Of course.'

Sir Amias Paulet had the keeping of that place, and of its present guest. Phelippes ranked Sir Amias close among his friends, had served with him in France, and counted him among the few men he could trust. Sir Amias was a man who did not shirk his charge. It was likely that the soldiers here belonged to him, and not to Robert Devereux. That, Hew considered, was in some way a relief. What concerned him, most of all, was the temper of the men, who were ill at ease. They reminded him of skittish, temperamental horses, that were quickly put to flight, and could not be relied upon. There was no knowing what might fright them, or where that fright might lead. It was hard not to find their nervousness infectious.

Hew followed to the castle, which had fallen into ruins. The moat that surrounded it, a clogged and brackish green, sank deeper than the lake which graced the nearby manor house, and its stagnant waters seeped into the rock. What remained of the walls had a penetrating dampness, and a bleak blank coldness that no sun could lift.

The keep to this castle was more or less intact, and within it Sir Amias Paulet had installed a kind of military quarter, for the purpose of defence. It contained the one strong, fortified vault in the Devereux estate, secure against a threat. Above this vault was a small council chamber, where Hew was taken now, and stripped of his clothes. His dagger and his purse were placed out on the board, with the letter he had brought, in its seal intact. A soldier took the knife, sliced the leather buttons cleanly from his coat, and slit them from their backs. 'I cannot imagine,' Hew said, 'what you think to find,' as another man prised the soles from his shoes, and let the blade slide through the silk of his cloak. In fact, he knew all of those tricks, and a dozen more besides, that were used by people who had things to hide, and thanked God he had none. He shivered as he waited, naked in his shirt in the dampness of that keep, for Sir Amias to arrive.

Sir Amias, when he came, did not still the fear. The burden of his charge had taken toll on him, showing in his slow arthritic gait, his face, blank from want of sleep, the dullness in his eyes. Recognising Hew from the tale he told, he sent the soldiers out before he asked. 'How did you come here?'

'On Grey Gelding, my horse. In truth, he is not my horse. He belongs to William Phillips – that is Tom Phelippes' father, as you know. That is a good horse, and his master is fond of him. I hope that your men, who have taken him from me, will see he is fed, and take proper care of him.' Hew answered full and cheerfully, with a smiling countenance, to encourage confidence.

This tactic failed to put the keeper at his ease. 'No, that is not possible. There are guards at every town within ten miles of here. No man may pass, and he is a stranger.'

'I did not come from the town.' Hew understood that what had caused the trouble was the breach in their security. 'I came across the field. A boy showed me the way. And I beg your pardon, if it inconvenienced you. I have an urgent letter, from William Phillips to his son.' He gestured at the letter lying on the board. Sir Amias looked at it, as though it were a thing he had not seen before, though Hew knew he must recognise the Phillips family seal.

'I can leave the letter, if you will. But I believe that his father will expect him to reply. I can tell you what it says. His wife Mary, has miscarried their child. The doctors believe she will not have another one.'

The keeper, it was clear, was moved by this. Sir Amias was a family man. He had brought his family with him to Chartley, finding them essential to the running of that house, not for profit or advantage to their interests there, but because he could not hope to serve so well without them. Without their close support, the burden of his charge would have crippled him completely, and become too hard to bear. He had in his keeping his elder grown son, with the young girl and ward he was soon to marry, and his youngest girl too, the bright baby daughter he had nicknamed his 'jewel'. He could not imagine what his life would be without them. Perhaps because of this, perhaps because he was uncertain what was right to do, he acted on his conscience. 'Take the letter to him. One of the soldiers will show you the way. We will look after your horse.' Sir Amias returned to Hew the letter and his purse. Since Hew's own were *futless*, he replaced his shoes. The dagger, he kept back.

Hew was taken to a place a mile or two from Chartley, to a farmhouse requisitioned from a Catholic lord. Soldiers had been quartered there; the great and ancient hall was cluttered with their gear, and several of them cleaned their weapons with its tablecloths. Others played at dice, and swilled down draughts of beer from blackened metal cups. Thomas Phelippes was not there among them. A young man in a blue wool coat answered to his name, and claimed to be his servant. Hew had not seen him before.

'You are not Tom Cassie.'

'No.' The boy had a bland, foolish face, placidly inscrutable. That he was Phelippes' agent Hew was willing to believe; he had been trained to give nothing away.

'I have a message for your master.'

'I will pass it on to him. He is not free, at present.'

Hew was aware of Paulet's soldiers, listening in. Neither he nor Phelippes' servant wished to give them anything to hear. 'I would prefer to deliver it myself.'

'Then, sir, you must wait, for he is occupied.'

'Is he here, is this house?' Hew persisted. The boy did not confirm this, nor deny it. 'If you will wait in the kitchen, I will let him know that you are here. The maid will give you food.'

It was less of a request than a command. The soldiers who stood by allowed no other course. Hew had ridden in the rough for many miles and hours, with no dinner but the bread he had wrapped up in a cloth, and the liquor in a flask he had brought from Grantham. He was chilled from his visit to the castle keep, and his limbs had stiffened to a leaden weariness. The prospect of a supper at the kitchen fire now seemed an enticing one. He followed at the heels of the bland, blue-coated boy, coming to a kitchen down a flight of stairs, where a single serving girl stood clearing dirty plates, polishing the pewter with a grimy cloth. The boy in the blue coat conferred with her quietly. Hew saw her nodding, weary in response.

The kitchen was large, and had once been, Hew thought, the wellspring and heartbeat of a country home. From the rafters hung sharp metal hooks, where he supposed had hung bacon and hams; long rows of shelves held stone crocks and jars designed to be filled with pickles and fruits. A small sprig of rosemary, puckered and grey, was all that remained of a banquet of herbs. The kitchen girl said, 'There is bread and cheese. The soldiers have had all the rest. There is plenty of beer, since the brewer came yesterday. But it will cost you to drink. The beer here is very expensive.'

He felt for his purse. 'Why is that?'

'I cannot say. Perhaps it is because the brewer comes from Burton.' The girl was very young, no more than a child. It was not stupidity, nor the serving man's impassiveness, that dulled her curiosity, it was the exhaustion of her service to those men. Hew asked her if she worked there on her own.

'There is a cook, but he has gone home.'

'I can help you clean the plates.'

'Do not be daft.'

She brought him a loaf of dry ravelled bread. He took out his purse, and bought himself a friend. 'Did you know,' she said, 'you have no buttons on your coat?' In answer, he asked for her name.

'Elizabeth. I was named for our sovereign lady queen.' She had it on her tongue, like a kind of catechism tripped out many times. Perhaps she was a relict of that ancient Catholic household, waiting for a master unavoidably detained. He asked her, had she ever chanced to see that *other* queen, kept up at the Hall, in the manor house at Chartley. 'For I met her, once.'

She stared at him, and shook her head. Hoping to have drawn her out, he had only frightened her.

'Do you know a man called Phelippes, who is staying in this house?'

But she was wary of him now, and would not play his game. 'I do not know the names of all of the soldiers.'

'He is not a soldier.'

'I do not know him, sir.'

He let her be at that, and while she worked, he watched, and brooded over three warm cups of Burton brewer's ale. Presently, he wandered back and up the spiral stair, to find there was a soldier stationed at the top. 'Wait down below sir, until you are called.'

He asked for the serving man in the blue coat, who had gone without leaving his name. The guard did not move. 'When you are wanted, you will be told.' There was nothing to be done but to go below and wait, where the young girl risked a smile at him. 'You can lie there, if you like.'

She showed to him a mat that was rolled out by the fire, with a woollen blanket, to make a sleeping place. Perhaps it was the journey he had taken through the scrub or the swilling in his belly of the Burton brewer's ale, but at that moment he was certain there was nowhere else on earth where he would rather lie, where every torn and straining sinew ached and longed to be. 'Perhaps, but for a while. You will wake me, when they come?'

'I will wake you,' she replied.

He did not resent the sour scent of the pillow, nor the heaving burrows of that bed without a sheet. Their torments did not touch him, for he was asleep.

He was woken by the light in the narrow kitchen casement, and the crowing of a cockerel somewhere in the yard. His limbs felt swollen, bruised and stiff, and rusted red pinpricks speckled his shirt. He would be scratching for days. The same young girl, Elizabeth, came in with a basket of freshly baked bread, the daily ration for the house. It did not look much.

'I robbed you of your bed,' he said, sorry for it now.

'It does not matter, sir.'

He wondered where she had slept, hoped it had not been with one of the soldiers. Her apron was grubby and torn. He watched, as she buttered a slice of the bread, which she set on a tray with a pitcher of ale. On impulse, he asked, 'Has Tom Phelippes broken his fast?'

'He has not had his supper yet.' She coloured as she realised what it was she said. 'I am busy, sir. I must take up the tray.'

'I will carry it for you.'

'No, you must not.'

But she could not prevent him from following upstairs. She did not turn at the top to enter the great hall, where the soldiers were quartered, but continued up a second flight, which opened at its head to a gallery of doors, all of which were closed. On the floor by one of them sat the tray of supper things.

'Let me hold the door for you.'

Trouble and confusion blotted her white face. 'Hush now, and be gone with you, you must wait below.'

Before he could come to her, Blue Coat appeared, his blue coat undone, woken in a flurry as he slept upon his watch. Swearing at the girl, he moved to raise his hand. Hew intercepted quietly, with just sufficient emphasis to show that it was meant, 'Know that if you strike her, I will knock you down.'

The boy lunged at Hew blindly, showing a fright that was not caused by him. 'You cannot go in there. You don't understand.'

'Let me see him now, or if he will not see me, let him send me away himself. What should I tell his father? That he does not speak or eat? Does he have the plague?' Hew inquired ironically. In truth, he found it strange. It pricked him into fear.

The boy was desperate now. 'It is not the plague. But there are soldiers in the house. They will hear you.' He waved at the girl, 'Go now, leave the breakfast things.' She dropped her tray and fled.

'There are soldiers in the house,' Hew repeated, 'whose attention you do not wish to attract. Why is that, I wonder?'

'It is not what you think. My master is engaged in an important work. He has given me instruction that he must not be disturbed.'

Phelippes had a temper, and was capable of sending his own servant damned to Hell. Hew felt a twinge of pity for the man. 'I do not believe that you have told him I am here. Was that your instruction from Sir Amias Paulet?'

Blue Coat answered miserably. 'Sir Amias does not know how vital this time is. And *he* is not my master, with respect.'

Hew said, 'Even so.' But before he could embark upon a more convincing argument, the door flew open from inside, and out came Thomas Phelippes, loud and in the life, calling for his boy. Hew found he was at last, absurdly pleased to see him.

Blue Coat stammered, 'Pardon, master, if we have disturbed you.'

Phelippes merely grinned at him. 'No matter, for the work is done. Run up to the house at Chartley. Tell Sir Amias to send down the post boy when he comes. For I have a packet for him.' He saw the boy's face, grey as the flap of his half-buttoned shirt. 'What is the matter, Hal?'

Hal stuttered, '*Him*', and Tom, for the first time, glanced towards Hew.

'Hew. *You*. Come, come inside. Come within, at once.'

Tom had a mind that worked quickly. But it could not, Hew understood, have come at that moment to the right conclusion, or he would never have allowed him to have stepped into that room. Tom believed, in that moment, that Walsingham had sent him. By what other means could he possibly have come? Perhaps it was from tiredness, or exhilaration, he let drop his guard. Perhaps the fault was Walsingham's, who chose to share so little of his workings with his principals, that they were never certain who was on their side. Perhaps it was, quite simply, that he trusted Hew. Whatever was the cause, he let him see the work he did, and, within a heartbeat, realised his mistake.

Thomas had not slept. If he had undressed, it was to still the sweat that trickled from his brow on a warm summer's night, his sleeves and doublet folded, cap upon its peg. The candles in their sockets had been burned down to their stumps, counting in the corpses fallen from their ranks the profits from their work. Phelippes through the night had been writing letters, though the letters he had left, in packets by the bed, meant more than what was said in them. Hew, who had spent hours on ciphers, understood at once.

The packets had been sealed, and tied up with thread. There were ways, Hew had learned, of breaking a thread, and a seal, so that the fracture might not be detected. There were methods, too, of tying a thread, and of folding a paper under its wax, that ensured that those fractures were not *un*detected, and he had no doubt that Phelippes had applied those methods when he made his seal. On the outside of the packet, he had written the direction. Besides it he had sketched, with the last flick of his pen, an image of a gallows. Hew understood the mark. It was a warning to the post boys, few of whom could read, that the packet was an urgent one; post haste for life, it meant, and no more than that. Yet Hew had the impression that those few concluding strokes might mark in their decisiveness the closing of a game, and end in hang-the-man. Phelippes had left out a letter set in cipher, too precious to be trusted to the common post. In places, it appeared the ink was wet, but that could not be so, for it was evident to Hew that it was one of the originals that Phelippes had transcribed. Besides it lay the alphabet, and both were written neatly in an unfamiliar hand. A fascination drew Hew to the desk. He could not help but whisper, 'Is that cipher *hers*?'

Phelippes asked, 'Why have you come?', his grey eyes drawn narrow with doubt.

'I have a letter for you, Tom. It concerns Mary. I am sorry to say that the news is not good.'

The colour fled from Phelippes' face. He looked blank, uncomprehending. 'Mary?'

'She has lost the child.'

Tom let slip a sound that was something like a sigh. He was thinking of that queen his purpose was to ruin, and in that moment had forgotten that he had a wife.

Chapter 5

The Lion and the Hare

That queen, Phelippes called her, sounding it like Cicero, accusing and direct, to mark her from the proper one, the Sovereign queen Elizabeth. Hew had met *that* queen in 1584. Though he had not expected it, it did not come about by chance. She had been in the keeping of the earl of Shrewsbury. And although she had complained of restrictions on her liberty, she was granted freedoms then which since had been withdrawn, and which she had already known were coming to their end. At that time, she had held hopes, of her son in Scotland and her friends in France, and Walsingham designed to penetrate those hopes, and shape them to his own, before he snuffed them out. To that end and purpose, he had ventured Hew.

For as long as Hew had known him, William Phillips had been plagued with a cruel arthritis. In the springtime of that year, a dampness from the river crept into his bones and ravelled them in knots. Clysters were prescribed, but offered no relief, and a raft of purging swept him to his bed, clinging to his blankets, through the bitter winds that blasted into March. Hew had written to his sister, asking for a remedy, and Meg sent by return a receipt for oil of comfrey, to be rubbed into the joints, and for nettle broth, infused with bittersweet. The old man was suspicious, and had baulked, at first. But Frances in her quiet way had followed Meg's instructions, ordering the ointment and the herbs from the apothecary, searching at the river banks and edges of the parks for the sweetest nettle leaves, with her tender fingers nipping out their hearts, gently steamed and simmered in a grassy stew. William had been melted by it, when the muddy potion he had sipped to please her brought a cooling solace to his aching limbs, while the rubbing ointment warmed and soothed his bones. In the month of June, Phelippes had proposed a trip to Buxton Spa, to take the waters there, to round off his recovery. 'Frances and my brother John will take care of the trade, while you shall take Hew, to attend to your needs. I should come too, were it not for the husting at Hastings.'

Phelippes had been standing for Parliament, as the member of Hastings, to which he was duly elected. He had been put up for the post by Lord Cobham, to whose younger brother Phelippes was attached during his embassy to France. It was not clear if Phelippes stood with Walsingham's approval or in spite of him, for Walsingham and Cobham grouped in different camps, but Hew had given up attempting to unravel it. He suspected Phelippes chased so many different threads that he did not know himself, when he doubled on his course.

William had resisted him at first. Derbyshire, he felt, was too far and remote. 'There is water at Hastings, is there not?'

'Not the healing sort.'

'Bath is a closer resort. And, I am told, very fine.'

Phelippes had impressed upon him that the trip to Buxton might not be refused. He had arranged it through Sir Francis, with the kind intervention of Lord Burghley himself, that his father should stay as the guest of the earl. The names of three great personages, in a single breath, had blown away William's objections.

In confidence to Hew, Phelippes had confessed the purpose of the stay. Derbyshire was known to be a papist enclave, and the well at Buxton, with its ancient superstitions, was a favoured watering place for hatching Catholic plots. 'There they may be lax, apt to let their secrets drop as loosely as their hose. Bathe with them. Drink with them, make yourself known to them. You an exile from Scotland, out of step with the king. Your father was a Catholic too, you understand their ways. Seek nothing out, but make yourself close to them, quiet, insinuate, earning their trust. Report all you hear of threat to our queen.'

Though Phelippes had not lied to him, he had not told the truth. Thomas had in mind a more prestigious prize. 'It is possible,' he mentioned just before they left, 'that someone in that house will attempt to contact you. If that happens, I would counsel you to follow your own heart, and what will out, will out.'

Hew had set out in a spirit of adventure, on a journey which had turned into an arduous one. William was not fitted to the rigours of the road, and had suffered a relapse, as soon as they arrived, taking to his bed. They had not been quartered in the Buxton hall – Thomas had exaggerated, or spent out his influence – but in a smaller lodging house, a short walk from the baths. Hew's sharp eyes had taken note of soldiers on the route; their papers were examined with a strict security that caused him some concern, but there was little sign of traffic or of bustle in the street. He had entered the earl's hall, to be welcomed by the porter who was stationed at the door, and who functioned also as the keeper of the baths.

'You must subscribe your name in the register, here, and beside it, the place you are come from. Next, you will see the doctor, who will make assessment of your present state of health, and will prescribe you your treatments. You pay for your treatment according to your rank, and to the charges there.'

The charges, which were painted on a board, ascended from a pittance for a pauper to considerable amounts for the highest in the land. A poor man paid fourpence, an archbishop, the sum of five pounds. The archbishop of St Andrews, the wily Patrick Adamson, had come to spend a winter in the south of England, 'for benefit of health'. His passport application, sent to Francis Walsingham and passed by Laurence Tomson, had been shown to Hew. So snivelling and villainous a missive from a Scotsman he had seldom seen. Scotland was too cold, he should have said too warm for him, to ensure his comfort at that present time. It tickled Hew to think that he might come to Buxton, and pay high for the privilege. Patrick's sparring partner, the reformer Andrew Melville had been driven down to England later that same year, fleeing the Black Acts. 'Also for his health,' Phelippes noted grimly. While Melville had found refuge among willing friends in Oxford, Hew felt relief that their paths had not crossed.

As to himself, he had felt at a loss. He did not feel equipped to call himself a gentleman. He had entered in the register, 'William Phillips of Leadenhall, London, customer of wool', and below that, 'Hew Cullan of St Andrews, lawyer, servant to the same', and handed back the quill. The physician, he was told, had been called out to the baths, but would soon return, if he cared to wait.

The keeper had for sale certain books and pamphlets to inform his guests, and Hew had bought two copies of a tract by Doctor Jones, on 'The Benefit of the Ancient Baths at Buckstanes which Cureth Most Grievous Sicknesses', one to keep himself, and one to give to Giles. It occurred to him that he might make a cipher of the text, and send a secret letter, under Phelippes' nose. Phelippes would no doubt have approved the sentiment, if not the act itself, as becoming to a spy.

At the back of the hall, where sunlight came glancing from several large windows, were set out some tables for board games and cards, and a shelf with a small row of books. There were several chairs, and a bright bow window seat, where Hew sat down to read. He had not gone much further than 'A Rule to Know when Exercise Should Begin' (the colour of the urine was apparently the key) when he had been distracted by the lighting of the sun upon a line of letters, delicate as frost, etched upon the window under which he sat. The gentle men and women who had watered in that place, having time and leisure on their hands, had whiled away the spare hours writing in the glass, with the pointed bezels of their diamond rings. There were verses, anagrams, among the hearts and flowers, the open secret record of a lover's trysts and tiffs. But what had held him rapt were those that bore the signature of the queen of Scots. For they were bitter notes, plaintive to the pith; not the tender linnet, singing in its cage, but the restless lion, rattling at the bars. It brought to mind the king of Scotland, and his pale menagerie.

'*Et dejecto insultant lepores leoni*', Even the hares will taunt a dead lion. The words were defiant and proud.

'I see you like to read. Perhaps you will excuse us for our lack of library? On command of our dear queen, our public shelves were stripped of all that might appeal to Roman Catholic tastes. Those interests were diverse, or else the censors scrupulous, for there is little left.'

Hew had been engrossed, and had not been aware of the approach of the physician. It was far from clear, from the doctor's tone, whether he approved or not of the queen's efficiency. Hew rose to take his hand. 'Are you Doctor Jones?'

'Alas, not. I am Samuel Forrester, the physician here. I am not so favoured as my famous colleague. It seems you are familiar with his work.'

'I have not got far with it,' Hew had admitted. 'According to the title, the waters in this place cure "most grievous sicknesses". What does that mean? *Most* grievous sicknesses, or *most grievous* sicknesses?'

The doctor had answered him, 'Indeed,' with the smooth prevarication Hew was well acquainted with in men of his profession. 'If you care to read the whole, you are sure to find it most apt and illuminating.' Despite his clipped English accent, and his pinched and narrow features, something in his manner had reminded Hew of Giles. He had felt – felt even now – a sudden lurch of homesickness.

'If you will follow to my cubicle,' the physician had proposed, 'there I can examine you.'

'Ah, it is not I, but my master is unwell. He has taken to his bed.'

'Where I shall see him presently. Oftentimes, the journey here exacerbates old ills. Do not be alarmed, for it will quickly pass. As for you yourself, you must be cleared of sickness before going to the baths. And, if I may say so, you do not look well. Have you lost weight?'

They were out of earshot now, in the doctor's cubicle, and Hew had dared to say, 'I was looking at the writing on the glass.'

'Hmm?' The doctor had his back to him, writing in a book.

'On the window pane.'

'A frivolous pursuit. Do you have a cough? The croup? Persistent rheum?'

'None of those. Am I right when I suppose that Mary, queen of Scots has written verses there?'

'That is more than likely. Have you ever suffered from the great or little pox?'

'Never, God be thanked. Is she often here?'

'Not so often, no.' The doctor had perused him sternly through his spectacles, and Hew had been expecting him to offer some rebuke, when he had remarked, 'If I were a man, who fished before a net, then I should place a wager she will come here very soon.'

'Why do you say that?'

'The house has been cleared, and guests turned away. That is a clear sign that she is expected. But sir, this cannot be news to you. No one who is properly a stranger to the earl could presently be here.'

'My master must have known of it,' Hew had reflected, 'while, I confess, I did not.' By master, to be sure, he had not meant William Phillips. He had felt the rising of a kind of sick excitement that would not be stilled. He had thought that Doctor Forrester, physician as he was, would feel beneath his shirt the leaping of his heart, the flexing in his belly that was writhing like a fish. But the doctor had said simply, 'Your master is assured of my best attention, since that lady, when she comes, will bring her own physician.'

'Who must consult with you at times?' Hew was fishing, quite shameless, for more than a hint.

That fish did not bite. The doctor cleared his throat, a harumph of reproach. 'Indeed, and if he did, that confidence is not one I should ever break. I shall want, from you both, samples of spittle, water and stool. Until such a time as a regimen is set for you, drink three pints a day of water from the spring. You shall enter in the bath when all has been evacuated and the piss runs clear. Now, sir, that is all.'

The days had seemed interminable. Twice, the doctor called, and Hew learned that the queen and her party had arrived by night, and were quartered in the hall, where no man might pass without permission of the guard. The baths were closed off while the queen had use of them; at other times, the gentlemen were given leave to bathe according to the regimen the doctor had set out for them. On the third day of their visit, William had felt well enough to descend into the water, with assistance from Hew.

The bath house was set out with steps of marbled stone and benches by the fire, where clothes were left to warm and hot towels were supplied. On the first occasion, they were quite alone, but on the second there were two men in the far end of the bath, who climbed out as they entered, and as quickly dressed, conversing with each other quietly in French. One had stopped to bow to them, politely, as he passed. Hew had begun to despair of the relentless regimen, of lying lapped in towels or under steaming bladders forcing out a sweat, and most of all of drinking water, from the Buxton well. He felt his humours had been balanced to the point of equilibrium, where they cancelled out, and nothing had remained in him except a listless vacancy, shallow and lukewarm.

He was drawn, all this while, to the letters in the glass. It was partly for the paradox; the meaning was opaque, and the medium clear. There was satisfaction too, in the knowledge they were written there to while away the time, in a leisurely resort that was a kind of tedium. But the verses that were made in captivity and exile, by the queen of Scots, had a resonance for him that was poignant and particular. She wrote her name in anagram, linked sometimes with her son's, in brittle slender strokes Hew's fingertips had traced. And so he had returned, and looked, and looked again, for something of significance, some message meant for him. He did not find one there. At last, he had been cornered by the keen-eyed Doctor Forrester, whose medicinal interventions he was trying to avoid.

'I see you have been captivated by the riddles there. Alas, though they perplex and occupy the mind, I cannot think the hours spent in their execution the most beneficial exercise. They are too inward-looking to be counted wholesome, to one who is by nature melancholically inclined. You, may I say so, look pale.'

Hew had answered vaguely, reluctant to be drawn, for fear of being sent to be blistered, bathed or bled. It had struck him as singular, when the doctor went on, 'If I may recommend to you a little light diversion, to relieve your present cares, I think that it would profit you to walk out in the gallery adjoining the bath house, this afternoon, at two o'clock. Yes, indeed, at two o'clock. Now I will bid good day to you. But I do warmly recommend that you should take that walk. Now sir, would you say, is it about to rain?'

Abruptly, he had left. And Hew, who had no doubt he had communicated secretly, had bustled William Phillips through his paces in the bath and had bundled him to bed with a hot bladder in a sack when the old man had suggested he would like to take a walk.

'Absolutely not. You will catch a cold. The doctor said this morning it was sure to rain.'

'Piffle. If Frances were here –' the old man had grumbled.

'She would say the same.'

The bath house had been closed, while the queen and her ladies took the waters there, but the keeper had allowed him access to the gallery, a long covered walkway looking to the hills. At its far end, he had found a group of children playing *trou madame*, throwing wooden balls into the holes cut in a board. Hew had watched them awhile, until one of the balls was bowled with such force that it broke from its boundary and rolled to his feet, whereupon he had bent to it, picking it up. The eldest of the girls stepped forward to retrieve it, holding out her hand.

'Merci, monsieur. Pardonnez-nous.'

'Je vous en prie, mademoiselle,' he had answered, with a smile.

She was more than a child, fifteen, perhaps, and wearing a gown of a dark ruffled silk, that marked her at once as a person of rank. The eyes that gazed at him were challenging and curious. He was encouraged by the fact that she spoke to him in French to suppose that she belonged to the household of that queen. She had turned her back on him, returning to the children with a conscious gracefulness that told him she well aware that he still stood and watched. Another child called 'Bess!', a light trill of alarm, and Hew saw Bess bend down to her and whisper in her ear. A startled burst of laughter, and the children ran, chattering like birds, headlong down the gallery through an open door, which swung closed behind them. Hew walked across the hallway to the other side, and looked out at the hills, thoughtful for a while. The message had been plain enough, that he was meant to follow them. It could not have been clearer had he been Tam Lin, asleep beneath a tree, and Bess the incarnation of a faerie queen. Once he would have followed, blindly. Now, he waited patiently, as he had been schooled.

And as he had supposed, he had not long to wait, the small door was opened, and there came in Bessie's place the elegant man he had seen in the baths, with his manicured nails and neat pointed beard, discreetly presentable in his court clothes. The man had approached him. 'Tell me, monsieur, do you speak French?'

'Certainly,' Hew had replied.

'You are Hew Cullan, come from St Andrews.'

'That is correct.'

'I am Claude Nau de la Boisseliere, secretary to the queen of Scots.'

'Très bien, monsieur. I have read your verses, written in the glass. I admire your Greek. I was under the impression that your name was James.'

'Jacques is a name I was given as a child. We have something in common, you and I. We are both men of the law.'

Hew had said, he did not practise now.

Nau had smiled at that. 'And, sir, nor do I. Let me come to the point. The queen is made aware of your name in the register, and is much intrigued at it. She does not often have the chance to discourse with strangers, and would like to speak with you. She is occupied at present, but tomorrow at this hour, I will meet with you here.'

There was no implication that he might refuse, nor did such an answer even cross Hew's mind. He had simply nodded. 'I will be there.'

'Her Majestie will speak with you in French or in Scots, whichever you prefer. Never, though in English, which she does not understand.'

'They are not so very different, as I thought,' Hew had answered.

Nau let slip a smile. 'To my French hearing, also. But she will not have it. Tell to me, monsieur, what is it brings you here?'

'My master, William Phillips, suffers with the gout.'

'No, I mean to England.' Men of all cloths came to Buxton to take the water, and that queen had met with them, in less troubled times. Therefore it was not strange to Nau that Hew had chanced to come there; for one who trusted God, it seemed a stroke of grace, an insubstantial spark to brighten those dark days. Nau had been aware the visit was her last. And Nau had told the queen of Hew's name in the register, which Sir Francis Walsingham had surely hoped he would.

'I am an exile, monsieur, fallen from grace with the king,' Hew had said.

This answer satisfied. Claude Nau had replied, 'Ah, your country is a cold and thankless one, monsieur. Myself, I had no quarter there.'

And Hew had marked him then, a gentle, civil Frenchman, faithful to his queen.

Chapter 6

La Reine Marie

Tom was writing furiously.

Hew said, 'You are not thinking straight.'

'The post will be here soon to pick up the letters.'

'If you send Mary a by-letter, it will not reach her for weeks.'

By-letters, as they called them, were carried by discretion of the queen's own posts, and at a heavy price. They mouldered for months in the post masters' bags, if they were not abandoned somewhere on the road.

'At least, let me take it to her, if you will not go yourself.'

'No.' Phelippes had completed his few lines, blotted them with paper, too peremptory for dust, warming up the wax for the impression of his ring. He had written the direction on it, spiderish and cruel. 'I have enclosed it in a note I have addressed to Laurence Tomson, who will redirect it, without alerting Walsingham. She will have it in good time.' He had closed down the expression on his face, to infuriating blankness. Only for a moment had he let it slip. Now, he had recovered, perfectly controlled.

'You will break her heart, Tom. It is not her fault.'

'Did I say it was? I never said, nor thought, that any fault was hers. She is my wife. And I will share her sorrow, if she cannot have a child. Yet that is not the end and purpose of her life. She knows I love her well, and will see her when I can. So much she understands. I am grateful to you, Hew, for coming with this news. But you must understand that you should not have come. And now that you are here, I cannot let you go. There are matters here outstanding, pertaining to that queen.'

The second time that Nau had met Hew in the gallery, he had taken him down through the heart of the baths to the underground trance leading back to the hall, descending a short flight of steps. That queen had her chamber on the lower floor, closest to the bath, since she was not well enough to climb up many stairs. There Nau had paused, and said reassuringly, 'We are not solemn here. You need not stand on state.'

It had not been true. That queen made her court inside a vaulted tiring chamber, slightly damp and chilly from its closeness to the baths. Perhaps she could not help but replicate the stage on which she faced the world, however far withdrawn from it, so much of her nature, it was in her blood. It struck Hew that her son might say, that he had no more liberty nor pleasure in his life than she had on that day, and that the king himself was not so blessed with people who well loved him, as the cast-off queen. She won their love, with constant show of courtesy and kindness, and through her assumption that it was her due. And there was no question that they were devoted to her. Some of them, who came to her as children, knew no other lives; some had formed alliances, in that closed-off world, like the purpled paroquets in the king's menagerie, breeding in captivity. Their offspring were the infants playing in the gallery.

She was sitting on a stage, in a high-backed chair, and for those short weeks that she was at the spa, had rigged up in a canopy the cloth of her estate. She wore a gown of dark green velvet, falling to a single, jewel-encrusted slipper of a matching shade. One foot was raised, resting on a stool, and she was swaddled from the waist in a swathe of blankets. Nestled in her lap, in lieu of a hot water bladder, was a little dog. On cushions flanked on either side, her gentlewomen sat, and bowed their heads to stitch and work at bright embroideries, while a maiden sang to her, the young girl from the gallery, in a clear, sweet voice.

Hew knelt as he approached her, thankful for the coolness of the stone, feeling on his face the fierceness of her fire.

'Hew Cullan, of St Andrews,' Claude Nau had announced.

That queen had smiled at him. 'It is some while since we had a visitor from Scotland. It was kind of Claude to think to fetch you here. Do you know, Master Cullan, that we have to do such things by a kind of subterfuge? It is a tedious necessity. But, when it succeeds, it brings with it a consummate and simple kind of pleasure.'

He had wondered then, how much she understood. He came to the conclusion she had been outplayed, a novice in the test of wits she pitched with Francis Walsingham. She could not hope to match the cunning of his game.

She had spoken French. And Hew had been taken with the lightness of her voice, which he had supposed to have been embittered, sad and sour, but which he found was humorous, lively, and affectionate. There was life still in her eyes, inquisitive and keen, and quick to rouse. He sensed that there was laughter sometimes in that place, that whatever she had suffered, still her spirit had survived, and still could be rekindled with a spark.

The girl had completed her song, and had bent down her head to receive that queen's blessing, which was bestowed with a kiss. The queen had spoken something in her ear, for the girl had nodded, lifting up the little dog, and brought it to the door, where she took it out with her. She did not glance at Hew, but made curtsy to Claude Nau, who had seemed to frown a little.

The queen had smiled at Hew. 'Come, and sit by us. You may kiss our hand. We do not stand apart, for we are nothing here.'

Her looks and manner gave the lie to everything she said, in her display, a queen. 'Our little family here has to entertain itself. We do not say, in truth, they are the poorer for it. Did you like Bessie's song?'

'Very much, your Grace.'

He had sensed there the slightest of movements from Claude, who stood close at his side, as though something tensed in him. Was it the girl? The queen had said, 'She has been a comfort to us, since

66

she was a child. She came in to our service when she was four years old. We love her as our own. Yet we must wonder if the time has come when we should look to part with her. Perhaps, she could be found preferment at the English court. What do you think, Monsieur Nau?'

Hew had thought the Frenchman seemed a little hesitant. Something in him strained. 'I cannot say, your Grace. But I should think that it would grieve her very much to be parted from your company.'

'As it would grieve our heart to have to part with her. But sometimes, we must set aside our feelings in considering such things, and do what may be best. That, Master Hew, is our responsibility. Bess is the granddaughter, besides, of the countess of Shrewsbury. And as she grows older, we wonder if she does not show a little of her grandmère's disposition, which makes us, we confess, less inclined to keep her here.'

'I had not noticed that, your Grace,' Nau said.

'No, indeed. You are *a man*.' Though the queen's tone was light, Hew had sensed a deeper nuance in her voice, a clear note of command. He had wondered, for a moment, what it must be like, to have served her through the years of captivity and exile, living in her court, a shadowed sort of life. Her servants doubtless suffered with their own concerns, as they were her satellites closed off from the world.

Nau had brought a stool for Hew, that placed him sitting closest to her swollen foot, gross beneath its cloth. He trained his eyes away from it, with nowhere else to look, fearful he might somehow knock it with his own.

The queen had said, 'You speak very good French. But would you prefer we spoke Scots?'

He had chosen French. She spoke Scots with a subtle accent, prettily refined, and he found it hard to hear it spoken here, stripped bare of its life.

'In St Andrews,' she informed him, 'we were happy once. And you are a lawyer there?'

'I was.' He told her he had given up the law, that he had found no justice there.

'Justice is a matter we should fight for, should we not? It is sometimes hard to find. If you do not practise law, what is it that you do? A young man of your kind must have certain talents.'

Did she take him for a spy? He had told her of the work he did, in keeping the king's peace. He had told the stories, of a merchant and a weaver and a dyer who was drowned; of a lawyer who was caught up in a deadly game of chase; of a windmill that was washed up in a shipwreck on a shore, while they had sat and listened, quiet in that place, her maids with open mouths. He had told that queen the story of the tree that she had planted, that had blossomed for the first time after twenty years. She did not recall it; she had planted many trees. But her eyes opened wide at the trick that had been played on it. 'Mon Dieu!' She had smiled. 'We should have liked to see your Master Melville's face! That was a wicked boy. We trust he has been punished for the ill deeds he has done.'

'I cannot say, your Grace.' The thought of home, of things undone, came flooding to his heart, and the queen took note of it. 'What brings you here, my dear?'

He had told her the truth, or a version of the truth that would not anger Walsingham, since anyone among them might have been his spy. 'I am in exile, your Grace, and sorely sick at heart, to have lost the faith and favour of my king. False men spoke against me, and won him with their lies.'

She had nodded. 'Then, we may be sorry for your plight. The king our son is young, and he is ill-advised. We pray to God that he may come to better judgement. Yet there have been times when we were moved to doubt it.'

One of the ladies who sat by her side had cried out at that, 'Ma Reine, keep strong your heart, and do not say alas, for God will hear your prayers.'

That queen had said simply, '*Perhaps.* Tell to me, monsieur, do you know our son? Have you met with him?'

'Once or twice, your Grace, when he was still a boy. Before the lord adventurers had placed their hands on him.'

She had shuddered at that. 'Praise be to God he is free of them now. We pray he will come to know his own mind.'

Hew had said amen to that. Then, she had held hopes still of the king her son, which now were surely dashed. James had signed a pact with Queen Elizabeth, on which, as Phelippes rode to Chartley, the ink had still been wet.

She had spoken then, with a mother's wistfulness. 'Tell us what you saw in him. For we should not know him now if he stepped into this chamber.'

'For certain, you would know him then, ma Reine,' her lady had exclaimed, 'as well as any mother knows her son, and if he saw you in this place then he would kneel and weep, and beg your Grace's pardon for the hurt that he has done, in sway of those whose minds are evilly disposed to you, who turn his heart against you.' The queen had smiled at her.

'God grant him the eyes and the heart to see, now that he is grown.'

'God,' the queen corrected, 'grant him the will. They tell me,' she had put to Hew, 'that he is ungracious and unmannerly. Do you find him so?'

He had struggled for a way to answer this. The young king had a restlessness, and could not sit at ease. His mother, by contrast, held a quiet dignity that marked her for a queen, however low she came, and however ill she looked.

'I have not, your Grace, seen the king at the court, but in such places where he has shown skill as a scholar; he has a sharp and clear, a penetrating mind, and is well-accomplished at his books,' he had replied at last.

'Then he is not a fool?'

'Not by any means.'

'But with the kind of books that they have filled his head, 'twere better for his own sake and that of the world, that he had been a dunce. Does he ride, and hunt?'

'As I understand.'

'Then he were advised to make most of that liberty, and use it while he can. We have a little picture painted in a glass, but we have not seen another since he was a child. They tell us he is loath to sit still for his likeness. Is he truly such a fidget?'

'He has, it may be said, a roaming sort of mind.'

She had seen through the flattery. 'That is a kindness, we think. Does he grow fair? Does he favour his father, Lord Darnley, at all?'

She did not call him king, the title she had granted to him while he was alive. Most likely she had never felt it in her heart. But she spoke of Darnley now, in a calm and loving voice. She did not sound like a woman who was troubled in her conscience, or in any way complicit in her husband's death. She seemed to look back on the years, wistfully detached, as if they were but matters she had come upon in books, memories of things that did not belong to her. 'That was a handsome young man.'

Hew had answered diplomatically. 'I cannot say, your Grace, if the king should favour him. I never saw a likeness of his lordship's face.'

'We suppose not.' There was mischief in her eyes. 'Not all men, after all, turn out like their fathers. And in Lord Darnley's case, it may not be desirable. But you, we dare say, may yet turn out like yours. You would not be the worse for it.'

'My father, your Grace?' He had not, for a moment, thought she would remember him. That was her trick, Phelippes would have said, of pulling people close, of drawing in their spirit and their courage and their confidence, and claiming them as hers.

'We knew him very well. He should have been our advocate, had times not turned against us. He helped us find our way, when we first came from France. Tell us, is he well?'

Hew had felt blood well up in his ears, like the water that streamed from the fount. He wanted her to stop.

'He has been dead for three years, your Grace.'

'Then we are sorry for it. That was a good, loving friend. And a good Catholic too. Did he build his house, on the land we gifted him?'

'What land was that?', he could not help but ask, and did not want to hear.

'It was land that had belonged to the archbishops of St Andrews, and had come into our hands. He would not have a title, or a place at court, but asked for leave to live out quiet in retirement; since that land had come to us, and was of little worth, we placed it in his hands, a small mark of our gratitude. Now, as we suppose, it must be yours. Did he not say?' she had asked, in her eyes a faint flicker of hurt. 'We suppose he did not, for it was not much.'

He had answered her, hollow, it was the world.

At Chartley, Phelippes said, 'I do not blame you, Hew. For your duty to my family, I must give you thanks. But the truth is you have come here at an awkward time. Your appearance has thrown Amias in a heightened state of fear. He does not dissemble well, and in his agitation may resort to such a rigour as will make the Scottish captive fearful for her life, which is not what we want, for we must console her with a smiling countenance, and keep her mind and spirit free from all suspicion. I can hope to still Amias, and make calm his fears, but until this work is done, I must keep you here. I am sorry for it, but I cannot let you go.'

'Then your family,' Hew objected, 'will despair of us both.' He had no wish to be kept as a prisoner at Chartley.

'I have written in the letter that you will remain here, to help me with my work, that we may the both of us more speedily return. Laurence will see that it finds its way to Mary, and that your coming here will not be known to Walsingham, until we have undone whatever harm it caused. He will hear it soon enough, and he will not be pleased. You have been irksome to him, from the very first. You must be aware, there is a net about to close, and I cannot run the risk of your warning the conspirators.'

'How should I warn them?' asked Hew, 'when I do not know who, or what they are? You know, upon my life, that I will take no part in a conspiracy, against either queen.'

'Trust me, when I say, we know that all too well. Therein lies the trouble, Hew.' Tom sighed. 'We do not want, besides, a second thief to fly.'

He was alluding to the fraud Hew had uncovered in the custom house. 'That is not fair,' Hew objected. 'The thief was alerted by the presence of a stranger. He would loup at a shadow. He was poised for flight.'

So much had been true. Yet when he thought of the face of that foolish young piker, nervous as a lute-string, no more than a boy, he could not have sworn he would not have forewarned him, had the frightened faulter given him the chance. He had not had the stomach for the taking of a thief. His heart was harder now.

'So much may be true of the conspirators. And if they were to fly, and you go out from here, what conclusion, think you, Walsingham would take from that? No matter if he knew you had no hand in it, you would pay the price. He would make you suffer for it. It is vexing to him, that he cannot put your talents to their best effect. Your conscience is a trial, and cannot help us here. Wherefore, you must stay, and we must watch and wait, till Walsingham sends word.'

Chapter 7

A Dead Man in Delft

Phelippes kept him close, for Hew's sake and his own. He hoped that Hew had good intentions, yet he could not take that risk. For though he knew him well, could capture to the life the manner of his speech, the letters from his hand, and frame them in a wink, he could not win his confidence, or see into his heart, as Laurence Tomson did.

Hew had never spoken with, or seen, that queen again. His journey to the spa had been judged successful. Phelippes had informed him that Walsingham was pleased with him. 'It is better than we hoped. She liked you. So much, in fact, that she has asked the earl for you to be enlisted in the service of her household. She says' – and he had smiled at this – 'that she wants a Scottish man of law, having for the present only someone French, and that *a friend* had told her, you were close at hand. The pity of it is, it cannot be agreed, for she cannot be allowed to think that she can have her way, nor to become suspicious of her will acceded easily. But, you can be attached to the household of whoever has the keeping of her when the earl demits it, the better to insinuate, and build upon her trust.'

It was rare enough that Phelippes showed his hand. Doubtless, it had been his own idea, to try Hew in that place, and he had been well satisfied, at first, with the result; that queen was taken in. The sticking place had been their confidence in Hew, who could not be trusted not to play a double game.

Hew had spilled his heart to Laurence Tomson, knowing as he did so it would go to Walsingham, that Laurence, in all conscience, could not recommend him.

'He is honest, in all ways, to his faith and country, that is to say, to his king. And where there is no conflict with his own beliefs, so far, we can trust him. He will not, I think collude in any manner of conspiracy, that threatens to unseat the Scottish king. There is no question of his faith. He could no sooner change it than the colour of his eyes. It is thorough and complete. But his quest for justice, of a personal kind, sometimes supersedes his allegiance to the state. He has confessed that he was moved by the appearance of that queen. That queen has a claim over him, through family ties, not easily thrown off. He will help us bring her down, if he sees her harm to us, yet may not be persuaded to it *by whatever means*; he will not see that the method may be justified by cause, and where it is our will her malice may betray itself, he may seek to mend, or put her on her guard,' Laurence might have said.

'She knew his father. Is that all?' Phelippes put contemptuously.

Laurence understood that it was enough.

Laurence had recommended Hew have nothing more to do with the queen of Scots, less likely in that cause to help them than to hinder it. 'What devil shall I do with him?' Walsingham asked then. His answer came emphatically, more bloody and more urgent, than he did expect.

It was Phelippes who had brought the news to the house at Leadenhall, not long after their return from Buxton spa. Aroused by the commotion, in smocks and linen caps, the older family members had been shaken from their beds. Hew had been going out, to see if Audrey would be willing to indulge in conversation on a sultry summer's night, while Frances sat alone, in solitary candlelight, transcribing for her uncle the accounts of business done by Phelippes and his brothers in his absence at the baths.

William, the Silent, of Orange-Nassau, stadholder in the Netherlands, was dead, shot through the stomach in his dining room at Delft. Phelippes had resounded every lasting note, harrowing and pitiless. The assassin had bought the weapon he had used with money that the stadholder had given him himself, to buy a pair of shoes; a

74

penniless fanatic, he had nothing in his pockets but the bladder of a pig – to keep himself afloat as he swam through the canals. With hopeless satisfaction, Phelippes had described the bodily afflictions that were practised on the perpetrator in the hours of anguish that were drawn out till his last, sparing no account, until his mother's shuddering and murmurs of disgust, and Frances' pale face, caused Hew to protest that this was not the place.

'Not the place?' Phelippes cried. 'You will say tis not the place, when we are overrun, and all that we hold dear is brought down in flames. There is not a woman nor a child would shrink to see sharp justice pinch and sear his flesh, and trail the flaming ribbons smarting through the crowd. Anyone who whimpered at it, would be flayed alive. And rightly so.'

Joan had whispered, *Tom*, and William had objected that the women did not like to hear speak of such things, so tender were their hearts.

'Then better they had learn to make them hard, against the terror that will strike them, that threatens all the world.' And brought to a standstill by a savage kind of grief, a fury wrought of impotence, the staid Thomas Phelippes, who had seemed impassible, had broken down in tears.

Though Hew had not wept, the cold grip of horror had clutched at his bowels, and left him sick at heart. The loss of that good prince had touched him in a personal way, over and above the damage it had done to what was right and civil in the Christian world. He had met the prince in 1582, on travels in the Netherlands, where William had been kind enough to treat to save his life, when Hew had found himself in hostile Spanish hands. The prince had been disfigured from a gunshot wound, and Hew had learned of courage, moderation, love, in the gentle contours of that ravaged face. So resolute a Calvinist, he would not take precautions to protect his life, nor close his gates and mind to those who meant him harm, for what would be, would be; and so, of course, it was.

Once Phelippes had departed, and the house was still again, and

Hew was drawn at last into a restless sleep – no more thought of Audrey – he had dreamt of that face, and felt upon his head the light touch of the blessing of that gentle prince. The hot-water bladders of the spa at Buxton were blown up into water wings, a fool's bladder bobbing on a Dutch canal, that became the swollen belly of a man upon a stick, spilling out its innards like a pudding in a flame. Hew had woken to a world that felt bleak and desolate, that no amount of rage, no spilling out of blood, could possibly assuage, a tidal wave of terror that had caught him in its flood.

That day, or the next, he was called to Seething Lane. It was clear to him that Laurence Tomson had not slept for days. It fell to Laurence to receive most of the correspondence from the Netherlands and France. Hew wondered whether he had had the task of breaking the news to Walsingham, which Walsingham himself had broken to the queen. There he saw letters from the embassy in France, warning that Elizabeth was now in mortal danger; he could only imagine the fresh flux of fear the news would discharge on the Scottish king James.

Walsingham was there, shivering in furs despite the summer heat, and seemed to shrink inside himself. His voice was hoarse and rasping, and he barely looked at Hew. He delivered his instruction, with a cold, distracted air. Hew was to take a paper, which Laurence had prepared for him, to the gaol at Newgate. Hew had felt quite sure the paper was the warrant for his own arrest. But Laurence, in his quiet way, had set his mind at peace. 'Take the letter, and this purse, to the keeper of the upper floor. He is a scoundrel, and will ask for more. When you have what we want, come back.'

Hew had asked, 'What is it that you want?'

Laurence had allowed the slightest twitching of a lip, too worn out to smile. 'To see my wife and daughter, and a good night's rest. Take courage, Hew, and heart. You will like what you find.'

Hew could not imagine what he could have found to please him in Newgate, a place that even Phelippes sidestepped, from a kind of superstition, when he showed to him the town, that had as many depths to it, as were sorts of men. It was unlikely such a place, where a seeping rot corroded every joint and sinew, should not infect the man who had the keeping of it, however well-intentioned he might once have been, and the keeper Hew had met was tainted with corruption long before he came. He had taken up the purse and turned it in his hand, and answered true to form, that it was not enough.

'For thy miching sclaunder, it is recompense. By order,' Hew had said, 'of the queen's ain secretaire.'

The man had scratched his head, baffled at the Scots, which Hew had delivered with an open countenance, keeping his face straight.

'This villain is a loose one. He is violent, see? This is little solace, for the trouble he has caused.'

'Then you will be thankful to see the back of him,' Hew had told him cheerfully. 'Else you will account to Mr Secretary Walsingham, fetch him up at once.'

Privately, he wondered what kind of a monster he had to recall up from Hell itself. The gaoler spat upon the floor, a slick gobbet of disgust. 'A bastard he is, like yourself. That is to say, a Scot.'

He had left Hew at the gate, returning in a while with a creature caked in filth, shaking out his limbs a little in the welcome air. The prisoner flexed his knuckles, which were bruised and bloodied. 'Well met, my auld friend.'

Hew had gaped at him. 'Robert Lachlan, can it be?'

Robert had answered with 'Whisht,' and pulled him out of earshot of the jealous guard. 'I could dae wi' a drink.'

'And a wash.'

'Now whit wad a man want wi' that? The pity is, there isnae time. We maun gang awa an play court tae your man.'

'But how did you end up in Newgate? What have you done?'

Robert had answered, his job.

Lachlan was a man for hire Hew had first met in Campvere. He had seen him last in St Andrews harbour, setting sail for Ghent.

'You did not tell me,' he accused, 'that you worked for Walsingham.'

Robert Lachlan shrugged. 'I telt you that I wasna working for Sir Andro Wood. And that is the truth. If they were in league togither, what was that to me? I never liked that man. But Walsingham, I serve fae time to time.'

He had been in Newgate, not for any crime, but to lie among the Catholics there, reporting on their plots. It was a role to which he had adapted naturally; in the Spanish wars, he had fought upon both sides, no more and no less than a man for hire. Most of the soldiers there were ordinary mercenaries, who bore little malice to the other side, and there was small distinction on the battlefield. Most of the fighters, on whichever side they fought, had admired the prince of Orange. Robert had the fortune to be entered in his service, earning his respect, and on one occasion, saving his life. He took it amiss that the life he had saved had been snatched while his own back was turned. When one of the papists in Newgate rejoiced at it, Robert had broken the vaunting man's face, and had had to be pulled from his quivering carcass. His shirt sleeves were stiff with the blood, and with it his cover was blown.

Walsingham was furious. 'Four months. Four months to win their confidence, and you give it all up. What those men might hide, we may never know.'

Robert said impassively, 'They had nothing to hide. Or I had found it out. You can hang them now.'

'Hang them, for what? Four months you had, and ran up exorbitant bills, for meat and strong drink.'

'The drink was to loosen their tongues.'

'And, when it did, you stopped them at once. God help you, man, I thought you could control yourself.'

'No man could control himself that was so sore provoked. Twas slander to the finest prince that lived,' Robert had declared.

Walsingham had snapped, 'Do not, I warn you, show such strong allegiances, that they amount to treason. Since you feel so strong, you will thank me for the chance to avenge that prince's death, and not be left to rot in the dungeon you deserve. Tis likely that her Majesty will wish to act on this, and send some fighting men. You two shall go ahead, as far south as you can, and send us back intelligence.

For you were there before, and served well in that place. God knows, I see no other hope for you.'

'I am not a soldier,' Hew had reminded him.

'And he is not a wit. Yet between the two of you, you may make a man.'

Audrey had a bloody streak. She liked to watch the puppet shows at Tyburn and Tower Hill, to catch wind of a scent that even Phelippes shrank from, wafting from the walls of Newgate and the Fleet. Audrey would not flinch, to see a man's flesh torn, nor shudder at his cries, 'if that man deserved it'. And yet she was not cruel. She pitied the poor fool, and would give a crust to any honest beggar she saw passing by. At the fair, she had wept, at a bear kept in chains. 'I am that tender at heart. It is not just, do you see?' she explained it to Hew, in the warmth of her bed. 'That poor bear had done nothing wrong.'

He lay with her all night, the night before he sailed, breathing in her perfume, pungent, rich and dark, closeted inside the whiteness of her flesh, pillowy and ponderous. Her plump fingers tickled the scar on his chest, counting the holes that the needle had made. When her husband had been killed, a knife had pieced his throat. 'No more than a prick. But you would not believe, how much there was of blood. His beard was like a brush with it, bristled stiff and black.'

He felt her weight upon him, and yielding to the warmth, the comfort of her thighs, he found himself more spent than sated, lunging into emptiness. 'Be sure and come right back,' she said.

And he had understood, that if he did return, it would not be to her.

Their ship had set sail at first light, and as they waited at the dock for the lighters to set out, Frances had appeared, with a bundle for them both, of blankets, beef and cheese, and a flask of beer. Hew had been moved by the sort of kindness that his sister would have shown. Frances had touched him, briefly on the cheek, and her touch was light and cool. 'I wish you to be careful, Hew. The stories that are told . . . I could not bear it if such cruelty should be done to you.'

Robert had said, through a mouthful of cheese, 'That is a lusty young lass.'

They had sailed to Middelburg, and found their slow way south, in close and covert paths betwixt the streams of refugees, thousands trudging north with a life's possessions bundled on their backs. The blockage of the Scheldt, where once Hew had sailed, had cut off the light of the fair and glorious towns that had been the envy of the merchant world, and left them cold and desolate. They made their way to Ghent, to find that it had fallen to the duke of Parma. The people in that town had no more will to fight, and abandoned to their deaths the beleaguered foreign forces who had come there to defend them. Hew and Robert had been sheltered from the occupying soldiers, by a group of nuns, and Robert for his part took two of them to bed, he said, 'for old times' sake'.

They had sent back, all this while, a clear and true intelligence, by what means they could. When Antwerp also fell, giving up the ghost of that devastated city with no more than a groan, the Spanish who had taken it had opened up the gates for the weary exodus of forty thousand Protestants, and Hew and Robert joined them on their straggled route, to the northern harbours and across the seas. They had returned to London, in 1585, in company among a ship of Flemish weavers, who found they were made welcome there, with others of their trade.

Their work had been acknowledged then, with money from the Crown, and more precious still to Hew, despatches from the Secretary to the Scottish court, reflecting on the service he had done to serve the cause of true religion, and to protect the mutual interests of the English and the Scots. Those interests had drawn closer in his absence overseas. James had consented to repeal the wicked acts that had sent the kirkmen fleeing into England, and permitted their return. He was moving closer to a new alliance with the English queen, to build upon the bond that might exist between them, to the disadvantage of the queen of Scots. John Colville, who had caused a charge to be levelled against Hew, had repaired his own relation with the Scottish king, and offered a retraction, owning to his fault. James had sent word that he was prepared to hear a plea from Hew, and send to him a passport, if he would go back. The tide had turned at last.

And yet, for all the longing he had felt to see his home and family, he had not returned. Scotland at that time was ravaged by the plague; the kirkmen said that it was God's wrath on the king for imposing those Black Acts upon the Presbyterians, but its sweep was indiscriminate; the court had crossed the country hoping to escape it from it, trailing in its wake, a black dog at its door. At St Andrews, the town was stripped bare to its bones. The colleges were closed. A single note from Giles, sent to Leadenhall, said no more than this: 'Do not come.' For months after that, Hew heard nothing more.

That, he thought now, was the worst. While he was abroad, he had thought little of his family, so intent and occupied in that present world. Meg had given birth, to a second child. The news had passed him by, with all the joy and terror it had meant for Giles, without a second thought. He had immersed himself in another life. And in that time, he had not considered all the months gone by when they had had no letters from him, when they had not known if he was still alive. The empty weeks were torment to him then; he had felt his exile brutally enforced at the very moment when it was revoked. Often, he had been upon the point of setting out, desperate to have the smallest scrap of news, when Walsingham's own spies retreated from the peste, like the puling lice that flee the cooling corpse. It was Frances, always, who had held him back.

'Trust your family, Hew. From what you say, your brother-in-law is a fine physician, and your sister is wise; trust them to keep themselves safe.'

'They can be trusted well enough,' Hew had answered grimly, 'to go out among the sick, and tend to them, in peril of their lives.'

'Then put your trust in God. He will not allow such good people to fall sick.'

Hew felt less than sure that God's will worked that way. He was more persuaded of her second argument.

'What good can it do you to go to them to now? You will carry the peste as you walk through that land. It follows a man wherever he travels. You will spread that plague wide, and fall sick yourself. What use were that?'

She had persuaded him to take up his old business in the custom house, and return to his old room, in her uncle's house. Phelippes was engaged on secret work for Walsingham. He appeared very close with a friend, Gilbert Gifford, who stayed at his house for a few weeks at Holborn. That year, Tom had married, and he and his wife had spent Christmas at Chartley, returning with Mary expecting his child. His father had begun to trade among the Flemish immigrants, where Hew helped to translate. When the work was done, he would walk with Frances in the gardens of the guild house, or call to speak with Laurence at the house in Seething Lane. This sedentary quietness helped put to rest the horrors he had witnessed in the Spanish Netherlands, and he felt more at peace. Robert Lachlan had returned to the London underworld, pensioned to a life of debauchery and drink. Hew met with him occasionally, in the Cock and Bull.

At last, a letter came, the plague had done its worst, and left his family safe. He gave up thanks to God. The way was clear at last, for him to go back home. By then, he had been snared, in such a slender web, he could not see the threads that bound and held him still.

Hew was kept at Chartley for the next five days. Phelippes showed no sign that he was nervous at the wait. He told Hew he had seen that queen, riding in her carriage at the manor gates, and that queen had smiled at him; whatever plots were hatched around her, she did not suspect. But when a letter came, with word returned from Walsingham, Tom became tight-lipped. They rode back to London, and to Seething Lane. Phelippes left at once, and went on to the court. Perhaps he found the time to call in on his wife. Perhaps though, he did not. Whatever happened then, did not trouble Hew. His own life had begun upon a different course.

Chapter 8

Frost of Cares

Hew was held at Seething Lane, and kept there from the sun, for a time in which he lost count of the days. He found himself interned where he had first had his beginning, which then was filled with wonder, now was dark with knowing, emptied of its hope. His innocence was gone, and could not be recovered in that kindless place. He was kept from sleep, and woken as he slept, for the purpose of interrogation, by the agent Francis Mylles, and on more than one occasion, by Walsingham himself. The questions, and the answers to them, did not ever change, but fell into a rhythm with a dull, familiar beat. Walsingham, he sensed, was simply marking time. For when he wished for an exactness of response, he had more exacting methods at his hands, and would not hesitate to use them. The conspirators, this while, had not yet been found. And while they were at large, the friction at the court, and in the steps of those who set their subtle snares for them, had become unbearable. Walsingham relieved a little of his share of it by picking over Hew, and took a vicious pleasure in that small distraction.

For what purpose had he taken it upon himself to ride to Chartley?

'To inform Thomas Phelippes of his wife's distress,' Hew returned each time.

Why had he not despatched the servant, Thomas Cassie, who was then in London?

That man could not be found.

Why had he not consulted Walsingham himself?

Because, Hew answered, looking at him, it had not occurred to him that office was concerned with so small a matter as the stillbirth of a child.

What acquaintance had he with the principal conspirators?

That he could not say; he did not know who they were. Of necessity, inquisitors will give their cause away, and so he learned, by inference, their method, and their names.

Had he ever met a man called Gilbert Gifford?

Certainly he had. He was Phelippes' protégé – he would not call him friend.

Had he been aware of Gifford taking letters to the queen of Scots? That he had been her courier?

Hew had not been aware of it. But now recalling Phelippes at his work at Chartley, he saw and understood.

Had he ever met the man they called Black Fortescue?

He could not help but smile at that, and it was seized upon.

He never heard that name. It struck him as ridiculous.

And if he met the devil, would he smile at him? Ballard was his proper name. He styled himself a priest. And he was the devil in a plain man's clothes. Had he heard of Savage?

They sounded like the stuff of country children's tales. It was duly pressed upon him that the threat was real.

Had he ever spoken with a man called Babington?

He was certain, not.

He must think again. Anthony Babington once was a page in the household of the earl of Shrewsbury. Hew had been at Buxton Hall, and had met *that queen*, and others of that house. Had he met or spoken with, or heard talk there of Babington, he must reveal it now.

He had spoken, he affirmed, with two men in that household, that was the doctor, who called himself Forrester, and Monsieur Claude Nau. Forrester, he thought, was working for that queen, or else for Francis Walsingham. *Which*, he did not know. It was not inconceivable that it was both. Nau, he thought true to his queen.

This Walsingham did not confirm, or otherwise deny. Had he had any contact with the queen of Scots, by any word or sign, or with any of her servants, such as Monsieur Nau, while he was at Chartley?

He had none at all, Phelippes saw to that.

And then, again, again, what purpose did he have, in riding to that place?

He felt his mind was stripped, clean of will and hope. It brought a kind of peace with it, desolate as death. He had, after all, nothing there to hide, and little to hold on to, in the bleakest hours.

Eventually, it seemed, Walsingham allowed him the benefit of doubt, or simply had grown weary of the line of questioning, had nothing more to ask. Perhaps he had allowed a little slack, so that Hew himself could tighten up the knot. The inquisition stopped, and he was detailed to help Laurence with his correspondence, back where he began. Perhaps it was Laurence who had spoken up for him. Perhaps it had been Phelippes, who despite appearances, deeply loved his wife. Perhaps it was that Walsingham, never really satisfied, had turned his mind a moment to the greater threat.

'There are letters from the earl of Leicester, and from Sir Philip Sidney, which I have not had time to read. Since you know the lie of the Low Countries, you can be of help to Laurence in drawing up a chart, to mark out the progress they have made.

'You may not, for the moment, leave this place,' Walsingham informed him, in his parting shot. 'Then, if your detention does arouse alarm, and cause to put to flight, the principal conspirators . . . well then, we shall know.'

This left Hew in a state of perpetual unease, for any small effect that might alert the principals, could be blamed on him. And wherever they were, it seemed likely that their enterprise would keep them poised for flight. They might bolt at any moment, unless they were innocent. And neither thought brought comfort to him.

As to what evidence there was of the conspiracy, apart from a letter stolen from that queen, he was in the dark. A scrap, he came upon by accident, hardly comprehending what it meant. Phelippes had returned, and left behind a letter to be entered in the files. Hew had found a draft, scribbled on a piece of paper, lying in the grate, of a line or two of cipher, like the one at Chartley. He took a moment to imprint it firm upon his memory. Then he left the paper to the solace of the flames.

Those last days he spent under Laurence Tomson's guard were among the longest and most irksome in his life. He struggled to attend to the work in hand, and to conceal from Laurence the disquiet in his mind. He felt like a child, who is kept at his books while his school friends run at play, and under the promise of worse penalties to come. The house appeared vacant and watchful; all of its agents were occupied abroad, and while the flow of traffic did not break or falter, it moved slow and stealthily, channelled underground. Hew could scarcely bear the ominous deep quietness, the storm about to break. Laurence was methodical, indifferent to the mood, and in no way altered from his normal self. His placidness unnerved. It was Laurence who informed him of the first arrest; Hew expected he was primed to look for a response. Black Fortescue, a priest, had been arrested quietly by those who had ostensibly no link to Francis Walsingham. But it had been enough to alarm his co-conspirators, all of whom had fled.

For nine days, Hew remained there, in a state of dread. On the tenth day, unexpectedly, he was free to leave. Laurence took him by the hand, and walked him to the door. There stood a man brought in by the guard, who, as they came to him, fell to his knees.

'For pity, my masters, for pity, please help me.'

Laurence asked mildly, 'How can we help you?'

'For that you have the means to speak out to the Secretary, I pray you, good masters, put my case to him, as I was promised, and put off, for days. It was never meant . . . I thought to tell him all, I was to tell him everything, but could not have the hearing of him, each time it was stayed. I swear upon the life of my infant child, it was understood.' The man broke down in tears. The water ran in rivers through some dark stuff he had rubbed to cover his fair face. He had cut his hair, and childishly dissembled in his servant's clothes, his cheeks were hollowed out from hunger and from fear, yet he could not disguise that he was a gentleman. Laurence placed a hand, calmly, on his shoulder. 'There, now, sir, be still.'

'It was my intent, always, to have told. That was what was meant. But when it was the time for it, then he would not hear.'

Hew felt pity swill, hollow in his bowels.

Laurence said soothingly, 'You shall tell it now. And he will hear it all. Fetch this man food, and something to drink. He will be here for a while.'

To Hew he remarked, as they moved on, 'He had not gone far, before his hunger forced him out into the air. He will fill his guts, and spill them in his eagerness. He will spew his tale, as easily to Walsingham, and upon the scaffold, spill them out again.' Compassion had evaporated to a cool complacency. Hew whispered, aghast, 'Who was that man?'

'He is Anthony Babington. And I give thanks to God, he did not seem to know you, more than you know him. For had he shown such sign, this day had ended differently, in sorrow for us both.' Laurence showed his old self, ghostly, in his smile. 'God love you, Hew. Go home.'

He had a cold homecoming to the house at Leadenhall. William Phillips had been without the convenience of the grey horse longer than he had been willing to excuse, until Thomas had returned it, without a word from Hew. Phelippes had reported that he might be gone awhile. 'Not a thought for us, or for your duty to us here.' Joan Phillips was disposed to have turned him from the house, but Frances intervened. 'He did not leave us, quite. We had the word of Tom.'

Tom's word, God knew, was far from satisfactory. Their son had been to visit twice, to spend time with his wife, and left her in their care. Mary bore her loss with a patient fortitude, her love for him undimmed. Hew wondered how much Thomas had confided to her; he suspected, everything. Even Phelippes could not keep his spiralling intrigues entirely to himself.

The grumbles of the Phillips family were founded in anxiety. In

Hew's absence, the house had been searched. In the hunt for fugitives, the store rooms at the Leadenhall were stripped bare of their felts and cloths, the sacks of wool were split, spilling out their fluff like dummies at the tilting yard, scattering the mice. In Hew's sleeping loft, the search was more methodical. His linen, books and writing things were taken from their chest and laid out on the counterpane, a purposeful display. The message was, we know you, we have read your thoughts. The letters he had had from Meg and Giles were cut free from their ribbons, open, neatly stacked. The riflers made their inquisition, clean, into his heart, and wanted him to feel the thorough, sharp incisions of their searching blades.

He folded up the letters and returned them to their chest. There was comfort in the fact that they could not have known the value of those words to him – that were no more than words, and held no hidden signs – the memories they stirred and brought back to his mind. There were no safe places that they could not find, prising out the conscience of a living man as though it were the pulp of a rotting tooth. A man might cling to his faith as close as to his bones, to find both rattled out.

Frances gave voice to the fear. 'You were gone for days. And I was afraid for you. Tom said you were helping Master Secretary with his enquiries.'

In Scotland, lists of malefactors to be brought to justice bore the name of *valentines*, a gallow- humoured twist upon the game of lots. So sinister could turn the simplest kind of phrase. Hew could not help but smile. 'He wished me to draw out a map, of the progress we make in the Low Countries.'

'Oh! Was that all? I was afraid you were caught up in some way in these dreadful conspiracies. Not that I thought . . .' Frances trailed off. 'Did you hear that Tom's friend, Gilbert Gifford, was involved with the conspirators? That he carried letters for them, to the queen of Scots? Can you imagine? He dined with Tom once, here at the house. He has fled to France. And Mary says, his father says – though he is professed a most devout Catholic recusant himself – he wished that his son had never been born. That is a thing, to have said of his son. Tom is heartsick too, to have been so deceived in him.'

Hew kept to himself his own thoughts on that. He had little doubt that Gifford had been pressed to the cause of Walsingham. Willingly or not. It struck him that the role that Gilbert Gifford played, he had once unwittingly auditioned for himself, when he was sent to Buxton to see the queen of Scots. Gifford had acquitted perfectly his part. He had fled just before the trap began to close, not trusting to the scruples of those experts who had played him, fearful that he also would be swept up in the net. So slippery a fish would doubtless have been prized. Had such a line been cast, and hooked the hapless Babington?

One of William's Flemish friends was at the house that day, the weaver Josef van Helst. Van Helst had brought samples of the lighter kinds of cloths his colleagues were producing, in which William had expressed an interest to invest, new draperies of bayes, broadcloth and fine wool. He stayed on to supper, of bacon collops, manchet, and a yellow cheese.

'A great terror is averted in this land today, but tomorrow, there will be a greater one. You must be prepared for it, vigilant. As to the perpetrators, no pain must be spared to them in exacting punishment. You people are too soft, womanish and faint. Your penalties are paltry, and do not go far enough. An eye for an eye, you will say. Pah. What for a man, who would bring down the state, dismember limb from limb, all that you believe in? No punishment on earth is too severe for that, whatever kind of recompense a brave man can devise. This bacon is good, is it not?'

He drank to the queen, in a fierce draught of ale, that left the Phillips family feeling they were somehow left behind, in their show of loyalty, faith and national pride. Josef was a shrewd, pugnacious little man, with a sharp glint in his eye. He had walked from Antwerp with his loom upon his back, when his business had been broken by the closing of the Scheldt. And no doubt he had suffered in the course of his displacement; but Josef had the force to set aside that life, and build himself a better one. To rise above the crowd, he climbed on other men. Not everyone who suffered, who was dispossessed, might in other circumstances have deserved respect. The self-appointed master of the Flemish refugees, Josef was a bully who had battled his way forth.

Bells were rung to mark the traitors' executions. On the day that they began, Hew discovered Frances sitting on her own. 'Is it very wrong?' she asked, 'not to watch them die?'

'Why should that be wrong?' he answered, touched that she should turn to him.

'It might seem ungracious to our lady queen.'

'It cannot be wrong, to pity someone young and foolish such a savage death. Frances, if you do not go, you will not be missed. There will be thousands there. Nor will their supporters, those who share their faith, choose to stay away. They will look to see them in the crowd, and die as martyrs, in their eyes. Absence does not mean your loyalty lies with them, if that is what you fear.'

She was troubled still. 'They are not martyrs, though. And they will go to Hell for what they did.'

'Perhaps. Most probably.'

'Then if they are condemned to Hell, why must their living deaths be made so cruel?'

'I do not know. Revenge. Or to put off the rest. Which it does not do. As a philosophy, in truth, it does not seem exact. But you need not go. You should stay with Mary. She is far from well enough to see the traitors hang.'

Frances nodded. 'You are right. Then I shall stay home. I thank you. For I was afraid you would think it weak, as Master Josef did.'

Joan and William Phillips went to see the executions, in the spirit that their Flemish neighbour had inspired in them. They returned with mixed reports. Since Tom had a house near St Giles-in-the-Fields, where the traitors were hanged, they had hoped for the advantage of a clearer view, which had been denied them by the pressing crowds. The speeches had varied in interest and in length;

the most affecting was a poet, tender still in years, who fitting to his words, took the longest time to die. The worst was from a man who did not in the least join in the spirit of the day; he had made no speech, saying he had come there not to argue but to die, and *that* had done ungraciously, coming to his God with the surliest of faces, departing very stubbornly, before his bowels were ripped. The whole day had been marred, when Joan had lost her pocket to a cutpurse in the crowd. It had not held very much – she had already bought a pie – but she had hoped to have a little tract of verses set down by the poet on the day before he died, which William, disapproving of it, had refused to buy for her. It did not seem worthwhile attending on the second day, so thick were the crowds. And since the queen, in her mercy, had remit the disembowelling, there was less to see.

Hew had left the house, in the full intention of following the crowd. But when he saw the feeling and the force with which it flowed, he did not have the heart for it. He found himself, instead, standing by the water of the brackish Thames, staring at its depths. At the close of day, he went to Laurence Tomson, and asked what was provided for the queen of Scots, when she came to trial. 'For she did ask once, if I might be of service of her, as her man of law. I would I might be offered to her, now, as counsel.'

Laurence stared at him. 'Have you lost your mind? She is indicted for treason.'

'In Scotland, all men have the right to counsel in the court, whatever is the crime.'

'This is not Scotland.'

'Yet, she is a Scot, and the mother of the king. The king will think it strange enough if no one comes to speak for her. I do not ask, you understand, from any preconception of her guilt or innocence, but because, in a case of this sort, it seems to be imperative that justice shall be done. Your queen Elizabeth would doubtless think the same, that no question could be put about the proper process, or about the evidence that comes before the court. It cannot be opaque.'

'Our laws,' Laurence said, 'are not the same as yours. As for evidence, you may be assured it will be fairly judged. It is sworn to, moreover, by Anthony Babington, and by her own secretaries, Claude Nau and Gilbert Curle.'

'Nau?' Hew shook his head. 'I do not believe that he would condemn her, unless it were under duress.'

'There you have your answer. For, I can promise you, he was treated with the utmost of kindness and courtesy. He is not under duress. Nor has he condemned her. That is for the court. You may be quite sure, that Nau has told the truth. Hew, you are my friend. And for the love of you, we have not had this conversation. It will take you to the Tower, if you mention it again.'

There was nothing more to say. As he left that place, Hew chanced to glance from the window, at Walsingham's garden of sallats and herbs. And there, by the bower of a rose, he saw Claude Nau himself, taking the air in the last of the sun.

That queen came to trial, where she was condemned. Elizabeth showed a great reluctance to sign the death warrant, taking time to confer with her own conscience, and with foreign princes, on what might be the consequence if she put to death a late anointed queen. She did not want that blood on her hands, or to set so close and discomfiting a precedent. She hinted that, should Mary's life be taken by one of those who had committed to that bond to protect and save her own life, that was not only lawful, but would be quite welcome. If Mary's life were snuffed out in hot blood, in defence of hers, no one would be blamed. Sir Amias Paulet, who had still the keeping of that queen, could not admit such a stain on his conscience, and he kept her with an honest rigour, more careful than before. Ambassadors were sent from Scotland, some more warm than others in their treating for that queen; her son's responses lagged, lukewarm and ambivalent. In those months, while Elizabeth hesitated, her own life was placed in a more urgent danger, more imminent, according to her councillors, than ever was before. Each day that the

Scottish queen breathed, under sentence of death, brought further risk. A terror watch was placed at every port, and guards patrolled the streets. London was on edge, nervous and alert, and foreigners were subject to a searching inquisition, irksome and uncomfortable. Rumours crept like fog, that Spanish troops had landed at the coast, that the stronghold had been stormed, and that the Scottish queen was freed, even that Elizabeth was murdered in the Tower. The council did their best to put down their source, but as quickly as they quelled them, other rumours spread. In midst of this, not long after Christmas, Hew received a letter in his office at the custom house, from the Scottish court. The king had called him home, and made claim upon his service there, in light, the letter said, 'of these strange events'. It was not the invitation Hew had had before, extending his good will, but a clear note of command.

He took the letter straight to Seething Lane. Walsingham by then was lying sick abed. He had done what he could, to ensure the Scots queen's downfall, and could do no more. His son-in-law, Sir Philip Sidney, had lately lost his life in service in the Netherlands, and he was burdened with the task of preparing for the funeral, and a raft of debts, which he had undersigned. In all this, he had no thanks, no word of help nor comfort from his queen. 'What? Still here?' he might have said, had he encountered Hew. But nothing, at that moment, could concern him less, had it been a flea he snuffed out with his fingertip or in a rare benignancy, brushed off from his cloak.

'Not before time,' Laurence said. 'This is no place for you now. If you can find in it your conscience, to send a letter here to tell us how things lie with your king in Scotland, Walsingham will thank you for it. And, if not . . .'. He shrugged. 'No matter. You have been repaid for your service in the Netherlands. I will arrange for your passport to Berwick. May I suggest that you take Robert Lachlan with you? He has drunk away what portion he was given by the Crown, and for idleness or want or sheer force of his stubbornness is likely now to find himself incarcerate again, in Newgate or the Fleet, procuring no one's downfall but his own. This is no time for a Scotsman to cry havoc in the streets.'

'Willingly,' said Hew. 'He shall come as my servant, or, if not, my friend. In truth, I do not blame him that he rages and reviles these filthsome streets, this air that grows thick with suspicion and hatred. This place, where I have stayed – for all I had the solace of your own sustaining friendship – never felt so fraught and bloody nor so strange to me, as it does now. I cannot for the world explain what force it was that kept me here, nor why I stayed so long.'

Laurence raised an eyebrow, sceptical and humorous. 'Can you not?' he said.

What Laurence had known now for several months came finally to Hew on the way to Leadenhall, as he realised that the time had come to say his last goodbyes. It was Frances that he looked for, first and last of all, and he found her on her own, sitting in the garden.

'It is cold here, to be sitting, at this time of year.'

'Yes.'

Her eyes were bright with tears, small shards of winter frost. He thought it was the chillness of the biting wind, that brought them there. It was not the wind. He thought perhaps that Phelippes had been there before him, had passed on the news of the letter at the custom house, and cursed himself at once, for his stupidity and arrogance. For why should he suppose that she should weep for him, or clearly see a loss that he had only dimly groped upon himself? The tears were not for him. The bitterest of winds had not yet blown that news.

'My uncle has sold me,' she said.

This was so unexpected he could make no sense of it. 'How can that be? You are not a black ewe, or a roll of blue cloth.'

'He has entered into a business arrangement, with Josef the Fleming. Josef will work in partnership with him, in return for my hand in marriage, for which he has solicited, over these past months. You may be assured, that I have not encouraged him. My uncle has agreed.'

'He cannot force you to marry,' Hew contended fiercely.

'I know that he cannot. But, if I do not consent to it, he will no longer keep me in his house. I have no other friend, and will be destitute. I have told him Josef is a man that I can never love. Yet he remains unmoved. My aunt says, that in time I may feel love. And that, in any case, I should not expect it. That many such a marriage was contracted out of honour, and among those was her own. That the match is a good one, and will keep us close and prosperous, that nothing I hold dear could possibly be lost to it, with everything to gain. And Tom says, tis a pity that I am not reconciled to it, but it cannot be helped.'

The tears were flowing freely now, for Frances, in her passion could not keep them in. And all that she saw blurred, was clear as day to Hew. He took her hands in his. 'You do not have to marry him. There is another way.'

Part II

Chapter 9

The Opened Bud

En ma fin git ma commencement
[In my end is my beginning]
MR

St Andrews, February 1587

'*When* will mine uncle come?' the small boy asked, again.

Meg Cullan sighed. 'We not do know. It may not be today.' She sympathised, in spirit, with her small son's restlessness. Three long years had passed, with no hope of Hew. A life could not be lived in constant agitation, for sickness was distilled in such a state of flux. Giles Locke warned against it: passion was a scourge upon the infant faculty, though Matthew was in temperament a solid, sanguine child. Martha was the kittil one, fickle as a fish.

'If you are done here,' Meg said, 'run out and play. The time will pass more quickly then.'

Matthew Locke considered. 'How will it do that?'

The children were making marchpanes, as a gift for Hew. Unless his tastes had changed, he did not care for sweetmeats, but the children did. An uncle from abroad was hard enough to grasp. Meg had baked crisp wafers, stippled from the iron, the cook had pounded almonds to a pestle paste, with sugar for the glaze; the children rolled it out, and cut it into shapes. Matthew had scored his, into a plaque of lozenges. In the centre of each one, he had placed a currant or a

99

sugared seed, measured and methodical, like a feathered quilt, or the diamond patterned doublet of a gentleman at court, padded and puffed out. Martha had gathered hers up in a ball, and was poking the almond nibs in through a hole. Her fingers were sticky and fragrant with rose, from the flask she had spilled. Meg wiped her hands. Martha said, 'Nuncle', her mouth full of currant and wafery crumbs.

Meg said, '*Uncle Hew*. When the marchpane is baked, you can colour it gold. It will be fit for a queen.'

'Fit for a king,' Matthew corrected.

Matthew Locke was four years old. A quisitive, pedantic bairn. It was not like him, Meg reflected, to be clinging to his mother. When he was not at his books – he had already learned to read – he was pestering the pigs, or tickling up the sticklebacks in the Kenly Burn, with the miller's boy, John Kintor. Now, he jumped up and ran from the kitchen, his steps light and purposeful on the stone stair. He returned with the hourglass from his uncle's library, heavy in its frame.

'Be careful with that.'

The boy set the glass on the board. 'Will mine uncle want to live with us?' he asked.

'Well,' reflected Meg, 'Kenly Green is his. We have only kept it for him, while he was away. And we have our new house, in the town; we shall move there presently, when the work is done.' She found that she was looking forward to that time. The new house on the South Street brought the gift of land, in the College of St Leonard near her father's grave. She would miss the gardens here, but could begin again. She would have her old life there, and more important still, the time to spend with Giles, who left before the sun was up and did not leave till late his college in the town, to start the long walk home. Meg had felt his absence in the year of plague.

'Will John Kintor come to the new house with us?' Matthew asked her now.

'By no means. John Kintor belongs at the mill.'

'Then I shall stay here. For, it is my mill, and my John Kintor. My uncle gave them to me.'

His mother sighed, again. 'He did not give you John. People do not belong to other people.'

Hew had gifted the mill, and the land on which it stood by the Kenly Water, to his little godson as a christening present. The land was in feu to the Kintor family; when the miller died, the working of the mill passed on to his eldest son, who was married with a child. Matthew was devoted to his brother John. John Kintor was thirteen years old, and close to leaving home, to begin an apprenticeship in another town. Meg did not know how to break the news to Matthew.

Matthew said kindly, misreading the signs, 'Do not be sad, Minnie. You can come and visit.'

He watched the sand a moment, running through the glass. 'I can hear horses.'

Meg wiped her hands on a cloth. 'You imagine it, my love. And watching the sand will not make time pass. It makes it run slow.'

'How can that be? Anyway, I *can*.'

And he did not imagine it. For Meg heard horses too, and voices at the door, and lifting Martha in her arms she ran out from the house, quickening in her heart, to see her brother coming, dusty from the road, his sweet, bewildered face breaking to a smile. She threw herself upon him, squeezing him so tightly that the infant Martha fluttered like a bird and beat upon his breast with small and flustered fists. Laughing, Hew stepped back. 'And who is this small fury? She has your temper, Meg.'

Matthew answered for her, solemn and important at his mother's side. 'She is Martha Locke. And she is my sister. She is not very big, and she does not ken much. I am Matthew Locke. You are my Uncle Hew, who gave to me the mill and my friend, John Kintor. We made you marchpanes.'

Hew said, 'How clever of you. I did not know it was March.'

'My Minnie says, English folk like them,' Matthew said, faintly reproachful. 'Who are those people behind?'

Hew's answer, meant for Meg, was filtered through the boy. 'I also

101

have some friends. And ye must excuse it that I have not mentioned them. This is Robert Lachlan, who is an old friend your mother kens well. And this is a new friend, close to my heart. Her name is Frances. And she is my wife.'

Giles Locke left his rooms as the light began to fail, and crossed the college courtyard to the dinner hall. The place was quiet now, dark and unfamiliar as he stepped inside. A voice spoke from the gloom. 'The painter went home with the light. And you will, I can fetch him.' The speaker was a graduand, aged seventeen, in a slate-coloured gown and a soiled yellow shirt, frayed at the cuffs. Doctor Locke frowned. 'No. Indeed. What do you do here? Supper will be set out in the common school.'

An inconvenient truth. The lecture hall smelt wearily of grease and cabbage kale, dispiriting to young and old, tormenting to the wits and to the hollow stomachs of the poorest boys.

'I know that, sir. Not yet.'

The young man did not bother to reply in Latin; nor did Doctor Locke, for they had come too far, and grown too close for that, this wanton boy's pale face as troubling as his own. Giles sniffed at the air. He caught a whiff of sulphur he had not smelled before, when the windows had been open to allow the light.

'There is sulphur, sir, and other things besides. The painter is a subtle kind of alchemist.'

And that alone, sufficient to explain the student's presence here, his ragged cuffs and fingers, with their yellow stains.

'Perhaps,' the student said, 'you have come here to look at the pictures?'

Giles felt foolish then, to understand how easily the young man read his mind. The student said, 'There is no shame in it. The drafts are very good. And he has caught the likeness of your spirit and your form. The prentice lad has craft, and skill, and he has caught the essence of you, in a piece of chalk. Your *solidness*, in fact. His master, I take to be some sort of juglar.'

'And you,' observed Giles, 'are an insolent loun.' His censure had little effect.

'Did you know, the prentice lad is deaf as well as dumb? That when his master speaks to him, he does so with his hands? It is a language, quite,' the student went on, seriously. 'And I should make a study of it, if I had the chance. The boy reads faces too, as well as the devil reads souls. Have you ever heard it said, that a man's mouth makes words when his head is cut off? That boy could probably read them.'

Giles retorted, 'Stuff.' Pretending to be cross, he was interested in this. He had once read in a book that it was possible to see from the moving of men's lips, what could not be heard. It was not a common thing, and the ancients did not mention it. He must look it up. But was that not this student's trick, to try to draw him in? 'Be that as it may,' he said, 'this place is out of bounds. You shall not vex the painters, nor distract them at their work. Go, attend to yours. You might profit from an extra hour or two of study. There is little time enough till your examination. Go to, and apply yourself.'

'It is hard to find the will,' the student said, 'when there is no purpose to it.'

'I will be the judge,' said Giles, 'whether there is purpose to it. You do as you're telt.'

The student lingered still. 'Has master Hew come home?'

'Not yet, to my ken. Be sure that ye will hear it when he does.' The doctor's tone was sharper than he felt, whittled on proplexity. His feelings were misread, for the boy said hopelessly, 'Then I will be gone.'

'That is by no means certain.'

'You will tell him what I said?'

'You must tell him that yourself. I will not give you false hope, though I will counsel as well as I can. But you should know, you must know, Hew is a good man.'

'As I am not.'

'Come, do not say that, I will not have that. Go now, to your books, and do not let me find you meddling with the painters.'

'Very good, professor. Will you come to supper, sir?' The student had a knack of changing tune precipitate, which Giles found disconcerting. His moods could be mercurial.

'No. Not tonight. I am going home. And shall go at once, for I must call in on the way to visit the archbishop, who has not been very well.'

'I can go in your place, if you like,' the young man suggested. 'And tell him you were called away, incontinent.'

'By no means,' answered Giles. He shooed the boy away, and stole a glance around. The dinner hall was stripped of plate, the stools and trestle tables racked up on one side. On the upper dais where the masters dined, the painter had set out a scene upon a stage, a green-backed chair and table with a pile of books, where Giles had been sitting, artfully arranged, all that afternoon. He had felt an itching, then, to look upon the paper where the boy had drawn, unconscious of the music he was making with his mouth, a stream of squeaks and squawks. The drafts lay on the table, covered with a cloth, but Giles had lost the will to look at them. 'Vanity, all vanity,' he muttered to himself. He locked the hall door and lodged the key with the porter, instructing him to lend it only to the painter, and for no other purpose to allow it from his sight.

The comfort of his supper by the fireside had to wait, for the doctor's journey took him first to the South Street town house of Archbishop Patrick Adamson, who had fallen back into the slurried troughs which plagued him through his life, brought on by drink and gluttony, and politics and posturing. The bishop had returned that morning from the Parliament, and had sunk at once into his old dyspepsia, claiming once again to have been 'poisoned by a witch'. Giles prescribed, as always, a severe and thorough abstinence, which Adamson, as always, worked hard to resist. 'I doubt it is a chill I caught upon the road, coupled with the blow of that most dreadful news, has set my bowel a-wammilling. A little aquavite will likely settle this.'

Giles snapped shut his case. 'Aye then, please yourself. What news was that?' he asked.

The answer chilled him too, and turned his stomach sour. By the time he set out, on the back of a mare who grew slower each day, the pale moon was masked in a bank of black cloud. It was past eight o'clock by the time that he reached home.

This did not damp down the spirits of his son, who met him at the door, shrieking with excitement, 'Mine uncle Hew is here! Did I not tell you, he would come today?'

Giles allowed, 'You did.' He ruffled the child's hair. 'And since you have telt me each day for a fortnight, logic demands it must sometime be true.'

'He has brought a soldier wi' him, and he has a wife. The soldier can kill a man, with his bare hands. An' he will tell to me and to John Kintor how we may do it.'

Giles said, 'Dear me,' raising an eyebrow at Meg, who had come in the wake of her wild little son.

'He brought Robert Lachlan,' Meg said.

'That, perhaps, accounts for it.'

'Robert took Matthew to see to the horses, for a moment only, while I talked to Hew. But it was long enough.'

'Ah. I see it all.' Giles surveyed the child. 'A surfeit of unsteadiness. The bairn has been exagitated to a hurkling heat. Bed is prescribed here, I think.'

Matthew pulled a face. 'It is not supper yet.'

'Go with Canny Bett, who will give you supper and a cooling drink. Your uncle will be here still in the morning,' Meg promised.

'And his soldier too?'

'As I fear and trust.'

The child was whisked away, and Giles returned to Meg, cheered by her embrace. 'Well,' the doctor said, 'where is the sorry prodigal?'

'They have gone to rest, worn out from their journey. Giles . . .'

'And who is Lachlan's wife? Can it be that Maude, that went with him to Ghent? For, as I had thought . . .'

'Whisht, and listen, Giles! The wife belongs to Hew. He met an

English lass. Her name is Frances Phillips. She seems the perfect choice. A match for him, I think.'

And that was like Meg, to depend on an instinct. She was not often wrong. But nature sometimes could be cast awry, and instinct blown adrift, by a malignant force. The doctor shook his head. 'Dearest, though it hurts my heart to be the one to say it, this is not good news.'

Frances lay quite still, watching as he washed. Someone had brought water, scented soap and towels, and a fire was lit, in a little brazier in the centre of the room, distilling the cool air into a soporific smoke. Hew was naked to his waist, moving round the chamber with a settled kind of ease. Folded in the press he found a linen shirt, fresh as the day on which he had left it, interleaved with dried petals and herbs. The scar on his chest shone in the lamplight. Frances had asked, 'Does this hurt you, still?' pricking it out with light careful fingers. She had not seen it before.

On their long journey north, they had not shared a bed. Hew had slept with Robert at his side, while Frances slept apart. So they had escaped the censure of the crowd, and slipped away unseen. 'She is a chaste piece,' Robert had said. 'You will not know where to start with her. It will be like bedding a nun.' Hew had replied, 'You should ken.'

The conversation, when it came, was tentative at first, hesitant and shy, for they were strangers still, and began upon it with a strange politeness, civil and reserved. But when they lost their shyness, they had come together deep, and known each other well, and there was meaning to it. Frances had unfolded like a rose and blossomed in his bed. She lay now, quite still, in a flowering of semen and blood, and wondered if that flux was how a child was made, for she had not been told. She remembered Mary, and her withered leaf, the tracery of veins.

Hew was washed and dressed. 'I hear Giles in the hall. We should go down.'

'You go on first. I will come after.'

She wanted to stay. In the coolness of the sheets, in the safe milk of his seed, for the rest of her life. 'I do not want them to know.'

She had the kind of skin that flamed and coloured easily, that bloomed into a blush, upon her breasts and cheeks. He kissed her once again. 'They will not know,' he said.

He came into the hall, glowing, from her bed, to find it home again. It was more than home, for Meg and Giles and their small bairns had kindled up the warmth it had when Matthew Cullan was alive, and fuelled it with their own. The hall was furnished with the drapes and hangings Hew remembered from his childhood, his parents' plate and furniture, burnished to a gleam in the blazing fire. On this winter night, the shutters had been closed and lamps and candles lit, illuminating gloom with confidential light. The board had been set out for supper for four, and a rich jug of claret, fresh from the cask, from which Meg poured a long draught for Hew.

'Come by the fire. Your travels were long, and the nights here are cold. Too long. Too cold.' Giles, for all his cares, for all the absent years that had made hard his hopes, could not help but clasp Hew close, and hold him to his heart. 'Here you are, intact, and back where you belong. God love you, how we missed you, Hew!'

For a moment, in that place, Hew felt overwhelmed. That part of his life, from which he had been snatched, and had come accustomed to have left behind, flooded him with feeling he could barely comprehend, when feeling was a thing he had been taught to hide.

It was Meg who rescued him. 'Your friend Robert Lachlan asked for bread and cheese. He spent the afternoon drinking with the groom, and has fallen asleep in the library.'

Her brother grinned at her. 'I will tell him to behave himself.'

'As I wish you would. Supper will be served, as soon as Frances comes.'

'She will not be long. Or I will go and fetch her.'

Meg nodded. 'Anyone can see that she is lovely, Hew. But why did you not tell us that you had a wife?'

'Because,' Hew confessed, 'it came about by chance. I did not know I loved her, till we came to part. We married in great haste, and after I had written to you I was coming home. And somehow, too, a letter did not seem the place, to tell to you the news. I knew that when you met her, you would like her too. The marriage was clandestine. It was, you understand, entirely lawful under English law. Frances is of age, and she knows her mind. But her uncle had intended she should wed another man.'

'Her uncle?' queried Meg.

'She is an orphan, too.'

Nothing in his friend's account brought peace of mind to Giles. 'When were you at Berwick, Hew?' he asked.

'Ten or twelve days ago. I should tell you, perhaps, that Frances did not travel with me as my wife. I have a friend in the office of the Master Secretary, Laurence Tomson, whose passport allowed me to bring out two servants. I requested the same from the king.'

'You slipped in on a thread,' Giles said. 'For since then, the border has closed.'

Hew asked, 'Why is that?' though in his heart he knew.

'The queen of Scots is dead.'

The words came sharp and cold, with nothing there to blunt or mitigate the force of them. And though Hew had expected it, though he understood a course had been embarked upon which nothing could have stayed, he was shaken to a depth for which he had not been prepared. Giles Locke, as he spoke, was visibly afflicted, which was shocking too, for Giles did not dread death. He was Catholic also, secret in his heart. And Catholics he attended to, in their dying hours, had the best of deaths, however hard they fell, whatever hurt was done to them, because they died in hope.

In the year of plague the dead kists were tipped out, and were filled again; the dead were left to moulder naked in their shrouds. Despite his best beliefs, the ravage of the peste had worn the doctor down. It had left him changed. The magnitude and scale of it was hard to understand. Yet the toll of that flood, counted in drops, insubstantial and small, did not amount to the loss of that queen, whose departure from life had been more than a death; more, to Giles Locke, than its sum.

'She was killed at the command of the English queen, Elizabeth. Her head was cut off from her neck. This news took a week to come to the king. Patrick says, he marvels at it greatly. Yet I have no doubt he must have expected it.'

'Once she was convicted, there could be no hope for her,' Hew said.

The doctor shook his head. 'Does Frances know,' he asked, 'what horror you have brought her to?'

Frances washed and dressed. She had no chest of clothes, no scented smock or shirt, so could do little more than shake her gown for dust, combing out her hair, and tucking it away into a linen cap, as wives were meant to do. Her shoes were worn out to the soles. On the stairway to the hall, she encountered Canny Bett, who put to her a question, and gave her some advice, at which she smiled and nodded, understanding none of it. Her heart was in her mouth as she entered the great hall. She understood at once that there was something wrong. 'What is the matter, Hew?'

'Ah, my love,' he said, 'I fear the queen is dead.'

Her hand flew to her face.

He realised his mistake, and hers. 'I do not mean Elizabeth. I mean the queen of Scots.'

Frances cried, 'Thank God!' and opened up a gulf between them in that room.

They were good, gentle people, and they did not leave it long, however deep the cracks they plastered over privately. Meg was the first to break into the awkwardness. 'We must eat. We have a kippil of cunyngs with mustard, and beef in a broth, and a tart, and marchpanes the children have made.'

Frances said, 'Kippil of . . . ?'

'It means a pair of coneys,' Hew explained. 'What the French call, lapin à la moutarde.' Giles did his best to recover his sangfroid, and came back with a quip, 'or in other words, cunning as mustard. It is Hew's favourite, and we are obliged to him, for not coming home on a fish day. Soon it will be Lent, with all the deprivations that entails. In the meantime, we are blessed with a surfeit of fresh meat, and I would call upon you both to help us make the most of it.'

The leprons had kept their sweet delicate flesh, their sauce refined and fragrant, with a subtle heat; the beef had been cooked on the bone, melting with its marrow to a mellow broth, sticky, dark and unctuous. The tart was filled with custard, laced with spice and quivering. There were brittle oatcakes, baked upon a skillet pan, that crumbled in the throat, but also good white bread, that Frances had been told was scarce enough in Scotland. She ate a little of the manchet, dipped in mustard sauce, and a little of the meat, and nibbled at the edge of a sliver of the tart. She sipped at the claret which was deep and dark, and the more of it she drank, she more she felt adrift, floundering in talk. Though Meg was kind in her attentions, and gentle in her speech, the words she used were singular, and hard to understand. Giles had travelled further, and had lived abroad, and had the content of his speech not been convolute and tortuous, she might have hoped to follow, but she found the language heavy, and the argument abstruse. Even Hew himself, whose gently tempered tones had lulled her from the start, was sometimes falling now into a deeper dialect, and she felt left behind; however long and patiently they broke off to explain to her, she never quite caught up. It was not just the words, but their world that was strange.

They were speaking of the college at the university where Giles Locke was the principal. One of the professors there, a man called Bartie Groat, had perished in the plague.

'What? Bartie gone?' Hew wailed.

'Bartie was the first,' Giles said. There came on him a weariness, wiping out all energy and weathering to quietness. 'The peste takes first the faltering, the fragile, frail and old, and sweeps them from its path, careless as the wind. He remained behind when the college was evacuated. Where else should he go? His life was at St Salvator's.

He had decided that his time had come. But you may be assured, Hew, he did not die alone.'

Frances dared not show the pity that she felt; their grief was closed to her. Far across the table, Meg reached for her hand. 'That was a hard time. The men from the college, who had nowhere else to go, came here to us. We were quarantined, and those who could afford to, fled the town. But Giles did not leave. He remained at the college, tending to the sick, and doing all he could to rein the sickness in, and to stop its spread. It was not long after Martha was born, and we did not see him for almost a year. Paul, who was our servant then, brought letters back and forth, together with supplies, which he left by the wall, not daring to enter the town. And we sent our herbs to them, and waters from the still, to help them where we could. Four hundred people here died in the plague. But were it not for Giles, it could have been four thousand.'

The doctor cleared his throat. 'Dear me. This a sad thing, to speak of on your first day home. If you will call in at the college, Hew, anytime you will, we can talk of matters, that we do not touch on now. Indeed, I think it best.'

Hew nodded. 'I can come tomorrow, if you like. For I have in mind to see my man of law.'

'That seems to me, a practical idea.'

Frances saw the men exchange a look she did not understand. 'I should like to see the town, very much,' she said.

Hew hesitated, 'And of course, you shall. Tomorrow, I expect that you will want to rest. Your journey here was long.'

'No longer,' Frances said, 'than it was for you.'

Meg said, 'They do not allow women in the university, Frances, for fear we will distract, and turn them from their books. Leave them to their law, and to their dead philosophy, and stay at home with me. In the summer, when the students have gone, you and I will go and look around the college. By then the pictures will be done.'

Hew latched upon this quickly, grateful for Meg's help. 'What pictures are those?'

'Did I not tell you? Giles is having his portrait painted, in recognition of the work he has done to help the town.'

'Stuff,' protested Giles. 'It is a piece of foolishness. The provost is persuaded that I saved his son. And in honour of the boy – a graduate of ours – he has paid a man to decorate our dinner hall, insisting that a likeness should be made of me. I do not count it much.'

'It is quite a lot. You will need one of those panels, that folds in three parts,' Hew teased, and the two of them fell to their old style of flyting, quite baffling to Frances, lifting the mood for the rest of the night.

Chapter 10

Ars et Natura

Frances woke up to a cold bed beside her, and lay a moment frozen in the stillness of the house. At Leadenhall, the markets would be coming to their close. She would have awoken to the raucous crowds, the greening herds of cattle and their doleful calves, the clamorous cacophony of birds. Except, she thought, the sounds would not have woken her, for she would not have been asleep. Never in her life, except when she had suffered with a mild strain of the small pox, had she stayed in bed beyond the waking hour. She felt, through slats of windows closed off to the sun, the fingers of a frost, that kept the world outside her prisoned in its clasp.

There was nothing in that bed that was left to her of Hew, but a stiffness in the sheet, and on her smock, a stain. She heard a light knocking, and Hew's sister Meg came into the room, with her arms full of cloths.

'I did not want to wake you, if you were asleep. But I thought you might be lying, fretting here alone. I brought you some towels, and clean linen smocks, and some of the rose water made in our still. It is meant for a kindness, and I hope won't offend you. Hew said you did not have so many things.'

'Thank you.' Frances sat up in the bed. Her instinct was to leave it at once; she felt ashamed to be found there so late in the day. She remembered the stain, and shrank back.

Meg said, 'It is cold in here. I will send someone in to make up the fire. Your servant, Robert Lachlan, has been quartered with the grooms. He has made friends with one of the kitchen maids. That is not a good thing.'

Frances felt a shiver of alarm. She wondered if she was expected, in Hew's absence, to effect some kind of discipline. She knew that Robert Lachlan was far out of her control. 'He does . . . he is . . . Hew is fond of him. But, as I confess, I do not understand anything he says.'

'That may be for the best,' said Meg. She set the things down on top of a chest, and stood back to watch what Frances did next. The fragrance of the rose seeped into the room. There was water in a bowl that the servant must have brought while Frances was asleep. Or maybe it was Hew. She had felt his touch, gentle on her cheek. The water would be cold.

'I shall not want a fire, for I will soon be up. I did not think I should have slept so long,' she said. 'But we were on the road so many days and weeks, and the places where we lay were sometimes very ill. I never had a mattress that was soft like this. In London, I sleep in a bed with my cousins. There are five of us, sometimes.'

As she spoke, she understood that she would never share a bed, or fall out with them, again, and her face fell in a cloud, which Meg observed at once. 'You must love Hew very much, to have left your friends to come with him so far.'

Frances was afraid of her. Meg dealt in natural remedies, and had, her brother said, a skill to bring to life the stubborn force of nature, and tame it to her will. She had suffered from the falling sickness since she was a child. 'For that reason, my father quit his work as advocate, at its very pinnacle, retiring to the country, for the sake of the reclusion that was wanted for her health.' Frances did not see how anyone with hair as dark as Meg's could have been Hew's sister; Hew was fair, like Giles. Meg's infant child, Martha, shared that same darkness; her curls were permitted to stream in a tangle of wildness, not combed, as they should be, and pinned. Frances was afraid that Meg might be a witch, an apprehension that she did not dare admit to Hew. She was fearful too of Doctor Locke. Hew insisted that he had a most loving generous heart, the kindest of his friends. But

Frances felt his gaze upon her searching, sharp and critical, his language was opaque and by sheer force of his bulk, a massiveness of intellect, of spirit, and of flesh, she was overwhelmed.

In spite of all these feelings, she confessed to Meg, knowing that without her, she was quite alone. 'I have loved him, I think, from the first day that he came to our house at Leadenhall. He told me things then about you and your husband, and of his home here, all of them true. But somehow, none of it is quite as I expected.'

'It must seem quite foreign to you. But you will get used to it.'

'So I hope. For I cannot go back.' The words sounded hollow, forlorn.

'He must love you too,' Meg, said, so kindly Frances was encouraged to confide in her.

'He did not seem to notice me, at first. He was taken with a woman by the name of Audrey, with open voluminous thighs, and a warm simple heart, who did not stake a claim on him. I fear, it was for pity that he took me.'

'That is like him,' said Meg. 'And it was clever of you, if you gave him that cause.'

'What you mean?'

'Pity is the way to move my brother's heart, where nothing strikes to terror quite as much as love. He must be caught obliquely in it, else he shies away. You will forgive the question, Frances, but are you with child?'

'No. I do not think so.' Frances hesitated. 'I have not known him long – that is to say, we have not been married for long. The truth is, there was no time to discuss such matters with my aunt, or my sister-in-law.'

'Then please do not forget, you have a sister now.' Meg smiled at her. 'The men have gone to town, and will not be back for hours. Matthew has his grammar lesson; Martha is with Canny Bett. We shall have some time to come to know each other.'

'Your little boy is young, to be put to school,' Frances said.

'He is his father's son. When you are dressed, I will show you the garden. You will say, that nothing green can come, from those beds of frost so obdurate and desolate, but I shall prove to you, that there is nothing further from that case.'

Hew spent the morning with his man of law. The consultation, as expected, did not go so well. The man had told him what in essence he had known already, had concealed from Frances, and did not wish to hear. His marriage, which under English law, had been lawful under extraordinary circumstance, was unlikely to be recognised in Scotland, under any circumstance at all. And even if it could be proved as lawful, it would never be accepted by the Scottish Kirk.

'You will not mind my saying, but you could not have chosen a less propitious time, nor a more contentious contract. Do you say, that she brought you no portion at all, no kind of tocher, that will secure her in case of your death?' the man put to him bluntly. He had dealt with Hew, and Hew's father too, as his father before him had done. That gave him the right to express himself forcefully. 'My advice to you is to call the banns in your parish kirk – that is St Leonard's, is it not? – and marry her again, as quickly as you can. That may not be as simple as it sounds. This contract was ill done. But you are a lawman. Ye ken that. And were your late father with us . . .'

Hew interrupted quickly, 'I will think upon your words. Can I be assured that you will keep this close?'

'As always,' the man sighed.

There was better news relating to the land, and the funds that had accrued from Hew's father's last investments. At the height of his career, Matthew Cullan had loaned a large sum of money to the Edinburgh council, at the common rate of ten per cent a year. Upon Hew's indictment on a charge of treason, the profits had been frozen by the Crown, but now that the attainder was removed, the funds had been released, and with the rents from several properties let out in the capital, had risen to a sizable amount. 'Indeed, if you would draw upon that capital,' the lawyer had advised, 'the council would be sorely pressed to meet the debt. You can be assured of relief in kind. Your credit there is sound.'

Hew asked for an account of the land at Kenly Green, and how the tenants there had prospered in his absence, conscious that their welfare might depend on his.

'There, you have been fortunate. For, as you recall, the title to the land was given to your sister Meg, when you were arraigned, to guard against the risk of seizure by the Crown. When that danger passed, it was put back in your name, and since your sister and her husband made no claim upon the rents, except what was required to keep up the estate, they also have accrued. They are good people, Hew. The rents from the mill have been placed in trust for your nephew Matthew Locke when he comes of age. All else there returns, in good sort, to you.'

'Tell me,' Hew asked then, 'for it never was made clear to me, how it was my father came to have that land.' This question had troubled him, even before he had met with the queen. Alison Peirson, the wife from Boarhills that Archbishop Adamson cried for a witch, had told him that his land had belonged to the archbishops, and would return to them yet. Though he gave little credence to that sad wifie's curse, he had feared that the land might be tainted with blood. And now that it *was*, through the death of that queen, he did not feel at ease in his claim to it.

The lawyer cleared his throat. 'The records do not show. As I understand, it was in payment of a debt.'

'What kind of debt? Was it money he had given? Or some kind of service?'

'I'm afraid I cannot tell you. My father may have known. But such small events of fact are buried in the past. The *de facto* case, is that it is now yours, and so may be left to your children.'

'Children?' Hew repeated. Children were a thing that never had occurred to him, despite his fondness for his godson, Matthew Locke.

'Should you be so blessed.'

'I confess, I did not think of that.' Had Frances, wondered Hew.

'For most men, when they marry, children are the matter foremost in their minds. The more so when they have possession of a large estate.' The lawyer had shaken his head. 'You, though, are perverse. There is, as I observe, a stubborn inclination to controversy in you, that your father, were he here, would no doubt have deplored, and which I cannot hope to ever understand. Though given all the trouble that your marriage has entailed, lack of any issue from it may prove an advantage.'

Hew departed there, cross and ill at ease, with this cold endorsement ringing in his ears. He had walked to town that morning, in company with Giles, coming to the harbour as the watered sunlight etched upon the bay its level greys and blues. There they had an argument, which threatened his affections for his closest friend. They had not gone far beyond the Kinkell Braes, when Hew had told Giles the matter on his mind. 'I learned something lately that I did not know before. My father obtained Kenly Green in the gift of the late queen of Scots.' He did not say how he had come by this information, and was thankful that Giles did not ask. His friend was silent for a moment; remembrance of the Scots queen's death was painful to him still. Then he said, 'I did not ken that. But though I did not know your father well or long, it does not surprise me, for he did not disguise the fact that he was of that party, God rest her Grace.'

Nor, at that moment, did Giles, who wrestled with a grief that showed clearly in his face. Hew was moved by his passion to admit, 'Had he lived to have looked on these recent events, they would have broken his heart. And had he ever thought that I might play a part...'

'Why should he think that? What part could you possibly play?' Giles interrupted, and the look in his eyes stopped Hew short.

'I could not, of course. But Giles ... I hope that you will not count Frances as somehow to blame. Because she is English, she is not England,' he said.

'You thought I felt that?' Giles shook his head. 'I should not for the world have you think me so uncivil, or in any way unkind, to fix that fault on her. If she felt a coolness in me, then I do confess, it comes upon my fear for her, not from mine own prejudice, but from that of the world.'

Hew answered, unconvinced, 'Do you not think, though, they might be the same?'

'They are not the same. You were not here, in the months after the late queen's arrest. And in that time, a great bruit and cry was raised among the people, on behalf of a monarch, whom they never loved, nor championed so well when she lived among them; and, at that same time, was brewed a hatred and abhorrence of all England and the English, and especially Queen Elizabeth. At our last winter fair, a pitiful old pedlar was pummelled to a pulp, because he did his prattling in an English tongue, and the powder court decided that there was no case to hear. The news of the queen's death spreads slowly, and has not yet been broken out in the streets. And, when it does, you may be sure that those who were the fiercest in calling for her blood, when she was hounded here, will be first to cry vengeance and to spill blood in defending her, now that she is dead. Your Frances is caught up, right at the heart of it. And I can only fear, that we cannot keep her safe,' his friend put forward, forcefully.

'That,' Hew accepted, 'must be my concern. But it is none of yours.'

'Stuff!' retorted Giles. 'And if you think for a moment we should leave you to it, you should not have come home. You are not blind to it, Hew. You have come here expecting a fight. Else why would you bring Robert Lachlan? But tell me, does Frances know? Has she the smallest idea, what she has come to?'

'I will tell you the truth, and only to you. The whole thing was not well thought out. And had I, for a moment, thought about the consequence, I should not have bought her so far from her home. But I do not repent it. I will not repent it. I love her, Giles.' Hew had meant it then, fierce and full in heart.

His passion reassured, and softened his old friend. 'Meg says, she is right for you. And if anyone knows, it is Meg. God love you, Hew, you never come but you bring trouble. And the trouble that you bring quickens my slow heart, and makes my spirits leap; it stirs a purpose in me that I would not be without, an energy of sorts, and meaning to this life. Our cares would be dull ones, without you.' They had parted friends, and close to their old terms, arranging to confer together later in the day.

Hew left the lawyer's house, and crossed into the South Street by the Holy Trinity. He had time to spare before he met with Giles, and chose to spend it walking round the town, to see how much had changed. The kirk, that was its heart, where all its people met to deal with their concerns, both spiritual and practical, was strangely quiet now, and its main doors closed. From a man that he met in the yard, Hew learned that the minister had died in the plague, and the kirk itself, lacking an incumbent, was closed for some repairs, open for the service at set times in the day, or when the kirk session convened to its court. It had lost its purpose as a meeting place. The services themselves were delivered by the readers, or by Patrick Adamson, when he put his mind to it. But the people, though they came, as kirk laws obliged, were fearful of a crowd, and did not linger long. The kirk had lost direction, and the town its soul. What solace for the fold, from the creeping peste, when God's only shepherd was the first he snatched away? And what hope of God?

Hew saw, for the first time, the force of the peste, and the devastation it had left behind. It had left its mark in the shuttered faces of the women and the men, their shrunken shoulders hunched, who hurried to their work, and did not break their step to gossip in the street, whose children had been swept and ravaged by that plague. It was Antwerp, again, though on a smaller scale. For the plague had an effect on the fabric of a town, and left it battle-scarred. Buildings, once abandoned, quickly fell to ruin, and on the leafy South Street, where bare branches trembled over tender buds, several homes stood derelict, stripped and gaping open to the bitter wind. The College of St Mary, opposite the kirk, had suffered with the worst. A chasm had appeared in Andrew Melville's roof, as though it had been smitten by the fretful bolt, of an indignant god.

St Mary's had been closed, long before the plague, by those Black Acts that had driven Andrew Melville to the south of England. His nephew James returned, to find the whole place gripped by God's revengeful scourge, while Andrew had been punished by a futless goose hunt, chasing after Jesuits in the wilds up north. He was not long back, and the college had begun to show some cautious signs of life. Students re-emerged and did the best they could, to patch the damage done to furniture and hope, with plaster, paint and truth.

Further to the east, the College of St Leonard had not fared so badly, sheltered from the storm within its high enclosing walls. Hew had been a student here; its chapel served the purpose of his country parish church, and would serve him now, to hear his wedding vows. Yet he had no will to share this world with Frances, until she was prepared to beard the Scottish Kirk, and hardened to its scrutiny. He was mindful of what Giles had said. And the lawyer had not kent the Scottish queen was dead, when he had dispensed his words of worldly gloom. How much more profound his prognostications then? A muddy surge of feeling swilled up in Hew's heart, complex and confused, for this place, that was dear to him, and harsh and strange to her. He hurried past it now. At this end of the street were new building works, and at the cathedral, where three streets converged, the spires had been stripped to a stark winter shadow, bearing up bleakly against the grey sky.

Hew turned in to the North Street at the Fisher Cross. The market had waned to a few listless haddocks, the fisher wives, hoarse and despondent, stood by their baskets blue-lipped. Soon, it would be Lent, and the fishermen would cast their newly mended nets and duck among the waves in freshly painted boats. For now, it was too cold, and no one wanted fish. Doubtless it was winter kept the children in, buttoned from the wind and off the quiet streets. The town was smaller and more desolate than Hew had remembered it, washed out in the sea spray to a sullen brown.

Giles was in St Salvator's, delivering a lecture. Hew spent half an hour in a lecture of his own, delivered by the porter who kept the college gate. Giles Locke had been elevated, to a living saint. 'He saved that many lives. And no one in the college fell except Professor Groat, who wouldna leave this place, so would he remain here, body and soul. His relict is here still, God rest him.'

'His relict?' echoed Hew. Poor Bartie had little to leave, but his books and his handkerchiefs.

'I mean, his spirit, sir.' The dereliction of its kirk had left the town free to revert, to what superstitions it chose for its comfort. The new minister, when he came, would have his work cut out.

'The pity is, we dinna have him here, to put him in the hall,' the porter said.

Hew asked, 'What do you mean?' He was relieved, when the porter replied. 'I mean, sir, his likeness to hang on the wall. Professor Locke would like to have his picture with the rest. Alas, it is too late, to take it "from the life", as the painter says. Did ye ken, there is a painter here? A likely, lusty fellow, doing up the walls. And I cannae tell ye why, but I dinna like him much.'

The porter's intuitions to one side – he was ill-disposed to strangers in the college – Hew could understand the importance of the painter, though Giles had played it down. His purpose was to bring back colour to the town, to restore a brightness that the peste had wiped from it, lifting up its spirits in a lick of paint.

Hew waited for his old friend in the turret tower, that housed the doctor's rooms. All that was familiar there, and much more that was strange, reminded him of Giles. He amused himself in looking round the shelves, to find a cornucopia of implements and instruments, pickle jars of body parts, entrails and an eye, grinning at him glassily from a butcher's block. Then there were the books, ranks of tall anatomies, lapidaries, herbals, travelogues and grammars, old religious tracts, all the lore and language of the natural world.

There was nothing in this place that did not hold a narrative, a history encased in paper, wood or brass or bone. There was nothing in this plethora of antic curiosities that did not have a purpose there, and nothing came by chance, but the objects held the measure, that was scattered, deep, of a scientific soul. On a folding table by the doctor's gossip chair lay a human skull and a little book, Alciato's *Emblemata*, which Hew recalled from childhood. He picked the volume up and settled down to read.

Returning to the tower, the doctor was confronted with the picture of his friend, carelessly disported in his favourite chair, buried in a book, as though he had been waiting for him all those absent years, and never left the place. Hew looked up and grinned. 'I had this, when I was a boy. Not this same edition, but a less explicit one. My father bought it for me, when I first learned Latin. It did not, as I recall, include this rather singular verse, "*contre les bougres*", as the French say. I have the copy still, somewhere back at home. Matthew might have it, for the pictures.'

'It is for the painter,' Giles explained, 'to make a series of panels for the dinner hall. I had thought, six virtues, on the one side, and six vices, on the other. As to the vices, you may be sure, the sin against nature will not be among them, nor any others rooted in the baser flesh, beyond a simple gluttony; for even what is meant to be prohibitive, our students are inclined to interpret as encouragement. And that, to be sure, is not what our benefactor has intended here. The work must be clean, to pass the provost's test.'

Alciato's *Emblemata* was a book of pictures, each one coupled with a Latin verse or epigram, which offered to the curious and contemplative eye a simple moral text, or sometimes a more complex one. The picture and the text became a kind of riddle interspersed; each showed up its meaning in the other's light. Sometimes, it was used as a painter's pattern book, in decorating ceilings, tapestries and walls.

'I thought,' continued Giles, 'to have the dozen pictures painted onto wood, and underneath the letters to be set in gold, in Latin as you see. To encourage the students to look to the morals, and take them to heart, I was thinking about a competition to turn the verses into Scots, with a prize for the most pleasing, apt and pithy one. What do you think?'

'I think it is an excellent idea. One word of advice,' said Hew, 'do not include the one on nicknames for professors, for fear they knock us openly, and not behind our backs. What is apt and pithy often brings offence.'

'I had foreseen that trap, and shall not fall for it. In seriousness, Hew, since you know the book, what pictures do you recommend?'

Hew considered this. 'Your six vices, and virtues, will do well enough. But I should have thought, the most apt of all of them, was this one, on art assisting nature: *ars naturam adiuvans*. It is the most affecting lesson to your students of philosophy. And if what is wanted is a tribute to your own effect with Meg's, of helping to assuage the terror of the plague, nothing were more apt. See.'

He showed his friend the picture in the book, of Hermes, the winged messenger, sitting on a cube, to represent the arts, while Fortune, blindfold, rested on her sphere, the world she turned to chance. Behind them raged a storm at sea.

Ut sphaerae Fortuna, cubo sic insidet Hermes:
Artibus hic variis, casibus illa praeest.
Adversus vim Fortunae est ars facta: sed artis
Cum Fortuna mala est, saepe requirit opem.
Disce bonas artes igitur studiosa iuventus,
Quae certae secum commoda sortis habent.

'As Fortune rests on her sphere, so Hermes sits on his cube. He presides over the arts; she over the varied chances of life. Art was developed to counteract the effect of Fortune, but when Fortune is bad it often needs the assistance of Art. Therefore, studious youths, learn good arts, which bring with them the benefits of an outcome not subject to chance,' translated Hew.

'That is perfect, and I thank you,' Giles exclaimed. 'With a little tweak – Fortune may require a more modest form of dress, while

Hermes wants a cover, for his manly breast – this will be our centrepiece. I shall take it to the painter right away, so that he can make a start on it.'

'Is the skull for him also?' asked Hew.

'Indeed. It is a property, with which I mean to sit. The mark of my trade, and also, of course, of that ultimate end that must come to us all, *memento mori, dicat,*' answered Giles.

It brought to mind the porter's tribute at the gate, 'So would he remain here, body and soul', and Hew could not help but ask, 'It is not Bartie, is it?'

The doctor blinked at him. 'Professor Groat? Bless my soul! You have a peculiar fondness for the grotesque, and very little grasp of the process of decay. Did you never see a corpse that was left out on a gibbet? This skull I should say is one hundred years old. Perhaps fifty, at least. I had it from – well, no matter where I had it; it is brought here for the painter, to put into his picture, as an ever present emblem of the permanence of death. I have no doubt that the provost will expose the work to scrutiny, and will want to know where his gift is spent. In truth, I have no time for it. It is difficult enough that the work is done in the middle of our most exacting term. The painter says it is the only time he has. It is not convenient. The ground that we lost when the college was closed, and the loss of poor Bartie and one of our regents, who left us last summer and was not replaced, leaves us sorely taxed to see our students through to their examination. Hew, there are two things I wanted to ask you. I notice you said, "For fear they knock *us* openly". Confess, in your heart, you are one of us still. Will you come back, and help us awhile?'

'Gladly,' said Hew, 'if I can. First I must go and make peace with the king, and swear my allegiance at court. God willing then, I shall serve to your cause.'

Giles nodded. 'When will you go?'

'Once Frances is settled. Which may be some time.' Hew pushed that thought from his mind. 'But you said there were two things. What was the second?'

Chapter 11

An Efficient Cause

The doctor's face darkened. 'That is more difficult. You have heard that I stayed here during the peste. The college was evacuated, as you are aware. Yet I was not alone. There was one that remained with me – Bartie besides – who would not be deterred, for all my remonstrations, promises, and threats. And the truth is, what I faced then wrung me limp and dry. You will smile, I doubt, to look upon me, here, still as large as life, and in no way dwindled from my former self, but I am shrunken, Hew. I could not have endured that horror on my own.'

Nothing that he said there tempted Hew to smile. He saw how the plague had diminished Giles, ravaged him in spirit, if not in the flesh.

'Someone washed and cooked for me, brought me to my bed, when I was exhausted, and where the path was pitiless, strengthened my resolve. And since he was your pupil too, I know you will remember him. His name is Roger Cunningham,' Giles said.

Roger. Richard's son. Hew had not forgotten what the boy had done. He could not come into that place without harking, and attending to it, however far he had let it slip back from his mind. *That was a wicked boy*, the tainted queen had said.

'Richard's son, indeed,' Giles said. 'The peste is borne by lice, battened on the blood of the dying and the dead. When the corpses are brought to the carts, the lice leave their bodies in waves, rising to the surface as the flesh grows cool. Meg sent camphor, rosemary, peppermint and sage, distilled into a water, repellent to the lice, to help to keep us safe. And Roger did not spare in coming to the sick. He went freely among the dying and the dead, assisting the clengars who brought the bodies out. He caught the plague himself, yet did not die from it. And in the throes of that sickness, he confessed to me, and heartily repented, that he had conspired to trick, and hurt you, Hew.'

'His brother, too,' Hew said.

The doctor stared at him. 'Do you say you knew?'

'I did not ken, at first. I knew that Roger blamed me for his father's death, and did not fault him then. I felt I owed a debt to him. That debt has been paid. By the time I understood the malice they had meant, the brothers had gone home. And, when they returned, I was gone myself.'

'Please tell me, Roger had no hand in those events that took you from us. He said he wrote a letter, with intent to do you harm, but that he did not think his letter had effect. He did not tell me what was in it. But he is ashamed of it, bitterly ashamed.'

'The letter that he wrote played no part in it,' said Hew. Events had swept him up, and Roger's infant fantasies had been incidental. 'He was just a bairn. I think he was encouraged in it, by his brother James. Where is the brother now?'

Giles said, 'That is a strange and sad tale. He left St Andrews back in 1584, after those Black Acts that moved against the presbyteries dashed his future hopes of coming to the Kirk. He could not, as he wished, pursue his studies at St Mary's, so he went abroad, to Geneva. There he became so fervent and fanatical, that even the strictest of the Calvinist professors found fault with his doctrine, and he was expelled. He travelled further north, and gathers round him acolytes most perverse and cruel, who do not conform to any Christian church. He has broken with his brother, and his mother too.'

'Did Roger tell you that?' Hew asked. For he was not disposed to take this word on trust. The doctor shook his head. 'I wrote to his mother, when he fell ill. Eleanor telt me. She was distraught. She lost her husband, as you know, in the most wretched circumstances. Now her eldest child. He wrote to her, vile words, of hateful accusation, calling her, her daughter too, a whore. I cannot help but think, there is a madness there, passing from the father, that infects the son; this cannot be of comfort to her. Her one hope, her bright light, is Roger, who was once the cause of her dismay. For the progress he has made, his helping with the plague, she is proud of him. I did not have the heart to tell her, what he had confessed to me. Understand me Hew, I do not tell you this to move you to my will, but to acquaint you with the facts. I am well aware the boy has done you ill, and should be punished for it. If I had known, then, what he had done, with what evil intent he came to this college, I should have dismissed him at once. I took him in, when he was expelled from St Leonard's, at your own request. We both saw how he blossomed here and how he has a gift for natural philosophy. There can be no doubt – has never been a doubt – that he has the makings of a fine physician. Yet if he had no moral sense, that would be nothing worth, and I would cast him off, without a second glance. I cannot think that the confession that I heard, on what he believed to be his own deathbed, was not truly repentant. Nor could I discount that time he spent with me, attending to the sick, careless of the risk, the danger to his life. Therefore, I have kept him here, and he has understood whatever lies ahead for him must depend on you. He is one of those preparing to graduate this spring, if you will allow him to proceed to the examination.'

'Then send him in to me,' Hew said, 'and I will hear him speak. Whatever is the outcome, he will not depart unheard.'

Roger was a strange and uncouth boy. He had a fascination with the workings of the flesh, with the nature of things, both living and dead, that under Giles Locke had been nurtured, and nourished. His interests could be harnessed to the good, or put to evil ends. What purpose could there be in severing the influence that kept him straight and sound, to lease him out disconsolate and raging at the world? If God intended Roger to be saved, then Giles Locke was his instrument. For that reason, Hew was willing to forgive, though not prepared to trust.

He had left behind a boy of fourteen, slight as a child. The young man who stood before him in the doctor's chamber looked him in the eye, even overstepped him by an inch or two. He was slender still, the willowing of youth or withering of sickness; his gaze was cool and frank, yet when Hew looked back, and did not speak, Roger's eyes dropped low, a late show of humility. 'I ask you to forgive the failings of a child, and if you will not, I submit to the correction that I have deserved.'

Hew said, 'Tell me, what you think you did.' He was interested to hear how much the boy would own. For, as he discerned, he had not told the whole of it to Giles.

'I wrote a letter, with intent to do you harm. The truth is that I blamed you for my father's death, though I know better now. They say I am like him, sir,' the boy replied. It was hard to know how much he cared or meant, for he had stripped all feeling from his tone.

'You may be like him, or not, as you choose.'

Roger said, 'I do not choose.' A statement that was bold in its ambivalence.

Hew responded with, 'You and your brother contrived of the trick with the hawthorn, that neither of you could effect alone. And the purpose of it was to draw me in; you knew that such a riddle would be irresistible. So great a hatred you conceived, that you conspired to do me harm. Where is your brother now?'

There was no question in Hew's mind that the two had worked together; he was interested to know which was the moving mind. Roger, filled with rage and the passion of a child? Or the older, calmer brother, as a more malignant force?

'I cannot tell you, sir. For, we do not speak. As far I have heard, he is still abroad, and stringent and fanatical in his beliefs. He distils a kind of hatred, fixed upon his God, and he has broken with my mother and myself, damning us to Hell for our affront to his faith.'

'And what affront is that?'

'For my mother, that she will not hide herself away, but does her best to live an honest, decent life, and to find hope for my sister; and for myself,' Roger answered more simply, 'that I do not believe in God.'

'For the God that he courts,' supposed Hew.

'In God, of any sort.'

A sharp glance up at Roger told Hew he was serious. Yet he did not believe it for the world. This cool young sapling still, filled with bluff and posturing, did his best to shock. If Giles Locke caught him at this play, Roger would repent of it. But he was not afraid to try his heresies on Hew. He was an intriguing, and exasperating boy.

'Stuff. If you do not believe in God, what moved you to confess, when you almost died?'

Roger said, 'Oh, *that*. That was Professor Locke. I kent that he believed in me, and thought that he should know what kind of man I was. What did ye think? I sought to save my soul? Are ye so sure, that I have one?'

'You bicker like a bairn, and are not worth the trouble of a rational argument,' Hew dismissed this game. 'The letter that ye wrote, did your brother think of that?'

Roger shook his head. 'That was my idea. And I was sorry for it, after it was done. My comfort was in that it did not do you harm. It did not, did it, sir?' His pleading seemed to show a genuine remorse.

'No harm to me, perhaps. But you cast a stain upon a woman's reputation, and caused suspicion in a husband, when his wife was blameless, and that is a transgression harder to forgive.'

Roger had sent his letter to the brother of the crownar. He had told Robert Wood that his wife Clare Buchanan *stirred the pot* with Hew. Robert saw at once it was a schoolboy's prank. But that did not affect his treatment of his wife, who had had to suffer for it.

The boy was startled then. For he had not known that Hew had found him out. And Hew was unkind enough to take a fleeting pleasure in it.

'How did you ken?' Roger asked.

'Andro Wood told me. He had the letter. It did not take a moment to guess it was you.'

'Yet you did not tell him my name?' The boy was nervous now. And if he was afeart of Andrew Wood, his instincts were impeccable. 'I don't know what to say,' he said, 'but that I am sorry for the things I did.'

'I am sorry too,' said Hew. 'Not for myself. For Clare.'

'I cannot help that, sir. I did my best, in truth, to make amends to her. It cannot hurt her now.'

'Why do you say that?' The feelings Hew had harboured, long ago, for Clare, had been so far eclipsed that he was unprepared to find them flooding back.

'Did ye not ken?' Roger said. 'I supposed the professor had telt you. It was from Clare that I caught the plague. The sickness was rife in Robert Wood's house. Robert died first, and Clare was afeart, so sorely afraid, that I took off the mask, which Doctor Locke said I must wear on my face. Then I was the friend of her brother George, and not, as she had looked on me, a harbinger of death. I held her hand, and spoke with her. I whispered in her ear, and telt to her my fault. She said it was forgotten now, that Robert Wood was dead, and you had been a true, a good and gentle man, a better friend to both of us than we did well deserve. I stayed there till the end. And after, I fell sick, and Doctor Locke took care of me, and brought me back to life.'

'What became of George?' Hew forced his mind to anything but Clare; he dared not show the boy the workings of his heart. He found it required all the strength he had; the courage and the fortitude he had from Seething Lane now seeming to evaporate. Phelippes could have toppled him, and floored him with a glance.

'George was sent home with the rest of the college. He had come into his father's estate. But when the college reconvened, he did not return. Freed from Robert Wood – a tyrannous curator – he lives there as he likes. He is foolish as he ever was; sometimes, he will write to me. He likes to play at caich, as he learned from you, and ride out with his hawks. Our regent says, it is a pity, for he had begun to show some promise at his books – the regent's hopes were dashed, of George's gifts and feasts, and a sumptuous banquet, at the end of term. To tell the truth I miss him, for I had never had so innocent a friend, so simple in his thoughts. Had you returned sooner, he might have come back. He was fond of you, especially,' Roger answered easily, blind to Hew's distraction. 'He never knew, of course, that I wrote that letter, though the thought behind it came at first from George. I think it is not something he could easily forgive. Can you forgive it, sir?'

The painter liked to watch his young apprentice. Sometimes, he would break off from the panel he was working on, to guide his hand or brush towards a small adjustment, for sake of that hand, compliant to his, that he knew had no need of a master's correction. And on those occasions, the prentice stood back, and showed no resentment, but smiled his slow smile. The prentice had a perfect eye. But the painter did not feel, as some masters did, jealous of his pupil's skill. In the six or seven years the apprentice had been with him, he had not progressed. He would never be a journeyman, nor set up as a master in the masons' gild, for he had never learned the basics of his craft. He would never leave the master painter's side, nor ever wish to stray beyond what he did perfectly, with natural intelligence, to imitate and draw, with clear and perfect line. His was a rare skill, which a painter might come upon once in a lifetime, and never at all if he stayed here in Scotland. The painter felt a pride in him, fierce, proprietorial; his feeling for the man was complex, in a way. It was simple, after all. It was a kind of love.

It was meant to be. The painter was quite sure they had not met by chance. There had been a purpose to it, and his luck had changed. The prentice had been mewling like a kitten in a barn; any other man would not have stopped to look. There he found a lad, no more than thirteen, filthy, frightened, starved. In the first year he had been with him, the boy had grown so much he had outstripped the painter, tall and straight and strong. He had strong, subtle fingers, great flapping lugs and a long slender tongue, that sometimes when he worked poked out from his mouth, like the tongue of a tomcat, supple and grooved. That was God's jest, for lugs and a tongue were little of use, when a man could not listen nor talk. Though God had his sport with him, he was not cruel. He gave that boy to compensate a perfect eye to see and a hand to draw, that he could catch a likeness in a few flicks of his wrist. The painter did not ken where the boy had come from, or what kind of people they were who abandoned him. Likely, they were dead. Nor, for a while, did he trouble with his name: since the laddie could not hear, he had little need for one. In their first year together, he would answer with a grin to anyone who asked, 'I dinna ken his name. He never telt me, see?' But later, when they took the boy to be the painter's brother, he had called him Mark, which seemed to him to fit, for *mark* was what he did, and what he could not do. As surname for them both, he had chosen Workman, solid and dependable, that had served them well. He had taught himself how to talk to the boy, with deft and quick movements, using his hands. The boy was no daftie, by no means at all. And fortune had smiled on them both, when she had brought him to the painter.

Not one man in a thousand would have lifted up the straw, and realised what he found. John Workman believed a man made his own luck. He was, at present, marking out a panel for the picture Doctor Locke had shown to him that morning, of art assisting fortune, which was the kind of sentiment he heartily approved. At Doctor Locke's request, he had veiled Lady Fortuna in a modest smock, and for Hermes had sketched in a tunic, to tone with his bright feathered helmet, lest the students at their board should find themselves aroused by naked globs of flesh. The letters underneath he would pick out in gold; colour was the essence of the painter's art, and he had in mind a particular device for the metal of the plate, which would capture it perfectly.

The prentice, meanwhile, worked on Doctor Locke. It had taken John Workman some little while to settle him down for his portrait, expert though he was in putting men at ease. Once he was relaxed, he could be left safely in the hands of the boy, who would capture a likeness almost too faithfully. A man of the middle rank, who had come on in the world, wanted his picture to reflect his achievements; he did not want to see, the sour twist in a mouth, the furrow in a brow or the slanting cast of a suspicious eye; therefore such a sitter must be set at rest.

Doctor Locke had been hard to settle, for there were a dozen places he would rather be, and a dozen things that he would rather do. He would not have considered that he was a vain man, but the capture of his likeness for and in perpetuity, occasioned him some anxious interest how it might appear. He was sitting on a chair, in his doctor's cap and gown, and his full beard neatly trimmed above a fresh starched ruff. ('You do not think the whole effect too solemn and severe? For I should like to show the picture to my bairns.') Behind him was a cloth, and the light from the window glanced across his face, on what he was persuaded was his better side. On the table by his side lay the human skull that symbolised where all of us, pictured in our prime, are certain to find end, as well as his particular and personal stock-in-trade. From his vast array of instruments he had brought along an hourglass and a clock – to warn his students that they were indebted, too, to time.

The apprentice had completed his first drafts, on thin sheets of paper bound in a book, which would be kept in case copies were called for, a pattern for forming a full-fleshed physician. To his panel portrait, drawn in black and white, he began to add a film of crimson lake, filling in the contours of the doctor's face. John Workman set down his own brush to watch, as the likeness, unmistakable, began to take its shape. He was conscious of a movement at the door behind him, and turned round.

The man at his back had an interesting face; sadness underlay a kind, appealing smile. The eyes were clear, intelligent. John Workman thought, this is a face the prentice should paint.

'I had hoped,' said the man, 'for a word with Giles Locke.'

The painter sighed. 'Can you speak with him now, while he sits? For it is hard to get him still for any length of time.'

'It is a private matter.'

'You need not fear my prentice. For you see, he cannot hear. And what he cannot hear, for sure he cannot tell.' The painter gave his most engaging smile. He knew well enough how to work his charm. For some reason, though, this man appeared indifferent to it. He was a fair and a civil-mannered man; it was not lack of patience that compelled him to persist with it, but some deep perplexion stirred up in his mind.

'Even so,' he said, 'And I do not doubt you, I would like to speak with him alone. Can you tell him I am here? Hew Cullan is my name. Ask him, if he will, if he can step outside.'

'No need for that,' the painter said. 'I will call my boy out; we shall take a break. Can you wait a moment, sir?' Once the doctor was unsettled from his place, there was no kenning when he would be settled back. John Workman hid his sigh, resigned to interruption, and moved to the sightline of the young apprentice, to catch his attention, without startling him. He was rewarded with a deep, good-natured smile, that split the concentration on the young man's face. His dark hair flopped forward, over his eyes, and the painter felt fiercely, the strength of his pride. He spoke to him, quickly and deftly, using his hands, in the language that they had made private between them. The young prentice nodded and set down his brush.

To the doctor, John Workman said, 'There is a scholar to see you. Mark and mysel' will be off for a drink, down to the buttery. And it please you to relax a little, do not leave your seat, for fear to lose your pose. We will back before long.'

He clapped the young apprentice fondly on the shoulder, and the two went out.

Hew, with his mind fixed elsewhere, glanced at the easel as he came past, and was momentarily distracted. 'He has your likeness, quite.'

Giles strained a little, affecting not to look. 'Indeed, it is an irksome thing, this sitting down for half the day. So much to be done. You look troubled, Hew. Do I take it you have come to your decision?'

'Yes. No,' Hew said, abruptly. 'You did not tell me Clare was dead.'

135

He half expected, even then, had hoped for, a reprieve. Roger had lied. Of course, he had lied. But the look on Giles' face told him all, and turned his hopes to ashes, choking in his throat. It was a look of drawn out, overwhelming weariness, a heaviness that superseded any sense of grief. 'Oh, my dear friend. I did not realise you had feelings for her still. There were so many lost, and most of them were friends. What did Roger say?'

'That he caught the plague from Clare Buchanan's house. That he took off his mask, and breathed it from her. Is that how it was?'

'Well,' reflected Giles, 'it is true enough, that she was among the last he attended to, shortly before he fell sick. The silly bairn, for taking off his mask. Why did he do that?'

'To make amends, he said. The letter that he sent was to her husband Robert Wood, accusing her of infidelity with me. You may be certain that she suffered for it.'

Giles looked at him, appalled. 'I did not know. But then I have to count myself in part to blame. For had I not allowed her into the college, had she not met with you, he could never have known such a thing.'

'He did not *know* it. He imagined it. And so bairnly and so feeble were his delusions that, Andrew Wood said, his brother Robert gave no credit to it. It was clear enough a student from the college.'

'My God,' whispered Giles, 'they should have come to me.'

'You were not responsible. And you are not now. And since you confirm that they died in the plague, the whole thing is now laid to rest,' Hew concluded bleakly.

'It is a sad, wretched, case. And I am sorry for it, Hew.'

'I am sorry, too.'

'What will you have me do? Shall I dismiss the boy?'

Hew decided not. For nothing he could do, could help the hurt he felt. And he would not pervert those feelings to revenge. 'Let him be examined at the black stane, still. I will not deprive him of his laureation. When he is a graduate, he may be more staid.'

'I thank you, with all my heart,' Giles sighed. 'For I did not want to sway you. But he has too much promise, too much hope by far, to throw away. Punish him, however else you will, and I will make sure that he accepts it meekly.'

'He caught the plague. Which seems to me, punishment enough.'

Clare was dead, and they was nothing else to say. Hew forgave the harm the boy had meant to him. But he would not forget, and would watch him still. He did not believe, with Giles, that Roger's risking his own life had been a sign of virtue, for someone who was careless with his life, he had learned at Seething Lane, could be someone very dangerous indeed.

The painter found the doctor sitting, just as he had left him. But however hard he tried, he could not coax his face into an equilibrium, or put him back at ease.

Chapter 12

Ash Wednesday

For days, they lived as lovers, closed off from the world. Hours were spent in bed together, velvet curtains drawn against the midnight air, where they found new lands, and kingdoms to explore. Sometimes, Frances woke up to the raging of a storm, and reached out in the darkness for her husband's hand. Sometimes, she looked out upon the sliver of a moon, shivered in the frost that rimed the leaded glass, thinking of the stars that shone on Leadenhall, until her husband, waking, called her back to bed. In the mornings, they slept late. In the afternoons, they went for winter walks, through brittle grass and silver streams, to the darkening shore, where Frances saw the sea that billowed in her dreams, smooth and still as glass. And rising in the distance on the far side of the bay she could see the town, kirk and spire and castle craning to the sky.

They knew it could not last. Hew should have gone, at once, to make his peace with James, to answer to the summons of the royal court. He invented reasons to remain at home; the weather was too cold, or else the road was wet. His horse had lost a shoe, he did not have a coat; he would not intrude upon an open grief, before that hurt had healed. Yet he was aware they could not stay for long, sheltered from the glare of a suspicious world. They must be forced apart. And on the first day in Lent, that was the first of March, the spell that bound them fast was broken by the coming of a far from welcome visitor.

Meg sat by the hearth, in a pool of lamplight, working on some drapery to furnish her new house. Her little daughter Martha, settled at her feet, sat playing with a box of brightly coloured threads. The boy was at his books, and Giles had left for town, through a drizzled sleet, against the kind of sky that never comes to light, but drags on from a sluggish dawn towards a dreary dusk. Hew and Frances finished off the last crumbs of a breakfast, leisurely and late, drinking cups of warm spiced ale beside a blazing fire. Frances leant from time to time, to find a scrap of silk, a button or a hook to dress a little puppet she was stitching for the child, while Hew watched the firelight flatter her soft cheek, and looked upon a book, he did not try to read. He found himself complete, and blissfully content. Their peace was broken then, jarring and abrupt, by an insistent hammering, resounding through the house. They were neither of them dressed to face the outside world, Frances in a kirtle loaned to her by Meg, of a soft blue wool, and Hew in shirt and slops, his coat and points undone. Meg set down her work. 'Something is amiss, to bring a body hurtling through the sleet and snaw.' Canny Bett appeared, to announce the coming of the crownar Andrew Wood, 'to consult wi' Mistress Meg, upon an urgent matter'. And Hew rose up at once, to face the coming storm. He looked upon Sir Andrew as a dark malevolence, brooding and intent, without a qualm or conscience to dilute his force. But he was stopped in his tracks when the crownar appeared, for slung in his cloak was the corpse of a child. Sir Andrew took no note of Hew, but went at once to Meg. 'The wee one isnae well.'

Meg was on her feet, and had lifted the little one out of his hands.

Hew thought, she is dead, for sure, that child is dead, the limbs that slipped lifeless, the white waxen face must surely be dead, void of all hope. But Meg brought her close to the heat of the fire. 'You did not bring her all this way, in the biting cold?'

'From St Andrews,' Andrew said. 'Since my brother's death, it is a convenience for me to lie at his house, that otherwise were vacant, when I come to town.'

That was like the man. He would not shed a tear to see a brother lost, or spare to let one hang. Though Robert Wood had been a brute, that few might mourn his passing, as a brother should. Sir Andrew lived at Largo, half a day's ride south; and in his role as sheriff travelled over Fife, as well as to the court, where he served as comptroller to the king's grace. His office was performed with calculated ruthlessness, uncannily at odds with this show of tenderness towards a little child. 'I wrapped her up in blankets, safe against the wind. Elizabeth was terrified that it might be the plague. She will not eat nor drink, and she is sic a fragile, insubstantial thing.'

The child had hair like flax, spun out in a thread. Her cheeks began to flutter with the smallest bloom of breath.

Meg said, 'It is not the plague. The cold air, as I think, has helped reduce a fire and fever in her brain. Do you see, sir, that her ear burns red and hot? I doubt there is infection there. So it will present itself, in a little one.'

'Can you cure her, then?' Sir Andrew was quiet, respectful to Meg. That was not like him, at all.

'Certainly,' she said. 'I have syrup to cool her, and coax back her appetite. She is a delicate thing. How old is she, now?'

'Not long turned three. Elizabeth thinks she is small for her age. But she had a difficult start.'

Meg nodded. 'She is delicate flower, that droops from the want of a drink. And, like a flower that is parched, you will marvel at how quickly she comes back to life. She shall have an onion, roasted in the fire, dropped into her ear, and a little poppy juice, to help relieve the pain. And it please you, sir, I will take her now to the kitchen and dispensary. Frances, will you come, and bring Martha too? I should like your help, and these men will want to talk.'

For the first time, Andrew Wood chose to notice Hew, and they eyed each other, warily. Together in a company, neither showed their thoughts. Once they were alone, Andrew spoke up first, 'I have come lately from court, where the king finds it strange you should be in Scotland, and yet fail to pay your respects. He has a pardon to give. He marvels that you seem too proud to come and beg it from him. Though I make no offer to dispose your life, it pains me to observe you throw away so carelessly, what has taken others such care to procure.'

Hew, who was aware that he was overdue at court, was irked to be reminded of it by Sir Andrew Wood. 'I had thought, sir, you had taken it upon yourself to dispose of my life, freely at your will, with no regard to mine.'

'If you mean, the efforts I engaged to save your stubborn carcass, thriftless though it was, and to protect your family, I accept your thanks,' the coroner replied.

'I think you mistook my poor life for your own, when you plucked me from Scotland and sent me to Walsingham. Perhaps you did confuse my treachery with yours.'

Sir Andrew seemed amused at that. 'Walsingham, in truth, repented for his part; and you and I could never hope to play that trick again.'

'As I assure you, sir, the trick was only yours. And so much should I swear to, if asked, by the king.'

'That will profit little, Hew, You should know, that I have that tract still, I took from the desk in your library. What was it, now? A translation of Buchanan's book, on the laws of kingship. That work has been banned. Its dissemination is a capital offence.'

The translation was made by Nicholas Colp, to occupy his fractious mind in his last days on this earth. No earthly harm was meant by it. And yet, by implication in it, Hew might stand accused. The coroner had kept it, as assurance that the king would never come to hear of his pact with Walsingham.

'Touching, was it not?' he sneered. 'And dedicat, to you. You may sometime have it back, when the time is right. That is not now, I think.'

'You are, for a traitor, sure of yourself.' Hew could not deny the force of Sir Andrew's argument. He felt a vicious pang, that the word against him had been forced from Nicholas, a flagrant violation of an honest friend. It was not fear of death that worked to stay his hand, his will to cut the sheriff from his safety at a stroke, but a fear for Frances, left alone behind. It was not a fear that he had felt before.

'I saw Robert Lachlan,' the crownar said then, 'at your stable outside. He gave me a look that he would have cut me there, down to the quick, had I not carried the child. And had I not carried the child, so I had done unto him. I never liked that man. And I do not commend you for your choice of friend.'

'No? When you work for Walsingham, you cannot be particular. All his men are cutthroats, renegats and thieves.' All but Laurence Tomson, Hew emended privately. 'Robert is among them the most worthy and most honest, since he does not pretend to be other than he is, a simple man for hire.'

Sir Andrew did not shrink, but smiled upon his rage. 'God love and keep you, Hew, can we not be friends? Can you not accept it, in your stubborn heart, I moved to save your life?'

'And you tell me why, then I may consider it,' said Hew. 'For I am not so vain, as to think that it was sentiment, or any love for me. Is it that you like to live your life at risk?'

'As to that, I find no solace in it, now that I grow old. Shall we say, perhaps, that you have influential friends? Let the thing rest, or we both shall repent of it. Time has moved on. For myself, I have done with the court. My tenure as comptroller there is coming to an end. And I am worn and spent. The king has squeezed me dry. And I swear to you, I never did betray his purpose or his cause, but with a good intent, to see him safe and sound. Whatever you may think of me, I had his good at heart. And what have I to show for it? My purse is worn to threads, and my dead brother's too. The king says, for that he kens he cannot ever pay to me the debt, that I have expended to settle his accounts, he will let me keep the lands that were mortgaged in his cause, and graciously bestows upon me, what was mine before. He serves the debt with thanks. The present crisis to our state and country should concern us now. For if he came to know, that either you or I had dared to deal with Walsingham, on any secret terms, we should both hang high. He is greatly perplexed at the death of the queen.'

Sir Andrew did seem wearied now. And Hew was quite prepared

to set aside their feud, to hear this present news, more pressing to his cause. 'How does it move him?' he asked.

'That is hard to say. Outwardly, of course, he claims himself much wronged, and grieved at it. He marvels that so strange and unkind a thing was done. Before the loving populace, he wrings out his tears, crying for revenge.'

'You think he does not feel that way, at heart?'

The coroner confessed, 'I think he is conflicted in it. He cannot help but feel the slight to him, since she was a mother, since she was a queen, no son nor king could help to feel a pang at that, and shiver at the blade that whistled close to him. He will be anxious too, lest any taint shall fall on him, through an association that was irksome while she lived. He will not wish to enrage, or lose the will of his own people, when they cry out for revenge. He will not wish to seem to them subservient or weak. And on the other hand, why should his Grace weep, for a Catholic mother he neither saw nor loved, who wished to see her own son toppled from his throne? Her death is, at best, a convenience to him. If he can show Elizabeth an honest, proper grief, he may hope to profit from a brave show of his righteousness, and win from her the hope that he has always dreamt of; he sees within his grasp the future English Crown.'

'Has he come so calculating, now?' This did not match Hew's picture of the fretful bairn who trembled at the footsteps of his watchful lords.

'He has grown beyond the boy you knew and fled from last. He has a shrewd intelligence, and knows he holds a fragile promise balanced in his hands. For that reason, it seems likely he will bide his time. He has broken off his embassy with England, and the queen's ambassador is kept at bay at Berwick, for the king protests he cannot keep him safe, nor send to him a passport at this present time, so fervent are the passions of the people in this country, at what they do conceive of as a monstrous crime. He might as well declare embarquements on all Englishmen, for his delay does nought but stir the people's flame. The borders have been closed, and Sir Francis

Walsingham must whistle for his spies. No one dares send news. And you bring none, I doubt?'

Hew said, 'Not for you.' He was encouraged, still, despite the dreadful news. If there was no word from England, Frances might be safe.

The crownar laughed at that. 'Still, you do persist, in thinking that our end and purpose cannot be the same. When will you be taught, our hopes are intertwined?'

Before Hew could retort, Meg returned with Frances and the children by her side. Sir Andrew Wood's small girl, so desolate of life, had made what seemed to Hew a miraculous recovery. She was walking now, barefoot and unsteadily, holding onto Meg's hand. Sir Andrew cried, 'God love you, Mistress Meg! I thought the lass was gone!' And Hew saw such a feeling flood that uncouth face, that he was startled and amazed, as though it were on Andrew Wood that Meg had worked her miracle, and not his little child.

'There is no wonder in it,' Meg said with a smile. 'It happens oft with little ones, that fall into decline, that they come round as quickly. I wish that it might always prove the case. Take this physic for her. In another day or two, she will be quite well.'

The small girl stumbled to Sir Andrew's side, holding up her arms. 'Dada,' she scolded, 'Whisht, do not cry.'

'Never, my pet.' He lifted her, and she settled on his shoulder, sucking at a thumb.

'She is a pretty thing,' Frances spoke up, in her clear English voice. 'She is lovely, sir. Is she not pretty, Hew? Such enormous eyes. I should hope to have a little girl like this.'

Sir Andrew turned towards her, thoughtful in his gaze. 'I thank you, mistress. As I do confess to you, she has brought us joy. Forgive my plainness here, but we were not introduced. I am Andrew Wood, crownar and sheriff in Fife. I keep the king's peace in this place. And while you are here, you may be assured, you will have my protection.'

'Shall I need it, sir?' Frances asked, bemused.

'As I should suppose. For you are a stranger, in a hostile place.

And, as I infer, you have come with him.' He glanced across at Hew, a clear and frank amusement lighting up his face. Hew glared back at him. He would not, for the world, let Frances understand that they had anything to hide. 'Frances is my wife,' he said, 'and wants no help but mine.'

'Now I understand what kept you from the court. What man would not be stayed by such a fair distraction? You must brace yourself, mistress, and wipe your soft tears, let your husband be torn from your side for a while, or the king will be cross with him. God love you Hew, as I do,' Sir Andrew answered, laughing, 'hurry to the court, before the king has wind of it you have an English wife. Else you will find good fortune, even such as yours, will not last for long. Now I must depart, and take this bairn back home, before my wife despairs of her. For, I do confess, she loves her as her own.'

Hew asked, compelled, 'Is she not yours?' He looked upon the child, her cool commanding gaze and hair like linen flax, spun out to a thread, the shadow of a bloom upon her dewy cheek.

Sir Andrew grinned at Frances, answering to Hew. 'Can ye not tell? She is Clare's.'

Frances had waited all day, until they lay naked in bed. When there was nothing but darkness between them, she asked, 'Who is Clare?'

Hew answered her, 'His brother's wife. They died in the plague.'

'That is sad. You liked her, I think.' Her voice sounded small. The curtains were closed, against the night air. He could feel her warmth close, though they did not touch.

He would not lie to her. 'I did like her, yes. But she had a husband. Robert Wood was cruel to her.'

'Oh. Did you pity her, then?'

He answered, 'I suppose I did,' and did not understand why she let slip a sigh, sorrowful, deep, in the dark of the bed.

'It is touching, I think, that Sir Andrew Wood cares for his dead brother's child. For tis clear that he loves her,' she said.

'What?' he was listening, half; her words made an impression

145

somewhere in the shadows spilling in his mind. Some vague idea disturbed him; he did not know what it was.

'It is good of him, Hew.'

'It is not goodness. It is . . .' Before he could grasp what it was – whatever it was there that had escaped him, for he would not admit to goodness in that man – he heard, and understood the reason for her wistfulness, 'He is not your uncle, my love. They are nothing alike.'

'No.' Her voice was hollow in the darkness, and he reached across the chasm that had opened up between them, to comfort as he could. Her head rested light on his chest, where she could feel the steady beating of his heart.

'I know you miss your family.'

Frances whispered, 'It is not only that. My uncle took me in, when I was very small. I have betrayed his trust, and failed him, in my duty as a child.'

'He failed in his, to you.'

A small shake of the head. He felt on his skin the ruffling of hair, and stroked it. He knew what she had lost, and felt the burden of his part in it. It was not regret. If they could lie forever in that bed, and keep the curtains closed against the rain and wind, if he could hold her in his arms to weather out that storm, then he could be content. He knew that he could not.

'Dearest, you know that I must go to court. Tomorrow, if I can.'

She whispered, 'So soon?'

'The sooner am I gone, the sooner my return. Know that I would take you, if I could.'

Her skin was light and soft. Her pale hair smelt of camomile.

'I have never yearned to come into the court. I never thought to meet a queen, or king. Besides,' she spoke bravely, a crack in her voice, 'I have nothing to wear.'

She had nothing at all. He had seen her in the gowns lent to her by Meg, thinking little other than how bonny she had looked. He had seen her quite bare, and had liked her just as well. Now he understood, and saw what she had lost.

'Meg will take you to the town. You shall have all that you want. Shoes. Gowns. Clothes. Buy something fine and fit, in popinjay or green.'

She was quiet a long while, and he did not know what she was thinking. Then she said, 'Green is not becoming to a pale complexion. For your sister, perhaps.'

'Sea-water, then. What you will think fit, for a wedding gown.'

'Were we not married, Hew?' she asked him then, tentative and serious. So much he had taken from her, and taken her from.

'Of course we were. An English marriage. But we will have a Scottish one, in a Scottish kirk. Then no man may say, twas not properly done.'

'Will they say that?'

'The kirkmen here are scrupulous, and will say almost anything, to damp down our hopes. We will not give them cause. But you know that we were married lawfully and in sight of God. Since you had no gown nor maiden at your side, and enjoyed no feast, you shall have them here.'

'I do not care for those.'

'Of course you do. You and Meg shall make schemes for it while I am gone. It will keep you amused. Women like such things.'

'Ah, Do they now? I shall show to you what women like. Do not pretend that you know,' she teased. If words were kept light, a heart could not break.

'What? And you were so innocent, so meek and mild last week. I blame it on Meg. What has she taught you, in that coven of her sisterhood, corrupting you, my sweet?' he teased her in his turn.

'Ah, you should like to know! I shall put you to school, very strictly, when you return. Let the fear of it hurry you on, and the hope of it hurry you back.'

Their playfulness made light, and hid the deep disquiet there. When they had made love, and lay still and content, he said to her. 'Take Robert Lachlan with you, when you go to town.'

'Robert? He does not look like a man with an eye to choose a gown.'

'He will keep you safe.'

'Did you never see the leather markets held at Leadenhall?. Are your market places ever quite so wild?'

'I had not thought so, once. But these are troubling times.'

Frances drifted off, and woke up in the night to find him still awake. She felt for his hand, sensing his absence there, even before he had left. 'What are you thinking?' she asked.

He lay silent still. But his breathing, measured, told her that he heard, and was not asleep.

'I wish that you would tell me,' she said. 'I am not afraid, when you speak the truth. When you are close, and secret, like Tom, it fills me with a kind of dread.'

For a moment, it seemed as though he would not answer her. Then he whispered, 'Please do not say that.'

'That you are like Tom? It is true, is it not? You have learned to lie, and to keep yourself close.'

He asked her, 'When have I lied?' And knew it was, instead, the things that were not said.

'I do not blame you for it. But if you cannot trust me now, then there is no hope for us. No hope for me,' she said, in a brittle voice, 'who have followed to a place where I am a stranger, and perceived a foe, and am bereft of friends. Then cold earth could not shape a colder marriage bed, and it were my grave.'

Her words were cold indeed, and moved his heart to pity, passion and remorse. 'Hush, you shall not be . . . Frances, all will be well, I will make it well.'

'How will you do that?'

'I do not know,' he said.

'That,' Frances said, 'is, at least, the truth. Talk to me, now. What is it that troubles you, Hew?'

And he found the courage, and the heart to answer her. 'It is what Thomas did at Chartley.'

Something in him gave, something in his heart he felt there, tight and physical, and he reached for her. In the darkness of that place, he understood what even Phelippes knew; a man could not place a lock upon conscience, and keep it always closed. And Hew, least of all, could be dark and distrustful, towards someone who had trusted him so far with her own life, and placed it in his hands. The thought of that filled him with the deepest kind of terror. And so he told her, all.

'You heard that Gilbert Gifford carried letters for that queen. As I believe he did. But he was not of her party. Tom trained him for the task, and both of them were agents for Sir Francis Walsingham. Gifford was not willing, but they had some hold on him. For that is how they work. And I believe, they meant his part for me, but found they could not trust me to it. Tom was at Chartley to decipher the letters the queen had entrusted to Gifford. To ensnare and ensure her destruction. To bring the queen down. And, as I suspect she was lured into the plot, and a web was spun. Since they had the letters from the start, they could have wiped out the conspirators, before they ever reached her. They did not do that. Instead, they let it run, intending to entrap, and catch her at its heart.'

Frances was a long while quiet then. But Hew felt calm, and peaceful in the silence that they shared. And presently, she told to him her thoughts, falling into place, sensible and clear, and he understood that he was not alone.

'They let her think it safe, to show her heart. She showed it, Hew, and it was black. What harm was there in that?'

'If it was true, there was none. Perhaps it was true. They made sure that it was. I do not think that there was any kind of justice there. The evidence was skewed. And the letters that they showed, I think that Tom may have altered, in his own hand.'

'Why would you think that?' she asked.

'Some writing that I saw. It does not amount to evidence.' He knew, had always known, it would not stand as evidence in any kind of court. And yet he believed it was true. 'Justice is a thing that we should fight for, is it not?' the queen of Scots had said.

'What are you saying, then? That that queen was blameless of the fault they killed her for?'

'Perhaps. Not even that. That guilty or not, they had determined that she would die for it. That it was prejudged, long before she ever put her name or mind to it. She was lost from the start, as the Calvinists might say. For her life was a threat to your queen, whether she meant it or not.

'You asked me, what secret weighs so heavy on my heart. And now I have told you. I see Giles Locke, a man who has the strength to face a thousand deaths, dash away a tear at the falling of his queen, and I feel a stain upon my conscience, dark as though I were complicit in the act. If I cannot look my friend straight into the eye, how can I look on my king?'

'You were not complicit, Hew, because you were a witness to it,' she said. 'You cannot act on forces such as these. Suppose you told the king? Would he want to hear? If you spoke the truth to him, his hopes could not be reconciled. What would that mean? There might be a war. And that queen will be dead still, whatever the truth. You cannot tell him, now.'

He answered her, 'I know. And I should not have burdened you.'

'You should. For that I am your wife. Else what was this for? I will not allow it to tear us apart.'

'Dear Frances,' he whispered. 'Are you not sorry you came?'

'Not for the world, now you tell me the truth. Are you sorry you brought me?'

His answer came soft, in a kiss.

Chapter 13

The Touchstone

He did not like to leave her, with no way of knowing when he might be back. He trusted Giles and Meg. Both of them were loved and respected in the town, the more so since the peste, and their protection would extenuate the feelings of the crowd. Yet he felt ashamed to leave his charge to them, and troubled by the conflict it had caused his friend. As a precaution, he left Robert Lachlan. He had found Robert Lachlan a house by the mill with a small plot of land. John Kintor had offered up three of the pigs, from the litter his brood-sow expected that month. To every hireling skrimmar there must come a time when he set down his sword. Yet Hew was under no illusion Robert would last long. His friend had entered an alliance with a rousie kitchen maid, that kept him, for the moment, busily content. But it would not be long before his restless bones would itch, and he would scrap again, until that fateful skirmish that would be his last.

'What am I, now? A nursemaid for wives?' Robert had complained.

'I cannot think to leave her in more careful hands.'

'And though that may be so, there is a fly in your reasoning. While I look after her, who looks out for you, and saves your feeble bane-house fae the devil's claws? You never gang a pace, but you fall into a pit. Your puir lass has nae hopes, but those she puts in you.'

Hew was well aware of that. 'If, for some reason, I do not come back, if, in that event, she will not stay here, can you take her home?'

'Jesu,' Robert said. 'I was jesting, Hew. Why in the name of God would you not come back? You are off to Edinburgh, not to the antipodes.'

Hew said, 'Even so.'

He had time to think about it on his journey south. At Edinburgh, he would buy a ring, a symbol of his love. They would be betrothed, and married in the Scottish Kirk, as soon as he returned.

Coming into Edinburgh, Hew felt once again on old, familiar ground. Here, he had spent the first years of his life, with his family at the Cowgate, while his father practised law at the justice court. Here he went to school, remaining with the master when his father had retired, until he had matriculated at St Leonard's College. The High School, in those days, had been his second home. The mile down which he walked, from the castle on its rock through the Netherbow and down into the Canongate, he knew and loved as well as any place on earth. He could live there with Frances, perhaps.

At Holyrood, he learned the court was at Dalkeith, in mourning for the queen. There, he would call on the following day, if it should please the king's grace. He found stabling for his horse, and a bed for the night, at an inn by the West Bow, close to the Grassmarket. The horse was a sprightly young bay. Dun Scottis, stubborn still, remained at Kenly Green, living out his days in a peaceful indolence. He let no one ride him now apart from Matthew Locke, whose affections he tolerated with a stolid gloom.

For the rest of the day, Hew wandered by the castle and the high kirk of St Giles. From a Lawnmarket tailor, he bought mourning clothes, of a kind and quality that were fit for court, yet did not overshoot his status and his rank. He chose a woollen broadcloth in a midnight shade, with black silk for his hat and the lining of his cloak, plain white ruff and gloves, and little else of ornament to brighten his black coat. The strength of the dye bore the cost, offset by the cut and cloth, resulting in a balance of refined restraint. The prick-louse assured him his suit would be done by the end of day.

The people took their lead and licence from their king. His grieving gave them leave to put on a display. For some, it was the chance to show their old allegiance to the Catholic queen, and to mourn her openly. The little shops and stalls clustered at St Giles, the luckenbuiths and krames, had filled their stands with doleful ribbons, brooches and black gloves. The hammermen had dulled their daggers; cold bright shards of metal darkened to a dusk were clad in velvet sheathes. Street sellers peddled their fruits, flowers and herbs. Rose*marie*, remember me, the bold among them cried, and the women bought sprigs of it, tied up in silks, to pin to their bonnets and shawls. Sad-coloured kerseys were whipped into cloaks, with which the willing poor could drape their workday clothes; grizzled greys and tans, melancholy bays, eclipsing greens and gold, washing out a landscape of yellow, pink and blue, as a north-east haar drains colour from a day.

The krames could not compete with the jewellers' shops in Cheapside, where lustred plate and trinkets glinting in the windows dazzled those who passed, to think the streets of London must be paved with gold. The Edinburgh goldsmiths did not flaunt their craft, but made their wares to order in the quiet ranks of unassuming workshops, closed off from the street. Here, Hew came at last, and hoped to buy his ring. By the Lady Steps, leading to St Giles, he remembered the shop of a goldsmith called Urquhart, who did business with his father and the lawyer Richard Cunningham. Urquhart's virtues were that he kept clients' secrets close, and the delicate touch he brought to his craft. His fault was the absence in him, of a moral intellect. He would deal with the devil if he counted profit in it. Perhaps, after all, the devil had returned to make a claim on him, for Urquhart was no more. Carved upon the lintel stone of what was once his door, were the words *George Heriot*. Hew recognised the name, as a goldsmith of repute. Therefore, he went in.

It was like looking down upon the throttle of a furnace, standing on its tongue while its hot breath bellowed out, and dribbled from its mow into a spittery of gold. The space in which he stood was six or eight feet square, lit at the back by a large open window, made secure with bars. There was space for little else, beside the blazing chimney built into a wall, but the goldsmith's board and stools, a cupboard with a lock, and a cabinet of shelves. In the centre of the room, a young man spun a thread, to infinite fineness, from a droplet of gold. He was stripped to his shirt, and a wide leather apron caught fragments of gold, that sheared from the wire in delicate flecks, like a bright shower of rain.

'A moment, if you will.' The goldsmith cut the wire, turning in his hands from a stream of lava to a silken strand. 'Now, can I help you?'

'I hope so,' Hew said. 'But I thought this was the workshop of a man called Urquhart.'

'Aye, so it was. He died in the plague, that ravaged through this street. Urquhart would not leave. My father telt me once, he thought his life was charmed.'

Hew remembered too. Urquhart had contrived to make himself invincible. 'It caught him in the end. Your father is George Heriot, I suppose.'

'He is,' the young man grinned. 'And so am I. Geordie, to my friends. If it is my faither that ye want, ye will not find him here. This is my shop.'

'Then,' answered Hew, 'you may do just as well. For I should like to buy a lady's finger ring.'

The goldsmith opened up his cabinet of trays, and brought out a small rack of rings. 'These are samples only, and are not for sale.'

The pieces were beautifully crafted, with delicate features wrought in the clasps, fruit, flowers and feathers, insects and birds, carved in the casing that held in its grasp a table ruby or emerald stone. One had been set with a sharp pointed diamond, and Hew picked it up. 'This is exquisite work.'

'That is a bezel for writing on glass,' George Heriot said. Hew nodded and put the ring back, finding it poignant in more ways than one. There were examples also of *memento mori* rings: an enamelled death's-head; vipers in a nest, flicking silver tongues; a tiny golden toad. There was one that was a dead kist, opening on a hinge, upon a bed of bones, one where a circle of skeletons danced, one where an eye, carved from weeping white opal, dropped dew-clustered diamonds as tears.

'Do you like those?' the young goldsmith asked. 'I had in my mind to send some to court, as a present for the king. My wife says tis presumptuousness, and like to cause offence. She is canny, see? I tell her that there is no profit, comes without a risk. What do you think?'

Not knowing the king's mind, Hew could not advise. 'The work is surely fine enough, to set before a king. Perhaps you could send your gift to one of his lords. Then, were it worn at the court, his Grace might take notice of it,' he suggested.

'That is an idea. Aye, perhaps I will. Thank you, sir,' the goldsmith smiled. 'I have had had some call for these, in the past few days. It is, as they say, an unco ill wind, though it may be a cruel one.' His frank and cheerful confidence Hew found as engaging as his subtle craft. 'I do not want a mourning ring, but one like this,' he said, lifting out a band with interlocking parts, which were held together by a clasp of hands.

'That is very apt and pleasing, both as a betrothal ring, and a wedding band. You can have two or three hoops, or as many as five, with a verse on each one, interlinked. And you may have it set with any colour stone, or enamel, as you choose,' the goldsmith said.

Hew preferred two parts, the inner one inscribed, and the outer circle carved with some intricate device. He had a picture in his mind, of petals intertwined, of pansies and columbine, a thistle and a rose.

The goldsmith made a note of this, in a table book. 'Have you any thought what poesie you would like? I have some written here, that are always popular.'

It felt a little false to Hew, to choose a lasting sentiment from the goldsmith's list. Some appeared acquisitive: 'All that's thine is mine'; some were less than chivalrous: 'If I think my wife is fair/why should other people care?'

'Something simple, perhaps, "Amour, toujours, tous les jours" or "My hand and heart in yours"?' The choosing of a ring, meant to last a lifetime, proved harder than expected. Geordie sympathised. 'I have not long been married mysel'. And the making of the band was the hardest part.'

'It must have been, for you, harder still to pass the lady's expectations. If you do not mind, I will give some thought to it. I have more idea about the raw material. My mistress is a stranger. I should like the gold to come from our native soil. Whatever else it is, it should be Scots,' decided Hew.

'Some folk,' Heriot said, 'make their wedding band from a melted coin. If you have a ducat, and a foreign crown, you might melt your piece with hers and intermingle currence, as you meld your hearts.'

Hew considered this. There was something in it pleased, the melding of the thrissel with the English rose. He had an English angel, still, inside his purse. But he was not prepared to venture it.

'That is a pretty idea. But I prefer that the gold should be pure.'

'Pure gold is too soft. It will not make a ring, or aught that will endure. The trouble with our coinage, on the other hand, is that in recent years it has become debased. Yet Scots gold, cut with silver, is quite fair and light, and a becoming colour to a lady's hand.'

That was not what Hew had meant. 'By pure, I do not mean unmingled, but rather, untouched. A coin has passed through many hands. I would like a gold, never wrought before. I have something in mind. It is foolish, perhaps. I heard there was an ancient mine, at Largo Law in Fife. That is not so far from where my home is now. They say it is the gold that gives the Largo sheep their yellow-tinted fleece.'

'Faerie gold, you want, then,' Geordie Heriot smiled.

'Then it is a myth?'

'Put it like this. If a man offers to sell you gold mined from Largo Law, bring your ain touchstane. Or else it is yourself, that will be fleeced. I will ask some questions, and see what can be found. But if there was ever gold there, outside of the fairy stories, it was long ago.'

Hew thanked him for his help. It would have been simple enough, for George Heriot to spin him a yarn, and pass off to him any old gold. It was to his credit that the goldsmith did not.

'I will draw some drafts for you, and work up some samples and costs. Can you come back in a day or two? In fact,' the goldsmith hesitated. 'Ach, what of it, then. Tis all but denner time. Can you spare a moment, sir, to witness an experiment? We maun go outside, for we cannot do it here.'

Young Heriot took off his apron, and folded it, from the outside in. He placed it with his tools, in a wide leather pocket nailed to the bench. He rinsed his hands in water, and dried them on a cloth.

'We shall need some water with us.' He poured a clean draught from a pitcher into a small flask, handing it to Hew, 'And a tinder box. And here, we have the matter, that will mak our trick.'

From the cupboard in the wall, he brought out a leather sack, a dish and pot of lead, and a glass retort, of the kind that Meg used in her still.

'And that is all, I think. Take care to wipe your feet as ye gang out.'

'Of what?' Hew discovered at the door a strip of metal grating above a leather mat, and complied with the request. The goldsmith winked at him. 'Of particles of gold. You will carry off as dust a little in your hair. But we do not charge for that. This air is filled with it. Do not be alarmed, for it cannot do you harm. Some say, tis as potent as the sun, her power in earthly balm, made gentle and benign. And it wants the sun to form in streams and hills, for, without that power, no seam of gold will grow. Physicians make their medicines from it, where it is more tolerated than the sweetest herbs. I know no sweeter substance in the living world, more malleable and ductile, more sympathetic to the human body. My wife tells me, Geordie, you have a heart of gold.'

If something in his manner had reminded Hew of Giles, it was his immersion in the substance of his craft. Gold was precious in itself, not for any riches it could bring to him. He did not strive, like alchemists, to find the secret in it of some rare elixir, for he had it in his hands, could beat it to a thinness of translucent airiness or spin it to a thread as bright as angel hair.

Hew followed him out to the lane, and down a narrow alley to a small back yard, behind a metal fence. George unlocked the gate. 'I rent this from the kirk.' In the corner was a burner built of brick, with a little bed of charcoal, onto which George struck his tinder, sparking up a flame, sheltered from the wind by the high wall of the kirk. 'Now,' the goldsmith said, 'open up the sack, and pour a little out into the flannel cloth.'

Hew opened up the sack, and found it full of dust. 'What kind of stuff is this?' he asked.

Geordie smiled at him. 'Does it look like gold?'

There was little sun in the bleached March sky to snatch at any glimmer that lay lurking in the dust. Perhaps it looked different to a practised eye? George admitted, to him it did not. 'For that purpose, dae you see, we maun put it to the test. This is the powder from a piece of rock that was given to my father by a certain Dutchman, painter to the king. Bronckhorst was his name. That man had an interest in a Scottish gold mine, six or eight years back, that, as I recall, came to the attention of the king's regent Morton, and Bronckhorst and his complices had little profit from it. My father gave some gold to him for gilding of a picture frame, and in return for it, the painter gave to him a sack full of the ore recovered from that mine – this is washed and pulverised, powdered to a dust, but not as yet refined. My father had no use for it, but as a curiosity. He has nor will not time to work up from the raw, and this – were there gold in it at all – would scarcely hold enough of quantity or quality to repay that effort. He gave it to me, when I took on this shop.

'This pot of lead holds quicksilver, which, ye may ken, is to a goldsmith his alchemist's stone. Pure gold will dissolve in it. Fine particles will cling to it, and leave behind the sand. It must be washed quite clean, or else it will not stick. The silver must not flower into a myriad particles, or else the fused amalgam never will be split.'

Hew watched the liquid silver chase and cluster on the cloth, fugitive and vacillating, like a living thing.

'Now,' Heriot said, 'we can squeeze the excess of the quicksilver out in the basin of water, and what is amalgamated, draw off in the still. For that reason, we are outdoors, for heating of the quicksilver gives off noxious fumes; it is harmless to swallow, but elusive where it spills, where it will gradually insinuate into a noisome air.

'What remains is dust. Now we shall still it, in a retort. The vapours that flow off, collecting in the cup, consolidate as mercury. What remains behind will be native gold.'

The nugget that remained, once the drops of quicksilver were carefully drawn off, and re-sealed inside their pot, was mottled, dark, and dull.

'It does not look like gold,' Hew said, disappointed.

'You are impatient, sir. It is not finished yet. There are other metals, precious in their kind, the mercury adheres to, that must be drawn off. This lump must be put to the fire, and heated seven times, before it will yield up its perfect heart of gold. And that may not be much. Come back in a day or two. I will show you what the molten fire has made of it, and ye may try it on the touchstone, whether it be pure or not. If you like it then, this dust may be incorporate into your lady's ring. Then you shall say, at least, there is a story to it, that you saw it forged, and sifted from the rock where ancient feet did walk.'

Their bargain was concluded in a tavern near the kirk, where the city merchants did their business at midday, over soused Lenten herrings and a stoup of mellow ale. Hew left there well content, to find a crowd had gathered at the mercat cross. His wam was warm and weak, full of drink and meat, and he could not stomach seeing harlots stripped or lusty beggars scourged. He was sloping off, shyly, to the Cowgate, when he heard the sounding of a herald's horn, and a speech read out. Before he could come close enough to try and catch the sense of it, it was at an end. The herald blew his horn again, and with this second flourish, nailed his proclamation staunchly to the cross.

'What was that?' Hew asked a man, who answered, 'Limmars to be dealt the blaw that is restanding tae them. High time, an' a',' and spat into the dust.

Hew waited for a moment for the crowd to disperse, which did not take long. The notice on the cross meant little to the multitude, for few of them could read. They viewed a piece of paper with a grim suspicion, for by such and such a scrap some of them were damned, with little understanding of the writing there. Had any of them dared, they would have torn it down, whatever was its sentiment, for fear that in its ciphers they would stand accused. And if they did not tear it down, bluntly from its nail, it was kenning that their lugs might be hammered in its place. Such papers were reviled, and were rarely read. They hung until they dropped, shrivelled into strips like the hanging skins of men, and were sidestepped in the mud, by superstitious feet.

Hew had both the will, and the skill to read, and he was the first who found the piece of paper pinned up to the cross, and took it to his heart. The proclamation said: 'No Scotsman shall have intercourse with any Englishman, upon pain of life, land and goods, without dispensation of his Majestie the King.'

Chapter 14

Peregrines

Frances, in his absence, did not sit and pine. She resolved to write a letter to her aunt and uncle, seeking their forgiveness for her dereliction, in the tender hope they might be reconciled. For what troubled her more deeply than the lack of Hew, in this far-off place, was the disappointment she had caused her friends. She had left to her family a short scribbled note, which she supposed her uncle would read out, in tones that were querulous, peeved and perplexed, to an incredulous Joan. 'I am now married to Hew, and have gone to Scotland. I am sorry for the nuisance this will cause to you, in your business with Josef, the Fleming. Your loving' – she had scribbled out the 'and obedient' which slipped out from the quill without a second thought – 'Your loving niece, Frances Phillips.' Conscious of the debt that duty owed to them, she had taken nothing with her but some yellowed linen, well-worn past its best, and her mother's wedding ring, the only thing that Frances had that she could call her own.

They were married at a church outside the city walls, where banns were not required, not far from Leadenhall. It was Robert Lachlan who had come across it, in a parish full of whores, with one or two of whom he had been well acquainted. London was the best place in the world, to enter into lawful, but clandestine marriage. Robert had put forth the Tower of London, Newgate or the Fleet, but Frances had not cared to fall as far as those. She hoped to have, at least, a slender veil of decency.

She could not, on the day, put on her finest clothes, and so had slipped away, in her workday drabs. Robert Lachlan, and Hew's friend, Laurence Tomson, had come along as witnesses. She had been concerned that Laurence would warn Tom, but Hew reassured her that he could be trusted. And afterwards, he had spoken to her words of such encouragement and kindness she had been moved to tears. He had given her a ribbon, and a book of prayers, as a present from his wife. And he had furnished passports for them all.

Now, she climbed the staircase leading to the tower, where paper, pens and ink were kept up in the library. She had been there once, in company with Hew. They had not lingered long. Though Hew did not prohibit her from looking through the shelves, he did not encourage her. 'Most are dry as dust, law books and the like. If there is something you would read, ask, and I will find it for you.'

Frances did not know where she might begin. Apart from in her song sheets and her uncle's ledgers, she was not well read. There was no music here. But she would not be daunted by a room of books.

She was a little troubled, though, to find the place was occupied. A young man with rumpled red hair sat on a stool by the secretar's desk, taking some notes from a leather bound tract. He looked up to speak. 'I took you for my little charge. Ye haena seen him, I suppose.'

Frances took a moment to make sense of the Scots. 'Are you Matthew's schoolmaster?'

'Gavan Baird.' He smiled at her. 'And you are a peregrine, I doubt.'

'A peregrine?'

'A foreigner. A stranger to these parts. A pilgrim, who has strayed.'

'I am Frances. Hew Cullan's wife.' The words brought her courage, and strength. She had not said them before.

'Then I beg your pardon, for I did not ken. Leastways, I had heard that yon master had come hame. I had not kent he brocht a wife wi' him.' He was forward in his manner, stretching out his legs, nothing in the least abashed. He might have owned the place.

'Matthew is in the garden, with his mother. I wonder that you did not see them as you came. I can send someone down to fetch him, if you like,' Frances said, hoping to impress upon him that she was the owner there, or at least, his wife.

Gavan yawned, and grinned. 'To speak the truth to you,' he confided then, 'I should not like, at all. I heard them in the gardens and crept by them here unseen. I came before my time, to steal a quiet moment with your husband's books. You have found me out. I confess my fault.' He did not seem, in any sense, ashamed of his confession. 'Will your husband mind it, do you think?'

'Perhaps you ought to ask him,' Frances said. In truth, she did not know. Though Hew appeared, at times, so careless of his wealth and comforts it astonished her, the contents of the library were closest to his heart. Whenever, in London, he had squirrelled some spare shillings, he had spent them at the booksellers, huddled round St Pauls. He had brought a stack of books back home from the Netherlands, salvaged from the wars, where other men preferred their spoils in silver or in gold. In the latter months, when his credit was assured, he had made them into parcels and had shipped them here; the crates were waiting still, for him to come and open them. The library, she understood, was linked to his father and his dead friend Nicholas, who had kept the books; the crownar, Sir Andrew Wood, had broken in upon it, desecrating memories that were bittersweet, and muddled still, for Hew.

'Are there no books at the university?' she put to Gavan Baird. For she had been told he was a student there.

'Not of this sort. Or they are locked away, and I am not to be trusted wi' them,' he answered, honestly.

'Why would they not trust you with them?' She looked for a sign that he was careless with the books; the young man was dishevelled, and his red hair was long. His shirt cuffs and ruff were a little worn and grubby, but his hands looked clean.

'The master does not like me, for I talk too much. There are books in this library banned by the statutes. Your man has been abroad, and likely does not know.'

'What books are those? Written by Jesuits?' Frances was alarmed. Many of the books on the shelves were in Latin, and could have any core of dark and sly intent.

'Not Jesuits,' Gavan smiled. 'Though the old man was a papist, and there are, I maun confess, some stirring sorts of tracts. Those in themselves kept quiet here will not do much harm, though at this time . . . when the wind blaws right, it may tak but a spark to light a fire. I do not count those. It is imperative to read what your enemy puts out, the better for to understand and countermand their thoughts. To come about their compass with a searching mind. Do you not think?'

Frances was not sure; her thoughts had turned to Hew, and what danger he was in, if wittingly or not, he disobeyed the law.

'I meant rather, books which in some degree, offend the king, though they are in step wi' the true religion, and are well regarded by the Kirk. Do not look dismayed, mistress, there is no crime here, in the sight of God. The pity is, since my little charge is moving to the town, I no more shall have the pleasure of this library, which has been a joy to me, you cannot understand, and that besides the value of the rare forbidden books. You have no bairns, I suppose?' Gavan asked.

Frances shook her head. 'We are not married long.' Her hand flew, unconsciously, down to her lap. And he inquired, shrewdly, 'How many months?'

'Sir, I am not . . .'

'You misunderstand me. When were you wed?'

'Not long after Christmastide.'

'Aye? Whereabouts?'

'At the Holy Trinity.'

'Here, in the town?' The tutor sounded sceptical.

'In Minories in London. At St Botulph's, without.' They called it, too, the chapel of St Clare. But Frances did not like to think of that.

'Without what?' The humour in his voice did not reach his eyes. He was watching her, thoughtful.

'It means without the . . .'

Gavan cut across her as she started to explain. 'You do not need to say it. Never mind. And you keep my secret, I will keep yours.'

'What secret?' Frances asked.

164

'That I have made free with your guid man's books.'

That was not what she had meant. But Gavan changed the subject. 'Was there something you looked for? Did you want a book?'

'Pen and paper,' she admitted. 'For I came to write a letter.' She was astonished at the confidence with which he shared the library, as if it was his own. He took up the key and unlocked the lettroun, setting out before her paper, pens and ink, powder and penknife, sand and sealing wax. Staring at the page, of finest French paper, she found she could not write, could not shape her thoughts, which were complex and troubling, with Gavan in the room.

He noticed her confusion, offering his help. 'I cannot pretend to a ladies' touch, though I have written letters for my sisters to their friends; for one, to her betrothed.'

Frances coloured deeply at the word, 'betrothed', and hoped he did not see into the trouble in her heart.

'Though I cannot speak as to the sentiment, if you will but dare to say the words, you will find in me the perfect scribe. I can assure you, mistress. Hardly any blots,' he smiled at her, encouraging.

'I thank you, sir. I do not need your help. I am well able to write.' It came out sharper than she meant, for he took it for offence.

'Your pardon, mistress, pray, excuse my ignorance. It is not common, in this land, that a woman kens to write, and no shame in a wife, howsoever she may read, that she should use a scribe, to set down her meaning in a practised hand. Perhaps it is different in England, where there is a queen. Perhaps, where you come from, all women can write.'

'No. It is not different.' She could not tell if he was teasing her or not.

'Then *you* must be different,' he said.

'My uncle had me taught, that I might be a help to him. His business is cloth. I wrote his letters, and kept his accounts.'

'He must miss you, very much.'

'He wished that I should marry. It was his resolve.'

So much was true. And untrue, Frances thought. To her dismay, she felt the prick of tears. She must not let the young man see them drop. He had the kind cleric's heart, and that was rare enough. To discourage him, she said. 'I will write the letters later in my chamber. Will there be a post?'

'A post?'

'Someone I can send them by?'

'If you bring them by me I can take them to the town. Where are they directed?'

'To my family, in London.'

'That is harder, then.' He was thoughtful for a moment. 'I can find out, if you like, how a letter can be sent to London, in this straitened time. Perhaps there is someone at the college who will know. You could ask Professor Locke.'

Frances said, 'I could,' doubtful in her heart. She gathered up the paper, penknife, pens and ink, to take back to her chamber, where she might start again with it, in a braver mind. She had no will to write a letter, difficult and painful, which might not be sent. What means had she of sending it? She did not have the courage in her to apply to Giles.

Gavan simply nodded, picking up his book. 'Good luck with your letter, then. I will be here the morn again, if you want some help.'

Meg was in the garden, the children by her side. Matthew lay flat on his tummy in the soil. 'Look at this ant. He is carrying a leaf.'

'Your schoolmaster is here,' Frances said.

The small boy shook his head. 'It is not time for that.'

'It is almost time.' Meg grasped his waist and pulled him up again. 'Go and wash your hands. Ask Master Gavan what the Latin is, for an ant and a leaf.'

'I know those words already,' Matthew said. 'Mind you do not crush him, with your babby feet,' he warned his little sister, as he scuttled off.

Meg smiled at Frances. 'So, you have met our master Gavan Baird. What did you think of him?'

'He seemed a little ... forward,' Frances said. 'Is he to be trusted?'

Meg said, 'I should think so, else he would not be here. Giles took a great deal of care with his appointment. He asked the archbishop, Patrick Adamson – who is chancellor also of the university – and the reformer, Andrew Melville, who is principal of St Mary's, to recommend a man from the bursars in that college, to read Latin with his son. He asked them both for a list of those who were most disciplined, earnest and devout, and fixed upon the cause of the true religion, to inform his choice. Their lists did not agree, for those men are at odds. There was one man, alone, was warned against by both, because he had a light and undermining playfulness, and a lively wit, that neither of them thought becoming in a minister. That was Gavan Baird, and so, the one we picked.'

Frances was perplexed, at reasoning so perverse. She began a question, and then bit her tongue. For in this foreign place, where almost all she met with baffled in its turn, she no longer knew what ought to count as strange.

Hew woke to the dawn at his West Bow inn, and dressed in mourning clothes, which were set out at his bedside, solemn as a shroud. There were dark ribbons too, for dressing up his horse, and a little pot of blacking, to be smeared upon his spurs, lest they should cause offence by glinting in the sun. It seemed to him so impudent and naked a hypocrisy he blushed to put them on. What might have brought his deep unease about the Scots queen's death, outwardly expressed, a small sense of relief, relapsed in him instead to a muddy slough of guilt.

Word had come from court that the king would receive him later in the day. He breakfasted on beer, so brooding and morose that the serving lass wished him good luck for his funeral. And it might as well have been his own.

He settled his account, and came out to the stable yard to saddle up his horse. There he came across a mercer and his boy talking with the innkeeper.

'I do not understand,' the mercer said.

He was the sort of man who dealt in haberdashery, who kept a little shop, in a burgh market place, and travelled to buy goods for it, once or twice a year. The young lad by his side stood buckled under sacks full of trinkets from the krames, and slung across his shoulders were a dozen pots and pans, tied up on a rope. Backpacks and saddlebags littered the ground.

'There is no helping it, Jock,' the keeper of the inn did not meet the mercer's eye, but answered him obliquely. 'It isna up to me.'

'Leave it, Faither,' the young boy urged, tugging at his cloak, and struggling to connect through his impediment of pans. 'Dinna fight it now. Or ye will mak it worse.'

'How can it be worse?' his father snapped. 'It does not make sense. I should let it be, if there were any reason to it.'

'I have telt you the reason,' the innkeeper said. 'Now, it is out of my hands.'

'Do you not know me, Jim? Have I not come here, for years? Have I not slept, in your best feather bed? Summer an' winter, for seventeen year. Before this young snapper was born?'

The innkeeper shrugged. 'It vexes me too. What can a man dae? It's no up tae me.'

'Then who is it up to?' asked Jock.

'It is the law, you see. I canna serve an Englishman, nor hire to him a horse.'

'What Englishman?' the mercer roared. 'We are come fae Peebles, man! And, at the last account, Peebles was in Scotland. This boy is a Scot.'

'He may be, by troth. I do not say, he's not. But you came fae a place that was south o' the border, afore ye did marry your lass. That maks us enemies, Jock.'

'Twenty years since!' The mercer spat, disgusted, out into the dust.

'It is a pity, Jock. I do not say that it is not a pity. But I cannot gie ye a horse. And ask where'er ye will, an ye will hear the same. My advice to you now, as a friend, is leave your stuff here and go home, as swift and as shy as you like. Let your boy do the talking, and you are found. For if you care to linger here, ye will be strung up.'

'Aye, very like,' the mercer said bitterly. 'And how should I do that, without I have a horse?'

'You will have to walk.'

The mercer looked about to speak, and then, this glimpse of human nature finally defeating him, he picked up what he could, and slung it on his back. Hew was moved to ask, 'Sir, can I help you?'

'You can sell me your horse,' the mercer answered back.

Hew hesitated then. He caught sight the innkeeper shaking his head, and knew that if he did, he could not have another one. With regret, he said. 'I cannot, sir. I would, but I must go at once to the court.'

'For certain, sir, you must. Why should it be otherwise? For no doubt this whole city has to go to court today. We should be thankful, I doubt, ye rebuff us politely, and do not kick us down, to crawl off in the dust,' the mercer said to that.

The young boy whispered urgently, 'Whist, will you, Faither, we *should.*'

The keeper shook his head to watch them straggle off, hampered by their load of trinkets, jingling in the dust, a wry, discordant trail. 'That man has been coming here for nigh on twenty years. I count him as a friend. God speed him safely home. He will not come again.'

'Then why, in God's name, did you treat him so harshly?' asked Hew.

'Because, when I woke up this morning, I found this was pinned up on my door. "A letter to be borne abroad, by traitors harboured here".'

The innkeeper opened his hand and showed Hew a small piece of paper crushed in his palm. Wrapped up inside was a noose, made from a thin cord of hemp. On the paper was written a verse.

'To jezebel that English whore
Receive this Scottish chain
As presage of her great malheur
For murthering of our queen.'

Chapter 15

The Lion's Den

The king was in the deer park of the Douglas family, at their castle at Dalkeith. In mourning clothes, in Lent, his band of men and dogs were sorely out of place. His servants warned his Grace, for he had grown beyond the bairn who might have been refused. The keeper of the Douglas game was grieved to see his startled does drop out their lifeless fawns. 'All things have their season, sire.'

James could not be swayed. He knew that this perverse anomaly of men, cloaking nature's greenery in uncouth swathes of black, was moving to the time. What was that compared to the killing of a queen, where God's rule was reversed, and natural law sent spinning, burled upon its head? Dark, portentous times, when storm clouds would eclipse the cold conflicted skies, and split them from the earth, overturning nature by those cruel events.

His people would have frowned, to see him at the hunt. They would not have understood. For that reason, he had left the King's Park, and come to Dalkeith, where the walls were high, and the walks obscured. He put on sombre dress, reflective of the mood, and a convenient mask, hiding from the world. Mourning clothes were conscious, clever in their kind; the wearer wore his heart pinned upon his sleeve, or as he preferred it, buried in his cloak. Those who were the closest to him did not know his mind. It was not want of purpose that drove James to the field. It was not distraction from affairs at hand. It was not that he yearned for the taste of fresh meat, not that he had wearied, so early on in Lent, of the fish and fowl his cunning cooks prepared for him. Nor was it his intent to deplete the Douglas stock, which he would replenish gladly from his own. But the sharp morning air, the crisp wind of March, the sliver of bone and the necklet of blood, that circled the throat of the delicate hind, the droplets of dew on its gingerline hair, all of those cooled and stilled in his mind the tremble of passion, and power and excitement, the leaping and flux of his own beating heart. An exaltation clarified, and helped to hold his mind in that place of balance where his course was clear, where he kept his nerve.

'Enough,' he told the gamekeeper. 'And sin it is the Lent, this deer shall feed the dogs.' He walked back to the house, his carnage left behind.

At Dalkeith, he had assembled with a small band of men. Maitland, the foremost in his government, secretar and chancellor, rarely left his side at this exacting time. There was set up a council chamber in the hall of the castle, where the lords could meet, and where Maitland read and attended to the business of the court. Beyond that were more private chambers, reserved for the use of the king, for what purpose could console him in his present grief. Here the king retired, to rest and change his clothes, which were a little spotted from the bleeding harts. On an ordinary day, he would not have cared. But he had lately learned, from a lady at the court, that the kings of France wore purple mourning dress, '*pour encourager les pauvres*, your Grace. A king should be solemn; he should not be sad.' He was struck by the idea to adopt it as his own, and his new velvet suit had only just arrived. He trusted it would lift him high above the crowd, and send a flutter of dismay to the English Queen Elizabeth.

Maitland came in, with papers in his hand, and if he was disturbed by the king's display of plumage, he was practised not to show it. 'We maun answer, your Grace, to the English queen's ambassadors, whether we will meet with them at Berwick. As I contend, we must.'

'We must, of course,' the king agreed. 'Not yet. This smart is too sore, too poignant and too raw to us. Tell them, we are thrawn by it, that we are compelled to settle the unrest it stirs up in our people, who marvel that a queen and mother of this house, thrown upon the mercy of a foreign state, should be captive there, and murdered by its prince, against the laws of nature, and of hospitality. Say, willing though we are to hear Elizabeth's excuse – for none shall be condemned, *by us*, without a proper trial – we cannot read her letter, at the present time. Nor, in good conscience, can we see her ambassadors, or allow them to pass, where we cannot vouch for safety of their lives.'

'Do I dare to ask,' the chancellor enquired, 'how long you intend to refuse the queen her letters?'

'As long as shall seem strange to her, and good enough to us. An envoy will be sent to the border in due course. But we shall not be quick to come to terms. The people would resent it, for one. And while their hot blood cools, her Grace shall have more time to think upon her fault, and how she may amend her broken trust with us,' the king replied, aloof. He was at that moment in complete control.

'Very good, your Grace.' Maitland hesitated. 'They tell me that the man is here, you were keen to see. I have the picture, too, sent down to us from Holyrood. But, sire, I cannot help but fear you think too much of it. It is a thriftless, trifling thing, of no import or consequence. Ye mauna be distracted by it, at this present time.'

James said, 'Believe me, we would not. But it is a thing that creeps into our mind, and causes the distraction there. And, as I believe, it cannot be assuaged, until the cause is found, and forcibly removed. You tell me, tis of no account. And yet, you cannot give me any explanation for it, to dispel the doubt. Your investigations, all of them, are worthless in this case, and your pleas are trumperous.'

Maitland said uneasily. 'We have tried, your Grace.'

'I did not say you had not tried. I said that you had failed. Wherefore, I have called a man who has a searching intellect, more acute than yours. Please me. Show him in.'

Hew was shown at last into the presence of the king. He had waited for three hours at the castle at Dalkeith, before he was admitted there. At the close of each hour, he was taken further in, and allowed to come a little closer to that place where he would be received if the king allowed him audience. It did not make a difference that he had been called.

He understood, of course, that this was more than he deserved. It was nothing untoward, and was not meant as an expression of the king's displeasure at his time away. It was not, in fact, to do with Hew at all, but simply the reflection, rather than reminder, that he was there to await the king's will, outranking any pleasure of his own. He was left to stand, and no one spoke to him, after he had passed through every level of obstruction, and cohort of defence, between him and his goal.

At the West Bow inn, he had dreamt, the night before, of a trance of doors, through which he had passed, endlessly and on, each one with a lock in which a key had turned, and each key had turned with a single sound that he had strained to hear, like a beetle's click that moving further off came quieter and quieter, until the key clicked soundlessly, but left an echo still, when all the doors were closed, and all the beetles gone. And where he came at last, he had found the king, standing on a box. The king had been a puppet, worked by Francis Walsingham.

This dream came back to him, so vivid in its shape as he knelt down to his lord, that he was grateful for the floor to swallow up his smile. He waited for the king to speak, to beckon and to welcome him, to offer him the wafting air around his hand to kiss, or to call in the guard, to have him clapped in irons. What happened next was none of those things. For it was Maitland who spoke. 'Mind me, your Grace, who is this man?'

The chancellor had come to power after James had freed himself from the lord enterprisers, and from Gowrie's governance. Most of the court was under his control; he would not lose his grip, nor permit a danger to pass by undetected, at this taxing time. The council was at best an uneasy coalition, on the brink of fracture; now it had been driven to the brittle edge. Maitland kept the whole intact, never lax or absent, so that nothing was put past without his seal or ken. It had brought him to exhaustion, wrung out in the interests of his country and his king. Then it was little wonder he suspected Hew.

'Your Grace maun have patience wi' me. I was not in office when this man defected. I have no understanding, what were his crimes.'

'He committed no crime. It was a misunderstanding. He was indicted on a false charge brought by John Colville. It was not maliciously meant. Since I have pardoned Colville, I have pardoned those lords who overstepped their mark to assist the earl of Gowrie, I have pardoned the irksome and unruly presbyters, and I have pardoned Hew. We have moved on,' the king said, and Hew, as he knelt on the cold of the stone, found his heart leapt at the words.

'Not without a trial,' Maitland insisted. 'None has been restored, without examination. He must go to trial. Or, at least, must give an account of himself, before the Privy Council.'

The king dismissed this, with a wave of his hand. 'Aye, I shall consider it, at some other time. My lord, and I thank you, you must go home. I fear you will fall ill for lack of rest. Go, and I pray you, good Maitland. I will do nothing, you maun ken, without your counsel. Our minds are alike, be assured.'

'As your Grace commands. I will wait without, for I shall not leave your side.' Maitland, as he bowed, turned his eye to Hew, critical and sceptical. 'Tell me, sir, were you one of those who followed after Ruthven, or one of those who threatened the episcopacy?'

'He was neither,' smiled the king. 'He is a lone adventurer, who follows his own heart, and is no one's man. He has shown himself full of spirit and courage. He has a knack of finding things out. And I mistook for treachery, what was the perplexity of a searching mind.'

Maitland said dryly, 'I look forward with some pleasure to hearing his adventures, in the council chamber. Where, I have no doubt, he will illuminate us all.'

As the chancellor departed, James regarded Hew, kneeling on the floor, several feet in front of him.

'Well. Here you are,' he said. Will you not rise up, and let me see your face. You mauna mind Maitland. He is perplexed, at this vexing time. As to whether you will go to face him at your trial, that must be a question for another day. I have something first that I would have you do. I ken no other man that shows himself as fit for it.'

The king had grown up from the bairn that Hew had known before. He had seen him last, a scared boy of sixteen by the lion house at Holyrood, cowering from the lords who harried him like crows. Now he sat in the house they had called 'the Lion's Den', when Morton had command, strategy, not cowardice, marking his retreat. He had grown through the years of frustration and rebellion to a shrewd, patient prince. He was nervous, slight, fair and slender still. Yet this was a young man on the verge of flight. The nervousness in him was no longer fear, but the pulsing of excitement. In three or four months' time, he would come to his majority. The queen of Scots was dead. He was owed a debt of conscience by Elizabeth; he saw the world ahead, tantalising, glinting, just beyond his grasp. If he kept his nerve, his confidence, and waited, it would come to him.

'I am glad to see you here,' he said. 'For you have the wit to solve a certain matter, troubling to my mind. Run boy,' he told a little page, who waited on his word, 'and bid the Lord Chancellor send in the picture.'

'What picture, your Grace?' Hew felt a shiver of fear. He could not have explained it. This was a calmer, more confident king, whose demeanour did not cause alarm.

'You shall see it, when it comes. Tell me, sir, is it not strange, that a queen take the life of an anointed monarch, trusted to her care?' the king turned back to him. 'They tell me, she will plead her innocence in this, that though she signed the warrant leading to the death, her council went against her, for it was not meant to be acted on presumptuously; it was but an assurance, to secure herself. So it is reported, for I have not found the time to attend to her ambassadors, to hear in her own words, how she might defend the singular unkindness of this wicked crime. You were in England. What have you heard? This wound is fresh to me. They telt me, they severed her neck, at the blow of that English queen's axe. Can it really be so?'

176

Hew could not meet his eye. 'I do not know, your Grace. It grieves my heart, to think it. When I was in England, I met with her Grace.'

'You met with Queen Elizabeth?'

The king's interpretation showed his true intent, where his thoughts had strayed, to that greater prize. And Hew did not know how to answer him.

'Not the Queen Elizabeth.' He thought, but could not say, I could not meet Elizabeth, for she moves in such spheres so far above my own – and yours – that I should be eclipsed by her, or dazzled by her sun, for such a frank confession would not sit well with the king. Hew had once caught a glimpse of the queen of England's barge, sedate and gilded paragon, gliding down the Thames, and that was bright enough. 'I was never,' he excused himself, 'at the English court.'

'But you served her, did you not, in the Netherlands? We had despatches sent, from her Secretary Walsingham. Will you tell me now, you never met with him?' James demanded then.

This was awkward too. But Hew could answer truthfully. 'I met with Frances Walsingham. He did not like me much.'

His answer pleased the king. 'Shall I confess a secret to you? Nor does he like me. Then we shall bask together, in the glare of his displeasure, for we do not like him. So. You did not meet Elizabeth. Who else did you meet?'

'Your Grace ... the queen of Scots.' Hew stumbled with the words. He could not think how to style the dead queen to her son. He had begun to say, to mean, 'Your Grace's lady mother,' when he realised that he could not call her that, that *mother* was too rude, too intimate a word, to say to such a king, of someone he had never loved, and barely ever met. He was twenty years old. His bairnly affections had grown, to a young man's indifference. His callousness had reached its prime; he had not been so hard before, nor would be again.

It was reckless, he knew. The king did not want to hear his mother's name, to fill the empty letters with her flesh and blood, not kenning her before, would want it all the less, now that she was dead. But Hew could not forget the shadow on her face, the shape of her voice as she spoke of her son. And James, despite himself, was readily enthralled, with a kind of horror, easily drawn in. 'Tell me.' All men follow ghosts, when they do not want to see, when they do not want to hear the whisper of their breath. They cannot help themselves. Hew felt that queen's hand, puffy, soft, on his. He felt upon his head the blessing she bestowed on him.

'It was at a place called Buckstanes, where folk go to take the waters. She had come there for her health. My employer, William Phillips, was afflicted with a palsy, and he required of me to take him to the baths. The guest house there belongs to the earl of Shrewsbury, who at that time had the keeping of her. I met her at the bath. She saw my name in the book, and asked to speak with me.'

'And I suppose,' James scowled, 'she made complaint to you. For what she wrote to us, was fulsome in complaint. Did she complain of me?'

'No, your Grace.' Hew was at a loss what to tell the king. He could not say, 'For when I saw her there, she still had hopes of you.' There seemed no tactful answer to the question. He answered therefore with another kind of truth. 'She asked after the health of your Grace. If you were well, and grew strong. She said she had your picture in a glass, but it was very old, and she would like another.'

'Did she say that?' James reflected, 'That is oddly pertinent. We had pictures made last year. As I believe, she asked for a copy through the French ambassador. I do not recall if one was ever sent. We had one of her. It was done some years ago, when I was a bairn. But no one seems to ken now where it might be kept. Put away, perhaps.'

His cool indifference to it moved Hew to remark, 'My mother died when I was six. I have no picture of her.' He could see that queen still, vivid in his mind.

James raised an eyebrow. 'So?'

'They say my sister Meg is the living image of her.'

'*Well*, then.' James did not say, I do not care about your mother, or your living sister. For he did not have to. 'This is better than I thought. Since you have seen the queen, more recently than most who are present at the court, you can offer an opinion on a matter of contention.'

He beckoned to his page, who had returned with a packet tied round with string. 'This is how it came to us. Take it up, and look. It was sealed with a small lump of wax, that bore no impression, and was broken off. All else about it was exactly as you see.'

Hew turned the packet over in his hands. A smudge of the wax remained still, daubed like a thumb prick of blood. Besides that, the paper was clean. It bore the direction, in a clear neat hand, 'To his mjty the king, in hansell for this good new year'.

'It came to us,' the king explained, 'as a New Year gift. The picture was left at the gatehouse at Holyrood, among a parcel of confitures and sweetmeats collected by the people who dwell by us in the Canongate, to be given out among the poor folk in the town. It was found by the guard, who brought it in to us. Open it.'

Wrapped up in the paper was a pleated picture, painted on a board a foot or so in length, furrowed into folds of lines of dark and light. Hew turned the panel side from side, yet could make no sense of it.

'And you would have perspective on it, gave it to the child,' said James. Hew passed the picture back to the little page, who lifted it aloft, and tilting it aslant a little turned it to the left, with an ease that demonstrated he was practised at the trick. The pleated strips of paint were smoothed into a plane, and a woman's face appeared, pallid, stiff and strange, but clear and unmistakable. A dark red coif of hair, a painted flush of colour at the cheek and lip, a fleshly jowl descending to a crisp starched ruff.

'Now,' said James, 'the other side.'

The child turned the panel smoothly to the right, so slick and sly a turn Hew scarcely saw the trick of it, as though the little boy had been the only conjuror. Before his captive gaze, the face became a skull, the ruff a piece of mantle cloth, the woman's velvet gown the board on which it sat. There were hollows in the place of those sad and knowing eyes, a jagged rope of bone in place of her prim smile.

The pictures were effected with a stark economy, that made their statement blunt, though none the less ambiguous.

'It is a turning picture. Of a woman and a death's-head. Is it not ingenious?' The king let slip a smile, no more than a flicker at the corner of his mouth, masking at its heart a hard core of distaste. 'And we should like to have the man who made it here at court, that we might try his wits, and find out what he meant by it. It appears quite singular, as a New Year's gift.'

'Most singular,' Hew agreed. 'You do not ken who sent it?'

'The sender and the painter of it we should like to ken, most dearly, I confess to you, for we are in the dark on it, and ignorant of both. And so, sir, to the question. Since you saw her last, and have her image printed freshly on your mind, is the likeness hers?'

Chapter 16

Perspectives

There was nothing in the portrait, sparse as it was, that led him to conclude it could not be the queen, though coarse and crudely drawn. The white of the skin, the height of the brow, the length of the nose, the slight fleshly sinking below the right cheek, could well be hers, as could the clear sad gaze, though stripped of any headpiece, artefact and ornament. And if she looked in truth a sober sort of Puritan, that was but the measure of the pleated picture, which would brook no brightness to inflect the skull. The palate was a simple one, the image plain and stark. Yet, for all its plainness, the meaning was obscure.

'I do not think,' Hew said, 'that this can be an image of the queen, *taken from the life*. It is hard to say, for any likeness there is thrawn by the device. There is no mark or sign identifying her. But that is not to say, that though whoever painted it never saw her Grace, it was not meant for her.' Its appearance at the court, he thought, made it more than likely. For even if the painter never had intended to depict the queen, her image was imprinted on it, irreversibly, by whoever brought it to the notice of the king.

The king was pleading, almost. 'Tell us what it means.' The picture had exerted an uneasy force on him, upsetting the resolve that settled in his mind. It made his heart unsure again.

Hew recalled the rings that he seen in Heriot's shop. 'Could it be, perhaps, a *memento mori* gift, offered to your Grace in mourning for the queen? That nothing might be meant, but a kindness there.'

'Aye, but at the New Year, she was not yet dead,' James reminded him.

Hew considered this. The queen, though not yet dead, was certain then to die. Seen in such a light, the painting might become a premonition, or a warning sign. What struck him most of all was its effect upon the king. Taken from its sphere, the picture spun eccentrically. It was not like a cipher, or a riddle to be read. Its meaning was impossible, opaque. In one sense, it was endlessly, essentially ambivalent. Should it be perceived to be a threat, a comfort or reproach? That depended solely on the colour of his mind, the spirit of the heart that was reflected in it. Then the painting was a glass, that held no other conscience but the one that looked in it. Yet in another sense, it was unequivocal. The message there was plain. It said simply, this is all you are, and all that you will be. Flesh and bone and dust.

'You wish me to find out, who sent this to your Grace, and with what intent,' he said. 'I will do my best.'

'Our fear is, there is witchcraft in it,' James confessed. 'For the strange effects it works upon our mind. We pray it is not so. And, we have been told, you have had some practice in unfolding strange events. For we have heard a story of a bleeding hawthorn tree, that they say was planted by this fated queen.'

The king knew in his heart the picture was bewitched. Or how could it prick and unsettle his conscience, when he knew that his mind was quite stern and fixed? And how could it awake him, clinging to his sheets, with the whistle of an axe, sheering through the white stem of a mother's neck? When it was nothing but a board, of paint and blood and bone.

Hew had caught a glimpse of the fragile bairn in him, surfacing again, and did the best he could to put his mind at rest. 'That was human mischief, sire. There was no witchcraft, there. And I will contend, there will be none here. Whatever is the source of this, I will find it out. Tell me, have you shown this to the painter at your court? Bronckhorst, is his name?'

'Bronckhorst?' James frowned. 'Why do you mention him? That was a man that painted here once, when I was a bairn. We have another now. And, as I believe, this was shown to him, but he could give no help. Maitland will inform you, and give you a paper, that will give you leave to act upon on our will.'

It was clear enough that the king's part in this was not to answer questions. Nor did he expect them. 'Take the picture too. Do it, for our thanks, and whatever gift that we can grant to you, to recompense the years when you were lost to us,' he offered in return, gracious in release.

'Your Grace,' Hew dared to say, 'there is one favour, I would ask of you. I hope to have a wife.'

'Aye, indeed you should. They tell me, wives are grand.' The relief upon the king, of the removal of the picture, was palpable to Hew, as though he had passed on some vicious threat or curse. Its transfer lightened him.

'She is the niece,' Hew went on, 'of a customer of wool.'

'And what is the niece of a customer of wool, to do with us?'

'She is an English lass, your Grace.'

James shook his head. 'Absolutely not. We cannot have that, now. Now, at this present time, that would be disastrous. It would cause an outrage, if we made a law, and another, just for you. Put that thought from your mind.'

'Then you maun call your guard, and have me put in chains. For I love her, sire.'

'You are,' sighed the king, 'a very stubborn loun. Is that your only price? You will not have a title, or a piece of land? I can make you deputy to Sir Andrew Wood.'

'Your Grace is kind, but no.'

'You will understand, we cannot grant you licence at this present time,' James said. 'But when you have resolved the matter in your hand, then we may consider it. You can look upon it,' he was merry now, relieved of the trouble he had passed to Hew, 'as a kind of quest.'

Hew departed there, hopeful in his heart, that leapt upon a mystery. He felt an old excitement that had not been stirred in him since he came from London, wiping for the moment all his other cares. Before he quit Dalkeith, the chancellor Maitland gave to him a paper with a seal confirming he was acting as an agent for the king. This should smooth his path, when he knew what path to take. The painter to the court seemed to him the place most likely to begin. Maitland was no help, and in no way had relaxed in his suspicions towards Hew. He drew up the document without a word. Only once he had ratified it, with the king's seal, did he condescend to interrogate him.

'Sir Andrew Wood reported that you were set upon, on your way to trial. The rebels confessed, and were hanged, I am told. It was thought they had left you for dead.'

'I thought so myself,' answered Hew, with more than a hint of the truth, for there had been a moment, when he was pulled from his horse in the black of Dysart muir, when he had despaired that he would even see the sun, before he had known they were Andrew Wood's men; nor had it reassured him, when he understood.

'Those are lawless parts. And Andrew Wood has fought well to have kept a hold on them. You were blessed,' Maitland said, 'to escape with your life.'

'Just so,' admitted Hew.

'But what I cannot understand – you maun help me here – is how you got away from there. Without you were helped. With neither sound nor sight of you, for all the hue and cry. How came you then to London?'

'My mother's kin had friends at Berwick, who helped me on my way,' said Hew. 'You will excuse it, I am sure, if I do not name their names.'

'Aye, but even so. It is a long walk to Berwick for a wanted man. A man who has no horse, no water or fresh clothes. A man who is weakened from his late imprisonment, and injured in an ambush – grievously injured, so we have been told, and doubtless is frail for want of food. Are we to suppose that such a man would walk to Berwick?'

'Many have walked there, on the old pedlars' route, pilgrims and cadgers, old men and paupers with loads on their backs. Through wind and hail, and with snow underfoot. Some of them died there, many did not,' answered Hew.

'Do you mean to say you joined the dustifutes?' Maitland looked incredulous. But it was not impossible. If Hew had lain low in the woods and fields, had lived on the land on the late autumn fruits, till the cry had died down and his fresh wounds had healed, he could have joined the packmen winding their way home from the last of the late autumn markets, once the bright branches were withered to black. What man would have questioned him then?

Hew risked a wink at him. 'What wad ye expect, of one who is a venturer?'

The secretary sniffed. 'What, indeed? And when ye tell us your adventures, in the council chamber, we shall be transfixed. You should ken, sir, that I hold out no hope that you shall solve this case. The council has made a thorough inquisition of it. Nothing came to light.'

'Perhaps,' suggested Hew, 'it wants a fresh perspective.'

Maitland stared at him. 'Do you find it merry, sir? Is that some sort of jest?'

'No. Indeed no. Can you tell me,' Hew capitulated hurriedly, 'is the king's painter at court?'

'Why would he be here? You think that he is wanted, at the present time? While the country is in turmoil, and the king beset with grief? Perhaps you think he should be painted in his mourning clothes?'

'Then can you tell me where I might find him?'

'Find him out yourself. Is that not your charge? Are you not, indeed, a kenning kind of man? Were you not employed, to sniff the devil out?'

Hew took his cue and parted from him, leaving with a bow.

The next morning, he returned to George Heriot's shop. George was pleased to see him. 'I had not expected you to come back so soon. I have from my father a pure lump of gold, from the Crawford mine, which I put with yours, and which will make for you the bonniest of rings.' He showed to Hew a piece of fair white gold, tried upon the touchstone. 'That is quite perfect,' Hew approved. 'And I have the verse.' It had come to him the night before, as he lay in bed. He had borrowed pen and paper from the West Bow innkeeper, and had set it down. Now he produced it shyly, as though it were a cipher to be torn to shreds by Phelippes. Heriot merely glanced at it, to make sure of the script. 'Nice. The last line only, will fit on the ring, unless you want four parts,' he said.

'That will do well enough,' answered Hew. 'I have some questions for you. You said you had a market for *memento mori* rings. I suppose you cannot tell me who you sold them to?'

Heriot said, 'On no account.'

Hew was not surprised. 'And suppose I put the question to you, on the king's authority?' It was well, he thought, to keep this till the last. For the paper with the king's seal was as likely to tie up a tongue, as it was to loosen it, coming between friends.

'The answer,' Heriot said, 'would be just the same. If the king wants to ken, let him come here himself, and sit on my bench, and I will tell to him the same thing I will say to you. I will not gie away my clients' names. Why, sir, would you have me tell the world about your English rose?'

Hew owned, he would not. He trusted that the goldsmith kept his word of secrecy, common to his trade. Urquhart kept his secrets too, and did not fear the king, for goldsmiths had the power to keep him in their debt, and in their close economy, their interests chimed with his. This Heriot was a novice in his craft, but Hew had little doubt that he would soon be master of it.

'Can you tell me this? Where could I go to buy a turning picture? One that plays upon perspective, like a prism in a glass?'

Geordie could not say. He was puzzled at the question, and Hew could believe that he had never come across the picture he described. 'I never saw a thing like that. You might ask the king's painter perhaps. I can tell you where to find him.'

Hew had hoped he might. He paid him for the ring, not knowing, for the moment, when he would be back for it.

'It will be ready in a week. If you have the time, to come and have a drink on it, I will tell you a grand tale, about your Largo gold. I had it fae my faither,' Heriot smiled.

'I will hear it, and will drink with you, when you have the ring. For now, I must be gone,' Hew said. 'The quicker to my business, the quicker to be done.'

The painter Adrian Vanson kept a house and shop close by the Netherbow, adjacent to the Canongate, where so many Flemish refugees had settled, and not far from the printer's shop, that once was Christian Hall's. Christian had left there to migrate to London. Hew had once looked out for her, wistful, at St Paul's, but had not found her there. In a little close, not far from the place where he had gone to school, the painter's house, without direction, would have proved impossible to find.

The door was opened by a woman in a loose linen kirtle, striped at the skirt in a pale shade of blue. She had straw coloured hair, pinned up in a cap, and a broad, plain face.

'Yes,' she said. 'What it is that you want?' in the clear and open manner of the Dutch.

'I am looking for Adrian Vanson, the painter,' said Hew.

'So. What do you want with him?'

'I have come from the king, on business of the court.' He showed her the letter, with the royal signature. The woman barely blinked at it, remaining unimpressed. 'So. You have come from the court. It is too much to hope, that you have brought the money with you that still is owed to us. Of course, you have not.'

'Is there money owed to you?'

'Of course. And of course, you have not come for that. Do not say, you will look into it.'

He bit back the promise shaping on his lips.

'Other men have promised that they will look into it. If they kept to their word, they have not done more than to look.'

'I am sorry for that,' answered Hew. 'But on the king's command, I must speak with Master Vanson.'

The woman sighed. 'So you have said. I am Susanna, his wife. You had better come in.'

He followed her into the house, a single chamber neat and clean with plain whitewashed walls. An iron pot bubbled on the hearth; Hew recognised the scent of Flemish beef or mutton, stewing in a broth of ale, deep and rich and black. The board was set for four with bowls and pewter spoons, a large loaf of bread and a pat of yellow butter, in a little dish of Flemish tin-glazed pottery. The windows were dressed with squares of white lace, and the shelves of the press were lined and trimmed with it. Onto one of the walls, where the light from the window fell, soft and aslant, the painter had nailed up a single small picture, of a woman's face. There was no doubt in Hew's mind that it was Susanna, in the bloom of youth.

'His workshop is across the yard. You have come at an opportune time. Tell him, his dinner is here. When he is fixed at his work, he will not remember to eat.'

The house backed on a yard, in which there stood a kiln and rows of jars and pots, leading to a shed. Inside, the painter stood, grinding yellow pigment on a slab of stone. Stacked against the walls were rows of boards and canvases, and among them, several further studies of the painter's wife, the swell of her broad hips and breasts, tenderly captured in chalk. At the back of the room, in the best of the light, two prentices sat at their work.

Hew introduced himself, and unwrapped the painting from its paper case. The painter sighed. 'Not that, again. As I told the council, I cannot help you here. I have no idea, where this thing is coming from.'

'What about your boys?' asked Hew.

Vanson chuckled. 'Them? You think that they are capable? Let me tell you, then. Come over here and see.'

Each had drawn an apple to be coloured in with paint, one from a painting pinned up on his board, and one from a pippin set out on a plate.

'The one is a copy and the other from the life,' Vanson explained. 'It is a test.' He did not say of what.

'It will be apparent to you, they know nothing yet. This one, it is true has a modicum of skill,' he gestured to the pupil sitting on the right, who was filling in his apple with a vivid shade of green, 'but he is a wastrel and an idle little sot. He would rather spend his time at the tavern with the wenches than do any work for me. The other one is diligent, and he says his prayers, but he is a dolt.' The boy on the left sat sucking on his paintbrush; he had muddled up his colours to a muddy shade of grey, and appeared uncertain how he should progress. The master painter sighed. 'It seems it must be beyond hope, that diligence and skill should meet in the one boy. What am I to do? You shall be a burgess and a freeman, so they told me, if you take apprentices, and teach our boys to paint. This is what they send me. What hope do I have? Am I to beat them? What good does it do? The doltish one will be a dolt, whatever I will do, because he cannot help it. The wicked one will mend his ways but for a day or two, and will grow resentful and sly. Besides, I have my work to do. I do not have time to beat unruly boys.'

Hew expressed his sympathy. 'How long have they been with you?'

'The stupid one, a year. His sluggard friend, five months. But since the one is simple-minded, and the other evil-minded, they are no further forward than the first day that they came.'

Hew felt a little sorry for the young apprentices, who listened all the while, but with so still an air of ease and cheerfulness he saw they were not hurt by it. Their master's verbal railings, surer than his blows, rained down on them unheard; one did not understand, the other did not heed. They accepted with good grace the failings he assigned to them. Quite likely understanding, that it was not meant. 'Wash off your palette, and begin again, with nothing but the green,' the master told the prentice who had muddled up his paints, with a patient kindness that laid bare his gentle heart.

The other boy leant back, turning on his stool. 'What d'ye think of mine?'

'Yours?' Vanson shook his head. 'I will tell you what I think of it, when you have redeemed yourself. When you have atoned for the thing that you have done. I will tell you what I think. And I will tell you now, that it will not be good.'

The young apprentice grinned at this, not at all abashed. It felt like the rehearsal of an old familiar comedy, played out to the gallery before a cheerful audience, to little great effect.

'What has he done, then?' asked Hew.

'Ask him, if you will. How many apples were there here this morning? He will not deny to you that there were two.'

Then for all the bluff, this boy was Vanson's favourite; he had taken both.

'I was hungry,' said the boy, with a seraphic smile.

'Hungry! Do we not feed you enough? You cannot conceive, sir, how these boys eat. They are like bird babies, with their open beaks. They feast at my table like the sons of kings. They turn up their noses at cabbage and pork fat. These must have manchet and meat.'

'Your wife said to tell you your dinner was ready,' Hew was reminded at that. The prentices looked up. And they might be hungry, Hew supposed; if they kept to the hours that were common to prentices, their dinner was half an hour late.

'We will not stop to eat while there is light to paint,' the painter asserted, deaf to the protests of the two apprentices. 'This gentle man has brought you a lesson in perspective. Come, take a look.'

Hew showed the pleated picture, and observing their reactions, came to the conclusion that neither was as doltish or as idle as their master had pretended, and that neither had ever seen the work before. They examined it together, with a will and curiosity, working out in minutes how the thing was made.

'Two pictures,' said one, 'cut into strips, and mounted onto prisms cut out from blocks.'

'Or else,' said the other, 'the triangles are set in a turning frame, and the pictures painted with the sides turned flat.'

Either method, Vanson said, was sound.

'Can we make one, too?'

'Not till you have mastered the basics of perspective. Go now, to your dinners. Tell Mistress Susanna I will be there in a while.'

'They are good boys,' he admitted as the young men clattered out. 'Though it does no good to let them hear me say it. They will, in due course, make passable painters. But neither of them has the skill to make a piece like that.'

Hew did not doubt him. 'Who has?'

'In Scotland?' Vanson pursed his lips. 'That I should not like to say. Any painter might, who had served his time, if it was a copy; but a thing of this kind had no beginning here. There is but one man in Scotland who can paint a portrait, sir, and you are looking at him. Be that as it may, I hope you will not think that a painting of mine could be so crude as that.'

And Hew, glancing at the sketches of his wife Susanna, found he did not think it, though he knew that Vanson's boasting could not be quite true. 'Are there no others here could invent such a trick?'

'Not,' answered Vanson, 'at this present time. Bronckhorst, perhaps, had he set his mind to it. But I would dare to swear to it, that it is not his work. And he is here no longer, since he left your country, three or four years back. He was not happy here. He was the king's painter, when he was a bairn. And that, you may be sure, was a thankless task.'

'Why do you say that?'

Vanson smiled. 'His Grace is a restless soul, who does not care to sit. And, when he does, he does not pay his bills.'

'But there are other painters, surely, at the court?'

'There are one or two. David Workman and his sons. And the Binnings too. And they are good, what you call, decorative painters. They can paint a coffin or a coat of arms. They can paint a door. If you want a banner, Binning is your man. But you will not find a Scotsman who can make a likeness. They do not have training for that. Who is to there to teach them? If I have a son, who wants to be a painter, I will send him to Italy. Not to Antwerp now. Antwerp is finished.'

'Is that where you are from? I was there last year. Antwerp is a ghost town. The Protestants have fled the town. And the Scheldt is blocked,' Hew said.

If Vanson was from Antwerp, then perhaps he had been part of the first and savage routing of the refugees, meeting with Susanna somewhere further north. Then, he might be drawn into a deeper confidence, if Hew could win his trust. For what he said about the Workman family could not quite be true. What about the boy, and his subtle brush, that snatching at Giles Locke, had caught him to the life? Perhaps Vanson's views were coloured, by professional jealousy?

Though Vanson's eyes were dimmed a little, he did not respond. Whatever he had left, he did not wish to be reminded of it. He shrugged his shoulders. 'I should care, now. Now my home is here. But Italy is where you will learn about perspective. Vignola has put it in a book, and I will have a copy sent for, for these idle boys, whenever they have mastered how to draw a piece of fruit. Which God knows for sure will not be some time soon. As for Antwerp, shall I tell you what will come from Antwerp? The engravers will be busy making pictures for the books, that will make a martyr of the Scottish queen. They will show the blade as it shivers her white neck, and every other mark of idolatrous hypocrisy. Whatever they come up with, it will not look like this, it will be, do you see, more subtle and insinuating, supple and persuasive as the serpent's tongue. Whatever you may think of it, however it may stir you, *this* is coarse and crude.'

'Which makes me think,' said Hew, 'it has not come so far. There is a John Workman at St Andrews, employed as a painter at the university.'

'Doubtless, Davy's son. Workman by name, workmen by nature,' Vanson said impassively. 'He will do a good job.'

'He is painting a portrait of our college principal.'

'That I find hard to believe. A Workman never painted such a likeness in his life. They are not portrait painters. For what reason should they be, since they are Scots? He is likely to make a poor fist of it.'

'He has with him a prentice boy, who is deaf and dumb. I heard that he can paint a little,' Hew ventured, carefully. Vanson stared at him. 'John Workman has a prentice, now? I had not heard of that. Now that, indeed, is news.'

Chapter 17

Painters' Colours

On market day, Meg left her children home with Canny Bett and walked with Frances to the town. They did not take Robert Lachlan, who, Meg insisted, would attract more trouble than he kept away. 'You will be safe enough with me.'

Frances was inclined to believe her. The country people who had called in at the house to consult with Meg looked upon her with a superstitious reverence. It was not because she was the wife of a physician, whose philosophy and art were not the same as hers; her remedies were based in nature, Giles Locke's on the art and understanding of the elemental humours, set down by the ancients. Often, they were brought together, in a pleasing concord, when Meg's own prescriptions chimed and tuned with his, and when that was the case, there was no one Giles Locke trusted better than his wife. Occasionally, they disagreed, on such contentious issues as the swaddling of a child, the cutting of a tooth, the colic or the croup, the danger to the infant stomach of a piece of fruit. On such occasions, generally, Meg had her way, and her little children were the safer and the stronger for it. Her physic she had learned from a country nurse, who when she was a child had taught her how to keep at bay the falling sickness to which she was thrawn. Frances had no doubt that woman was a witch.

The plants that Meg grew in the Kenly Green gardens formed the basis of her herbal remedies, and she showed to Frances the beds of herbs and flowers, the jars in the distillery, and in the drying room. The spices and the oils, she bought from the apothecar. June was the month when the medicines were made, the herbs in full flower, the pickle jars filled with bright buds of broom. By March, the stocks which had lasted through bleak months of winter were thin, and the shelves of the still house threadbare. Meg had made a shopping list of button thread and silks, and several yards of cloth, of sugar loaf and saffron, which were running low. 'Those we shall have at the apothecar. He is a stranger here, and not much liked in town. He came in, a newcomer, after the plague.'

Her words caused a pang of discomfit in Frances. Were all strangers unwelcome here? In London, she had met with a melling mix, of Muscovites and Frenchman, blackamoors and Turks. Though some people looked upon them with suspicion, they brought music and song with them, stories and dance.

She was thankful, still, to come at last to town. They walked inland, through the fields, and along a narrow track, where the country people came with their butter and their cheese, and the candle makers with their tallow wax, and through a busy harbour choked with little boats, where the shrieking gulls picked trails of fish from slabs. They came out from an archway that was called the Pends, to the apex of a wide uncluttered street, lined upon each side by an avenue of trees, shaking out their green buds, in a brisk sea breeze. This, Meg explained, was the South Gate. To its east, the ruin of the cathedral yearned towards a sky of billowing white cloud, from which the town swept west in three converging thoroughfares, and four converging streets – the South Street and the Mercat Gate, the North Street and the Swallow Gate, falling to the cliffs and its castle on its rock. Between them were the run and rigs that held an inner life, of cookshops, inns and taverns, gardens, sheds and shops, and in this grid enclosed the compass of the town.

They walked from the cathedral to the college of St Leonard, closed behind its walls. 'We cannot go in, now, or we shall find the students at their private prayers. But on Sundays, we can come into the chapel there, which is our parish kirk. Then the college sits apart. It is a kinder kirk, than the Holy Trinity,' said Meg. 'For the elders there are searching, keen to pick out faults. It is a very strict and unforgiving church.'

The houses in this street were built of stone from the cathedral, stripped bare of its slates. They were merchant houses, opulent and fair, but seemed to Frances quite forbidding, sitting squat and grim. Between the college of St Leonard, and the college of St Mary – the new college, Meg called it – was the house that was given to Giles and his family, where his ongoing practice might benefit the town. It had at its back a small distillery, and gardens that stretched as far as the burn.

'Here we shall do very well,' said Meg, 'if we can fend off the New College dows.' The doves had flown off when the college closed; now they had returned, and were launching an offence upon St Leonard's College crops. Meg said the doves were presbyters.

The house was not far from the land where Matthew Cullan, and Nicholas Colp, had been laid to rest, on the very cusp of the chapel kirkyard, in a quiet glade. Here, Meg knelt, to gather up the weeds around her father's grave. Shy snowdrops had lifted their heads, and primroses too, that Meg had coaxed out from the frost. Frances felt like an intruder, in another person's life, that had somehow been mistaken for her own. 'Does Hew like to come here?' she asked.

Meg smiled at that. 'Hew is confused, in some things. But I think that he does, in his heart.'

Frances found this new world difficult to grasp. On a busy market day, the town seemed stripped of life, stony-faced and desolate. The colleges, that were home from home, and half a life to Hew and Giles, were closed to her and Meg. 'Where do women go?' she asked. In London, they could walk abroad, through gardens and through parks. They had more freedom there, than anywhere on earth. There was laughter and music, Burbage's theatre, revels and plays, dancing and skating, card games and bowls. Here entertainments were forbidden by the Kirk, and no one danced in rounds or played upon the lute. Frances, in the hours she spent upon her uncle's books, had never felt the life she lived was profligate or frivolous. But Joan and her five daughters liked to laugh and play, to entertain and sing, and gossip with their friends. St Andrews seemed to Frances now a cold and barren place. Some people who went past spoke a word to Meg, and looked at Frances carefully. They were civil and polite, gentle to her face. But when they had gone by, she felt their eyes upon her back, and heard them start to mutter in discordant, foreign tongues. By St Mary's, they encountered Matthew's tutor Gavan Baird, with a pudding for his dinner in a paper cloth. The ruffle of his hair brightened the grey town, and he smiled and raised his hat to them, a spark of warmth and friendliness that brought a little cheer, before he disappeared behind the college gate.

'The kirk is the place where people like to congregate. And beside the mills,' Meg said. 'You have not come to see the town when it is at its best. In another month, when the sun has warmed the colour in the sand, and softened the brisk breeze, you will come to see how beautiful it is. Our little town was ravaged sorely in the plague. But it has begun upon a brave recovery.'

'You do not find it quiet here?'

'Not in the least. But I am not inclined to living in a crowd. It brings the sickness on.'

Meg bustled Frances by the kirk of Holy Trinity, and quickly from the sight of its indignant glare, to the market place. Not far from the town house was the former weaver's shop, that now was owned and run by his daughter Tibbie, whose husband had a business dyeing woollen cloth. Tibbie Strachan had some lengths of wool for sale, of several weights and thicknesses, some in workday colours that were dull and serviceable, and some that were plain, and could be dyed in any shade. She kept some trays of silks, and smaller haberdashery, and, locked out of sight, a range of finer cloths, that could be had at cost. There was little that Tibbie could not put her hands on, whatever were the laws against excess in dress. She could cloak an earl, or whip up fancy dress, for Archbishop Adamson to wear in his sculduddery. Here Frances found at last a kind of kindred spirit, for there was nothing she knew better than the cloth trade.

With Tibbie, Meg was blunt. 'This is Frances Phillips, who will marry Hew. She wants some satin silk, to make a wedding gown.'

And Tibbie said, 'You have a guid man, there. What colour will you have? I should say, a rose, to flatter your fair face.'

Frances hesitated. Hew had said, sea-water blue, which seemed to her a washed out, melancholy shade. The morning sea was grey, reflecting layers of cloud. But when she mentioned it, both Meg and Tibbie cried, 'That would be perfect, of course. And subtle, in the silk,' and that appeared to settle it.

'When will you want it?' Tibbie asked. 'For I doubt we do not have the silk you need as yet, though we have the other cloth. We are low on stock, until the Senzie fair.'

'That is some weeks off. The banns have not been read, and we must wait for Hew.' Meg squeezed her hand. 'What do you think?'

Frances did not know what to think. She felt alone, adrift. For she had no kenning, when Hew would be back. She took between her fingers a length of russet kersey, of a price and quality her uncle would approve. 'This one is fine.'

Both women laughed. Tibbie said, 'Leave it to me.' And Meg bought fine broadcloth in willow and grey, in flax blue and primrose, carnation and straw, and yard upon yard of cambric and lawn, to make sheets and smocks, handkerchiefs and caps. '*That* is an outreiking,' Tibbie remarked. And afterwards, Meg said to Frances, 'There, you may be sure, you have found a friend.'

They came last to the apothecary by the market cross, a little shop with a distillery and oven at the back. Two young men, as customers, were standing at the counter, one gazing up upon a shelf of jars, a frown upon his face, as though for some elixir he could never find, however hard he looked. The other was engaged in a dispute with the poticar, jiggling with his arms, in an agitated dance. It was not a dispute of the ordinary kind, for there were no real words in it. The young man pointed furiously to a cup of red powder next to the scale, while the apothecary mirrored his movements, by vigorously shaking his head. He snatched up a paper from the young man's hand, and pointed at a word on it, then back at the cup. The young man responded with a stream of squawks, rising to a pitch of sheer and shrill indignance. 'Look, son,' the poticar said, 'That is what he asked for, and that is what it is. Awa. Shoo. Gang.' This was said aggressively, in the young man's face, and accompanied by gestures that could not be misread.

Frustrated, the customer picked up the pot, and emptied it over the counter. A powder ran out, of a muddy red brown.

'Now why wad ye do that, ye daft dummy?' The poticar took up a pen, and wrote a line or two upon the piece of paper, which he pushed back in his hand. 'Tak that to your master. Now then, out ye gang.' He came out from his stall, and physically and roughly, bundled the boy out. The boy was strong enough, indeed, to have resisted him; but he seemed a little sheepish at his own display of temper, and went quietly enough, withdrawn into the silence of a stubborn scowl. 'Your pardon, ladies,' the apothecar excused himself, 'But that man is a fool. And sometimes, wi' these naturals, they want a helping hand, for they will not be telt.'

At this, his other customer, turning from the jars, spoke up in defence of the boy he had thrown out. 'He is not a fool. And ye have no cause to speak to him like that.'

'He does not understand it.' The apothecary scraped the powder up upon a piece of paper, and funnelled it back into the pot. It left a stain on the counter, like a scab of blood.

'He understands perfectly. Not only can he see the contempt upon your face, he can read it in your lips.'

'You are as daft as he,' the poticar asserted.

'You do not believe me? You do not think, that in his twenty years he has not ever heard the words *daft* and *dummy*, so that he kens their shape? You think you are first, to speak to him like that?'

'He is a dummy, isn't he? Or will ye tell me next, that he can speak an' a'? You can be gone, too. I am weary of your coming here, with your countless questions. And I will not sell you ratsbane, argent vive, or brimstone, or whatever else you hark for in your daft experiments. I do not believe for a moment you have come from Doctor Locke. If he wants a powder, he will have to send a paper for it. Or come here himself.'

'Mebbe,' said the boy, 'I am sent here by the council, to experiment on you. Mebbe they had wind of your sophistication.'

The man said, clearly rattled, 'That is slander, sir.'

'Is it? For tis plain, that is what the painter's boy had come here to complain of. What did you mix into his vermillion? Red lead, was it? Rust? Or mebbe it was blood? Ye should take me on, as your apprentice. I could show you tricks that you have never dreamt of.'

'Get out of it, ye loun. And do not come again. I will make complaint of you, to Professor Locke.'

Meg interrupted then. 'It is Roger, isn't it? Roger Cunningham?'

The student turned to her. His courage lost its flame, and he looked abashed. 'Your pardon, mistress. For I do not ken you.'

'I am Meg Cullan, wife to Doctor Locke.'

'On my life, you are, Mistress,' he admitted then, plainly ill at ease.

'Does Professor Locke know you are here?'

A sly look of triumph had crossed the apothecary's face. Frances felt sorry for the truant student. Had he not spoken up for the dummel?

'I think he will have guessed it, if I have been missed,' Roger answered honestly. 'But your point is pertinent. Tis time for me to go.'

'You might like to tell him you were here,' suggested Meg.

'I thank you for your kindness. And I will.' The young man bowed to them. His swagger petered out. But at the door, he turned. 'Ladies, beware, and make sure to sift whatever you will buy from him for sweepings from the floor.'

'That boy is a menace,' the apothecary said, 'and I would bid you speak to Doctor Locke agin him, as I shall myself. Pay no heed to his slanders. He is wrath with me, for I refused to sell him what he wants to buy.'

'What does he want to buy?' asked Meg.

'He makes some experiments. And sometimes, he has licence for it from Professor Locke. Without such licence, I insist, I will never sell to him. For, it is my suspicion he makes his own medicines, and peddles them, illicitly, when he has not the kenning for it, nor indeed the skill. Doctor Locke is lax with him, because he was a help in the year of plague. That credit, to be sure, maun sometime soon run out. Now, ladies, I am sorry to have troubled you with this. What more can I do for you?'

'An ounce of your saffron, if you please,' said Meg.

The apothecary hesitated. 'Now, that is a pity. For of the best saffron we have quite run out. The painter had it all, to make his yellow pigment. What is left is of a quality so poor, it cannot serve for you. And there will be no more of it, before the Senzie fair.'

Meg asked. 'May we not see what you have, and judge the quality ourselves?'

'I will be honest with you, Mistress, I should be ashamed to show it up to you. I cannot sell sic dregs.'

'We shall have to do without,' Meg sighed, as they left the shop. 'Until the Senzie fair. That is the great Easter market held in the cloisters of the auld cathedral, by the synod house, that gives the fair its name. If Hew will hold off your wedding till then, it would be as well, for we shall find lace there, and pearls, and fresh fruits and spices, to put to the banquet. This is the worst time of year, when the cup has been drunk to its dregs. In April, 'twill be filled again.'

'I see,' Frances said, 'why that man is not liked in the town. Does he cheat his customers, as the young man says?'

'I believe he does. But he is clever enough not to palm off his dregs on myself or on Giles, who would well be wise to it. We have both had patients who had physic from him, which is very weak and adulterate. Yet when he is charged with it, he will maintain they cut it themselves, to make it go further, and therefore halve the cost of it. Wherefore his frauds are hard to test and prove. I have no doubt that he has some saffron still, and will sell to another sadly mixed and cut, what he dare not sell to us. There is no love between him and my husband, to speak plain. Giles does not care for those who fleece the poor and sick.'

'Then did Professor Locke send this student there, to spy on him?' Frances asked.

'Giles would not do that. But Roger is an agent, and acts upon a conscience, entirely of his own. He is a difficult boy. Still, Giles is fond of him, and finds hope and merit in his cunning for philosophy. Hew was his guardian, and paid for his tuition here.'

Frances echoed, 'Hew did that?' She had not heard that Hew was ever guardian to a boy, for he had never mentioned it, at Leadenhall or here.

'Aye. Did he not say? There is something between them, I think. Roger is the son of Richard Cunningham, who was our own father's pupil, and Hew's master at the bar, when he trained to be an advocate. That was a man who had a troubled heart – either it was madness, or a native evil in it – and he came at last to an unhappy end. His history has had a hard effect on Hew. It was Richard that caused that wound in his breast, for he would have killed him, if he could.'

'I did not know.' Frances was shocked. She had thought that the scar, a silvery line where the hair did not grow, had come from the battles Hew had fought in the Netherlands. She had never asked, and he had never said. So much there was, she thought, she did not know of Hew, though they had shared a house, at Leadenhall, for years. His mystery confounded her, opening up new layers like petals of a flower; the closer she became to him, the more remote she felt.

'The deaf boy, I suppose, is prentice to the painter, and the one who makes the likeness now of Giles. Tis likely that the poticar has mixed dust into his colours, and his master has complained of it,' said Meg.

'Will you tell the doctor this?'

'Perhaps. He will hear it first from Roger, for, you may be sure, he will be quick enough to plead to him the facts of his own case. He is a subtle soul, and wisely kens to play. And though Giles is not foolish or lax in his indulgences, he has always had a soft spot for that boy.'

The painter's apprentice made his way back through the town, to the barn he had leased with his master by the burn. It was less than a house; two tiny chambers in a ramshackle roof, with a window and a door, open to the elements, made secure at night by a flap of leather, tied and nailed across. The painter had made his own window, to keep his colours clean from the dirt and dust that blew in on the breeze, from a sheet of parchment, reinforced with glue, allowing in the light, and keeping out the wind. Here, he ground his colours, with water from the stream, linseed oil or tempera, on a marbled porphyry, until they reached a temper of a satisfying clarity, when he would decant them into cups or walnut shells, and put them in a box, ready to be used. He found a certain solace in the rhythm of the grinding, and the cutting of the water from the sparkling burn; the longer that he spent at it, the purer was the shade of black or white or green, of ochre or azure, that eventually emerged. Colour was the painter's art, the instinct that he did not share with his young apprentice, for if the boy had learned the secret of his trade, he would be equipped to make his way alone; that sense would overcome the flaw of those deficiencies that God had wrought in him, and he would be the master of his craft. He would have the skill to leave his master then; the painter would not have that for the world.

He heard the boy returning from his errand in the town. Unconscious of the sound he made, he did not wander quietly but chuntered as he came, a strident, whistling sound. He clattered where he ran, noisily and clumsily; a wonder that his muckle hands could take and hold so sensitive a pen with which to draw.

The boy was in a mood, the painter sensed at once. And he had been like that, of late, though this huffing and puffing was not in his nature, it was not like him at all. Something had filled him with stubbornness; something had stirred him to rage.

'What is it, now?' he asked.

The prentice boy showed him the paper he had kept crushed in his hand. The painter had to smooth it out to read it, criss-crossed with lines of the bearer's displeasure.

'Ach. Dinna fash. Ye mauna tak it to heart.' The paper bore the note he had sent to the apothecar. 'Send vermillion crystal, the pigment ye sent was cut with red lead.'

The apothecar had put, 'What I sent was pure. And if it was contaminat, somehow in your workshop, speir to your prentice boy, what hand he may have had in it, if you can make the dummy understand. Which, as I maun tell you, I cannot. I will charge to your account the spillage in my shop that your boy has done. As for the pigment, ye had all I have.'

'And what he has is *shite*,' the painter said. Although the prentice saw the shape of that word, as it formed on his lips, and kent it full well, it did not raise a smile. The painter pulled his thumb out crudely from his fist, and for a comical effect, made a straining face. Even that did not force the sullen boy to smile. 'It does not matter, see? We have colours of our own.'

His own mood had changed, sharp and suddenly. He shooed the prentice out to fetch water from the stream, angry with the glower that soured his gentle face. He would send him back again, to the college with the coals, and keep him on his toes, and that would teach the lad to come back in a sulk. He held no grudge against the town apothecary. That he was a swingeour, there could be no doubt, and it was wrong of him to try to blame the boy. Yet the painter did not fault him for his fraud. It took a cunning thief, to ken another thief, and they were of a kind. They could come to an agreement, pleasing to them both, for the painter's fee included the cost of the materials. He would not, even so, put that shit up on the wall, or in a year or two, the pictures would turn black. Thankfully, he had some colours of his own, that he had kept back, for a purpose such as this. He had guarded them so long, he felt a guilty pang to break on them at last, as a miser frets to spend his pot of gold, but he was aware it was a wise investment. And what joy, what pleasure he would have, at breaking out the colour from unconsummated stone, where nature needed no more than a little help? The pictures on the college wall, the portrait of the doctor there, the best the boy had done, would make their names for them. The art and fortune painting was a beauty, was it not? It would be the consummation of the painter's craft, what he had been born to, what was *meant* for him; Hermes in his silver spurs, fly wings on his feet, who made fate his captive, supple, sly, and fleet, patron friend to fugitives, renegats and thieves.

Chapter 18

Memento Mori

Hew returned to St Andrews with the pleated picture wrapped up in his saddle bag. His next move was to try it on the painter Workman, as he had on Vanson, and, in particular, on the painter's prentice, who, despite what Vanson said, had a clear understanding of portraiture. For this, he was aware, he would require the help of an interpreter, in speaking to a person who was deaf and dumb.

This did not discourage him. Interpretation, he saw clearly, was the key. For the meaning of the picture, unlike the meaning in a cipher, did not lie in the pleats or the lines of paint, or even in the mind of the man who had created them, but in their effect in the mind of the person who regarded it.

He had noticed this, in the effect the painting had, palpably, on James. The young king was afraid of it. And since Hew did not allow that the picture was bewitched – would not, at this stage – then the reason must lie within the king's own conscience; the painting had shown up the conflict deep within, had mirrored and had brought to light, what was already there.

This Hew understood, for he was aware the picture had exerted such a charm on him. But the effect was not the same, for he was not afraid of it. Rather, it allowed him to express, and in some way amend, the discord in his mind that rose from an ambivalence; his muddled guilt and pity for the Scottish queen. He had the vague sense that by solving this mystery, he could set to rest that queen's unhappy death, and his uncertain part in it, and make something that was perilous because it vacillated, somehow firm and fixed, even if it fused into a constant grief. The idea of a quest, that proved his loyalty to the king, laid to rest that queen, *and* assured his love, very much appealed to him. Had he been honest with himself, he would have understood that the keenness with which he had embraced the challenge, and his general tendency to wander after mysteries, were an attempt to occupy and distract his mind, with riddles that were convolute, intricate and pleasing, and had certain ends, from those greater powers and mysteries of feeling, of human love, and God, which threw him into terror and could not be solved. His introspection, though, did not take him quite so far.

Coming home from Edinburgh, he went straight away to Giles Locke at St Salvator's, before returning home to his wife at Kenly Green. He showed him the painting, which Giles was much taken with. 'Ah, a turning picture. I like that. Indeed. I like that very much.'

'Do you think,' said Hew, 'that it was intended to represent the queen?'

'Quite possibly,' said Giles. 'Though by no means necessarily.'

That was the painting's charm for him. Its ambivalence reflected how he saw the world, a balance of two halves, and Giles, in his deliberations, rarely came emphatically upon a certain side. His conclusions were generally, 'So it will be, or otherwise, not.' A paradox was bread and butter, meat and drink, to Doctor Locke. It did not disturb him in the least to see the flesh and bone rotated in a wink. He collected prisms and perspectives, which reflected back on the reflecting eye, distracted and dissected in a myriad forms, the image it observed.

'This is a *memento mori* likeness, as I think, reminding us, how so fair we bloom, of our own mortality. And I should like to have it, or else something like it, for my own collection.'

'Why not ask your painter here if he can make a copy?' Hew suggested. 'I should like to ask him, what he makes of it.'

'That,' considered Giles, 'is a good idea. And I will come along, if you do not mind. For I have an itch to see into the dinner hall, and to find out how his painting has progressed. Since the boy has finished with me, sitting for the draft, and is working up his copy, his master is evasive, secretive and shy, and does all that he can, not to be observed. It is a curious thing, this subtle change in him, as I suppose, a jealousy, attending to his craft.'

It was true enough, the painter's mood had changed. For as the work went on, he had withdrawn with his boy into a private world, that occupied them, utterly.

They came early in the morning, while the students straggled yawning to their prayers, and hurried past the porter with no smile or word, but to have the key. They brought in the colours required for that day, in small pots and shells, and pencils that were made from squirrel tail or miniver, tapered to a point. The painter locked the door, and sometimes sent the boy for water, eggs or ale from the college buttery, a scribbled scrap of paper scrunched up in his hand, but would not go himself. He shrank from curious scholars, dawdling in the court, who racked their necks to peep at him; and while he had been happy, several weeks before, to prepare his panels out among the cloisters, sanding down the wood, and treating it with size, breaking off to chat with anyone who passed, now he was inclined to keep his work indoors, safe from the inspection of a squinting sun.

They had made good progress with the work. The boy had worked up the sketches he had drawn of Professor Locke, upon a panel broad enough to do his subject proud. The figure was complete, and he could do the rest, the backcloth and effects, without the help or hindrance of a sitter by his side. He was working now upon the antique skull, with the tints of ochre, orpiment and white the painter had prepared for him, elucidating bone in layers of yellow paint.

Ars et Natura was almost complete, and to the painter's eye, persuasive in its art. This picture would establish him. He had called for help, from his willing boy, in drawing the proportions of the figures on the board. The temper of the paint and the colours were his own. And colour was the essence and the heart of it, for him.

The painter was disturbed by an intrusive knocking at the

chamber door. For as long as he could, he went on ignoring it, trusting the intrusion would give up and go away. And the knocking, of course, did not disturb the boy, who painted on, oblivious. The rapping, though, did not let up, and was backed up in due course, by the imprecations of Professor Locke, muffled through the barrier of the chamber door, a solid mass of iron and oak, strong enough to stand against belligerent attack, but failing to protect against an irritating hum. 'Now, I must insist,' the doctor cried.

The painter called, 'One moment, sir,' the time it took to cover Art and Nature with a cloth, and resigned to all, opened up the door to them, albeit just a crack. He saw the doctor, and his friend, standing on the stair. 'Will you let us in?'

'Aye, and if ye must,' the painter said, reluctantly. 'And that your business does not keep, and hold us from our work.'

'It will not tak long. But, sir, I must protest, that you lock the door. For it cannot be allowed, that ye invade our college and shut fast her gates against us,' Doctor Locke complained.

'I am sorry for that. But it has been necessary. We are plagued, in our work, by some of your students, who will not desist, to keek and lour at us. They are craning at the windows, while we are at work,' the painter said.

'Really?' Giles replied, perplexed; the more so since the dinner hall was on the upper floor.

'Really. They are, if I may say, uncanny and uncouth for educated men. They pester my poor boy, and mock him his afflictions.'

Doctor Locke was vexed at this. 'Then, sir, I am sorry for it. You may have my word that I will amend it. I had no idea that they played at that. They will be telt, severely.'

'There is one, sir, in particular, haunts us at our work, and follows us incessantly; he has a fascination with the way we talk. It is not kind nor mannerly.'

Giles conceded with a sigh, 'Ah, that will be Roger. Then I take the point, and apologise for him. I may say in his defence, he does not mean a spite, or malice to your boy. His interest in his case is scholarly and genuine. Yet, I apprehend, it is an annoyance to you, and you have my word, he will not come again. I will speak to him.'

'I thank you, sir, If that is all . . .' the painter was about to close the door again, when Giles objected quickly, that that was not all. 'Please, sir, let us in. My friend here has a question he would put to you.'

The painter left the door, and they followed him inside. Hew had the pleated picture, wrapped up in his hand. 'Do you have a scaffold?' he inquired.

His question caused the painter a small shiver of alarm. 'A what?'

'A frame to stand a picture, like that one over there.' He pointed to the easel where the prentice stood, working on the portrait he had made of Doctor Locke.

Wordlessly, the painter looked around. He found a second scaffold, folded by the wall, and handed it to Hew, who set it up. He unwrapped the picture, with its prism pleats, and set it at a slant, well disposed to show its double aspect off.

'What devil's work is that?' the painter asked.

'Then you have not seen it before?' Hew was interested to read into the painter's eyes. Whatever the man looked at, or believed he saw, he did not like it much.

'Never in my life. It is a hideous thing. Why do you bring it here?'

'At the command of the king, who admires it greatly. He has asked me to find a painter with the skill to make a copy of it. Could you do that, do you think?'

The painter shook his head. He could not, Hew observed, take his eyes from the picture. Whether he had recognised it, it was hard to say. But there was something in it drew him in, willingly or not.

'It is not,' he said at last, 'my kind of thing.'

'That is a pity, then, for Doctor Locke had hoped to have one too. Can you tell us, then, what painter might have made this? Could it be Arnold Bronckhorst, perhaps?'

'Bronckhorst?' This shot in the dark had drawn a clear reaction Hew was interested to see. The painter looked afraid. 'Why do you say that? What maks ye think of him?'

'Because I spoke with Adrian Vanson, who is the king's painter. And he telt me there were only two painters, in the whole of Scotland, who could make a portrait likeness, Bronckhorst, and himself. This picture, he asserts, was not done by him.' Hew looked meaningfully over at the painter's boy. But the painter seemed relieved, and his face relaxed. 'Vanson would say that. Did he tell you it was Bronckhorst?'

'He telt me, that in his opinion, it was likely not.'

'Well,' the painter shrugged. 'You have your answer, then. And as to the rest, it is not a portrait, but a trick.'

'Well,' considered Hew. 'I think it *is* a portrait, of a kind. Though it may not be a portrait of the woman it depicts.'

'You have lost me there. I will leave sic reason to you twa philosophers, and get back to my work.' The painter turned his back on them, and on the painting too. But Hew did not desist. 'If you do not mind, I have not finished yet. You will understand, I put these questions to you at the king's request, which Giles Locke will confirm.'

'Aye, indeed,' said Giles.

The painter turned again. 'What is it you want, now?'

'To put the question of this picture to your boy.'

'For that, there is no call. For he does not ken.'

'Ask him, if you please.'

The painter, since he saw that Hew would not give up, and was supported in his suit by Doctor Locke, had no option but to come up and disturb the boy, where he painted still, blissfully absorbed. The painter showed his face and touched him on the shoulder, as he always did. The prentice shook him off, and scowled upon his hand, a thing that left the painter troubled and distressed, for never had the boy rejected him before. He knew no good could come of it.

He did as he was told. He made the boy come up, where he could see the picture. The prentice picked it up, and turned it in his hands, interested and curious to see how it was made. And it was plain to Hew that he was not afraid of it.

'He likes it,' he observes. 'Then I shall leave it here, and see if he will try to make a copy of it.'

'He does not have the time,' the painter said. 'And nor, in truth, do I. For after he has finished with Professor Locke, and the platform piece, we have all the virtues and the vices still.'

'There is no hurry,' answered Hew. He put the picture back on its easel frame, where it seemed to exercise a small and quiet mastery over the large chamber, like the queen herself. He followed the boy back, to look upon the portrait he had made of Giles. The doctor's face looked out, from a naked panel that was bare behind, with an uncanny prescience. For floating in that void was Giles Locke's gentle soul, his broad face filled with kind and humorous intelligence. There was something else, a deep and sad proplexity Hew had not seen before, or noticed to have aged his dear friend's living face, but as he looked upon it, recognised it now. 'Your boy is possessed of an extraordinary talent.'

The painter did not answer this. But, 'Will you take your picture, sir?' he asked uneasily.

'I will leave it here. It sits well, I think. Bear in mind, it belongs to the king, so we must be careful that no harm should come to it.'

He was not sure, after all, why he left it there. The painter, it was plain, did not want him to. But it seemed to fit. 'Did you know Bronckhorst?' he asked. 'Vanson said, he left; I wondered if you kent what might have become of him?'

The painter shook his head. 'I cannot tell ye, sir. I never met the man.'

After they had gone, the painter could not rest, though the boy returned to work upon his easel portrait. The woman and the skull seemed to watch the painter as he tried to work. From the corner of his eye, he could see them both, conflated and confused, so there was a bloom upon a piece of bone, or an eye winked from a skull, in an empty socket where it should not be. There was nothing else of art or colour there; the colours that were used were chosen for the trick, so that what was there of red, to mark the living flesh, was no more than a streak of thinly trickled cinnabar, dripping from a crease, like a line of blood. He covered up the turning picture with a cloth, but he could feel it still, burning at his back. The room was filled with skulls. The mark of his mortality meant nothing to the boy, who kent nought of Hell, but everything to him. He could not put the horror of it cleanly from his mind.

The prentice could not help. The painter sensed a change, a difference in the boy. His humours had grown dark, and his sweet nature soured. What devil could corrupt, and turn his heart against the master he had loved? What menace could intrude upon that secret, silent world?

And there was Bronckhorst, too. The painter opened up the picture from its cloth, and looked at it again. For there was something there, that would not be kept in. Nothing in the figure bore the mark of him. Then why had he come up? What impulse had returned him, after all these years?

He found peace at last, in the work in hand. The colours in his painting – vivid blues and reds, lifted and encouraged him. He painted the wings on the sandals and helmet, feathery light, with a feather itself, and found himself calmed by their delicate brightness. The helmet and the water he would leave till last, for in their sheer illuminance, his painting would be done, and he would prove himself, the master of his craft.

Hew came home to Frances, welcomed with a warmth that he had seldom felt before, and which he returned to her, with a loving heart. And yet, Frances felt, he was absent still, as though a part of him had wandered off elsewhere, and had forgotten to return. He told her what had happened with the king. 'The pity is,' he said, 'we may not marry yet.'

It did not seem to Frances that he minded much, Perhaps it was the chase, that mattered most to him. It distracted him, at least, from the trouble to his conscience at the Scots queen's death, and so much she was grateful for. And they were married still, whatever happened here.

'But you believe the king will grant us leave?' she asked.

'I'm sure he will.'

'What happens if you do not ever find the answer to his question?'

He would not think of that. And Frances understood, the trial that he was put to did not count, to him, as any trial at all; for it was what he knew, and what his spirit yearned for, and what he could do best.

'It will not matter, much. Meg says, we will have more things, and a better choice, if we are not wed before the Senzie fair.' Frances was surprised, how natural it felt, to shape a word in Scots for which she had no sound. 'The *Senzie* fair.'

He did not seem to notice it. 'That is perfect, then.' He grinned at her. 'You will like the fair. And I would like to take you to it, if I am still here.'

'Where else would you be?'

'Wherever I must go, to find this matter out. You will not mind it, Frances, to stay here with Meg? She likes you very much. I must go again, to Edinburgh, first, to question the king's servants, who found the turning picture at the gate at Holyrood. For I have no doubt, one of them kens something, that he does not want to ken, or that he does not want the rest of us to know.'

His confidence and pleasure in it filled her with a sadness she could not express. 'Must you go again, when you have just returned?'

He hesitated, then. 'I need not go, at once. For nothing can be hurt by it, to leave it for a while.'

And for the next three days, while he remained with her, he did not let the picture slip into his mind.

On the fourth day, he was asked by Giles to come back into the college to help, as he had promised, with the students who were due to graduate that year, whose studies had been interrupted by the year of plague. 'If you could hear their practice in the disputations, that would be of help. Some will have their laureation shortly, at the Pasque, others are not ready for it, and must wait till June. Roger is the student I am most concerned about. I will be indebted to you, if you hear his argument.'

'Gladly,' answered Hew. 'Though I should not have thought he needed help in arguing.'

'His arguing is faultless in its presentation. It is in the content that it lets him down.'

'As when he says, for instance, that there is no God,' said Hew.

The doctor groaned. 'Did he say that? The wicked boy. But he does not believe that, Hew.'

'I supposed as much.'

'I have been too soft with him. But these are public examinations, and he will not, he cannot, pervert them to his own misgoverned ends. What he wants is someone who will argue properly, and who will be quite firm with him.'

'That, I can do. In fact, I should find pleasure in it,' Hew said with a smile.

'I had hoped you might.'

They walked together into town, coming to the college shortly after eight. The porter at the gate called them to him urgently. 'There is an unco problem, sir. The denner hall is locked, and the painter man inside, and we hae chapped and roared, but he will not let us in.'

'Again?' The doctor sighed. 'I hoped that he had done with that. He has become quite strange, and is no longer reasonable. I must, I think, take measures to address the man myself.'

'I doubt ye ought to, sir. He was there all night. And not a peep fae him, nor yet his dummel boy. I ken he cannae hear us, sir, but often we hear him; the more so, sin he disnae ken the clatter that he makes.'

'All night?' repeated Giles. 'Now, that does seem strange.' He looked askance at Hew, who wondered, 'Has he stayed before?'

'Never, in the night,' the porter said. 'For he has a workshop, somewhere in the town, where he gangs to sleep. He does not ever stay here when it is not light, for then, ye see, he cannot see to paint. But when the daylight fades, he quits the denner hall, and brings the key to me. Last night, he did not. Nor, as I maun swear to you, did he pass the gate. And no one here has seen him or his prentice boy.'

Hew looked back at Giles. 'I do not like this much.'

The doctor was suddenly brisk. 'Now, I have a key, somewhere in the tower. It is an old and rusted one, and may not be of use to us. But I propose to fetch it down, and try it out, at once.'

Giles was the first to look in. He took a step back. 'Ah, dear me, dear me. Now, William,' he said to the porter, 'there are students outside. I want you to tell to their regents, to call them all in, and to the lecture hall. They must keep them there, until I send them word. Tell them to read to them, from the disputations, and then to put them all to work upon a paradox, whatever class they're in. And if they are kept long, and past the dinner hour, the bursar will attend to them, and send them meat and drink. And for their pleas of nature, show them to the pot. Lock the college gate, and send out to the tolbuith whether Andro Wood the sheriff is in town, for we may want his help. You, Hew, with me.'

The porter left them then, and the students were dispersed, all of them but one, and that was Roger Cunningham, who came up the stair and followed Giles and Hew, unheeding and unseen.

Ars et Natura was complete. The painter had hung up his painting, a panel in three parts that measured four by five, in the very centre of the long back wall. And in the hall in front of it, he had hanged himself.

Chapter 19

Speaking Pictures

It made sense to Hew, only as a scene. He could see it with his eyes, but could not understand what it was he saw, fractured and diffused, confusing to his mind, like a false perspective in a picture or a prism. Yet the images in front of him were not at all distorted, presenting with a clarity that could not be misread. And yet, and yet, his brain refused to comprehend the whole, but splintered into parts the horrors it beheld, could only apprehend them, broken, through a glass. It was like the tears, that cannot grasp a grief, divided and discharged, reflected in a thousand places in their blurry shards. The tableau that unfolded there took some time to print itself entire upon his consciousness. And, when it did, he did not think it likely it would ever be erased.

Art assisting Nature, fixed upon the wall, cast its shadow foremost over all else there. The figures in the painting did not have much depth. *Hermes et Fortuna* had nothing to distinguish the expressions in their faces, which bore none of the elusive, wary sensitivity the painter's boy had shown, but were bland and smooth. The draping of the clothes around their limbs and torsos, standing on their pedestals awkwardly and stiff, was flatter than the panel where they were depicted, which they could not lift. It was hard to imagine they were of the gods, who, with their vacant, inscrutable faces, could influence the storm clouds painted at their back, tipping out the listless vessels in a stolid sea. The sails of the ships, the curved piece of cloth in Fortuna's hands, were as fixed as wood, and carried in their solid folds as little there of movement. But what brought the picture out, to a transcendent brilliance, was the clarity and colour in the pigments that were used. Deep, mellow ochres, fresh and verdant greens, oozing, venous reds and florid, fleshy pinks, scintillating blues. The eyes of the serpents, wound round Hermes' rod, were a penetrating black; the wings on his helmet and his heavy feet were pure and white and clean. Nature's earth was coloured with a hot, honeyed dust long ago baked dry in an Asiatic sun. The colours of the sea, tempered greens and greys, were not swirled together in a muddy froth. Rather, they rose up, in little tufted curls, each one clear, discrete, white-flecked at its peak. The letters underneath, and the scroll on Hermes' helmet, were inscribed in leaf of glinting, brittle gold. And the pewter of the helmet, and the sea beyond, had a subtle shimmer to it, an effervescent sheen, that when the sunlight fell on it, made the metal and the water feel translucent and ethereal. So the painter's art had brought the work to life.

Nature's colours, to the painter, had been less than kind. A rush of blood and bile had pooled behind his face, swelling out the flesh, in a livid hue. He had hanged himself with the same wire he had used for the picture, strong enough to hold his painting's weight, and sharp enough, almost, to sever his own throat. His corpus had discoloured to a mottled splurge of purpled and heaving, bilious red. No clarity at all remained to him in death.

Though Hew's eyes were compelled, and held against his will, to look upon that place that was the painter's signature, his signing out of life, he became aware that it was not complete. There was another part to it, further up the hall. On the dais where the doctor had been sitting for his portrait, lay the painter's boy, figured as he fell, like an actor on the stage. He was covered over, half, by the backcloth to his painting, pulled down in his flight, and in the crook of his arm, toppled from its perch, lay the doctor's skull. The portrait of the doctor had been painted out, its gentle face obliterated in a mask of cinnabar. On the floor in front of it, with the paint and brush, was the hammer that was used, in assisting Art and Nature to their place upon the wall, and upon the boy, whose face appeared, to Hew, the one thing in that room to have no colour in it; but a thin fluid leaking from the dead boy's ear, turned up from the ground, kept a faint taint of pink, as though its stream of blood was long ago washed out.

Looking over all, quiet and impassive on its scaffold still, with its back to the door and its eye upon the set, was the king's turning picture, mindful, as always, of what it meant to die.

He heard Giles say, 'We must leave this scene untouched, to wait for Andrew Wood, if he is in town.'

His own voice answered then, reluctantly, absurd. 'We have no want of him.'

The doctor reasoned, calm, 'Ah, I think we do. We need the king's man, to help us deal with this. So will he do, efficiently and quietly. If what appears is true – and I do not say it is, before we ken the facts – but going by appearances, we have a man here who is murdered, and a man who murdered him, and has killed himself, which is a sin against nature, and God.'

And that, considered Hew, was what the speaking picture seemed to want to say, what his mind perceived, and Giles put into words. It seemed that the painter had murdered his boy, and then murdered himself, in a fit of remorse. As to what had happened first in the sequence of events, in the damage to the portrait, the hanging of the painting and the killing of the boy, the picture did not say. Nor was there a clue to what drove him to the act. One thing though was clear. All of this took place before the painter hanged himself, and so the painter ended this unhappy chain, wherever it did start. Or so it must have been, if what appeared was true, for without certain proof, Hew could not swear it was. The painting had been staged, the painter in its frame. Cold reason must dictate, that there was no one else. Yet he had placed himself at the centre of his painting, where Art and Nature turned, and cast their gaze on him, and they could not discount the disturbing possibility, that the painter was compelled by some other, stranger force, to commit a crime that seemed quite inexplicable.

'I cannot understand it,' Giles Locke said. 'For in the hours I spent with them, sitting for my picture, I never saw a cross or an uncanny look between them. So close and sympathetic was the understanding there, they moved and worked as one.'

'Perhaps that does explain the strength of a remorse, that drives a man to hang himself,' said Hew.

'Remorse, aye, but not this show of violence. This painter was, I never thought, a violent sort of man. He was not a man, that had that passion in him,' Giles Locke answered sadly. 'This is a terrible thing. But we cannot let our horror at it blur the practicalities, or deflect us from our duty in this case. The provost must be told, and this man's kin informed. I have a college full of students, who must be protected here, and this is not a thing we can handle on our own. It is too much for us. Andrew Wood must witness this, before we cut him down. This picture must be firm imprinted on our minds, before it is disturbed.'

It was imprinted now, on Hew, who thought he never would again accept an invitation to a dinner in that hall. The scene though, was disturbed, before the crownar Andrew Wood had had the chance to look at it. For it was broken up by Roger Cunningham. Roger had slipped in unseen, unnoticed and undaunted by the gruesome scene. He did not stand to gawp, but put his practised science into good effect, by lifting up the head of the broken painter's boy. He interrupted, urgently, 'Sir. Professor Locke. This man has a fractured skull. But he is not dead.'

They carried the boy, between them, to Bartie's room, which had lain vacant since his death. The room had been stripped bare and scrubbed, but Giles found from somewhere a folding camp bed, of the sort that soldiers used, and in this sling of canvas they set down the boy. And Hew was thankful to depart from the garish dinner hall.

Giles said, 'I have sent for the surgeon. But I will tell you now, this boy will not live.'

The boy's skull was dented, hollowed on one side, cracked upon itself like the splintered eggshell of a soft boiled egg. A little fluid dribbled on a napkin underneath, as though the egg had not been left long in the fire.

'We should shave his head,' Roger said.

'Leave it, for the surgeon. You should not be here,' said Giles. So dull and heavy were his words they lost in transit all their force, and Roger paid no heed to them. Instead, he fetched a razor, water, towels and soap, and shivered off the boy's black hair until a narrow bracelet circumscribed the dint in it, where the white bone dipped, and sunk upon itself. The boy was still, unconscious all the while.

The surgeon came at last. But there was very little that the man could do. 'There are fragments of bone depressed upon the brain. It requires an instrument to lift them out, of a particular kind, and I do not have that instrument,' he said.

The surgeon drew teeth, and let blood. He detached limbs, that were withered or gangrenous, and sometimes he sold those limbs, for purpose of dissection, to Professor Locke, who was a skilled anatomist. But he had never probed before into a living brain. He had not seen a wound like this on anyone alive.

Roger said, 'Professor Locke has an instrument like that.'

'I? You are mistaken.' Giles replied, perplexed.

'Aye, sir, you do. It is the tower, among the other instruments.'

'In truth . . . it may be possible,' Giles conceded slowly. 'There is something there. But it is not for use.'

'Not for use?' The surgeon challenged him, direct. 'Why should ye have such a thing, and it were *not for use*?' Why should you have, he intended, such a tool at all, which belongs to my profession, not to yours.

'I am an anatomist, sir, as well as a physician, and I have a collection of some objects to do with cadavers. I have an interest, explicitly, in skulls. And, it is possible, that among the items that are there accumulated, there may be something similar to what you have described.'

'May I fetch it, sir?' Roger asked.

'Aye, perhaps you should.'

The instrument with which the boy returned made the last sour dregs in Hew's raw stomach churn, just to look at it. It was a kind of clamp, that fitted on the head, through which there passed a screw that could be lowered down to elevate the parts impacted on the brain, rotated and pressed down to screw into the bone.

The surgeon hesitated. 'This is hard to do, without causing damage to the membranes of the brain. And I have not tried it before. I cannot do this well alone. Someone must assist.'

'I am willing to advise. But I cannot put my hand in it,' said Giles.

'Aye, God forbid,' the surgeon answered bitterly, 'that ever a physician soiled his hands.'

'Come, you know full well, that I have not been trained to it. And you would be the first to complain of the trespass.'

'It is your instrument.'

'It is your profession.'

Roger urged, 'Please, will you not try?'

'There is no help for him, son. For he is certain to die,' the surgeon explained.

'Then what can be lost, in the practice? If you will not, then I will.'

Hew did not stay to help. But he could not turn his back upon the horror there, for the porter had returned with the crownar Andrew Wood, having chanced to find him at his brother's house. Hew was obliged to take him to the dining hall, in the absence of Giles, and revisit the scene they had found there. Here Andrew Wood came uncannily into his own, for he was little moved to look upon a hanged man, having hanged enough of them himself. He cut the painter down, and laid his body out upon a trestle board, with an efficiency that was, oddly, reassuring, as though it were the matter of an ordinary day, and nothing untoward. And though his handling of the corpse was brisk, and businesslike, it did not want for courtesy, or for the respect, deserving to the dead. He covered up the painter with a cloth. And Hew felt grateful to him, calmed by his authority.

'Giles Locke must make what arrangements he can to dispose of this body, for, if he died at his own hand, as the evidence suggests, he cannot have the solace of a Christian burial. Sometimes, in such cases, it is a kindness to keep it from the Kirk. Where is the other victim? Is he dead?' the crownar said.

'He is not dead.' Giles Locke had joined them, white-faced, wiping his hands on a cloth, in defiance of the charge that he did not get them dirty. 'Yet. The operation was, to some extent, a success.'

'Then you found the way to turn the implement?' Hew asked.

'Roger did. He is with the boy now, and refuses to leave him. The surgeon has left. And what happens next must lie in God's hands.'

'We must hope that he recovers, and can tell us what has happened here,' Sir Andrew said.

'He will not do that. For even if his brain can heal intact, he cannot speak,' said Giles.

The crownar rubbed his beard. 'Then I must leave you to work out, whatever way you can, to determine what might move a man to such a dreadful act. For my part, I will go to Edinburgh, and inform this man's family of his death in Fife.'

As he left, he saw the pleated picture on its scaffold still, and picked it up. 'What is this?'

Giles said, 'It is a perspective picture, belonging to the king. He has given it to Hew, in hope to find its origin.'

'The king believes that it may be bewitched,' said Hew.

The crownar placed the picture quickly back. He wiped his fingers on his coat, the fingers that had lately lifted down the corpse, and set it on the board without a qualm, and retreated nervously. 'The signs are clear enough,' he said, 'that the king was right.'

He left behind a silence in that room, which Hew was first to break. 'But we do not believe that.'

'No.' Giles did not sound sure. But then, he was distracted by the horror that had happened in the college, by the practicalities of dealing with a corpse, and a mortal causality, without disruption to the students who were in his care. He was distracted also, by this senseless loss of life. He did not believe, could not have believed, that the picture of a death's head, who might have been a queen, had any kind of magic in it, over and above the painter's craft.

Hew looked round the room. 'The answer must be here. It must, in truth, be here.'

223

He knew it must be there. But, for all the world, he could not find it there.

The horror of the painter's death, for the college of St Salvator, was not the death itself, but that fact that he had died at his own unhappy hand. The corpse was taken out by night, when the college was asleep. The porter had insisted it be taken through the window, since a person who died at his own hand would infect a whole house, if he departed there using the door. In practice, this did not prove practical, and a compromise was reached, in using the back channel out from the latrines, which opened to the Swallow Gate, avoiding both the chapel and the college gate. It was buried in the dark, in unconsecrated land, far beyond the comfort of a hostile kirk. And if the doctor knelt, and said a private prayer, then no one was offended there but God.

'If there is a chance,' Hew said, 'this painter did not die by his own unaided hand, howsoever small, then for his family's sake, we ought now to search for it.' Doctor Locke agreed. He could however, find no clue, nothing in that place appearing untoward. It was, if anything too neat, too tidy for the work the painter had produced in it. Hew remembered Vanson's shop, and Vanson's training of his own apprentices, which, it seemed to him, was nothing like this boy's. He looked among the brushes and the pots of paint, which were small, and few.

'Where did the painter mix his paints?' he asked, and was told there was a workshop somewhere in the town, but no one there could tell him where it was.

Roger looked after the boy, for ten more days through which he drifted in and out of consciousness, by the grace of God, blissfully asleep, and in his waking moments, Roger fed him milk and pottage from a spoon. The spittle on the spoon, when Roger pulled it out, was often flecked with blood. From time to time, the surgeon called. The Easter disputations were put back till June, and Giles Locke did his best to dissipate the gloom which darkened the whole college, and to quell the superstitions of the fearful boys. Self-slaughter in a college was a rare event, and a perverse and strange one. The dinner hall was locked. The turning picture was removed to Giles Locke's room, and covered with a cloth. It filled Hew with a deep unease, not because he feared it was the devil's work, but for the power he knew it held in it, to move a troubled mind. He hoped and prayed that Andrew Wood would not relate this horror to the king, before he had an answer to the riddle there.

Andrew Wood returned, and brought with him some news that troubled even more. He had broken the news of the death to the Workman family, with his usual brusqueness. This had not been well received by John Workman's mother, the more so since her son was at that moment up a ladder, patching up the plaster in the Edinburgh tolbuith. When his brother was despatched, to inform him of his death, he almost fell from it. It did not take Andrew long to establish unequivocally that the Workman men were every one accounted for, and that there was no member of the mason's gild who ever had a prentice who was deaf and dumb. It turned out Vanson's scepticism had a solid core.

Chapter 20

The Doctrine of Signatures

The provost, who had engaged the painter, could furnish no clue as to his identity. His provenance was vague. He had surfaced in Cupar, in the first wave of peste in 1585. There, a man was charged with painting the lids of the burgh coffins black. After several months he succumbed to the plague, and among the painters in the masons' gild, none had shown a keenness to replace him. Workman had turned up, fortuitous and out of the blue, offering his services. He had claimed to be a member of the long-established family living still at Edinburgh, though the provost had been hazy quite what the relation was. He had a boy with him, who was deaf and dumb, and who the provost took to be a younger brother. Under those extraordinary circumstances, and on demonstrating in his work a modicum of competence, the contract was drawn up, and no one dared dispute the painter's title to it. In the year of the plague, the strict laws of the gilds were far more lax and fluid. People were displaced, there were vacant posts, requiring to be filled, and for anyone who wished to reinvent themselves, there were opportunities. At the end of the year, the provost had employed the painter in his own house at Dairsie, on works both plain and decorative. The painter had presented him a picture of his wife. And the provost was impressed with the result. *Ars naturam adiuvans*, thought Hew. Or, as the goldsmith had said, it was an unco ill wind.

On the eleventh day following the painter's death, the college of St Salvator was shaken from its sleep by an unearthly wailing sound. It echoed through the cloisters and billowed through the court, plaintive, keen and melancholy. The students who were woken by it fell upon their knees, all but Roger Cunningham, who slipped out from his bed and to the little chamber that was Bartie Groat's, where he found the painter's boy at long last awake, and lowing like a bull-calf in this disparate world, in which he had no sense of any sound he made. Roger soothed him then, by taking in his lap the great lolling head, with its fluff and stubble, cavities and shafts, and stroking with his hands the wet slabs of his cheeks, that were crazed with tears, until the noise diminished to a burn-like babble, bubbling from his throat.

The painter's boy was locked, imprisoned in a glass, where he could be seen and heard, but could not be reached. Roger had amended this, as far as was possible, through the sense of touch, revealing in his hands a sympathetic power. Later in the day, when Giles and Hew arrived, and came in to examine him, Giles found his state of health was not at all discouraging; less certain, more concerning, was that of his mind.

'Poor man. There is no way to tell what damage has been done to his unfettered brain.'

Roger disagreed. 'I do not believe it has been harmed at all. His distress is not derangement. It is his frustration, that he cannot find a way to make his feelings kent. He has lost the man who was his window on the world. And I think it probable he does not ken it yet. It does not seem very likely that he was conscious still, when the painter died.'

If what they had supposed was so, that the painter hanged himself, remorseful for the death blow he had dealt the boy, then that was no doubt true. 'Perhaps he does not ken what happened there at all? We could take him to the hall, and see if it revives in him the glimmer of a memory,' suggested Hew.

'We *cannot*,' Roger said. 'For what he might remember there would drive a man to madness, if he had no way to make it understood, or to have explained to him the questions in his mind.'

Doctor Locke agreed with him, impressed by this display of passion and sound reason, which justified his trust. 'Yet how can we know, that he is not mad now?'

Roger gave an answer that was unexpected. 'Because he has his language still.' He demonstrated to them, that the twitching of the hands, which were loose and agitated, rarely ever still, were attempts to speak. 'I have been watching him, now, for a while. I watched him when he was in conference with the painter. I have not got far. But these are the signs he makes for brush, and paper, this for bread, and meat, and this for the pot, when he wants to piss. He is hungry, now.'

'That is quite remarkable,' said Giles. 'He shall have at once, something from the buttery. Anything he likes. Can he tell you what?'

'I expect he can, though my kenning of the signs is not yet so refined. I only began on it, properly, this morning. And, you understand, he does not have a grammar. Something soft, I doubt. He finds it hard to eat. His teeth are somewhat loose, and some are rattled out.'

'Really?' tutted Giles. 'Let me take a look.'

Roger coaxed the painter's boy to open up his mouth, and Doctor Locke probed gingerly among the cracks and cavities. 'Has the surgeon seen this? What does he say?'

'That the blow from the hammer rippled through the jaw, resounding through the teeth, and shook them from their sockets.'

'Hmm. I will prescribe a paste, of alum and black pepper, and a little salt, that will help to strengthen them. You have done well here, Roger. Many other men would have given up, but you did not despair of him. Now, it is time to return to your studies. You will have till June, to prepare for the black stane, but that is not long. The bones in his skull will take that time to heal. Others can take care of him. You have done your part.'

Roger protested, as they knew he would. 'I can manage both.'

And it was Hew who came down on his side, knowing that Giles Locke was minded to refuse. 'Let him,' he urged, and Giles acquiesced, trusting to his friend.

Hew had already drafted something in his mind, that he thought to try. From a stationer in town, he bought two table books; one large and blank, and a second small and lined. He bought a box of chalks, in red, black and white, and the stationer cut for him four slender reeds, into which he could slide the soft strips of chalk, and sharpened them up to a point, showing to him how he could make his own. He took them back to Bartie's room. The smaller of the books he gave to Roger Cunningham. 'I want you to make a dictionary, of all the words you learn, or that you invent, in your talk with him. Write a description, and, if you can, draw the shape of every sign you use, and write the meaning next to it, in whatever language that you can, as well as Scots, since we have no kenning where he comes from. Then others can have access to his private world, and he will not be closed in it. The other tablet is for him, for it is high time he shared with us what happened here, and tells us what he knows.'

'Sir, he cannot write,' Roger pointed out.

'No. But he can draw.'

Roger began to make his book, as the painter's boy continued his recovery. For the first few days, the prentice showed no interest in the chalks, and his book was blank. Then, something moved him to take up the coloured sticks, and he began to draw, fervently and furiously, with delicate fine lines, until every stick was slivered down to dust, and every page was filled. Roger, the atheist, looked at the pictures, and was taken aback. He passed the book to Doctor Locke, by no means an atheist, who was equally perturbed, and passed it on to Hew. 'Either that poor boy has become deranged, or this was what he saw.'

Hew was not willing to allow the second possibility. For on every page, the picture was the same. And in every picture he had drawn the devil.

The painter's art was imitation. Yet, Hew considered, it was more than that, for it was possible to recognise, from images or words, the likeness of a thing that was never seen before, and yet was unmistakeable. The devil was a spectre never manifest to Hew, and yet he kent at once what he was looking at. He knew him from his books, and most evocative of all, from stories that were stilled in him from his early childhood, legends and descriptions, which he was aware, no one could have told the painter's boy. The painter's boy depicted only what he saw, for all else in the world, and in the other world, was closed to him. Yet Hew would not believe, did not want to countenance, that the painter's boy had witnessed what he drew.

The devil was depicted in a goatish form, standing on two legs, with every shaft of hair upon them intricately drawn, tapered to the hooves that were cloven at his feet, polished shiny smooth with a piece of chalk that the boy had whittled to a jet black dust. The devil had a tail that was barbed and splayed, swishing from his buttocks like the cruellest kind of whip. The devil had two horns, little buds of bone that sprouted from the furrows of his human forehead; his human head and torso had been coloured red, layer upon layer of the grinding of a chalk, thick and deep as blood, on every turning page.

In the corner of each page, on every one identical, the painter's boy had drawn a figure, cowering from the devil who was bearing down upon him. The cowering figure had, in every single case, the same imploring look upon his frightened face.

Hew spent a long time looking at the book, and did not say a word. Giles Locke understood the struggle in his mind, and, for a while, he left him to his thoughts. Eventually he asked, 'What, then, do you think?'

Hew's answer circumscribed, and would not admit, the image of the devil that appeared in every place. He concentrated, rather, on the human he oppressed. 'I was thinking,' he replied, 'how uncanny a likeness our poor boy has made, of his late master, the painter.'

Refusing to submit to the devil in their midst, Hew began a course that was clear and practical. He admitted, privately, that he did not think that it would work. But the implementing of it occupied his mind, and kept it from a trouble he would not admit. He asked Roger Cunningham to use what means he could to persuade the boy to draw a likeness of the painter that was straight and true, and did not have the devil in it. He had no idea how Roger might effect this. But somehow, Roger did.

The finished picture Hew had sent to a city printer, where it was engraved, and printed copies made, at his own expense. He affixed a note, that offered a reward of fifty Scottish pounds to anyone with knowledge of the painter and his name, and the crownar's men pinned a copy up in every town and burgh market place in Fife.

He had little hope that good would come from this. He knew full well, himself, that people did not care to look at papers on the cross, and even if they did, the chance that anyone would recognise the painter from the deaf boy's likeness, uncanny though it was, was surely slim. But it was all he had, and it kept his mind for the moment from his riddle of the picture, to which, he was aware, he had no clue at all. The money, too, might help.

The answer, he supposed, must lie somewhere in the works themselves, for it was plain to him that they were meant to speak. He went back to the dinner hall, to look again at the finished piece, art assisting nature, that was hanging on the wall, and spent an afternoon staring at its depths, the scintillating shades of its sparkling waves, elusive and ethereal, and wondered what the picture meant, what it had to tell him. He was there, still, when Giles Locke came to say that it was nearing suppertime, and he was going home. 'You maun leave it, now. Do you even ken what you are looking for?' Giles asked.

'I was looking,' answered Hew, 'for the painter's signature. For it does seem strange, that a man should make a work as beautiful as this, and not put his name to it. I thought it might be hidden somewhere in the waves, in these flecks and curls; but I have stared for hours, and have not found it there. I cannot help but think, that somewhere in this picture there must be a clue. Why did he take his life, so poignantly, in front of it? He made himself a part of it, suspended on a thread, caught up in the flux of art assisting nature. It is a captivating image, with a quality in it which is almost fugitive, that I believe did far transcend that simple painter's craft. And I am not willing, I do not wish, I will not say, that there is magic in it.

231

Reason and my faith insist, that there can be no magic there, that there must be another, human explanation, but I cannot see it, Giles. I cannot see it.'

The doctor no longer attended to him. His mind had been captured elsewhere. 'Say again,' he said, 'what you hoped to find.'

'A signature,' said Hew. 'But it was in vain. For he has not signed it.'

'Ah, has he not!' the doctor exclaimed. 'You are ingenious, Hew!'

'I thank you. But I am in the dark, how this may be manifest.'

'The surgeon is a fool,' said Giles. 'I always said he was.'

Hew was baffled now. 'In what respect?'

'In all respects. But, specifically, in believing that a blow to the skull with a hack-hammer loosened that boy's teeth. His condition goes deeper than that. It is one that I have treated, many times, when it has been caused by those same idiot surgeons, in their reckless treatment of the pox.'

'Then was it the grandgore, that caused the afflictions that poor boy was born with?' asked Hew.

Giles paused to consider this, 'That is an interesting perspective on it, and one I had not taken into account. On balance, though, I think the damage to the teeth – or more properly, the gums, is more recent and acute. And I have good hopes that it may be cured. The same may not be said of the disruption of his faculties, which, as I believe, have been with him since birth. They are compensated, quite, by his ability to draw. As to whether that ability is a quirk of nature, or the gift of God, I, as a physician, prefer not to assess. I ken what Meg would say.'

'Then he has the grandgore, now?' asked Hew.

'He has never had the grandgore. Please keep up. The answer lies in signatures. *Signatura rerum.*

'As God marks each plant, each herb,' Giles said, 'with the signature of its purpose, to guide the physician in its use, so that it resembles that part, that place in the body where is it effective, treating like with like. I saw the painter paint the wings on Hermes' sandals. And when he hoped to catch those little tufts and fronds, to capture speed and flight, he put aside his brush and painted with a feather. With a *feather*, do you see?'

And Hew did see. For he remembered Heriot, in his goldsmith's shop. He closed his eyes, and gave up thanks to God, that whatever fortune had beset the painter, in his poor distracted heart, the pleated picture Hew had brought there from the king had no active part in it; its power was not to shape, but rather to reflect.

At home at Kenly Green, they explained it all to Frances and to Meg.

'Tomorrow,' Giles concluded, 'we must find the painter's workshop, where we will no doubt find the conclusive evidence. The pity is, that no one kens, to tell us where it is. He was in life, and death, reclusive and most secretive.'

'Can the boy not show you?' asked Meg.

'Perhaps, when he is well enough. I do not ken how Roger will communicate to him our will to find the place. It is a hard thing, to put into signs. And, I doubt, it is not safe for him to go there.'

Frances said, quietly, 'It is on the bank of the Kinnessburn.'

Hew and Giles stared at her, blankly, as though she were speaking in tongues. 'Forgive me,' said Hew, 'but how can you know that?'

'Because it is not far from the place where Will Dyer, Tibbie's husband has his dyeing shop. It is an old barn, belonging to him. And Tibbie Strachan says, the painter owed them rent, that was never paid. She complained about it, when I went to see about the dyeing of our cloth. She said Will would go down, to clear the barn out, and maybe take back what was owed.'

'He must not,' exclaimed Giles. 'Indeed, he must not.'

Frances was bemused by the change she saw in Hew. He was so much absorbed in the riddle of the painter, his mind had little room to think about much else. When they were in bed, she said, 'I do not understand the doctrine of the signatures. How are they reflected in this case?'

'They are not in themselves,' Hew explained. 'It is a kind of parallel. The painter painted like with like. And so it was the work he did that drove him to distraction. It was not, you see, the painting from the king.'

'Then did you think it was?' she asked.

'It is not important what I think, or thought. What matters is the king, who must not come to think his painting is bewitched. I have to reassure him everything is well. This is good news, Frances. Horror though it is, the painter's death now has a rational explanation.'

'Then I am content. And more so since I chanced to be of help. But there is one thing,' Frances said, 'I do not understand. Why did the painter's boy draw pictures of the devil? For he could not have seen into the painter's mind. And how could he have drawn, what he has never seen? Signatures, or not?'

That question troubled Hew, and kept him still awake, long into the night.

The next morning, Giles and Hew returned to town. At St Salvator's, they found the painter's boy had spent a restless night. Roger let him out, for exercise and air, and he had wandered mournfully, from door to door and from room to room, chapping at the students to keep them from their rest with his plaintive cries. 'He has been like this,' Roger admitted, 'since you took the picture from him he drew of the painter. I kept him, for the first while, in his room, but it does not seem right to keep him prisoned there. Therefore, I resolved to let him out, but to keep him close inside the college grounds. He goes back, again and again, to the dinner hall, rattling at the lock. I think that he is looking for the painter. I do not think he kens that he is dead. And I do not ken the language for to tell him. And if I did, I would not ken, how to make him understand. What can he ken of death?'

And Hew, looking at the boy's dishevelled, mournful face, saw in it a feeling that was raw and unsophisticated, unsullied and unshaped by any hope or faith, and saw that what he felt, that did not shape itself in any kind of words, was a desolation deeper than a death, that had no understanding, but was an abandonment. And he was engulfed in pity for the boy.

It was their intention to set out to the Kinnessburn, to find the painter's shop. But they were distracted, before they could depart, by the arrival of the crownar Andrew Wood. With him he brought one of his own tenants, whose father had a farm, in the lea of Largo Law. This tenant clutched a picture in his hand, of the painter Andrew Wood had only just nailed up, on the outside door of his own parish kirk. The farmer's son had come to claim his fifty pounds. And he had a tale to tell. Sir Andrew Wood assumed that his credentials were impeccable, for it was a foolish man who spun a yarn to him, or plucked him for a fraud, and a brave one who had spent the last few hours with him, subject to a most exacting inquisition. Andrew, at the last, was utterly convinced, and he had brought to them what shadow there was left, wrung out from his tenant, to collect his prize.

'You will want to hear this for yourself,' he informed them grimly.

The four of them retreated to the turret tower, where Giles provided chairs, and a cup of brandy wine to encourage the informant, who was deathly pale. 'I ken this man,' he said, gulping at the drink, 'his name is Pieter Kemp.'

Hew said, 'Are you sure?'

'I ken that face. I see it my dreams. And a thing like that, a man does not forget. Pieter Kemp is dead.'

'We know that he is dead,' said Hew. 'What more do you know of him?'

'That he is in Hell.'

The farmer glanced at Andrew Wood, a real and creeping terror shadowed in his eyes. But it was not the crownar that he seemed to fear; he was grasping for support.

'I saw him die, you see. He died on Largo Law.'

'Then you are mistaken. This is not your friend. This man died here at the college,' Hew replied.

'Wait, hear him out,' the crownar said.

'This is Pieter Kemp,' the man insistently stubbornly. 'I would ken him anywhere. I saw him die. He died on Largo Law. The devil came an' plucked him, howling, from that place.'

Chapter 21

A Devil Incarnate

Sir Andrew Wood said, 'Tell these men your history. For it will relieve that load upon your soul. And you know you want to.'

The tenant took a gulp of the brandy in the cup. The amber liquid stilled in him both courage and a kind of fear. And he began a tale of treachery and greed, that as it was unfolded there made perfect sense to Hew, dreadful though it was.

It had begun, long ago, when the tenant's grandsire had been but a bairn; long before that time, the tenant thought. The devil sets his snares to trip up silly bairns, who fall into his traps, guilelessly and greedily. When Sir Andrew's tenant was a mewling bairn, his grandsire gave to him a rugged piece of rock. And running though that rock, hidden in its core like the seeds inside a pear, were little grains of gold.

The gold was from a mine at Largo Law, that had been buried deep since ancient times. So deep inside the hill that the grains of gold did not surface in the soil, or cluster in the streams that rippled at its foot, but was close encased inside that core of rock. But when the grandfather's grandfather had been a boy, that mine was opened up, and every chink of rock extracted from its core had given up its seed, its solid core of gold, until one day, the stories said, the man who found it drilled too far, and in he slipped and fell, deep into the heart of it, and lost his life to greed, and seeking after gold. Twas said, the devil came, and closed the mine again. And he set a ghost – the ghost of the dead man – to guard the entrance to it, so that the hot hewn rock, riven to its core, should never feel again the sair strak

236

of the pick that seared its living heart. And that was no surprise, for was it not well kent that evil spirits bide and watch by hoards of gold?

'One day,' the tenant said, 'a shepherd came, who dared to brave the ghost, in hope to have that gold, and asked him where it was. And that ghost said, he would show him that the place, if the cock did not crow, and the horn did not blow in the valley at Balmain, which was near that place. And that,' the tenant said, 'was as much as to say, I will tell it on a day when the sun does not rise, and the shepherd should have kent, no good could ever come of a day like that. But he was wily, see, and thought to trick that ghost. And he did gang awa, and slaughtered all the cocks, that crowed for miles around. And he telt the herder there, that came to graze his flock at Balmain by the Law, that God would strike him down, if he dared blow his horn. And so he came to that ghost, blustering and brave, and thought to have his gold, when the herder forgot, or neglected what was told, and blasted on his horn, and that ghost did cry, "Woe to the man that blew on the horn, for out of the spot he shall never be borne". The ghost disappeared, and was not seen again. And so that wily shepherd did not find his gold. But the herder was struck dead on the spot. And however hard they tried, they could not shift his corpse, as though it had fixed into the rock itself, and that was unco strange, for that herder was a weak and insubstantial man. And when his friends could not shift nor bury that body, they covered it with stones, and made of it a cairn, where it stands still.'

'Aye, that is true,' Andrew Wood confirmed. 'I have seen the cairn.' He was conscious, perhaps, of the doubt in Giles and Hew, as they turned their gaze on him, for he added, 'And, I have heard the tale which is, ye must know, well-kent in Largo.'

'I did not believe the tale,' his tenant said, unexpectedly, 'about the Largo Law. And I did not believe, the devil bides there too, until I saw it for myself, for I was like that shepherd, and a greedy, reckless boy. I thought the stories were made up, by those who hoped to have the gold themselves. I knew there was a mine, for my grandfather's grandfather saw it himself, and my grandfather gave me a piece of that gold, and there is no legend true or compelling as the one before your eyes. I will not lie to you, I wanted a part of that gold for myself, even back then, when I was a bairn. I helped my father on the land. We used to graze our sheep on the low slopes of the Law. The golden sun would shine on them, and they had yellow-tinted fells, from gazing on the grass that grew above the gold. And when I was a boy, I used to climb the Law, and look for the entrance to the ancient mine. I never found it, then.

'My father bade me bide by him, and help him work the land. But I knew in my heart, I was not meant for that. When I was eighteen, I went to Wanlockheid, far awa in Galloway, where they were mining lead, and gold and silver too. I thought, the skills I learned there I could bring back home with me, to open up the seam in Largo Law. That there must be a safer way to sink a shaft; and with that kenning I might mak a fortune of my own. There were, at that time, several mines in that place, and upwards of three hundred men were employed there, crushing the stones and washing for gold. And it was there that I met with Pieter Kemp. He was working for a man called Arnold Bronckhorst, who had come fae England to open up a mine. And Bronckhorst's mine was fu of gold.'

'Bronckhorst?' asked Hew, looking up at this. 'Bronckhorst, the painter? Was Pieter Kemp his prentice, then?' For that would seem to fit, if Pieter Kemp and Workman were one and the same.

'Bronckhorst was a painter. He was after painter to the king, when he was a bairn, though I heard it said he had no profit from it. It was the regent Morton forced him to the place, and you cannot, as I think, make a painter paint, more than you can make a captive linnet sing. Bronckhorst had no pleasure from the place, though he did paint that king, and that Morton too, that was stiff and arrogant, until they made him swing for it, and cut him doon to size. That is what I heard, and had from Pieter Kemp, when I saw him last,' the tenant said. 'Pieter Kemp was not his prentice, quite. He had begun, with him, no doubt, to come up in the craft, but Bronckhorst thocht that Pieter showed no art or skill for it. Bronckhorst was a man who was particular, ye see. He liked his work, just so. And though he would let Pieter grind and wash his colours for him, cook and clean his cloths, he did not have the patience to train him to his craft, and so what Pieter kent of painting, he had taught himself, and that was not so much.'

'It seems you knew him well,' Giles said.

'I did ken him well,' the tenant agreed. 'For he was a brave kind of bully to me, and he was a friend. And he took care of me, when I was not well, and the work was hard, and I was far from home. I was eighteen. He was, I doubt, older by five or six years and he took me under his wing. He defended me, from Bronckhorst, when on one occasion I had taken gold, to put by for myself. He swore the theft was his, and he was punished for it.'

'Why would he do that?' asked Hew.

'Because we were friends,' the tenant said simply. 'I was saving the gold, to put to the cost of working the mine, which one day, I knew would be mine. And Pieter kent that too, for I had telt him all about the gold on Largo Law. You must see, sirs, that it was not stealing from him, as Bronckhorst would have. And all of us tapped off what drops of it we could, for why else had we come, but to make our fortunes from it? The ground and streams were full of it; you might as well call theft the dipping in a burn or drinking in the air. But Bronckhorst was a jealous man, who thought the earth was his. And little did he gain from it, for when the regent Morton found him at his spoils, a peregrine abroad who pillaged Scottish crops, he took the whole in charge.'

It seemed to Hew that gold released a greed in men, that ran through like a seam, a fault inside their bones. 'This Pieter Kemp,' he asked, 'was he, like Bronckhorst, a Dutchman?' For the painter they had known, calling himself Workman, had surely been a Scot.

'His father was,' the tenant said. 'His mother was a Scot. And Pieter himself, he had the kind of wit, his manner and his voice, that kens to shift and slip – it was, *enchanting*, do you ken?' He looked a little foolish, then, flushing at the word, but persisted stubbornly. 'So did I think then, and now I know, I ken, enchanting is the word. I did not see it then, what menace might be meant in it.'

'That,' said Andrew Wood, 'is how the devil works, to snare folk in his charm.'

The tenant said, uneasily, 'I dinna ken, but there was something in him that was likeable. A flitting kind of wit, and something that was quick, and malleable in him. I did not ken for why I was attracted to it. For I did not ken, what the man had done, to make himself like that.'

Hew asked, 'What had he done?'

'He had made a compact, with the devil.' The tenant faltered then, and flapped about so fearfully that it was only the threat of the fiercest retribution, from Sir Andrew Wood, and the promise of a pocket full of coins, from Hew, and the comfort of another cup full of his sugar brandy, from Professor Locke, could induce him to go on.

'Then, my masters,' he spilled out at last, trembling in his cup, 'Master Bronckhorst flew into a rage, and beat Pieter Kemp, and dismissed him on the spot. Pieter quit that place. And after he had gone, Bronckhorst said that he had robbed him of a quantity of gold, and some of his colours, as he said, that were particular to him; and he was wrath and furious, and said the colours he had taken were the purest of their kind, and could not be replaced. And that like that man, for who can grudge a man a drop of colour for his eye, would snatch from him the air, or very earth he walks upon. But Bronckhorst seemed to think this was a heinous crime, for he swore that Pieter niver would hae joy from them, but they would serve him ill. And he said Pieter would be sorry, if ever he did dare to cross his path again. And that, I did think strange, for the colours Pieter took were but dirty clumps of rock, and could be nothing worse.'

Hew glanced at Giles, a picture clearing in his mind, the answer to a question there. 'Aye,' he said, 'go on.'

'Well,' said Pieter's friend, 'not long after that, the king's regent Morton found what Bronckhorst did there, and pressed him to his service, and the mine was closed. I came home to my father, then, to help him on the farm. And it irked me, to be sure, to have to come again to graze my yellow sheep, no closer to the fortune they kept underground. I had some gold put by, that I had squirrelled there, and where I could, I saved and added to that pile, thinking, one day, I wad hae enough to entice a man to try to sink a shaft with me; for, as you maun ken, gold begets gold.'

'And that man,' Hew supposed, 'was Pieter Kemp. How did you find him again?'

'Pieter Kemp found me. He came to my father's house, four years ago, that was four years after I had seen him last; and he telt me that he had been thinking all this while, about the gold mine I had telt him was on Largo Law, and that he had a pact, with a certain friend, to excavate the mine, and that, for the friendship he had kept with me, he was well disposed to cut me into it. His friend had found the entrance to the ancient shaft, and would show us where it was, but he wanted gold for it. And he said, if I was willing to invest my gold, and whatever else I had, he would do the same, and we should have our fortunes replicated there, a hunner thousand fold.'

'The upshot is,' Sir Andrew said, 'he gave the loun his money.'

'And wherefore, should I not?' the fearful tenant cried. 'He was my billie, then. I trusted him. I could not know the friend, with whom he made his pact. But he telt me that the friend was jealous and suspicious, and to win his trust, we should take the money to him at the Largo Law, and to the secret place, where his excavation shortly would begin.'

'Convenient,' murmured Giles.

'It was not convenient, sir,' the man said, misunderstanding him. 'But it was what the friend required. And when you come to know, the nature of his friend, you will understood. Pieter said that he was sorry that it had to be like that. But as proof of his faith, we must both do the same; he showed me his part of it, and I showed him mine. It was all of the gold I had kept from the mine, and all that I had saved, besides some that my father had put by him in a kist, and some rings and plate, and we took it with us climbing Largo Law, and I found it heavy, and the going hard, but his appeared quite light, and that he said was for the bargain he had made, and he was well content with it.'

'Ah,' Giles sighed. 'No doubt.'

'Well, masters, then,' the tenant's voice accelerated, hurtling to a precipice, as he came at last to the climax of his tale, 'he said we must go right to the top, for there his friend would wait for us, and take us to the entrance to the mine, which could be measured only from that place they called the devil's chair, which has seven steps, and there we should wait for him. There, tis steep, and I was glad to rest, and put down my sack. And there . . . and there . . . the devil came, and took him, sirs. And since I saw it there, I ken that he is dead.' Abruptly, he stopped.

Hew pressed him on, 'What was the devil like?'

'He was like a beast, louping on twa legs, with a great lolling tongue, and skin that was bright red, and horns to his head, and a thrashing tail. Oh, do not ask me masters, to remember more. He came out from the heart, the deep core of that rock, where, God is my witness, no place is to hide. And Pieter, when he saw him, fell upon his knees, and wept, "Pity, master, pity, for I paid my debt." And he showed up the gold, but the devil did not care, for he swept poor Pieter up, and Pieter screamed a scream I never heard before, and never, as I live, would want to hear again. And it would split the ears of any mortal man, but that devil did not flinch at it, but dragged poor Pieter off.'

'Where did they go? Where could they go?' wondered Hew.

'I do not ken. My heart was beating then, and when I had the courage to climb up there and look, they were gone from there. Pieter sold the devil his soul,' the man concluded bleakly, 'in return for the key to that gold. He thought, that with my gold, he might buy the devil off. It was not enough. For with the devil, see, it never is enough. And I was unco fearful he would come for me, and so I quit that place.'

Hew showed to him the picture the painter's boy had drawn. 'Is this what you saw?'

The farmer shrank from it. 'Exactly so,' he whispered. 'That is him, to the life. And there is Pieter, too. I do not ken how anyone could make so true a likeness, and he were not there.'

'Perhaps,' said Hew, 'he was.'

The man was fortified, and mollified with gold; for all his frights and fears, his avaricious nature had not quite been cured by what had happened to his friend. But he was sent off quivering, clutching at his sack, and sending nervous glances all around his back.

'And let us hope,' said Giles, 'he will be more cautious now where he invests his gains.'

Sir Andrew Wood said, shakily, 'Pray God the devil does not come again for him.'

Both men stared at him. 'Tell me,' Hew enquired, 'what you think has happened here?'

'It is plain enough,' the coroner explained, 'that this Pieter stole the gold from him, to pay the devil back. The devil spared him then, but came for him at last, in the college hall. The dummel witnessed it.'

'Dear me,' muttered Giles, 'if that is what you think, what hope can there be for the common man?'

'What do you think, then?' Sir Andrew put to them.

'We think,' said Hew, 'the devil was a man dressed up.'

The crownar shook his head, 'No. It cannot be. For where, then, did they go, with that poor man's gold? You heard him say there was no place to hide.'

'This is true, and pertinent,' said Hew. 'Perhaps there *was* a mine, or a fissure in the rock, and Pieter Kemp had found it. Or perhaps our friend was so afeart he did not stay to see, in spite of what he says. You might take your men, and climb up there to look.'

The crownar swore at him. 'Never, on my life,' he said. 'No man, fearing God, would pull a trick like that. To dress up as the devil there, in order to deceive, would call upon himself a fury straight from Hell itself. That is a haunted place.'

Superstition had the better of him then; and that was not so rare, for all men kenned the devil watches over gold, and that evil spirits linger in the air of country vales and hills. And who but the devil could drive a man, to such a bleak and godless end, the taking of his life?

'What God-fearing soul could dare do such a thing?'

'Perhaps it was a man,' said Hew, 'who was not troubled by a God, that he had never heard.'

The tenant's account made it seem more imperative still, that they should discover the dead painter's workshop. They were in two minds whether it was safe to take the boy with them. Hew believed they should. 'We may never ken, unless he comes to show us. And in coming to that place, he may understand that his friend is lost to him, and will not come again.' Roger, when he heard, insisted to come too. And, conceded Giles, there was a certain sense to it. He knew as much of alchemy as any one of them, and far more than Hew. 'If the truth of it is what we do expect, the air will be noisome,' he warned. 'We must all take care.'

It was Roger who suggested they should take the plague masks, and they were at last a grim little party that came through the town, past the South Street colleges and down towards the Kinnessburn, where the painter's boy broke free from Roger's careful hands, and ran towards the barn, which, had they allowed, he could have shown them all the while. And there they found the relicts of the master painter's life, and the stolen colours, which had brought about his death.

And Hew, from his experiment at Geordie Heriot's shop, could understand it well, without the explanations of the subtle alchemists. Bronckhorst's red was cinnabar, a compound in the rock of mercury and sulphur, in its natural state. The painter had extracted from it its component parts, to bubble in a pot and amalgamate again, to distil into vermillion clear and pure and deep. He had used the *argent vive*, extracted from the cinnabar, to purify the gold he shivered into leaf, and, using like for like, to paint into his picture, mercury for Mercury, or Hermes in the Greek, god of thieves, and fugitives, shifting, sly and fleet. The painter stilled his colours, secretly, and jealously, closed inside his shop. And the mercury he stilled had crept its noxious fumes, silently, insistently, where he worked and slept. Its poison had made loose the teeth of the apprentice boy, sheltered at some distance from it; and closer, more insidious, it had worked its poison in the painter's mind.

The painter's boy showed them the kist, where they found the costume that his master made for him, and coaxed him to put on, to perpetrate his fraud: the hairskin hose and tail, the make-up of red lake. The boy could not have kent, thought Hew, what it was it meant. But had the horror of it come to haunt the man? Had he tried to wipe that horror from his face? Had he felt remorse, that he had made a boy who had no kenning of the devil or the word of God, dress up in his garb? Or had the devil, in his madness, come again, for him?

They could never know. The painter's boy, shown to the place, understood at last, that he was quite alone. And by the kist that held his uncouth devil's costume, he knelt down and howled.

'The pity is,' said Giles, later at St Salvator's, 'I think we must destroy this painting. Else the mercury in it may leach out into the air, and poison us all, gradually. Art has not assisted nature here, at all.'

'That is sad,' said Hew. 'And I am sorry too, that the picture that the prentice made of you was ruined. Perhaps, when he is well enough, he will make another.'

The doctor shook his head. 'I do not think so. I never felt at ease with it. And what is a likeness, after all, but a poorer imitation of the life?'

'That is true enough.' Hew smiled. 'And, we still have you. Who, in your uniqueness, bear no imitations.'

He was teasing now, but Giles continued seriously, 'What would be the purpose of it? None, while I am here. And after I am gone, in a hundred years, in fifty years, or less, it would be no more than a pattern of a man, of some old physician, long ago forgotten. Better now, by far, to have a picture of the skull. *Memento mori*, Hew, for that is all we are.'

When the painter's boy was well enough, Hew relieved Roger of his care, and took him down to Edinburgh. Roger was aggrieved at this. 'I have not finished with him, yet. He has more to learn.'

Hew said, 'He is not your pet. And you have your own work, now, to attend to.' He felt that Roger's influence on the painter's boy had come quite far enough. He took with him the book of signs, and the book of sketches that the boy had done, and set the painter's boy before him on his horse. The boy did not resist. He had given up his searching for the painter, and had lapsed into a placid, solitary quietness, allowing himself to be led, with little hope or care. The medicines that Giles had given him had washed away, perhaps, the last trace of poison that had hurt his body, but the damage to his mind was harder to expel, and difficult to mend.

Hew took him, and the books, to Adrian Vanson's house. 'What is this, you bring me?' Vanson said. 'Have I not enough of hopeless boys?'

The painter's boy did seem a hopeless case. He had a hollow dint in one side of his head, and the stubble that grew back there was an odd shade to the rest. He was large and shambling, and with his poking tongue and useless muckle lugs he might have looked quite comical, but for the sad intelligence that showed behind his eyes. 'So,' Vanson said. 'Another futless hulk. Break it to me, now, what this one cannot do.'

'He cannot hear,' said Hew, 'so he will not heed you when you rail at him. And he cannot speak, so he will not cheek you, like your own boys do. He cannot trim a brush, or wash a board with size. He does not ken at all, how to grind the colours to make into paint. But, he can draw.'

He gave Vanson the books with the drawings and signs, and Vanson turned the pages, looking through the drafts. He was quiet for a moment. Then he answered. 'So. Drawing is a start.' He looked at Susanna, and smiled. 'What do you think?'

'I think,' Susanna said, 'that he must be hungry. Boys are always hungry. And, since our dinner is done, he has come at an opportune time.'

Hew went to Heriot's shop, to collect his wedding ring. And Heriot told to him the story he had heard, about a seeker after gold who was taken by the devil from a mine at Largo Law. It seemed Sir Andrew's tenant had not been the only man that Pieter Kemp had fleeced, for there were several more. 'The devil claims his ain, then, after all,' Geordie said.

'I should have heard you, then,' said Hew, 'and spared myself a trail.'

He put the ring in its pouch in his pocket to keep safe. They had come no closer to the calling of the banns, for he had made no progress at all in finding out the source of the king's pleated picture. He made extensive enquiries, at Holyrood and Canongate, but to no avail. And he was forced to acknowledge that Maitland had been right, the council had already made a searching inquisition, there was no stone in that city that had not been overturned. It irked him when he found a dead end to each path, not willing to admit his failure to the king. He felt he had to prove himself, his faith and trust, to James, and that he owed a debt of some sort to that queen, that he could not explain. He was certain, in his heart, that the answer lay with Bronckhorst. But Bronckhorst had left Scotland years before, and all trail of him had long grown cold. At least, the picture had not caused the death of Pieter Kemp, in any crucial sense.

For Frances' sake, he was less alarmed. The king had moved towards a concord with Elizabeth, and Andrew Wood believed it likely they would come to terms. Whatever Hew felt privately about the crownar now, he was a useful source of information, from both the Scottish and the English courts. It seemed likely that the law would be relaxed in time, as the people's heat and temper simmered down, and that he and Frances would be let to live in peace. And Frances, if not welcomed, had at least been tolerated, when she went to town. St Andrews had relaxed, he thought, the fierceness of its ministry, had mellowed in the plague. Perhaps the town would let, and leave the lovers be? So he had hoped and thought, as he returned back home. So did he misjudge the temper of that Kirk.

Chapter 22

Letters Home

At the chapel of St Leonard's in St Andrews, the principal arose, uneasily, from prayer that brought his troubled mind as little resolution as if he had said bah to it, and spent the hour in bed. As the students filed before him, to begin upon their day in a muddled morning haar, he pushed past them to waylay the regent Robert Black, before he opened up his Aristotle. 'I wanted to ask you,' he said, 'whether you were free to take the prayers tonight. There is, you see, an extraordinary meeting this evening of the kirk session, that I am compelled to attend.'

Robert said, of course. The implication that he might not have been free, to attend to an event that circumscribed his waking life, was so preposterous he felt there must be something more his principal had meant by it, and that it was a cloak, for what he had to say to him. And so he waited, meekly there, in certain fear and hope the principal would wrestle out the substance of a closer confidence. His patience was rewarded when the master said, 'The truth is, if I could, I would rather stay, for the matter is a case that is vexing to me. It concerns the household of a friend of yours, Hew Cullan, up at Kenly Green. You may have heard, or not, that he is home again. That young man courts trouble as a papist courts controversy.'

'I heard that he was home. I have not seen him yet. What has he done now?' asked Robert Black.

'I do not have the details, yet, to hand. But it concerns, it seems a case of fornication, that is far from straight, and marriage of a sort, not entirely regular, and an errant stranger, harboured in his house.

I have to say, I do not like it much. He is a contentious soul, and his wrangling in the past has brought a trouble here, I would not well contend with in the college. And yet, I do confess, there is some goodness in him. Do you recall that boy, the wry unruly student we expelled from here?'

'Roger,' Robert said.

'Aye, twas Roger Cunningham. We all were quite convicted that he was a hopeless case, but Hew kept faith with him, and took him to St Salvator's, and now, I understand, his honour is restored. Giles Locke thinks the world of him. It was the elder brother had us all deceived. You heard how he turned out? And butter would not melt, in that sly limmar's mouth, sleek fish as he was. Hew is quite a searching kind of man, to flush a matter out, and I am inclined to trust his better judgement. My worry is, you see, that his involvement in this case will bring us in dispute, and worse, to disrepute, in kirk and university. Then will Andro Melville wag his lofty brow at us, and say that we are wanting in our own morality.'

'But surely,' Robert said, 'it is matter for the parish, not the college. Hew Cullan is no longer an assistant here.'

The principal was gratified. 'You are right, of course. And I maun thank you, Robert, that you bring it to my mind. He shall be treated as a member of this kirk, and not of our community, which will free my judgement from preferential prejudice. Thank you for your help.'

It occurred to Robert Black that he might send a word to Hew, in order to prepare him for unpleasantness to come. On balance, he decided, he would rather not. When Hew required his help, he sought it soon enough, and not without a cost of inconvenience to him. Robert was a man who liked a quiet life. He had stayed a regent there for many happy terms, without aspiring ever to progress to a professor, and he believed that stagnant waters should be left unstirred.

At six o'clock, the principal left St Leonard's college for the Holy Trinity. In the absence of its own incumbent, he was called to moderate the session of the elders of the parish kirk. It was not a role that he had entered warmly, or with relish. The kirk session had not met through the months of plague. When the threat died down, the court had met sporadically, and without conviction. Perhaps the people who survived were too afflicted to offend, or perhaps the session felt they had been scourged enough, by the effects of the plague. Their own chastisements were eclipsed and all but made superfluous, trumped in scale by God's. They were hindered, too, by the lack of a minister. The bishop had stepped in, but found himself at odds, and often excommunicated by the vengeful presbyters. The principal lost track of whether Patrick Adamson was lately out or in. Whatever stage the bishop reached, in favour or disgrace, did not deflect him from his preaching in the kirk. But it did deter some of his flock, who drifted away to hear Andrew Melville, even though he had not been ordained. The fabric showed signs of a fracture. To keep the kirk whole, and to restore morale and spirit in the gloomy town, the elders of the kirk had endeavoured to restore those lively entertainments which had been the highlight of the Sunday service, the cuckstool and the jougs and the parading there of penitents, and the fleshly celebration of the people's sins. The St Leonard's principal did not care for that. He had no will to see a lassie shiver in her shift, all for the sake of a man she had kissed. The people would have said, he looked down his nose; but he was better suited to his dead philosophy than to the rough and rumpus of a living kirk.

Therefore, he had qualms when he came to Holy Trinity, where the elders met. The case they put before him was delicate and strange and not at all what he had been expecting. He tried, in vain, to cite Leviticus, 'And if a stranger sojourn with thee in your land, ye shall not vex him. But the stranger that dwelleth with you, shall be as one of yourselves, and thou shalt love him as thyself.' Leviticus had opened up Pandora's Box of tricks. And he could not deny that action must be taken. They could not allow such flagrant immorality to go unobserved.

'They are living openly, and as man and wife,' an elder said.

'But,' he countered feebly, 'how can we sure the act has taken place?'

The man to his right, a broad-shouldered baxter, leant over to him kindly, and whispered in his ear, respectful of his feelings as the sort of clergyman who had spent his whole life sheltered in a college. He blinked at the words. 'Ah, then, I see. Does she indeed. Then I approve of it, quite.'

A summons was drawn up, and the principal agreed, heavy in his heart, that he would go himself, to serve it in the place complicit in offence. The house at Kenly Green was within his parish boundaries, and all of its inhabitants fell under his own charge.

Hew, not expecting this visit from the master of the college that was close and dear to him, received him well and cordially. He allowed the man to say what he had to say, without attempting to distract him, or to put up a defence. And when, at the last, the principal concluded, 'And there it is. I must say, I am sorry for it. But it can't be helped.' Hew acceded quietly, accepting the summons that was in the master's hand.

When the man had gone, Hew turned the letter over in his hand. He sat thoughtful a moment. When resolution came, he did not call to Frances, who had gone upstairs, nor indeed to Meg, but left the house, and walked, by the garden walls, to the Kenly stable, where his horse was kept. There, he found Robert Lachlan talking with the groom. And he served Robert Lachlan with the summons from the kirk, to compear before the session on the first of May, where he stood accused, of carnal conversation with the servant, Bella Frew.

Canny Bett, in the kitchen, scolded the serving maid. 'You silly bisum, Bella, why would ye tell them that ye were with child?'

Bella answered, with a flounce. 'Mebbe, I am.'

'You cannot ken that yet.'

'Aye, mebbe not. But, if I am not, I will be in time. The kirk will not hurt me for it, if I am with bairn. And he will have to marry me.'

'He is marrit now, you silly, silly loun.'

Canny Bett had witnessed, when Robert married Maude, the

keeper of the harbour inn, before they left for Ghent. There, he had entrusted her to the Flemish nuns. But only Hew knew that.

'Aye, to a nun. It was never consummated.'

'He telt you that? Then you are dafter, Bella, even than I thought.'

But Bella was not daft.

Robert Lachlan came to the kirk of Holy Trinity, to compear before the session, as the court required, on the 1st of May. Some among the council were surprised to see him there. Others were dismayed. And one or two were quickened to exaggerated pride and pleasure to have caught so fierce and stout a fish, in their hopeful net.

Robert was a stranger there. And as a stranger to the parish, of a rough demeanour and a tendency to drink, and to corrupt the lassies, powerless to his charms, some had held the hope their writ would see him off, without he had to linger there, to darken their bright kirk. The hammer in the spoke had been Bella Frew, who if she had a bairn, would look to some support. And whatever sustenance could not be squeezed from him, would default on them.

The sight of this soldier, captive like Samson, shorn in their midst, caused the fainter-hearted there a frisson of alarm, and the braggardly, a pride that blew out in a blast. They could not conceive that they had caught him quietly.

Some of them, indeed, were put out to discover that he had not come alone, but had brought a friend to speak in his defence. It was not usual for a man to come before the session with his lawyer with him. 'Do ye think,' one of the elders had put to him, 'you will hae an advocate, in your final judgement, when you come to God? When you greet and tremble, on your knees before him, to quimper in the dust? Believe me, you will not.'

But Hew had put the case. Since Robert Lachlan was a stranger to the parish, he required a person of estate to vouch for his good character. Such a one was he. Secondly, he refuted, absolutely, the accusation of adultery, that was put to him. The session kent full well that Robert Lachlan had a wife, for he had married in that parish, five years before, Maude Benet of the harbour inn. Unless he could show proof to them that the wife was dead, he was an adulter, and a villain therefore of a heinous kind. Hew bore witness that the premise to this charge was false, with what appeared to be an extraordinary defence. Robert Lachlan's wife had left him on his wedding night, and gone to be a nun.

The elders were blawn out at this, deflated of their wind. 'Dear me,' one consoled, 'a most unhappy man.'

Robert Lachlan hung his head, and did not say a word.

At last, when Hew concluded making his defence, and bumbaized and bemused them with piercing points of law, they were agreed, that in view of the delinquent's plain and abject penitence, and Bella's parlous state, the charge would be reduced, to the lesser one of anti-nuptial fornication, and the couple would be married, after standing up on seven separate Sundays, repenting, at the kirk. This sentence Robert Lachlan took upon himself with so calm a meekness it drove many from their pleasure at it to a silent fear, and those who saw him standing, naked in his shirt, thoughtful as the lion chained up in its stall, did not stop to stare, but hurried past uneasily. Bella, for her part, stood by him bold and proud, and not a bit abashed.

Robert Lachlan's answer had astonished Hew, for never had he known him turn off from a challenge or resist a fight. 'What will you do?' he had asked, when Bella's indiscretion first had come to light. And Robert had replied, 'Marry her, I doubt.'

Robert was, quite plainly, not the marrying sort. His marriage to Maude Benet had been a convenience, which, as it turned out, was not convenient now.

'Do you think,' Hew pressed, 'tis true that she's with child?'

Robert had shrugged. 'Probably not.'

'And you do not care?'

'Probably not.' Robert had leaned back against the stable wall, sucking at a straw he bit between his teeth, as though he had no trouble to disturb him in the world.

'The truth is,' he allowed, 'I like the little lass. She has a kind of spark to her.'

'But she has trapped you here. She has telt tales on you, to the kirk session,' Hew had pointed out.

'Aye, I ken.' Robert grinned. 'Canny, is she not?'

And so he held his peace, and stood to bow his head, for seven Sundays dry and wet, barefoot in the church. The avaricious kirkmen triumphed in his fall. But it was not their kirk, that held him humbled there. It was Bella Frew.

For Hew's own case with Frances, peaceful resolution did not come so easily. At the close of Robert's trial, Hew had begged a word, private and in confidence, with the college principal. What he had to say there darkened that man's face. 'I cannot help you, Hew. I will not read the banns without the king's consent, and while we are at odds with all who are from England, I cannot marry you. I cannot, do you see, implicate the college. The best I can do, is to turn a blind eye. And since you are remote, and do not live in town, the chance is you may live there free from jealous scrutiny, unless and until your wife should fall with child. For then, I think, some questions may be asked.'

There was little Hew could do, and he left there malcontent and furious in mind, that he could not solve the riddle and appease the king. The weeks he spent with Frances, closed at Kenly Green, were heady and idyllic, and for a snatch at paradise, might well have sufficed. But they were both aware, they did not make a life.

It was Frances who resolved it, in the end. It was early June, and the lace and silks that she and Meg had brought home from the Senzie fair had long since been cut up and stitched into a dress, that was put away, with petals and sweet herbs to chase away the moths. She and Hew were lying, close in bed together, in a still contentment that required no words, and where, for several minutes, neither of them spoke. Then Frances mentioned, quietly and tentative, 'I have found something out. And, you were right. Bronckhorst is the answer to your pleated painting.'

Her husband smiled at her. He had begun to grow used to her shy intelligence. Frances was thoughtful, quiet, and contemplative. She noticed and observed, and over a long while, worked out her thoughts. But he did not expect much to come of this. There was no scrap or clue he had not worked up in his mind, thoroughly and endlessly. 'And how have you done that?' he asked.

She hesitated then. 'I wrote of it to Tom. I have written to him several other times. The first, when you went south to see the king.'

'You wrote to Tom? To *Tom*?'

And though he understood it was not meant for treachery, he felt, with every stretching sinew of his heart, betrayed.

'And what were wrong with that? He is my cousin, Hew,' Frances said defensively.

'A cousin such as that ... you do not *like* him, Frances,' he exclaimed.

'I had not thought I did. But things take different colours far away from home.'

He saw her tremble then, and was overcome with pity and with guilt, to hide from her his fears. 'Of course they do. Forgive me. Tell me, Frances.' He dared not conceive the damage she had done. For none knew more than he, the end result of letters that were sent to Tom, what weapons they became, in Thomas Phelippes' hands. Had Frances fallen in, so helplessly and guilelessly? 'Why did you write to *him*?'

Frances said, 'It was not him, at first. I wrote to my uncle and aunt. I asked for their forgiveness, which they did not grant. Only Tom replied. He wrote such words of kindness, Hew. He said he understood, and he admired my courage. I think it did amuse him, that we snatched away behind my uncle's back. He promised he would treat for me, with my aunt and uncle, and that in due course, we might be reconciled. He gave me his support, and encouraged me to write.'

'Of course he did.' Hew suppressed the bitter words that gathered in his mind. He understood her homesickness, had gone through it himself. Then Frances had helped him. When she was alone, he had been absent, looking for painters. And Phelippes understood, precisely how to prey upon that vulnerability. It made Hew sick at heart. 'The most revealing letters,' Laurence had once told him, 'are those of the wives.' And none was more adept at reading them than Phelippes.

'But how did you send them?' he asked. By what skew means had Frances found a post, when all lines were closed? It did not quite seem credible.

'Matthew's tutor sent them from St Mary's College. And he brought Tom's back with him.'

He stared at her. 'What? You trusted your letters to a foreign kirkman? Why would you do that?'

'Because he offered, Hew. And there was no one else. You had gone away. And I could not be sure, if you would come back.'

'Of course I would come back. Did I not tell you? Why not ask Giles?'

'Because I was not sure that I could trust him.'

'Not trust Giles? The dearest truest friend that ever lived? Yet you trust a kirkman you have barely met?'

'Giles Locke was a man I had barely met. You must understand, I made a leap of faith in coming here with you. I kept my faith, but when you were not here, I was on my own. I did not think that Giles was friendly to my kind. I thought him to be ... of that queen's party.'

'And even if he were, he would never let that colour or impair his judgement. He is not that kind of man. If you sensed a distance in him, it was that he feared some harm might come to you, troubled at the time; he never was the source of it,' Hew cried. He was far less guarded now, less civil in his tone to her, appalled at what he heard.

'I understand that now,' she said. 'I did not see it then.'

'The tutor, who sent on your letters. What was in it for him?'

'Some books in your library he wanted to read. He said they were rare.'

'Did he, now indeed?'

Frances stared at him. 'What are you, Hew, my uncle, now? Am I not made aware, that I belong to you? That all I have is yours? And that were little, too.' Her eyes were pricked and wet, with scathing, angry tears. 'Are you so jealous, Hew?'

'It is not that.' He would not for the world have her reduced to tears, or bowed before his will.

'Not in the way that you think. Tom Phelippes is a spy, for the English Crown. Our countries are now facing a crisis of security. If all the while, you have sent him word about our king . . . the secrets I have told you, while we were in bed . . .'

'You think I have no sense, to have told him that? That I would blab and spill, the secrets of your heart?' she cried.

'Not willingly, perhaps. But he has the skill, to tease and penetrate. Your cousin Tom has strung you, like the lute you used to play.'

It was a sharp enough thrust, and Frances flinched from it. She answered him coldly. 'You are so fixed upon conspiracies that it has made you cruel. I did not think you cruel, Hew, else I would not have come. How did you come so cruel?'

His heart pricked with remorse. He did not want to quarrel with her over Tom. At the same time, she cried, 'Oh, let us be friends! I cannot bear it, if we are at odds!'

And what did it matter, in truth? What more harm was done, now that all was out? That queen, as someone bold had pointed out to James, in nature's course, was bound to die ahead, and leave her son to mourn; once dead, her death by weeping or by force, could never be undone. And letters that were sent, could not be unsent, what damage they might do, was already done.

Frances thought the same. 'Do you not want to ken?' she asked softly, 'What Thomas said?'

'Tell me then,' he sighed.

'I told him that you had the picture from the king. I did not say, understand, what strange effect it had upon his Grace, only that you put your mind to know where it had come from. And he said, he could help you with that. He had seen something like it himself.'

It was possible, Hew thought, that Phelippes played a game with them. It was likely too, that he might tell the truth. And he could not deny, that he would like to know.

'Do you remember that he stood for Parliament in Hastings? He was put up for it by Lord Cobham, who is warden of the Cinque Ports. Sir Francis, I think, was not the best pleased with him. In September last year, after the traitors were hanged, he took Mary down to Hastings to recuperate. Do you recall?' Frances said.

Phelippes had absented himself, in the month of the queen of Scots' trial, a careful retreat. His concern for his wife, and the state of her health, was poignant and fixed in its coming, more than three month after the miscarriage.

'They spent some time with Lord Cobham, as his guests. And Lord Cobham asked Tom for advice, on a man who had lately come into his charge, detained at Dover as he tried to cross to France, with some papers that he had for a man called Mauvissiere, or Castelnau.'

'I have heard of that man. He was once ambassador, to the queen Elizabeth,' reflected Hew. He was listening now, his anger had evaporated, and had been replaced by a growing interest, and by hope, in the intrigue.

'The man detained at Dover was a follower of his. But he was not French. He was a Dutch painter, called Aart van Bronckhorst.'

'Arnold Bronckhorst,' Hew corrected. 'Can it be the same?'

'Tom believes it was. This Bronckhorst carried, as well as the papers for Castelnau, pencils and some colours, and a small perspective painting of a woman and a skull. Lord Cobham had the picture in his house. He showed it to Tom, as a curiosity, and Tom thinks, it may be the same as ours. It did not occur to them that it was the queen, who had not come to trial. Bronckhorst said, it was a prentice piece, an essay in perspective done by a pupil of his, that he was to send to Castelnau, to see if it pleased him, to give the boy favour in France. It was a composite, he said, of the painter's wit, and not intended to depict a woman from the life. Lord Cobham was careful, you will see, to avoid the spread of rumour or unrest to France, and for that reason he detained the painter, who was denied his passport, and referred the papers that he carried back to Francis Walsingham. In due course, he was freed, and allowed to return to his own house in London. The picture and the colours were returned to him, since they were essential to his trade. Since then, he is kept under watch, and may not have licence to pass overseas. When Tom read my letter, he took it on himself to call him in for questioning.'

Hew interjected, still resentful, 'That was good of him!'

Frances said, 'It *was*. Bronckhorst says he gave the picture, which he could not send himself, to a Frenchman who had leave to pass home overseas, to bring it home to Castelnau. So much he had promised to his boy, who was hoping to have made a name in France. If that Frenchman brought it here, to the king of Scots, and left it at the court, he is baffled by the cause, but solemnly avows tis nought to do with him. When Tom pressed him further, he supposed that the Frenchman, secretly of that queen's party, found in that painting a likeness to her *that the painter had never intended*, and brought it to the court, hoping so to prick at the conscience of the king. Tom thinks, Bronckhorst may be more involved in this, than he is willing to admit, and meant some mischief here, to nurse a private grudge. But so much he could not make him admit.'

'I have no doubt he does. But we shall never know. The man who brought the picture to the Scottish court, willingly or not, is doubtless home in France,' Hew said. He thought it apt, and strange, the answer to it all should have come from Tom, and written in a letter, open and unguarded, by an ordinary post. He could not help but smile at it.

Frances reached out for his hand. 'Then are you still sorry that I wrote to Tom?'

He let her hand settle in his. 'I will tell you that, when I have spoken with the king.'

He need not have feared. The king was well disposed to listen to his tale, when he gave him audience, two weeks on, in Holyrood.

'It is not bewitched. And it was never meant to be a portrait of the queen. And yet, it does possess a magic, of a kind. It turns a man's mind in upon himself, when he is perplexed, to find out what it means, and where he is disturbed, and troubled in his conscience, it will find him out. For, it will remind him of his own mortality, and what must come to him, when all is said and done.'

So Hew did believe. Giles Locke liked the picture, and it held no fears for him. His mind was at home in it, contented with controversy. In Hew it had produced a curious kind of peace; it mirrored and exposed a conflict in his heart, and made him more at ease, at seeing it expressed. But in the painter it had roused the torment of his guilt, that he had brought the devil to a helpless boy, and that, for his sin, he surely must be damned.

'It was not the pleated picture, but the poison in the mercury, that drove the painter mad,' as Hew explained to James. 'And yet, I think, the picture may have had a part in it, in what turned out to be the final cause. You need not fear it, sire. For it can do no harm. It merely shows us what we know, and what was always there.'

James was looking at the painting Hew had now returned to him, propped up on a board in his hall at Holyrood. It looked crude and small. 'However it was meant,' he said, 'we do not want it here. Since it was meant for France, we shall send it there; mebbe, to the king, to work its charm on him. I never took to Bronckhorst. Tell to me, now, how you found him out?'

Hew took a deep breath. 'My wife . . . the woman I would marry . . . has a cousin who works for Lord Cobham, the warden of the Cinque Ports. He picked Bronckhorst up as he travelled to France. He will verify all, if you write.'

'Ah, is that so?' James smiled. 'How useful it may be, to have an *English* wife. Go marry her, at once. She can spy for us.

'We are grateful to you, that you do our best to put our mind at rest. But your account of the picture, your assertion that it cannot be in any way bewitched, is not, for certain, proved, for your reason has a flaw.'

'What flaw is that?' asked Hew.

'You say it has no power but to stir up a man's conscience. That cannot be true. For, it worked on me. It made me feel unease. And, as you must ken, my conscience is quite clear.'

Hew left that place, lifted in his heart, with the Scots king's promise safely in his hands. Returning to St Andrews, he came straight away to the college of St Leonard's to instruct the principal to call his marriage banns. He crossed to the cathedral, and came down by the harbour, to walk home by shore, in the breezy sunshine of a summer's day. He watched the white gulls circle, high above the cliffs. As he crossed the sands, he looked out to the sea. And there he saw a ghost.

Chapter 23

Queen and Country

The image that he saw was imprinted on the landscape, fused into the line between the shore and sea, so narrow that it closed in the blinking of an eye, so broad that it stretched on, endless in extremity, the falling of the sand into the line of sea, the sea against the sky, the circling of the gulls, the water rolling back, infinite and on.

The tide was out. And on the shoreline by the sea, in the darkling sand, a little child was crouched, her billowing white smock lifted from the water's edge, dabbling in a pool for limpets or a crab, where sunlight caught the flaxen strands floating from her linen cap. A mother bent beside her, *fixed*; this picture had a fluid, transitory permanence, returning there, and on, for as long as the waters patiently revolved, for as long as the sea spray washed over the town to weather the stone to a pale yellow sand, and water pooled among the rocks and washed ashore its trail of crabs and barnacles and salt encrusted seaweeds dried out in the sun, and were drenched again, and the gulls fulfilled their circuits, mournful, round the bay, and began again.

A woman, who had taken off her stockings and her shoes and hitched her kirtle from the sand that clung to her bare legs. Whose own pale hair streamed loosened to the bright sea breeze. Whose pale cheeks coloured in the sunlight. Clare.

Clare.

She looked at him, and smiled. 'Hew. They tell me you were home.'

He felt his voice, strange and hard, rising in his throat as if it were a rock. 'They tell me you were dead.'

He could feel the life in her, the soft wind in her hair, the warmth of her breath touching his. He saw every part of her, transitory, fixed, the wet sand that clung to the fold of her dress, the salt on her lips, the bloom on her cheek where the bright sun had warmed her, the slender white cusp of her bare feet and neck.

Her eyes opened wide in wonder. 'Who would tell you that?'

'Roger Cunningham.'

'Oh, that naughty boy. He was a wicked boy. But you must not be cross with him. Did Andrew not say? It was Robert who died.'

He had never spoken of her with Sir Andrew Wood. Never to that man, would he say her name. Now he could not recall what Andrew Wood had said, could not see the sense, or shape his mind around it. He was feeling, through a fog.

'Roger saved my life,' she said. 'And he fell sick himself. For that, we must forgive him, think you not? As soon as I was well enough, I went to live with George. For I am curator now, of the land and wealth he had from our father, and it is a task, to see he does not squander it. He is still, I fear, an unco silly boy. You should come and see him, sometime. He is fond of you. Perhaps you can persuade him to return to the college, long enough to graduate.' Her composure and complacency astonished him. But Clare had known, always, he was there. And all that she had asked of him, when he felt so close to her, had been help for George.

'Your little child,' he said, 'why does he keep your child?' He could not comprehend why she sent her child to live with Andrew Wood, when she could live with George. Hew would not have wished a dog upon the crownar. And yet, he thought, *and yet*.

She looked down fondly at the child, who dabbled on, oblivious to them, in her little rock pool, in a private world. The child looked well, content. Her fevered cheeks had rounded to a stolid plumpness. She was lovely, still; the paradigm of Clare.

'She has lived with Andrew and Elizabeth, since she was born,' Clare explained. 'Robert never took to her. And, after Robert died, it did not seem right to take her from a place where she was wanted, loved.'

'Then you have . . . you are . . . alone?'

She answered him simply, 'I have my brother George. Now, look at you. You look well, and fine. And Andrew tells me that you have a wife.'

There was sadness in her voice. And he did not like the way she spoke the crownar's name, the closeness it implied.

'We are not married, quite,' he felt compelled to say.

'No? Then, I wish you well of it. She is fortunate, your wife. And Andrew says you met her in London. Then I doubt a good thing may have come of it. I am sorry, Hew, for what we did to you. You did not deserve that. But I knew no other way how to amend it. It was Roger's letter cost us both, and Andrew could conceive no other way. Robert thought the bairn was yours. For though he gave no credit to that silly boy, he knew she was not his.'

Hew echoed, uncomprehending, 'She is not his?'

'No. Did you not ken?' She is Andrew's child. Had Robert ever kent that, it would have destroyed him. His brother had everything, in Robert's eyes. He has only to wink at Elizabeth, and she is full with his bairn. Andrew is a man who is strong and venerous. For that reason, only, did he stray from her, for he has needs, that she cannot always fulfil. All of us have needs,' she admitted wryly.

He would not believe, that Clare had carnal converse with Sir Andrew Wood. 'No.'

'I'm sorry, Hew,' she sighed. 'I thought you must have worked it out. Andrew said, twas certain that you would. For you are a searching kind of man.'

'Then are you still . . . ?'

She shook her head. Sorrowful, he thought. 'Not still. He was quite aggrieved. He said, I blackmailed him. For he was not inclined to save your life. I telt him, if he did not want our secret blabbed, to Robert and Elizabeth, he must make sure no harm did come to you. We owed that much to you. I did not have a say in the way that he did it. He did the best he could. But he was not best pleased, and will not trust me now.' She laughed, lightly, and bitterly. 'Well, he did not do so badly from it, for he has his child, and he has Elizabeth. And they are better parents to her, both, than Robert and I could have been.'

'I do not believe that, of you,' he contended fiercely.

'You ought to believe it. You are too good to me, Hew. Now I must take her home, for Elizabeth is fearful when they are apart too long. She loves her very much. Their last little one died, did you know?'

Clare bent over the child, drying her hands on a cloth. Standing again, she moved towards Hew, and kissed him on the cheek. 'You always were too good,' she said. 'I wish she had been yours.'

Hew ran, his cheeks aflame, headlong up Kirk Heugh and to the college of St Salvator's where he launched himself, in furious dismay, on Giles Locke in his tower. Giles was reading quietly, when Hew burst in upon him. 'Where is Roger Cunningham?'

The doctor closed his book, at once alert and curious. 'At this hour, I should say, at his lecture.'

'Send for him.'

Taking in the look upon his close friend's face, Giles did not resist. Roger came, as called, calm and unperturbed. He glanced from Hew to Giles, and back again to Hew, with an expression that contrived to be submissive and aloof, both at the same time. Giles leant back in his chair, and watched with careful interest what was to unfold.

'Why did you tell me Clare Buchanan was dead?' demanded Hew.

A flicker of expression crossed the student's face, transitory, fleet, that seemed to Hew the shadow of a satisfaction, intimate and shrewd. In a moment, it was gone, and he could not have sworn to it. Roger's answer, when it came, was cool and supercilious. 'I do not think I did.'

Giles interrupted, 'Is this true, Hew? Can it be true?' his voice filled with trouble and doubt.

'I saw her on the beach. I spoke with her,' Hew said.

'Dear God, then I am sorry. I assumed...' the doctor said, dismayed.

'She has been living with her brother George, since her husband died.'

'Yes, I see. That makes a certain sense. That is such a consequence, as happens in the plague. People are displaced, and caught up in the flux, and it is hard to ken, what has truly happened to them. Did Andrew Wood not say?'

'We did not discuss it,' Hew reported shortly.

'Yes, I see, I see. But Roger, perhaps, was mistaken too? He fell ill himself. He could hardly ken, what became of Clare, when even I did not,' Giles conceded then. And Roger at his pleading let slip a small smile, unhidden from Hew.

'He knew,' Hew said starkly. 'He writes letters to George.'

'Roger, is this this true?' Giles asked.

'I do not recall,' Roger answered, 'that I ever telt him that. What, sir,' he asked Hew, 'were the actual words, that you believe I said?' He could not keep his pleasure in his subtle triumph meekly there subdued, and Hew was astounded at the malice in the boy.

'You said you were with Clare, when she had the plague, and stayed there till the last.'

'Stayed there till the last,' Roger mimicked carefully. 'Is that the same as saying, "Clare is dead?"'

'You knew it was. It was your intention to deceive. You allowed me to think . . .'

'*Allowed you to think*, sir?' Roger's tone now was scornful, superior. 'I did not tell you Clare was dead. And I cannot be held to account for it, if that was what you *thought* I said, in your disordered mind. You might as well say, it was you who murdered the painter, when you put the picture there that tipped him into madness. And we both ken, sir, that was not the case.'

Giles said, 'Stop,' in a voice of such cold restraint and rage as Hew had never heard from him before. 'Stop. For I will listen no longer to this sophistry.'

'It is not sophistry.' Roger turned to him. 'It is disputation. And you teach it in your schools, though, as I contend, you do not teach it well. I do not understand,' he said again, to Hew, 'why you are upset. You have a wife, of your own. Or is it that you *want* Clare to be dead?'

'That is enough. Pack your bag, and go. For you are expelled,' Giles said. A look of abject weariness settled on his face.

'Do you mean,' Roger asked, 'I shall not progress to my examination?'

'That is what I mean.' Hew had never seen his old friend so unmoved, no hint of vacillation in his kindly eyes, resolute as stone. This sentence seemed harsh, even to him, and he was almost moved to speak in his defence, when the boy said feelingly, *'Thank you. Thank you. For, sir, I did not know how to tell you. You have been so kind. But I did not intend to attend the laureation. The surgeon has offered to take me on as his apprentice, and I have agreed to it. It is far better suited to my knowledge and my skill. I have, sir, no desire for any further study to become a physician. I have no interest in Galen, or in Paracelsus, or all the other paragons among your dead philosophers. And what good is your philosophy, if it cannot put its hand inside a living head, and mend a broken skull? What use are your signatures, then? That sir, is what I would do. I would hold a living heart, while it is beating still, and mend it with the mettle of my own ingenious hand. You have been generous, in sharing your knowledge, and I have been grateful for that. But you should ken, that what you believe, for the most part, is worthless, and wrong.'

'This is sublimely arrogant,' Giles retorted then, choking on the words. 'What, Roger, would you be God?'

Roger grinned at that. 'I will let you know. For in our line of work, our paths are sure to cross. I am grateful to you both, for all that you have taught me. It has been illuminating.'

He bowed to them, and turned to leave the tower, before he was dismissed. At the door he said, 'I will tell the porter where to send my things.'

Giles concluded, *'Well!'*

Hew found himself convulsed, inexplicably, with laughter. He felt he could not stop. Giles, whose face had transformed itself through a series of conflicting and comical emotions, glared at him severely.

'This is not the reaction I expect from you. I thought, at one stage, and from the look on your face, you would strike him down.'

'And so I should have done, had I not felt it would give to him a kind of satisfaction. I am sorry, Giles. I do not mean to laugh. But I cannot help it.'

'So do I see. Your humours are quite thrawn, and dangerously unbalanced. If you do not stop, I will have you purged; precipitate, and from both ends at once.'

Hew composed himself. 'Thank you, I am balanced now, I promise you, quite well.'

When he was quite sober, he described to Giles everything that Clare had told him in the street. At the end he said. 'Though I do not like to say it, Roger may be right, I have no cause to feel concern that Clare lives still, and well.'

'Do you have feelings for her, still?' Giles asked, 'Conflicting with the feelings that you have for Frances?'

Hew did not reply. Instead, he said. 'Do you realise what this means? I telt you Roger's letter had no bearing on my going down to London. But the truth is, that it did. It was the moving force, that made Clare use her influence to charm Sir Andrew Wood to keep me safe from harm. And so it was the force that brought me close to Frances. Roger was, in this respect, the efficient cause.'

Giles snorted. 'Stuff. Then we can only hope that Roger never hears of it. For he is quite puffed up and surquidous enough.'

He came home, to find Frances at last. If there were to be no secrets between them, then he knew he must tell her about Clare. That would be hard. He did not know where to begin. And he could not trust his powers over his feelings, for he was not sure what those feelings were.

She read, at once, the tremor of disquiet in his face. He could guard his passions well enough. He had been schooled in it at Seething Lane. But not from her. Not from her.

'Is something wrong? Did your suit go badly with the king?'

He shook his head. 'Not at all. All is well. We have leave to be married in the kirk, in three weeks' time.'

'Then that is good. For, I have something to tell you.'

'Yes.' He felt a dullness in his heart. 'I, also.'

'Yes?'

'You shall speak first.'

She nodded. 'Very well. We have not spent much time together, in the last few months.'

He swallowed. 'No. I have neglected you. And I am sorry for it.'

'I do not blame you, Hew. You have been finding things out. And while you have been occupied, I have found things out too.'

'What have you found out?'

'I have been talking with your servants, and the factor here, about the running of this household, and of your estate. For Meg will leave here soon, and it will fall to me. I hope you do not mind.'

'Mind? Why should I mind?' This was not at all what he had expected. From a clear relief, he could barely take it in.

'You have a lot of land, but not all of it is put to good effect. The factor thinks it could be more productive. There are fallow fields, that could be given over to more sheep.'

'Sheep?' he echoed foolishly.

'You could increase the yield threefold. Tibbie Strachan says that she can find a market for the wool.'

'Tibbie Strachan. Does she?'

'Yes. I think one of the flocks you should give to Robert Lachlan. He will need something to occupy him, to keep him at home and constant to Bella. Else he will stray again. The miller's boy's pigs are a start, but not enough, I think.

'Your factor is a good man, and willing, but he is growing old. He feels he will no longer be able to manage your estates to their best efficiency, and it is a concern to him. He served your father a good while.

'He says that you have little interest in the management of your estate, and leave it all to him. He has kept it well, but now it grows too much for him. He wants an assistant.

'I hope you will not think it presumptuous, but I have someone here in mind. John Kintor, the miller's son. I have spoken with him. He is about to be apprenticed to a stonemason, for his brother's mill cannot sustain two millers. He tells me, he does not wish to be a mason, but to stay on the land, where he was born. He knows a great deal about your estate.'

'That is true,' reflected Hew. 'But he is only thirteen.'

'Thirteen is a good age to begin. You should send him to school for two years, to teach him to read and to write, and in particular, to keep the accounts. Then he can be prenticed to your factor, and eventually, in some years' time, take over the management himself. His young age is an advantage, since he can be trusted in the post for many years to come. He has an affinity for livestock, and he knows the land. He knows all the plants that grow in Meg's garden, and he can help to look after them, after she has gone. The surplus he can take to the town, and sell to the apothecar. He is not, I know, the best of apothecars, but with a little supervision he may yet be amended. The money that John makes will help to pay for his schooling. He will be an excellent factor. And an advantage is that he is very fond of you; he will not let you down. And it will a comfort to Matthew, as he grows older, to have his advice in running the mill. The facts and the figures I have worked out myself. How many sheep will be wanted for what quantity of land, and what will be the yield. The cost of John's schooling, and the value, as I count, of the return on it. You will want to look at them.'

She showed him a book, with the figures worked, which he accepted with a look of astonished blank bewilderment. 'You have done all this?'

'Yes. Are you cross?' she smiled at him, confident and pleased, for she was in her element.

'Not cross, at all. I am delighted, and amazed, that you have found so much to do,' he answered honestly. 'Tell me, is this all?'

'Well,' she hesitated, 'it is not quite all. I thought that you could employ Gavan Baird, to work in your library.'

This he did object to. 'Why would I do that?'

'Because you want a secretar. The books are in disorder there, and you do not have time, or the inclination, to sort them out. Nicholas Colp began to make a catalogue, but he could not finish it. There are the books, too, that you brought back from the Low Countries, which are still in their boxes. They need to be unpacked, and put on the shelves. They need to be found a place in their new home,' she told him.

'But why Gavan Baird?'

'Gavan Baird is clever, humorous and kind. He can keep a confidence. No one in the kirk will employ him as a minister. And he is a friend. You will like him very much, when you overcome your prejudice.'

Frances was so earnest, so serious in this that he burst out laughing. 'Should I be jealous of him?'

'You should not. I do not love Gavan Baird. But he has been a friend to me, as Laurence was to you. He was the first person, outside your own family, who made me feel at home here.'

'In that case, I shall set aside my feud, and make peace with him.'

Though he was teasing now, she did not smile. 'You *should*. For Meg, and Giles, and the children will be gone from here soon. They will take Canny Bett. This house will be empty without them. These are large estates, and they will not look after themselves. We need to people them, with people we can trust. We need Robert Lachlan and Bella Frew. We need John Kintor and Gavan Baird, who will look after the things that you love and hold dear, while you are away, chasing after mysteries, as I know and trust that you will always do. While you are in peril there, these things will endure, kept constant, waiting for you, when you will return for them. They will be secure, and kept safe for our children. For this land and estate is more than we can be. It was here before, and will be here after, long after, we have both gone.'

He felt, at her words, inexplicably moved, and to hide from her the flood of feeling he could not explain, he caught her in a kiss.

'Do I take it then,' she asked of him, unfolding from his arms, 'that you have approved of it?'

'You can take it for approval,' he informed her gravely. 'Though I will, of course, have to look more closely at your figures, later on in bed.'

'What was the thing,' she said, 'you had to say to me?'

'It does not matter, now.'

In the chapel of St Leonard, on a fair summer's day towards the end of June, they made their covenant with God. And the Scottish kirk looked kindly on a stranger there, and shuffled over, gruffly, to let her slip among them, quiet in their midst. There was little ceremony, and little to deflect from the common ordinary, but the vows they made, quiet in their hearts, and open to that God, whose minister accepted them, hopeful and bemused.

And after, when they came again to Kenly Green, they found the house prepared for them. They walked together through an avenue of trees, the holly and the rowan boughs that bent their watchful branches, heavy with their leaves, and where the drooping rose distilled its heady scent, lifted by the bees, and came to the house that was filled with flowers, and with row upon row of honeycomb candles, to colour dark corners in sweet friendly light. And Frances wore a gown the colour of the sea, of blues and greys and turquoise greens all shimmered in a watered silk, falling into waves, that flowed and gathered perfectly. The house was filled with people then, and with talk and laughter, and the trestles groaned with syllabubs and tarts, capons, salmons, roasted kid and laprons in a green herb sauce, gingerbreads and marchpanes, sugared flowers and fruits, strawberries and biscuit bread, with mound upon mound of butter and cream that Canny Bett and Bella Frew had whipped up to a froth; and there were wines and aquavite, of the finest sort.

And then, when all was gone, the guests went home to bed, the servants slipped away, and they were left alone, quite still, and centred in that house. The bed was turned back, sprinkled with lavender; rose petals perfumed the sheets. Hew crossed to the window.

'Leave the shutters open,' Frances said. 'For I want the moon to look at us.'

'How wanton you become,' he laughed. 'I have something for you, here. I found it at the krames.'

'It is a lute!' Frances cried, as he brought it from its box. 'I did not think,' she teased him, 'a lute would be allowed here.'

'There is nothing,' answered Hew, 'that is not allowed here. For this is *our place*.' He took her hand in his, and by her mother's ring, closest to her heart, he slipped on his own, and the sliver of moonlight that fell through the window fell softly, askance, on the pale band of gold, with its clasp of two hands, and its bright lines of flowers. 'There is a verse inside.'

'Is it a riddle?' Frances smiled. 'A cipher, to be solved?'

He did not reply, but showed her what was written there, that was true, and plain, and spoken from the heart.

> *My hand in yours shall never roam*
> *In fear of lands that lie unseen*
> *For where thou art, that place is home*
> *Thou art my country, and my queen.*

Notes and Attributions

The earl of Shrewsbury's guest house in Buxton spa survives, in part, in the Old Hall Hotel, which claims to be perhaps the oldest in England. In 2012, the hotel commissioned a reproduction feature window to illustrate the writing on the glass left by Mary, queen of Scots and other noble guests between 1573 and 1584, based on a handwritten copy of the original, kept among the Portland papers at Longleat in Wiltshire.

A transcription and translation of the writing there was also published by Patrick Chapman in the same year, in his *Things Written in the Glasse Windowes at Buxstons*.

My translations of the two proverbs quoted here differ very slightly from his.

The title of Chapter 7, 'Frost of Cares', is taken from Chidiock Tichborne's elegy, 'My prime of youth is but a frost of cares'. Tichborne is the young poet who made the longest speech upon the scaffold, and who, according to report, took the longest time to die. The conspirator who came 'not to argue but to die' was Charles Tilney. There were in all fourteen executions, on the 20th and 21st September 1586.

The title of Chapter 8, 'The Opened Bud' is an allusion to Robert Southwell's poem depicting Mary, queen of Scots as a Catholic martyr: 'the bud was opened to let out the rose'.

The often-quoted 'In my end is my beginning' is from Mary's cloth of estate, embroidered by her in captivity.

The wording of the proclamation at the mercat cross in Edinburgh, and the squib against Elizabeth, in chapters 13 and 14 are quoted verbatim from contemporary letters in the Elizabethan state papers.

The Latin verse quoted by Laurence Tomson in chapter 2 is alluded to in a letter by Thomas Phelippes, written in his final days at Chartley.

The 'turning picture' is inspired by the one currently on display in the library of the Scottish National Portrait Gallery, Queen Street, Edinburgh.

The text and translation of 'Ars naturam adiuvans' is quoted, for convenience, from the 1591 edition of Alciato's Emblemata, but Glasgow University offers digital access to 22 editions, from 1531–1621, in their fantastic Alciato at Glasgow project: http://www.emblems.arts.gla.ac.uk/alciato/index.php

The samples of verse in George Heriot's shop are from actual poesy rings. But Hew's is entirely his own.

Historical Figures

Mary Stewart, queen of Scots

Mother of James VI. Exiled and imprisoned in England from 1568. Implicated, in letters to Anthony Babington, in conspiracy against the English queen Elizabeth. Convicted in October, 1586 and executed at Fotheringhay Castle on 8 February 1587

James VI of Scotland

Son of Mary Stewart and Henry Stewart, Lord Darnley. Born 1566. King of Scotland from 1567–1625. King of England (as James I) from 1603–1625

Patrick Adamson

Archbishop of St Andrews

Anthony Babington

Catholic conspirator against Queen Elizabeth whose letters to Mary, queen of Scots were intercepted by Sir Francis Walsingham. A page in the household of the earl of Shrewsbury at Sheffield. Executed September 1586

John Ballard

Jesuit priest 'Black Fortescue'. Instigator of the Babington plot. Executed September 1586

Robert Beale

Diplomat. Deputy to Sir Francis Walsingham

Binning family
Edinburgh painters active from c.1538–1633

William Cecil, first baron Burghley
Lord Treasurer of England

Arnold or Arthur Bronckhorst
Court painter to King James VI c.1580–1583. Identified as gold prospector in Scotland c.1579 by Stephen Atkinson [gold miner, 1616]. Living in London by 1583. May be identified as 'Aart' detained for questioning by Lord Cobham at Dover in September 1586

Burton Brewer
Supplied ale to Chartley Manor. Smuggled letters to and from Mary, queen of Scots in beer barrels, at the instigation of Sir Francis Walsingham

Tom Cassie
Servant of Thomas Phelippes

William Brooke, tenth baron Cobham
Lord warden of the Cinque Ports and constable of Dover Castle. Close friend and political ally of William Cecil

John Colville
Scottish Presbyterian minister and supporter of the Ruthven raid. Spied for Sir Francis Walsingham

Gilbert Gifford
Acted as courier for letters to and from Mary, queen of Scots, at the instigation of Sir Francis Walsingham

William Ruthven, earl of Gowrie
Former Lord High Treasurer of Scotland and chief instigator of the Ruthven Raid, the detention of King James VI in 1582. Executed for treason in 1584

George Heriot
Edinburgh goldsmith; later goldsmith to Queen Anne of Denmark, wife of James VI. Founder of George Heriot's school

John Maitland, first Lord Maitland of Thirlestane
Lord Chancellor of Scotland

Andrew Melville
Scottish reformer and principal of St Mary's College, St Andrews

Francis Mylles
Secretary and agent of Sir Francis Walsingham

Claude Nau
French secretary to Mary, queen of Scots. Accused by some of a part in her downfall. Sought to marry Bessie Pierrepoint, the granddaughter of the Countess of Shrewsbury

Sir Amias Paulet
Keeper of Mary, queen of Scots from April 1585 until her death in February 1587. Close friend of Thomas Phelippes

Thomas Phelippes
Principal cryptographer for Sir Francis Walsingham. Deciphered letters sent by and to Mary, queen of Scots. Son of William Phillips, cloth merchant and customer of wool for the port of London. Married Mary, in or before 1586; no surviving children. Identified with Thomas Phillips, MP for Hastings, 1584 and 1586. Served Sir Amias

Paulet and Henry Brooke, brother of Lord Cobham, in embassy to France

John Savage
Conspirator against Queen Elizabeth. Executed September 1586

George Talbot, sixth earl of Shrewsbury
Keeper of Mary, queen of Scots from 1569 to September 1584. Patron of the baths; built Buxton Hall

Laurence Tomson
Secretary to Sir Frances Walsingham. Puritan author and scholar. Married to Jane

Adrian Vanson
Official court portrait painter to King James VI from 1584. Married to Susanna of Colone. Made burgess of Edinburgh, on condition he take on apprentices

Sir Francis Walsingham
Principal Secretary and spymaster to Queen Elizabeth

Sir Andrew Wood of Largo
Crownar and sheriff of Fife. Comptroller until July 1587

Workman family
Painter burgesses of Edinburgh c.1554–1664

Glossary

Aquavite	whisky
Argent vive	quicksilver
Bailie	[Scotland] a town magistrate
Bangster	a bully
Baxter	a baker
Billie	a close friend or comrade [Scots. cf English *Bully*]
Black Acts	laws passed by the Scottish Parliament in 1584 condemning presbyteries, endorsing the rights of the bishops and asserting the supreme power of the king over the reformed Scots Kirk
Black Stane	stone, on which students sat to take public examinations in the ancient Scottish universities; the examination itself
Blaw	to blow
Broadcloth	a kind of fine wool cloth
Bully	in early modern English, a term of endearment towards a good friend
Bumbaize	to confound
Butts	mounts for holding targets for archery practice
Cadger	a carrier of goods
Caich	the game of real tennis, played with racquet or hand
Campvere	Veere, in Zeeland, the Scots staple in the Netherlands
Canny	cautious or prudent
Chap	to knock
Cinnabar	red pigment
Clengar	a cleanser of infected places
Comptroller	Crown officer in charge of personal expenditure, who checks the Treasurer's accounts
Confitures	confectionary
Cots	cottages
Court of Dustifute	[Scotland] court appointed to deal with disputes during a fair
Coventry thread	blue thread made in Coventry in the 16th century,

	famous for the permanence of its colour; proverbial origin of 'true blue'
Crownar	[Scotland] a coroner or king's officer in charge of protecting the interests of the Crown in a particular district, often combined with the office of sheriff
Cunyng	a rabbit
Dead kist	a coffin
Dow	a dove
Dummel	one who cannot speak
Dummy	a dumb person
Dustifute	a pedlar
Embarquement	placing under embargo
Exagitated	stirred up, excited
Fash	to worry, trouble
Feu	a feudal tenure of land
Flyting	a contest, between poets, of mutual abuse; here, a playful exchange of insults
Forestall	to buy up merchandise before it comes to market
Friar-fly	an idler, someone up to no good
Futless	footless, useless
Gang	to go
Gild	[Scotland] a merchant guild or brotherhood
Gingerline	a red-brown colour
Goif stok, goifs	a pillory
Gossip chair	a curved wooden armchair with wide wooden seat; a *caquetoire*
Graduand	a student on the point of graduation; a final year student
Grandgore	the great pox, or syphilis
Haar	a sea-mist on the east coast of Scotland
Hammermen	metal-workers
Hansell	a good-luck gift given at New Year
Hurkling	colliding violently
Impassible	incapable of suffering
Incontinent	immediately, at once
Jougs	an iron collar fastened round the neck, fixed to a post, used as a kind of pillory
Juglar	a conjuror
Ken	to know
Kersey	a kind of coarse woollen cloth

Kippil	a pair or brace (of poultry or game)
Kirk	a church; the reformed Church of Scotland
Kirtle	a woman's close frock, worn under a gown; a simple smock
Kist	a chest
Kittil	sensitive or skittish
Krames	shops or stalls, in particular those on the High Street of Edinburgh, next to the Kirk of St Giles
Laureation	graduation
Leman	a lover or sweetheart
Lepron	a young rabbit
Lettroun	a lockable writing desk
Limmar	a villain or rogue
Loun	a ruffian
Luckenbuiths	shops which are fixed and lockable, particularly those by the High Kirk of St Giles on Edinburgh High Street
Lugs	ears
Lusty	cheerful or agreeable
Manchet	the finest white bread
Marchpane	marzipan; a confection of almond paste, rolled onto wafers and baked, glazed and decorated, sometimes with gold leaf
Maun	must
Mauna	must not
Memento mori	an object symbolising mortality. Lit. 'remember to die'
Mercer	a small trader or dealer
Miching	thieving
Minnie	child's name for mother
the Morn	tomorrow
Mow	the mouth
Muckle	large
Noisome	harmful, noxious
Orpiment	a gold or yellow pigment
Outreiking	fitting out or equipping
Pasque	Easter
Peregrine	a pilgrim; a foreigner
Peste	any virulent epidemic disease; here, possibly, typhus rather than bubonic plague

Pie-powder court	a court established for the duration of a fair; cf *court of dustifute*; from French, *pieds poudrés*
Points	holes in clothes through which laces were threaded to fasten them
Poticar	an apothecary
Prick-louse	disparaging term for a tailor
Proplexity	anxiety
Regent	a university teacher
Renegats	deserters
Restanding	owing, not yet paid
Rousie	wild, easily aroused
Rusty bully	disparaging term for a Englishman; *rusty* = morally corrupt, but playing also on the English fondness for roast beef
Sclaunder	slander
Sculduddery	lewd behaviour
Senzie fair	fair held in the cloisters of St Andrews Cathedral, at Easter time
Sic	such
Sin	since
Skrimmar	a swordsman, fighter
Slops	wide, baggy breeches fashionable in the late 16th century
Snaw	snow
Speir	to ask
Surquidous	arrogant
Swingeour	a scoundrel
Thrawn	twisted, distorted; thrown out or down
Thriftless	worthless
Thrissel	a thistle
Tocher	a marriage dowry
Tolbuith	town hall
Trumperous	stupid or worthless
Uncanny	malicious, threatening
Unco = uncouth	
Uncouth	strange, uncanny, unfamiliar; also an intensifier
Wammill	to feel queasy; *wammilling* = heaving